# OUTRUN

## IVY BRONSON

Seven Bodies™ is an imprint of Feral Turtle Media

Published by Seven Bodies Publishing





ISBN 979-8-9993467–0-4

For all you Battle Moms out there.

# PROLOGUE

**April 20, 2009**
**Prague, Czechia**

WE ALWAYS assumed someone was listening. It was one of the first things we were taught. Jonathan's voice came through my earpiece, interrupting the distracting thoughts I couldn't keep at bay. "I'll walk the dog. You take out the trash." It wasn't a sophisticated code, but we found that we worked best together when we kept things simple.

We stood back to back at the end of a dark hallway in a nondescript office building. The weekend janitorial staff had left hours ago, and the rest of our team was parked around the corner.

My task was to watch the elevator and the stairway door while Jonathan moved ahead, making him the first to encounter any potential dangers coming down the hallway. If someone attacked from his end, I could take cover around the corner. Of course, this meant Jonathan was heading down the fatal funnel alone.

Jonathan crept down the shadowy corridor, while I maintained my position and waited for his all-clear signal. My mind began to wander again, and I was unsure of the best approach to the situation despite a decade of experience devising and executing plans. The tail end of Jonathan's communication snapped me back to the current mission. Not hearing his full transmission, I glanced in his direction and saw he had reached the intersecting hallway at the other end. I scolded myself for losing focus and planned to address the situation when we were back in the States.

I attached the silencer to my 9mm, which I should have already done, and walked backward, closing the gap between me and Jonathan. Now it was my turn to proceed down the hallway alone. Although our backs were facing each other, I knew when I was within arm's reach. No visual confirmation was necessary.

My body responded the way it always did whenever I was in his presence.

Eagle's voice came through my radio earpiece. "Phoenix, you two lovebirds have ten days to get hitched."

"Copy," I whispered back.

I tapped Jonathan on his shoulder and held up ten fingers. We set the timers on our Casios, and Jonathan waited for my go-ahead. On my nod, we began the countdown in unison. He went left, and I went right.

The first door I encountered had a blank nameplate and was unlocked. The streetlight filtering through the blinds provided enough light to illuminate the empty room. Without making a sound, I approached the office across the hall, stealing a glance at Jonathan as he picked the lock on a door further down the hall.

I tried my door, which, according to the nameplate, belonged to Mr. Amato.

Locked. I holstered my weapon and tapped the light on my vest, illuminating Mr. Amato's nameplate for the video recording on my body camera.

"Mr. Amato. Got it," came Eagle's voice through my earpiece.

I worked the lock in four seconds and was about to enter the office when a clicking door lock caught my attention. I watched

Jonathan disappear through a doorway as I did the same. We were always in sync, always on the same page.

Mr. Amato's office was twice the size of the previous one. It had all the features of an executive office: walnut paneling, a mahogany desk with a plush leather chair, and stale cigar smoke lingering in the air. A wave of nausea hit me again for the second time since breakfast. This wasn't the office of a computer hacker.

Those guys wore hoodies and worked from their mom's basement. But our intel indicated that the computer virus had been traced to this location.

I began my search with the bookcases and then moved on to the file cabinets. A sudden flash appeared on the wall ahead as I approached the desk. However, when I turned around, I found myself alone. I glanced at my Casio. Five minutes left. I rummaged through the top desk drawer, making sure to put everything back just as I had found it. There was no flash drive.

When I opened the bottom drawer, a loud thud echoed. I froze and listened to the silence, wondering if I was the cause. A softer thud followed, coming from behind me.

Upon facing the walnut paneling behind the desk, I noticed a thin beam of light peeking through a gap between two panels. As I moved closer, I could hear a muffled noise coming from the other side. I gently pressed along the smooth seams of the paneling, and the noise stopped. Frozen once more, I strained my ears to confirm that I wasn't imagining things. I exhaled and continued to push the seams with both hands. Four minutes left.

On my last push, I heard a click and felt the pressure of the panels releasing toward me. I drew my 9mm and opened the hidden door.

It led to a short hallway that wasn't on the schematics, and pursuing it further meant facing potential danger. We were taught to resist the urge to flee from danger, but for the past eight years, it had never been difficult for me. Danger had always been welcome.

But now, my feet were uncooperative and felt like they had

become one with the concrete floor.

I pushed aside my emotions, reverted to my training, and crept down the hallway.

"Eagle, I need confirmation on the northeast corner," I said. No response. "Eagle, come in." Still nothing. That's when I noticed the walls were covered in metal sheets. Somebody had made sure radio transmissions were impossible in this undocumented area of the building. Three minutes left.

I managed to will myself down the dark, cold hallway, one foot following the other like I'd been trained to do. As my eyes adjusted to the darkness, I saw a dimly lit room in the distance. When I reached the end of the hallway, an overturned metal chair came into view next to an open door. The concrete walls and lack of windows created a stale and musty odor. Another wave of nausea hit me.

A whisper came from the corner to my left. "Pomoc." It was one of the few Polish words I learned before landing in Europe. I assumed one of our team members might scream it if things went sideways. But this was no violent scream. This was a quiet, desperate plea.

I turned toward the voice and saw a teenage girl. She sat in the corner, hugging her legs, her clothes ripped and stained. Her hair was matted, and her eyes were swollen from crying or from injury. I couldn't tell which. I lowered my gun.

I tried the radio again, but still nothing. As I approached the girl, something moving in my peripheral vision stopped me cold. A greasy, shirtless man with a hairy beer belly and his pants undone stood in the doorway across the room. I twisted to my right and aimed my 9mm at his chest as he took a long swig from a clear glass liquor bottle.

Using the bottle, he pointed to the girl, unaware that they were no longer alone. "You're very mature for your age. That's what I like about you." Despite the slurred words, it was apparent he was American. He took another pull from the bottle. "You don't scream and cry like the others. Gives me a headache."

I glanced back at the girl, now clutching a dirty teddy bear with matted fur. It was either well-loved or well-abused.

I stepped into the light, and he slowly raised his arms when he registered the red dot on his chest along with my presence. He had come unprepared for a firefight, yet his eyes showed no fear. I was familiar with the look he gave. He was above the law, and this interaction between us would end as nothing more than an inconvenience for him. He was a man without consequences.

I turned back to the girl and held her gaze so she wouldn't look at the man as I pulled the trigger.

The cacophony of the gunshot reverberating off the metal walls, his body hitting the concrete floor, and the shattering of the glass bottle shocked me back to the reality of my actions.

I flinched when Jonathan appeared next to me. "I don't think my comm is working," he said. He held up a purple three-inch flash drive. "Target acqu—" He stopped when he saw the body. He followed my eyes to the girl in the corner.

"I didn't have a choice," I said.

Jonathan examined the body. "Alex, where's his gun?"

"I didn't have a choice."

# ONE

January 16, 2026
Las Vegas, NV

JESSIE BALTIMORE fights the urge to scream at her teenage son as she sits in the passenger seat of her Ford Explorer, gripping the grab handle above her head with a white-knuckle intensity. The rear end of a silver Toyota Camry is getting alarmingly close. "You need to slow down," she says, noticing that the Camry isn't moving while the Explorer hasn't slowed. "Slow down now." Jessie smashes her Nike into the floorboard against an imaginary brake. "Right now." She presses with such force that she levitates above her seat. The rear end of the Camry fills her view. "STOP!"

The Explorer comes to a sudden stop, slamming her back into her seat as her seatbelt locks. Her heart tries to escape her chest, and she starts box breathing. It's a technique Dr. Smith had taught her when she woke up from a two-week coma three days after her eighteenth birthday. The news that both of her parents had died in the car accident, leaving her all alone, had induced a panic attack.

With her heart rate slowing to normal, Jessie takes one last deep breath and turns to Max in the driver's seat.

"You need to start slowing down much sooner," she says.

"Mom, we were perfectly fine. I wasn't even close to hitting that car." Max's argument comes quickly.

Jessie matches his pace. "Then why did you slam on the brakes if we were perfectly fine?"

"Because you yelled at me, and I panicked!" Max says.

She turns toward the backseat. "Are you okay?"

Sean sits in the middle of the back seat, wearing a purple hockey helmet with a crown logo on each side. This close encounter will either be brushed off as insignificant or cause a full-fledged meltdown.

It's been almost a year since they've had to deal with the screaming and the crying and Sean hitting himself. It's been peaceful and a welcome respite as Jessie navigates the treacherous teenage years with Max. But at Sean's twelve-year-old checkup six months ago, the pediatrician warned Jessie that puberty could trigger more meltdowns.

Sean removes his helmet and brushes the hair out of his soft brown eyes, patting it in place. Unlike Max, Sean has his mother's straight brown hair. Nick offered to take him to his haircut appointment last week so Jessie could get a much-needed massage, but an intense game of Gran Turismo caused them to miss the appointment.

Jessie has offered several times to take Sean to get his hair cut, but each time, he reassures her that he is fine and that it can wait. He prefers dealing with the annoyance of hair in his face for the next two and a half weeks if it means getting his hair cut on the fourth of the month, like it's supposed to happen.

Sean hands the helmet to Jessie. "You probably need this more than I do. Statistically, this is the safest place to sit in a vehicle." She waves away the offer. "If I worked at the Department of Motor Vehicles, I would *not* give him a license. He's probably going to kill someone," Sean says.

"How bout I kill you!" Max says. He glares at Sean in the rearview mirror.

"Nobody's killing anyone!" Jessie says.

The Camry navigates through the intersection, passing a faded sign for the mall and an analog clock tower that reads twelve-fifteen. Three years ago, the clock tower at the mall's main entrance was remodeled and updated with a digital clock that also displays the date and the weather. In contrast, the clock and signage on the backside of the mall have yet to be updated, giving the exterior a Jekyll and Hyde appearance.

The Camry driver signals and pulls into the rear parking lot.

Jessie points to the Camry. "Follow—"

"I know," Max grumbles.

"I can't wait until July ninth when I'm officially a teenager and I know everything," Sean says.

Max brakes hard, causing Sean to lurch forward. He glares at Sean in the rearview mirror. "Oops."

Jessie gives Max the Mom Stare and motions for him to turn down an approaching aisle. He does. "You didn't signal," she says.

"There is literally no one to signal to. This is why I want to practice with Dad," Max says.

"Then Dad shouldn't have scheduled your test until you logged all your hours. And he's not here, so you're stuck with me," Jessie says.

The familiar frustration builds in her chest. Nick's pattern is always the same: grand gestures and good intentions followed by forgotten details and missed follow-through, like the time they finally had a night free from school, work, or hockey commitments and decided to go on a date. Jessie had dusted off her makeup palette and was pleasantly surprised when her ancient curling iron still worked. She even decided to wear a pair of heels she found in the back of her closet. But when Nick gave the restaurant hostess his name, he realized he had never made the reservation.

This time, Nick remembered to schedule an appointment,

and Max would be testing for his license next week. Only he didn't make sure that Max had logged the required number of driving hours, so the responsibility has fallen to her, like this weekend trip to his parents' house.

Max rolls his eyes and huffs as he pulls into the parking spot in front of the Camry near the mall entrance. He doesn't unbuckle fast enough to avoid the inevitable lecture, and Jessie watches him stare longingly at the Camry driver, who walks to the mall entrance, laptop under his arm, without having to endure a nagging mother.

"The bad habits you create now will—" Jessie lowers her voice and regains her composure. "You want me to trust you driving on your own, but you aren't showing me you're ready."

"The average car weighs 4,000 pounds. That's *two tons*, Max. You could definitely kill someone," Sean says.

"Sean, shut up!" Max says.

"Max, don't talk to him like that." Jessie turns to Sean. "And you, stop talking about your brother killing people."

Sean puts on his hockey helmet and picks at his fingers, his telltale sign of rising anxiety.

A ding sounds as a light illuminates on the dashboard.

"I didn't do anything. I swear," Max says. He lifts his hand in innocence.

"It's the tire pressure warning light." Jessie sighs. Under her breath, she voices her irritation with Nick for not getting the tire fixed last week when he said he would. "We'll have to fill it on our way out of town."

Max kills the engine and slams the door behind him. Jessie rolls her window down. "Make sure they don't charge you. Dad already paid for the repairs." He nods. "Do you need me to go with you?"

"Seriously?" Max rolls his eyes and heads inside the mall.

Jessie walks the tightrope of giving Max more freedom as he gets older while ensuring he knows she's still there if he needs her.

And every day, she feels like she's about to fall off.

She takes a breath, wishing she could rewind the last ten minutes and handle his driving lesson with more patience. Another moment she can't take back.

A person's life is measured in years, yet it happens in moments. A single moment can end a person's life or change it forever.

*You're pregnant. I love you. It's an opportunity. They didn't survive.*

Jessie turns to the backseat. "Hey, you should download a couple of movies onto your iPad because we won't have cell service for half of the drive."

"Except for Zyzyx," Sean says.

"Yes, but that only works for a few minutes." During one of their trips, the boys stumbled upon one spot in the middle of Nowhere where they could get a cell signal for a few minutes. Nowhere is the name Sean gave the stretch of the Mojave Desert on the way to Grandma's house that doesn't have cell service.

At the halfway point through Nowhere is a random road named Zyzyx, that, as far as they can tell, leads to, ironically, nowhere. The signal is weak and unreliable, but they always catch a few bars around Zyzyx Road.

On their previous trip, the boys had a contest to see who could download a movie before they lost the signal. It was a draw.

"A couple is two. You want me to download two movies?" Sean asks. Assumptions and inferences bring Sean discomfort.

"Yes," Jessie says.

Jessie hears Sean tapping away in the backseat, no doubt scrolling through Netflix again. A moment later, he mentions something about downloading episodes from the Unknown series—The Lost Pyramid and Killer Robots. She remembers him studying the pyramids in fifth grade, and she can almost hear his logic now: how could anyone lose something hundreds of feet tall?

As for the robots, Sean had gone on a rant just yesterday because an AI grammar checker had tried changing all his verbs from present to past tense. Now he's convinced that robots can't be trusted.

"Downloads are complete," he announces.

With a five-hour drive looming, Jessie should download some entertainment for herself. Nick was supposed to be driving, and she was supposed to be napping. She'd better find something to listen to after they lose the radio signal at Nowhere; driving in silence is a sure-fire way to lull her to sleep.

For the past month, her friend, Tina, has been raving about a podcast called *The Five-Year Fraud*. It's about a man who passed himself off as an uber-wealthy heir of a foreign shipping magnate. Tina had said he lived this lie "for *five* years!" before someone questioned his legitimacy. She couldn't believe that even his so-called best friend had no clue he wasn't who he said he was. That's when Jessie changed the subject.

Five episodes should be plenty for the duration of the trip, but Jessie downloads six. She listens to the podcast trailer while she waits for each episode to download. The voice of prison inmate Theodore Munson sounds hollow and desperate.

"I didn't mean to hurt anyone. I never intended to become that kind of person, I swear. I just got caught up in the lie." Jessie hears regret in his voice. Theodore takes a long pause.

"I had an opportunity to become someone else, and I took it."

Jessie can relate.

# TWO

A MAN with salt and pepper hair sits in a worn vinyl booth in the back corner. It's been a decade since his first visit to the diner. He had sought solitude after the funeral and found himself driving in the opposite direction of home until he could no longer see through his tears. He turned into an empty alley, hiding from the world collapsing around him and seeking refuge from the harsh reality he couldn't confront.

After he had stopped shaking and his tears had dried, he wiped the crusted blood off the dashboard and walked around the corner to the diner.

The young waitress gave him a bag of ice for his swollen knuckles and sat him in the booth he sits in now. She let him sit for hours, keeping his water glass full and never asking if he was okay. She knew he was not. He's been a regular at the diner ever since.

The neighborhood is neglected, and the food is only decent, but the service keeps him coming back. His leathered hand caresses a gold crucifix around his neck, a wedding gift from his late wife,

Marta.

Papa stares at the faded family photograph resting against the aluminum napkin dispenser. Its edges are worn, and a corner is bent from the wear and tear of living in his wallet. A younger version of him in a cowboy hat stands next to two dark-haired teenage boys. Marta stands on the other side of the boys, her wavy chestnut hair cascading over the bright embroidered flowers of her Campesina dress. It's a happy family in the photo.

He looks across the table at Victor, seeing too much of Marta in his youngest son's face. The amber eyes, the way he unconsciously taps his lips when he's thinking. It's both a comfort and a torment, especially today.

--- ·· - ·-· ·· --·

Victor catches his father's tear-filled eyes staring at him, and the burden he knows all too well finds its place again. The last ten years have aged him twenty. His life is far from where he imagined it would be at thirty-two years old. He has his father's jet-black hair and his mother's amber eyes. His left arm crosses over his torso, and his chin rests in his right hand as he taps his lips, just like she used to do.

Unaware of his tapping, he stares at the family photo, and her Campesina dress transports him back to the night of his fifth birthday. His mother wore that dress when he asked her why he was born. As she pulled him into her lap, he traced the embroidered flowers with his finger while he listened. With her soft voice, she whispered a secret meant only for them. Victor's birth was her way of sharing her abundant love and happiness with the world. Remembering those words makes him feel just as special today as they did when he first heard them.

He will never stop missing his mother.

Victor grabs a menu despite having no appetite and catches his father's tear-filled eyes staring at him. Being a constant reminder of Marta becomes twice as burdensome for Victor on this day.

But every year, he dutifully sits with his father in this booth and they talk about everything except the day his mother and older brother died.

Victor's phone chimes, and he reads a text. "Change of plan. We need to get there earlier." He receives another text and hesitates before relaying the message, his eyes apologetic. "He'll be there in fifteen minutes."

This is the first time Papa and Victor have worked a job on the anniversary. It's another reminder of the unpleasant change Victor sees in his father.

Papa used to be strict about honoring their lost loved ones and spending time together remembering them. Usually, they linger in the diner for hours after the plates have been cleared, but Papa was adamant about doing this job today.

Papa curses under his breath and furrows his brow.

His father's business has been a double-edged sword for Victor. He wants Papa to leave it all behind, but he refuses to walk away unless Victor takes over, and Victor has no desire to continue this life. When Papa started his new endeavor, he said he had met a group of out-of-town investors at a bar. After a few drinks, one mentioned needing a resident familiar with the area to join his team. Papa had recently retired after thirty years at the post office and needed a reason to stay away from the bars. It was a happy coincidence that the two of them met. Or maybe it wasn't. After six months with the group, the jobs became more clandestine, with the pay increasing accordingly. By then, it was clear the investment group was a front, and it became another topic Papa and Victor never discussed.

Victor graduated from college a month later and was scheduled to start a job at the same accounting firm where he had interned. The night before his departure, Papa had invited Victor to join him in the garage. There sat his 1948 cherry red Chevy truck.

When Victor was young, he longed for an invitation to work on the truck alongside Papa and his older brother. When dropping hints failed, his brother proposed the idea on his behalf, but Papa consistently found reasons to reject it. Victor was too short and couldn't see inside the hood. He might clumsily drop a crucial piece with his small hands, losing it forever. Besides, he was too young to understand how engines worked.

Victor was a man standing over the hood as the odor of grease and solvent made him feel like a kid again. Without a word, Papa handed him a tattered rag and a wooden-handled screwdriver, and they started working. It was just as magical as Victor had always imagined it would be until he handed Papa a combination wrench instead of a crescent wrench. Papa's subtle comparison to his brother opened old wounds of jealousy, and the moment was over.

The next morning, Papa asked Victor if he would stay and help him with his new business. Victor didn't know if the invitation was an apology or if Papa feared being alone, but Victor didn't care.

His father needed him, and he accepted, not knowing the cost.

Every year, a bit more of Papa is replaced by someone Victor doesn't recognize. The short fuse, foul language, and quick judgments. This is the new Papa.

Marta would not believe this was the father of her boys. Victor decided this morning to plead his case again for Papa to quit this life. He'll even use Papa's love for Marta if necessary.

"You stay. Let me handle it," Victor says.

Today, Victor will demonstrate his ability to take over the business. And when Papa is comfortable in retirement, Victor will gradually dismantle and abandon the business entirely.

Papa mulls over the idea and agrees, but insists that he take Oscar and Charlie. It's not the ideal situation, but Victor doesn't argue.

It's a sign that Papa is ready to step away. That's all Victor wants.

He steals a glance at the family photo and hopes that someday the happy memories will outweigh the grief and Papa will turn back

into his old self. Then Victor can, too.
They aren't these men they've become.

# THREE

ASIDE FROM the See's Candies store, Computer Repair is the only other original tenant since the mall's opening. It has remained relevant over the past twenty years by offering mobile device services and catering to the needs of gamers and coders. Max scrolls through his social media while waiting for his turn behind the Camry driver.

Camry Man places his laptop on the counter and asks the young man if Chase is available. The young man informs him that Chase called in sick, but he is more than happy to assist. Camry Man glances at his watch and hesitates before mentioning that he needs the hard drive cleaned up.

The young man asks his usual set of questions, delivered in a monotone voice: Will Camry Man be leaving the laptop with a power cord, case, or mouse? Camry Man responds "no" to each question, provides his information, agrees to receive a digital receipt, and then leaves.

Max steps up to the counter, exchanges greetings with the young man, and shows the receipt on his phone, along with his

Nevada Instruction Permit as identification. In a week, he'll trade that permit in for a full-fledged driver's license.

The young man eyes Max's ID, checks the name against the receipt, and gives a quick nod. Without a word, he grabs Camry Man's laptop and disappears into the back.

Max waits.

He hears faint shuffling from behind the half-door, the creak of a cabinet, something small hitting the floor. A moment later, the employee returns with Max's laptop.

He sets it on the counter and slides it forward. "If you have any problems, give us a call. And if everything looks good, we'd really appreciate a Yelp review. It helps us out a lot." His tone is flat and rehearsed.

Max thanks him, takes his laptop, and leaves.

He's almost at the mall's exit when someone calls out his name. He turns and sees several of his classmates sitting at a table. He gives a wave and is about to leave when he recognizes the shiny strawberry blonde hair that always smells like lavender and vanilla. Max changes course and makes a beeline for the group.

Today, he will have the courage to talk to Katie Bridgewater.

▬▬▬ ▪▪▬ ▬ ▪▬▪ ▪▪▬ ▬▪

Victor would have already been at the pickup location if Papa hadn't insisted that he pick up Oscar and Charlie. Oscar sits in the passenger seat of the dark grey Range Rover with his elbow propped up on the door. He's six years older than Victor, with streaks of grey hair peeking through his ponytail. He pulls out a cigarette and lights it. Reason number 342 why Victor didn't want Oscar to come.

Victor gags as smoke billows in front of his face. "Seriously?" he says.

Oscar lowers his window and hangs the cigarette out the window. "Better, princess?" Victor rolls his eyes. "You don't hear..." Oscar turns toward the backseat.

"What's your name again?"

"Uh, Charlie."

"You don't hear Uh Charlie complaining." He takes a long drag and exhales into the windshield. Victor resists a cough. "You don't mind, do you, Uh Charlie?"

"Oh, u—I'm fine," Charlie squeaks out.

Charlie's the new guy on Papa's crew. Victor has only known him for a few weeks, but he reminds Victor of himself when he was twenty-two and had his whole life ahead of him.

Tomorrow, Victor plans to tell Charlie that Papa no longer needs him, and he'll tell Papa that Charlie decided to work with his dad somewhere and help care for an ailing mother that may or may not exist. It's not too late for Charlie.

Oscar takes a drag. "Daddy finally let you off the leash?" he says, before exhaling.

Victor ignores him. Oscar has been a thorn in his side ever since Papa brought him on board. He was surprised when Papa told him he had hired a new person on his crew, and he couldn't hide his shock when that person turned out to be his older brother's childhood friend.

And now there's Charlie. Young, naive, Charlie. Victor does not like where things are headed.

Oscar continues, "I told him business and family don't mix." He pulls down his visor and murmurs, "Foolish old man doesn't listen."

Victor shoots Oscar a look, but he's taming stray hairs in the mirror and doesn't notice.

Oscar slams the visor up. "You know, if he thought you could actually do this job, I wouldn't be here. Wake me when you have it." He tosses his cigarette butt and closes his eyes as he reclines his seat back encroaching on Charlie who is sitting behind him.

Charlie scoots into the middle seat and leans forward. "What's on it?" he asks.

Oscar chuckles. "Don't ever ask about details. Papa doesn't even know what's on it," he says.

Victor turns into the mall parking lot just as the Camry is leaving. He parks near the parking lot exit, far from the mall entrance. "I'll be back."

He hears Oscar mock him in the Terminator's voice as he slams the door shut.

Victor enters the mall and passes a group of teenagers sitting around a table engaged in loud conversation about usual teenage things.

He greets the young man at Computer Repair and shows him the electronic receipt he received minutes ago via a text message, which he altered to match the name on his ID. He completes the transaction and leaves when he notices the empty USB port. As panic sets in, he opens the picture of the laptop that was sent with the receipt. The serial number of the laptop in his hand matches the same serial number on the receipt, and the USB port in the picture clearly shows what he came for. Victor knows the receipt was sent from a burner phone that has probably already been tossed, but he texts the number anyway.

He receives an immediate response: Message failed to deliver.

He takes a deep breath before sending his next text.

--- ··- - ·-· ··- -·

Papa lights up when he sees Sonja approach his booth, ready to take his order. She's in her mid-thirties with flawless skin and thick, wavy hair. She reminds him of Marta at that age. "I'm so sorry about the wait. There was a minor emergency in the kitchen. No Victor today?" Her Spanish accent has faded over the years, and he tries to remember what she sounded like when they first met. He tries to remember a lot of things on this day. And each year it gets harder.

"He had to leave. Work to do."

She glances at the photo, and pity settles on her face. He notices and changes the subject.

"How is Mateo? What is he... eight or nine now?"

Sonja lets out a little laugh. "Ten. He already needs new shoes again. He won't stop growing," she says.

"They tend to do that if you're lucky," Papa says. He gives Sonja his order, explaining it will be a quick visit today, and she returns with what she has learned over the years was Marta's favorite, a root beer float with two cherries on top so the boys wouldn't fight. A large group enters, waiting to be seated, and Sonja leaves the check with a quick smile before scurrying off.

Before Papa can unwrap his straw, he receives a text from Victor.

As he reads, his face hardens, and he pushes the root beer float away. He snatches up the family photo, returns it to its resting place inside his wallet, and takes out two crisp one-hundred-dollar bills. He places them under the check and scribbles a note: Shoes are expensive.

As he leaves the diner, a beggar approaches him with his palms out, muttering for spare change. Papa ignores him and continues to walk down the alley toward a blacked-out Mercedes G Wagon parked in the lot.

The homeless man maintains his pursuit, so Papa pulls out his phone, hoping the beggar will get the point and bug off. With the beggar hot on his heels, Papa quickens his pace, takes out his car fob, and clicks the button. The car lights flash.

The beggar catches up, and Papa can smell the nauseating odor of alcohol emanating from his pores.

*The driver was intoxicated.*

He whips around and they lock eyes for a moment before Papa plunges a knife into the poor man's torso.

# FOUR

A SHADOW crosses over Oscar as he sits reclined in the passenger seat of the Range Rover. He peeks with one eye and sits up when he sees Papa's Mercedes parked in front of them. He watches as Papa exits and stands by the driver's side door. The plan was to meet Papa later after they completed the drop-off. Oscar checks his phone for any missed messages that might explain why Papa is here now. Victor didn't mention a change of plans, but he's tried to cut Oscar out of the loop in the past. When he doesn't know what's going on, he feels stupid. Worse, he looks stupid. He instructs Charlie to stay put, emphasizing with a glare, and exits.

He leans against the quarter panel, props his foot on the tire, and lights up a cigarette, giving him time to assess how to approach the situation. He'll mention they're running on schedule and see if Papa offers any new information. Before he has time to exhale, Victor emerges from the mall and heads in their direction. Oscar has seen Victor irritated, mad, annoyed, and a range of other emotions, but as Victor nears, he can't accurately describe what he's witnessing.

Papa eyes the laptop under Victor's arm. "You said there was a problem?"

Charlie cracks the window and immediately starts coughing from Oscar's cigarette smoke.

Oscar pushes himself off the tire and stands next to Papa and Victor.

"It's gone." Victor shows Papa the side of the laptop and the empty USB port.

"Maybe you have the wrong laptop," Papa says.

Oscar holds back a smile, hoping that's the case.

Victor shows Papa the text message from the courier, which includes a picture of a laptop with a flash drive plugged into its USB port. The laptop's serial number ends with "R2DW." Victor then flips the laptop over and points out the serial number to Papa: "R2DW. I have the right one."

"I can't believe this." Papa throws his hands in the air wildly as he paces between the Mercedes and the Range Rover. He pounds his fist on the hood of the Range Rover, cursing.

Oscar sees Charlie jump inside the Rover, smirks, and takes a drag.

"The kid working the counter said three laptops were picked up today. He wouldn't give me any other information." Victor says.

Papa stops and looks at Victor, but does not respond.

He bites his lip and resumes pacing.

Oscar flicks his cigarette butt onto the ground and steps right up to Victor, invading his personal space to stamp it out. "Did you retrace your steps? Maybe you dropped it," he says, speaking to Victor as if he were a five-year-old searching for his special rock. "I'm sure it will turn up." Oscar's condescension is palpable; he's fully aware of the consequences if they fail to deliver the flash drive on time. He takes a quiet satisfaction in now knowing what Victor looks like when he's scared.

Victor ignores Oscar and turns to Papa. "We arrived within five minutes of getting the text confirmation. The flash drive has to be nearby. I could've been here sooner..." This makes Papa stop in his tracks. Victor doesn't finish his thought.

"If it fell out," Victor says, glaring at Oscar, "and was put in the wrong laptop, we should be able to track it as soon as the owner turns it on."

Papa gets in Victor's face. "And what if they don't turn it on for days? We don't have days. We have hours."

Although Oscar relishes the sight of Victor getting scolded, he sees an opportunity and slinks around to the back of the Range Rover. He pauses for a moment to bask in Victor's misery as a sly grin creeps onto his face. He pulls out his phone and dials a number, listening to the low ring while he steals another glance at the drama unfolding nearby.

Oscar notices Charlie trying to hear his phone conversation through the back window, and shoots him a warning glare. Charlie quickly scoots to the other side and fumbles with the handle, trying to exit. His hoodie string gets tangled with the seatbelt, jerking him back. After a brief struggle, Charlie frees himself and exits the Range Rover, lingering near the rear corner panel.

Papa paces again, wild-eyed. "We need a full sweep of the store as soon as possible. Victor, contact the cleaning crew and set it up. This is a priority," he says. His face reddens as veins become visible.

"If it's in a laptop, I'm sure the owner will probably power it up to check if it works, and that's when we can trace it," Victor says. But Oscar watches Victor's face change as he seems to realize he's just outlined the worst-case scenario. Victor quickly backtracks. "More likely, it just fell out and is still in the store."

Oscar can see that Victor is trying to keep Papa calm. He's witnessed Victor navigate Papa's anger before, but this feels different. Papa seems more volatile, more dangerous. His rage has gotten worse since the funeral, and Oscar can tell Victor doesn't know how to tame this new beast.

Oscar finishes his phone call and opens the tailgate, startling

Charlie. He pulls a GPS unit from a weathered nylon tactical bag and slams the tailgate, making Charlie flinch again. Oscar walks over to Papa and gestures with the GPS unit. "I called Mike," Oscar says as if he's in charge. "He's setting up manual tracking for the flash drive. It'll take about an hour to get a lock." He shoots a glare at Victor. "Unless, of course, it's in a laptop and someone turns it on." Oscar's smugness lands on Victor as he lights another cigarette.

Victor steps away and texts the cleaning crew.

Charlie hesitantly joins Papa and Oscar while he fidgets with his hands inside the front pocket of his hoodie. He rocks side to side and picks at the seam of his sleeve when he catches Oscar eyeing him.

Oscar takes a step toward him. "Do you want to say something, Uh Charlie?"

Charlie pauses and seems unsure if he should continue, but he does anyway. "Uh, what about the store's security cameras or the parking lot cameras?" He nods to the nearby light pole. A grey camera sits atop, pointing to the entrance of the mall. He's too focused on awaiting Papa's response to notice the man striding with purpose in his direction. The man looks about Charlie's age and wears faded baggy jeans and an oversized Metallica t-shirt. Drugs have done a number on his skin and teeth, and he's due for a shower. Registering the group's sudden silence, Charlie follows their gaze and does a double-take at the man closing in on him. Panic takes over, and he tries to head back into the Range Rover, but it's too late.

The Metallica fan continues toward Charlie

"Jason Porter! No way!" he says, his excitement mimicking that of a game show contestant.

Charlie ignores him and turns his head just as his long-lost high school acquaintance claps him on the back.

"Yo! Jay, I can't believe it's you. Wow, dude. I heard you and your brother split town a while back."

Oscar stands next to Charlie, grinning from ear to ear. First, Victor gets reamed by Papa. And now, Charlie's true identity is revealed by a washed-up nobody. "So, Jason. Who's your friend here?" Oscar asks.

"Yo! I'm Freddie," he says. He scratches at invisible bugs crawling on his skin and fails to control his rapid blinking as he shifts his weight from side to side. "Me and Jay go way back. Remember that time we—"

Papa steps in. "Hello, Freddie. I'm sure you think this is your friend... what did you call him? Jason? But I assure you, he is not. People confuse my nephew here for someone else all the time. Just one of those faces, I guess." He takes a step closer, causing Freddie to stiffen. "Freddie, you don't look well. Perhaps you need some... medicine." Papa slips a folded twenty-dollar bill in Freddie's palm.

Freddie stares at the twenty like it might bite him.

His eyes shift between the bill and Papa, his brow furrowed in deep concentration. He mumbles something under his breath, then gives a slow nod, as if the money itself had explained the situation. "Yeah. My mistake," he says before wandering off, unsure which one of them was right.

Oscar notices the subtle shift in Victor's posture, like tension has just been drained. He actually looks relieved as if strung-out Freddie just did him a favor.

Victor leans close to Papa and lowers his voice.

"Now that we all know Charlie is actually Jason Porter, I'll let him know we can't keep him on. No real names."

"No need. I trust everyone here," Papa says. He pats Victor on the shoulder and steps away. The interruption has brought Papa from DEFCON 1 back to a rational human being. He motions to the light pole. "Can we use these cameras?"

"I already thought of that," Victor says, shaking his head. "The employee won't show me any of their surveillance videos without a warrant, and the same goes for mall security. Said I could be a psycho ex-husband."

Oscar looks Victor up and down. "I can see that."

Victor steps into Oscar's personal space. "What's your

problem, man?"

Oscar drops his cigarette butt next to Victor's foot and grinds it out with his heel. "My problem is you don't know what the hell you're doing."

Victor gets loud. "I don't know what I'm doing? I'm not the one who lost the flash drive." He turns to Papa. "Maybe it's not even lost. Maybe the courier decided to make some quick cash." Victor looks Papa in the eyes.

"How well do you know this new guy, anyway?"

"I've never met him," Papa says.

"What do you mean you've never met him? He works for you," Victor says.

Oscar chuckles.

"The courier works for Romeo. And he isn't the new guy. We are."

Victor raises his eyebrows. "Who in the hell is Romeo?"

# FIVE

JESSIE STARTS to roll up her window but stops when she hears yelling coming from the other end of the parking lot. This parking lot, located at the back of the mall, is quite empty, allowing the voices to carry easily in the cool January air. The area near the parking lot's exit has witnessed its fair share of ex-couples exchanging custody of a child. Sometimes the child leaves in tears, while other times they run into the arms of the other parent.

Last month, Nick went to the mall to pick up a box of See's Candies for a coworker. As he was leaving, he noticed police arriving at what looked like a tense child custody exchange. When Jessie later pressed him for details, he was no help—he'd already been pulling out of the parking lot before the officer even stepped out of the cruiser. She briefly considered asking why he hadn't stayed to make sure the child was okay, but stopped herself.

Not everyone lives with the same instincts for suspicion.

Nick wrapped up the non-story with a shrug, saying he was sure the cops had it under control.

The sun's glare obscures their faces, but from their builds and voices, Jessie can tell the argument is between three men. There's no sign of a woman or child, so it probably isn't a custody exchange. They're gathered near two SUVs parked close to the exit. One of the taller men appears to be playing peacemaker, trying to calm another who's visibly agitated. The third man, unfazed by the shouting and animated gestures, walks slowly behind the grey SUV. Jessie rolls up the window and slides into the driver's seat, keeping an eye on the scene.

With a better view of the altercation, she opens the window and strains to catch a few words of the argument, but the swooshing breezes carry their words away from her. If they were closer, she might be able to make out some of the conversation by reading their lips—a skill she learned long ago. Despite her failed attempts, she mentally notes each man's approximate height. Old habits die hard.

"Mom, can you put the window up? I'm cold." Sean's words pull her attention away from the men and to the rearview mirror.

A grin creeps across her face when she notices Sean wearing the T-shirt they bought last week—evidence of progress. Her face falls when she notices his athletic shorts. They are clearly two sizes too small—evidence of resisting change.

"Sean, I told you to put on some pants before we left."

"I checked the weather for today. It will be a high of 52. I'm fine. It won't get super cold until after sunset, which will happen at 4:50 p.m. We'll be at Grandma's house by that time. I'm fine, as long as the windows are up."

Sean covers his legs with his pillow and continues to hunt for the word *kaleidoscope* in his Word Search puzzle book. Jessie bought it for him on Monday, and she knows that once he finds *kaleidoscope,* he'll be asking for another puzzle book. Maybe she'll switch things up and have him try Sudoku. He's always liked numbers.

His new obsession costs more than Jessie's coffee habit, and she misses the days when his hobby was collecting the free things he found on the ground.

Jessie abandons listening to the men arguing and rolls the window up. Whatever their issue is, it isn't her problem. People argue. It's normal. Just like her life, now. Her only job is to raise her boys and make sure they don't kill each other along the way. And occasionally she has to take them to their Grandparents' house.

"Hey, Sean. Look at me." She waits as he finishes circling *kaleidoscope* before he obeys. "It's a long trip to Grandma's house. I would appreciate it if you would lay off your brother. You've been kind of a jerk lately."

"I don't lay on him. And he's a jerk to me first. We're supposed to treat people the way they treat us," Sean says. His words aren't defensive or mean. They are a matter of fact.

Jessie sighs. "No, that's not the saying. It's: treat others the way you want to be treated. If you want Max to be nice to you, then you need to be nicer to him."

"Well, Max is not a good driver, and I was just telling him the truth. You say we should always tell the truth," Sean says.

She can't argue with that.

Sean's problem isn't telling the truth. He's the one she asks when she wants a truthful assessment of her outfit. He doesn't hesitate to point out when her make-up is too heavy, or when she has coffee breath, or if the person in line ahead of them has body odor. She has hidden or fled from many public places, sometimes in mid-transaction, after one of Sean's truthful observations. Sean's problem is that he doesn't know when not to tell the truth.

"I know. But sometimes, the truth isn't helpful. Especially when it hurts someone's feelings," Jessie says.

Sean ponders her words. A moment later, he says 'okay' and puts his completed puzzle book in his backpack. With Sean, sometimes things are that easy. Sometimes they are much more difficult.

Jessie's phone rings and she answers it over Bluetooth.

There's a pause before Nick's voice comes through the

Explorer's speakers. "Hey... I was actually about to leave you a message. Figured you were probably in the dead zone by now."

"We aren't even on the road yet. There was a missing iPad charger followed by a long phone call from your mother that kept us from getting out the door." Jessie almost hadn't answered the call, knowing she would be held hostage. But the possibility of it being important niggled in her mind until she hit the green button on her phone. His mother was calling to inform them of the road construction on the highway. Jessie thanked her, and before thinking, told her she and the boys would see them soon.

The moment she mentioned Nick wasn't coming with them, Jessie knew she was stuck with no one to pay her ransom.

When questioned, Jessie quickly explained that Nick had a work obligation (she didn't mention that he scheduled it for today because he forgot about the trip) and would be driving separately, which prompted a proud monologue from his mother about Nick's stellar sense of responsibility that started with his position on his elementary school's student council and ended with his latest job promotion. Because apparently, fourth grade is when a mother can predict what kind of provider her son will be for his future family. Jessie couldn't argue that Nick was a good provider, so she allowed his mother to finish boasting while she impatiently watched the minutes tick by. After what seemed like an eternity, but was only twelve minutes, they were finally out the door and on the road.

Jessie recognizes the way Nick says 'hey' and braces herself for disappointment before asking, "How much longer do you think you'll be?" Her eyes wander to the men near the SUVs, more out of habit than genuine curiosity.

"Maybe an hour. The IT guy said they're almost done getting the servers back up. Then it's just a couple of quick signatures and I'll be on my way," Nick says. He agrees to call her when he's on the road, and they say goodbye.

Jessie debates going back home and waiting for Nick so they can all leave together, but she knows technology is fickle and can't be trusted. That's why she avoids it as much as possible.

Jessie sends a text to Max: Hue Mitch longer? She hates autocorrect. She tries again, double-checking before she hits send: How much longer?

Max responds with: omw

She shows the screen to Sean.

"On my way," Sean says.

Max walks toward the Explorer, laptop in hand, ready to hit the road. His smile drops when he sees Jessie in the driver's seat. He climbs into the passenger seat and slams the door.

"You said I could drive to Grandma's so I could get the rest of my hours in."

His driver's license test is next week, and he seems more than excited; he seems desperate. Jessie wonders if it has something to do with a girl.

"And Dad said he would get the tire fixed. I don't want you driving until I know it's safe." She sees his disappointment and remembers her excitement when learning to drive and the anticipation of getting her license. "If the tire pressure holds after we fill it, we'll switch spots at the Lee Canyon exit."

"Fine," Max says. It's a step up from his usual 'whatever'.

As they drive toward the parking lot's exit, Jessie notices a fourth man in a hoodie has since joined the men who were arguing, along with another young man who can't stand still. The situation isn't volatile, but something about it doesn't sit right with her.

# SIX

THE CHEVRON is the last gas station before leaving the city. It's not as busy as expected for a holiday weekend, but most travelers probably left the city hours ago to make the most of the short winter daylight hours. A crisp breeze rustles Jessie's hair as she opens her door and tells Max to come around to her side. She twists in her seat and points to the label on the door frame. "This is where you can find the required tire psi." She waits for an acknowledgment, which she doesn't get, then motions him to the front passenger tire.

As she gets out, she notices his Mario Wasted t-shirt. She doesn't recognize the band's name and stops herself from making the Nintendo joke that is on the tip of her tongue. Max doesn't appreciate her jokes anymore. Jessie doesn't appreciate his blonde wavy hair giving off cool surfer vibes after just crawling out of bed. His untamed hair and ocean-blue eyes make him look like a Quick Silver model. Her untamed hair makes her look like she travels by broomstick. In this moment, Jessie notices how much Max is starting to resemble his dad. His broadening shoulders and patchy facial hair send her an obvious message.

Her baby is growing up, with or without her consent.

"It's also in the app," he says.

Jessie misses what he said, her thoughts spiraling at the realization that Max will be leaving for college in eighteen months. She has only a little more than two years left with him. And each year passes by faster than the last. Has she soaked up as many moments as she could with him? How did he become a man in the blink of an eye? "What did you say?" she asks, trying to mask the sadness in her voice.

"You can find the psi requirement in the app."

"You don't have the app." She still has parental controls set on his phone, which require her permission for him to download apps. None of his friends have roadblocks on their phones, something he likes to remind her of when he's being *crispy*. It's a term she's come up with to describe a particular attitude Max has fine-tuned. A disrespectful jerk, she can punish with justification. However, a crispy teenager skirts the line that warrants a reprimand.

"I'll download it once I get my license."

Jessie doesn't like his tit-for-tat tone, but she can't give him the "we'll see" response she sometimes gives when he wants to download new apps because they both know she will want him to have it once he starts driving. "Sometimes apps don't work. Or your phone might be dead." Despite Max stealing her phone charger daily, along with her backup charger, his phone is in a perpetual state of: about to die.

"The infotainment system has the manual. I can get it there."

Jessie hadn't bothered to learn more than the basics of the touchscreen, also known as the infotainment system. Anything beyond the radio, navigation, and Bluetooth has been ignored. "If the battery's dead, the touchscreen won't work."

"If the battery's dead, the tire pressure won't be my first concern," Max says.

Jessie concedes. "We need to fill the tire to thirty-five psi." She kneels beside the wheel and demonstrates how to check the tire pressure using an old orange metal gauge. It has three black stripes on the bottom and chipped paint along the edges, but it still works perfectly.

Twelve years ago, she was flipping through paperbacks at a garage sale when a grey-haired man beside her pulled the gauge from a cardboard box labeled "25 cents each" in bold black marker on the flap. She offered him ten dollars for it, and he laughed, saying she could buy a brand new one for less. Before allowing him to accept or decline her offer, she pulled out another ten-dollar bill and handed both bills to him. He shrugged and happily took the money in exchange for the gauge.

It's identical to the one Dr. Smith used during The Agency's Evasive and Emergency Vehicle Operation training, dubbed Speed Week by the recruits. The tire pressure gauge is the closest thing Jessie has to a keepsake from that chapter of her life.

The gauge pops up to the line marked twenty-six.

Max doesn't seem impressed when Jessie reads the number and confirms what they already know. The tire needs air.

Jessie makes a face when she sees a digital screen on the air pump displaying a two-dollar fee. A sticker shows five different ways she can pay, and Visa is the only one she's familiar with. "Air used to be free. Let me grab my card." As Jessie turns, she hears the clanging of the air pump and turns back around.

Max waves his phone. "Apple Pay." It's another thing Jessie hasn't taken the time to figure out how to use. Max grabs the air hose, fills the tire, and checks the pressure readout on the pump's digital screen. Satisfied when it reaches thirty-five pounds, he caps the tire's valve and hangs up the hose.

"I didn't know you knew how to fill a tire."

"You didn't ask." Max gets in the car and starts scrolling on his phone.

Jessie pulls out of the Chevron, and seven minutes later, they are traveling north on US Route 95. She hates driving at night, and they are cutting it close if they are going to arrive at her in-laws' house before dark. The day after she turned forty, her night vision took a nosedive. She thinks WTF should stand for What The Forties because everything changes after that magical number: digestion, eyesight, hormones. Why does so much change after forty? She has five hours to ponder that question. And if Sean hadn't interrupted her endless rabbit hole of thinking, she would have.

"I think Dad should have to drive. Grandma is his mom. So he should have to drive to his mom's house. And you should have to drive to your mom's house."

After a moment, he adds, "But you don't have a mom."

Max, wide-eyed, turns and glares at Sean.

"So you don't ever have to drive to her house," Sean says. He looks puzzled by Max's glare.

"That's not how it works. How have you survived 7$^{th}$ grade this long?" Max says.

"As long as Max isn't driving," Sean says.

"Shut up." He swats at Sean, who blocks the attempt with his hockey stick.

"Guys, enough." Jessie eyes the stick through the rearview mirror. "Sean, I told you not to bring that."

"But I need to practice."

"You're not even a player, you're a goalie," Max says.

"It doesn't matter, Max. I still practice every day. What am I supposed to do? Not practice and become terrible?"

Despite his lack of finesse in day-to-day physical activities, Sean has become a rather good hockey goalie to everyone's surprise. The traits that once concerned Jessie—his fearlessness, need for proprioceptive stimuli, and tendency to be antisocial—have served Sean well in the position. The heaviness of the equipment and the act of throwing himself into butterfly or a diving poke check provide him with the body awareness his brain craves. Playing goalie allows him to hang out in a designated area all by himself.

His focus is always on the puck, which doesn't leave much

room for human eye contact, and he doesn't take shifts, so he never has to talk to anyone on the bench. Sean loves being a hockey goalie.

Jessie attempts to redirect the conversation, if it can be called that. "Grandpa said he wants to teach you how to drive the tractor. That'll be fun."

"I bet I drive better—" He catches Jessie's glare in the mirror. Occasionally, he has been a passenger while Max practices driving, and he speaks from experience.

"You can show him how it's done," Jessie tells Max, remembering how he always begs Grandpa to let him drive the tractor before they have even unpacked. "I've got stuff to do." Max pats his laptop.

Max's interests seemed to shift overnight. Tractors gave way to technology, and the make-believe battles between Monster Mom's terrifying tickles and Super Max's laser-beam eyes morphed into real-life standoffs. Jessie was still the villain, but now she faced death glares and eye rolls.

"I don't want your nose buried in a screen all weekend. We'll probably only make it back one or two more times, and...you'll be off to college soon."

She catches Max's response under his breath, "Thank God."

Jessie lets it slide.

"I think you should just enjoy hanging out with your grandparents without the distraction."

"Mom, I can monitor my usage," Max says. "It's just like with driving. You have to control everything. You always tell me what to do before I can even think about making a decision." Max sees her resolve cracking. "Plus, I was FaceTiming with Grandpa last week, well, trying to anyway, and I was explaining to him the program I've been working on for the last six months. But he couldn't really follow along with what I was saying. So, I told him I would bring my laptop and show him."

"Okay. But whatever activities your grandpa has planned, you do them without complaint," she says.

"Deal. Poor Grandpa thinks coding is like Morse code or something."

Morse code. Jessie hasn't heard, seen, or used Morse code in what feels like a lifetime. The first Morse code message she ever deciphered was from a fellow recruit. His message said she was pretty. Even at eighteen, it made her feel like a giddy middle schooler finding out her crush liked her.

# SEVEN

A STEADY stream of cars flows into the mall parking lot, gradually encroaching on where Papa and his crew linger. Victor stands with his hands in his jacket pockets, scanning the influx of people. A breeze carries the chatter of excited teenagers taking advantage of the extra day off from school. A handful of office workers on their lunch break engage in banal conversation as they spill out of a hatchback. Nothing to be concerned about. No one so much as glances in their direction.

Victor scowls and gestures toward Oscar. "Papa, what is he talking about? Who's Romeo?" Victor didn't condone what Papa's business had become, but he felt it was finally running its course, and he planned to coax Papa into retirement by promising to take over. Then, after a year, maybe two, he would dissolve the business and rejoin the financial world.

But now Papa was working for others? When did this happen? And for how long?

"Just a guy I started working with. He pays well."

"That's an understatement," Oscar mumbles.

"Papa, you said you were going to run your own business. Be your own boss," Victor says, his voice low and edged with frustration. He continues to watch the ebb and flow of strangers, avoiding eye contact with Papa. With the revelation of a new player in the picture, Victor worries his plan is jeopardized, and he has no idea how deeply Papa is entwined in the criminal underworld.

"I am running my own business." Papa glares at Victor.

"Then why are you working for someone else? What do we know about this guy? Can we trust him?" Victor asks in one breath.

"*We* don't have to trust him. *I* do." Papa locks eyes with Victor.

Victor shifts, taking a step back as tension rises in his shoulders.

This conversation can wait, but the job has a deadline. He runs his hands through his hair and exhales deeply as he turns and steps away from Papa. If he can get this job back on track, it will solidify his capabilities as a worthy successor. Victor turns to Oscar, his voice firm. "Oscar, have Mike hack into the security cameras."

"He's working on setting up the GPS tracking," Oscar says.

"He can do both. And if he can't, we'll find someone who can."

The approving twinkle in Papa's eye unsettles Victor. It conveys to him, "that's my boy," but Victor doesn't want to emulate his father in this way. Papa's silence encourages Victor to continue. He talks while typing on his phone. "Getting an update from the cleaning crew now. They'll let me know when they're on their way."

"Mike should focus on the GPS signaling, not the cameras," Oscar says. "That's our best bet for finding the flash drive."

"And if the GPS tells us it's in the mall moving around, how will we know who we are looking for if we don't know what they look like? Just make the call," Victor says.

Victor catches a flicker of amusement in Papa's eyes— approval maybe. It's something he's wanted for many years, but not for a reason like this.

Oscar hesitates before acquiescing to Victor's command.

Victor's phone buzzes, and he reads a text. "The cleaning crew is thirty minutes out."

"Why so long? Did you tell them this was a priority?" Papa asks.

"They're finishing a job on the other side of town, but they're packing up now."

Charlie glances at Oscar, who is talking on the phone, and steps closer to Victor and Papa. He hunches his shoulders and leans in. "Should we, uh, split up and start looking?"

"For what?" Victor asks.

"I don't know—someone with a laptop. Or, like, someone that looks like they stole a laptop," Charlie says.

His voice trails off at the suggestion.

"And what would someone like that look like?"

Victor gestures to the members of their group. "A senior citizen? A college-aged kid? A middle-aged high school dropout in desperate need of a haircut?"

Oscar flips off Victor at the last description.

"Relax, Victor. He's just trying to be helpful," Papa says. "I appreciate your ambition, Charlie, but it's best if we stay together. If the team separates, it will slow us down when we're ready to move. Besides, Victor's right. We don't know what we should be looking for." Papa sets his jaw. "Unfortunately, the only thing we can do now is wait."

# EIGHT

As the last city buildings become specks in Jessie's rearview mirror, the low tire pressure light remains off. The highway begins to curve, and the glaring afternoon sun finds its way back to Jessie. She pulls down her visor and pushes it to the side, shielding her eyes from the blinding rays.

In a few hours, the sun will no longer be a problem as it settles behind Sheep Mountain, home to ski slopes and a small cabin community twenty miles off the highway. The scenery for the next few hundred miles will consist of dry, cracked dirt dotted with Joshua trees. Deeper in the desert lie plateaus with drop-offs that are only noticeable up close. From the highway, they blend into the desolate landscape. The few plants that dare to exhibit any shade of green are overwhelmed by a sea of brown. This is the beautiful Mojave Desert.

Before the city's rapid growth, drivers often had to stop and let wild burros cross the two-lane highway. Now, it's rare to see a squirrel scampering across the four-lane expansion. Besides the highway's new width and the remodeled rest stop at the Lee Canyon exit, the long stretch of desert from Las Vegas to Grandma's house hasn't changed. Jessie hates making this drive, but she appreciates that in a world where boys become men overnight and passwords change every month, she can count on it to be exactly what it has always been.

Brown, dry, and lifeless.

Unlike the rest of the world, this drive remains constant and predictable.

They've only been on the road for thirty minutes, and Jessie already feels like a trapped hamster that will never reach its destination. There's a truck ahead of them, and what looks like a van or SUV farther along in the fast lane. She wonders if those drivers are just as bored and antsy as she is. Living in a society with instant access to everything has conditioned her to resent the fact that flying cars still don't exist, even if she thinks the idea is preposterous. Accepting that she lacks the superpower to speed up time or teleport, she sighs and starts the first episode of *The Five-Year Fraud* podcast just as the Top 40 radio station crackles to static.

After the dramatic music fades and introductions are made, the host grills Theodore Munson for the first ten minutes of the show. She recalls his lies and the devastation he caused to those close to him, and disregards what can only be described as a tragic and neglectful childhood. There's a long silence before Theodore explains the origin story of his alter ego. "I know my mom and dad loved me, but…"

As Theodore's voice trails off, it's replaced by the voices of Jessie's mom and dad—and the haunting memory of the last time she saw them alive. A loud pop had grabbed her attention, and when she looked out the window from the back seat, she saw a green car barreling down the alleyway toward her. She remembers the sounds of metal folding and glass breaking, as well as the nauseating smell of wet pennies and gasoline. And then nothing.

The Explorer's collision alarm and Max yelling her name

startle Jessie. She brakes hard, coming within a car's length of the truck in front of them. The near collision serves as a reminder of her inability to forget her past and the influence it has on her.

Sean's iPad flies out of his hands and slides underneath Max's seat. "You know, Mom, maybe you should let Dad teach Max how to drive. I don't think it's Max's fault he's a terrible driver."

"You need to start slowing down much sooner," Max says mockingly.

Jessie regroups and sets the cruise control. "Sorry, guys. I was —" What is she going to tell them? That she was thinking about the day that drove her to become a big fat liar, just like Theodore Munson? It's been years since memories of her past have infiltrated her present life, but today it seems everything is triggering memories of what she lost, who she became, and the choices she made.

She looks at Max and regrets nothing.

Max presses the power button on his laptop and rubs his temples.

"What's wrong?" Jessie asks.

"Nothing."

"Mom, who is your favorite son?" Sean asks.

"You," Max scoffs.

"That's not true. I don't have a favorite son."

"In school yesterday, we had to write about our family pet or favorite animal if we don't have a pet. And sons are kind of like pets because you have to feed them and play with them. And give them exercise, like hockey. I told my teacher that I don't have any pets and I don't have a favorite animal. I told her I have a favorite TV show, and I have a favorite book, and I have a favorite hockey player. But not a favorite animal. And she said I had to pick one to be my favorite. So, pick which one is your favorite. Me or Max?"

"Sean, just like you don't have a favorite animal, I don't have a favorite son," Jessie says.

Max snorts.

"Well, I don't have a favorite animal because I don't care

about animals. They don't do anything. I don't get why zoos exist. I wish people would spend money to watch me lay around all day," Sean says.

"Animals do lots of cool stuff. Some of them can camouflage themselves and hide from dangerous predators," Jessie says.

"All I ever see is neighbors walking their dogs. That's it. They just walk. And poop. And then walk some more. So boring."

"Well, that's because those are domesticated animals. The rules are different in the wild."

"Like what?" Sean asks.

"It's simple: hide, hunt, or die."

Jessie checks her cell phone. "Download some shows from the National Geographic Channel. I bet you'll change your mind. It looks like we still have service, so download them now before we're out of range."

Sean pulls his iPad from underneath Max's seat and starts searching for shows.

Jessie knows that Sean receives more attention, which has become a major source of her guilt. Six years ago, Nick and Jessie explained to Max that Sean was diagnosed with some neurological differences. At ten years old, Max couldn't understand why his younger brother got away with stuff that he didn't. She hopes that as Max matures, he will better understand the situation and will not grow to resent Sean. Or her.

Jessie believed bonding with children came naturally to most mothers, while a father had to put in work. When Max was a toddler, she allowed Nick and Max to forge their relationship. Now, she's wondering if she had pulled back too much.

She hopes the rift between her and Max isn't solely because of Sean and likes to think that puberty plays a role. Some days, she thinks there's more to it and wonders if he somehow knows.

Now that Sean is older and needs less attention, Jessie has tried to spend more time with Max, but he would rather be on his computer or texting friends. It might be too late.

When Jessie shared her concerns with Nick, he reassured her that "all teenagers are like this." She told Nick that they seemed fine and were thick as thieves. He told her that sons and fathers are different. She still doesn't know what he meant. Jessie feels like the window of opportunity to reconnect with Max is closing fast, and there's nothing she can do to stop it. He no longer wishes he had laser beam eyes or tickles from his mom, but Jessie hopes they can find a common interest on this trip to fill the void she feels in her heart.

"When did you learn how to fill a tire?" Jessie asks.

"Two weeks ago."

"Did Dad show you?" Knowing better, she adds, "Or was it TikTok?"

"It was in Driver's Ed at school," Max says. "What's with the interrogation?"

"No, I'm not... I was just curious. If I had known, I wouldn't have done the whole —" Jessie makes an awkward gesture with her hands, which Max doesn't see because he's staring at the black screen on his laptop. "I would've just let you do it." It's hard for her to accept that with each new day, he needs her less, and he's becoming his own person. His own man. Jessie keeps her eyes on the road, swallowing the lump in her throat.

Max presses the power button on his laptop again, this time with more force. Based on physical appearance alone, one would assume Max was the hockey player and Sean was the computer geek, not the other way around. He straightens in his seat and repeatedly taps the Enter key, but despite doing so, it doesn't make the laptop boot up any faster. Jessie can tell Max desperately wants an escape. While waiting for the laptop, he rubs his temples and asks Jessie if she has Tylenol.

"Sean, hand my purse to Max," Jessie says.

Sean passes her purse between the front seats without looking up from his iPad. From the corner of her eye, Jessie sees a cheetah racing across the screen in pursuit of a gazelle. Sean stays locked in, clearly impressed by the gazelle's zigzagging escape and sheer determination.

Max places her purse on his laptop, rummages inside, and finds a small plastic bag containing four yellow capsules.

"These?" Max asks, holding up the baggie.

Jessie glances over at Max and snatches the bag. "Where was that?"

Max stiffens.

"It was just at the bottom of your purse."

Jessie peers inside and notices that the lining concealing the hidden pocket has come undone. Lifting her right hip, she shoves the baggie into her jeans' back pocket. "There should be a small bottle of Tylenol in there."

Max pops two capsules in his mouth, takes a drink, and swallows the pills like a pro. Not that long ago, he had to use a straw to swallow pills.

Jessie hits a pothole, and water jostles from Max's bottle, spilling onto his laptop.

He recaps the bottle and scrambles for napkins in the glove box. "If it got ruined, I'm going to be so mad. I literally just got it fixed."

"That's called irony," Sean pipes in from the back seat.

Max is on the verge of telling Sean to shut up, but Jessie's look stops him. She's confident he'd fall out of the car if he rolled his eyes any harder. After wiping up the water, Max pounds away at the Enter key, then switches to clicking the trackpad in frustration. "I don't know why it's not booting up."

"I'm sure it's fine. Just give it a minute," Jessie says.

A moment later, a melodic chime sounds from the laptop, and the cursor appears, blinking in the top left-hand corner.

"Finally," Max says. He kicks off his shoes and crosses his legs underneath his laptop.

"See, everything's fine."

# NINE

OSCAR LEANS against the Range Rover while finishing a soft pretzel from the mall food court. Charlie's stomach rumbles, chastising him for not getting food when he had the chance, but he avoids being alone with Oscar, and Papa hadn't looked pleased when Oscar announced he was leaving to get a snack. Standing between the two SUVs, Charlie zones out, trying to remember if he ate anything that morning. He startles when the Mercedes door opens. Papa has entered and exited the vehicle at least three times now.

The first time, Charlie followed his lead and got in the Range Rover, thinking he had missed a conversation in which they decided to leave. After a few minutes of sitting alone in silence, Charlie watched as Papa exited the Mercedes, so he did the same. The second time Papa got in the Mercedes, Victor got in the Range Rover, so Charlie again followed suit. But it turned out Victor was retrieving his portable cellphone battery, while Papa quenched his thirst. Charlie exited again, realizing they still weren't leaving. The third time Papa went back to the Mercedes, Charlie waited. When it was obvious Victor and Oscar weren't budging, he stayed outside too.

Papa exits the Mercedes, checks the time on his phone, and asks Victor for an update on the cleaning crew. Victor checks his phone and tells him that the team is eight minutes out. Papa asks for an update from Oscar, who tells him that Mike is approximately fifteen to twenty minutes away from getting the manual tracking online. He's still attempting to hack into the mall's interior and parking lot security cameras, but it's surprisingly more difficult with the older system. Charlie's cousin has become really good at manipulating older electronics because most of the places he targets don't use state-of-the-art equipment. For a moment, he considers offering this information, wanting to contribute to the team, but ultimately decides his cousin can't be trusted.

So he remains silent.

The four men continue to stand around in silence, waiting. Victor incessantly checks his phone for updates that never come. Papa seemingly stares out into nowhere, hardly shifting his body weight, which Charlie finds impressive, considering he can barely stay still fighting the boredom. As Oscar lights up, Charlie moves away, evading the cigarette smoke.

"I wish it were in someone's laptop and they would just turn the stupid thing on already," Charlie accidentally says aloud.

Oscar pushes off the Range Rover and throws his pretzel wrapper to the ground. "They just did." He shows Papa the GPS unit.

Papa's trance has been broken, and his eyes blaze.

Charlie resists the temptation to pick up the pretzel wrapper as he walks up behind Oscar and looks over his shoulder. The GPS screen displays a red dot moving steadily along the highway. Papa tosses the Mercedes keys to Oscar, startling Charlie and causing him to lose his balance and stumble.

He scurries off to the Range Rover, trying to camouflage his near fall and hoping Oscar didn't notice.

Victor starts the Range Rover and shifts it into drive. He

looks toward the swishing sound made by Charlie's bouncing leg as it rubs against the pocket in the door panel. He throws the Range Rover into park and turns to Charlie. "What is it, Charlie?"

Charlie hesitates before answering. "What will Papa do to the person with the flash drive?"

Victor looks ahead and throws the SUV back into drive.

"I don't know."

# TEN

BRIGHT ORANGE construction signs line the highway, warning drivers of the roadwork ahead. Jessie grips the steering wheel a little tighter and glances at the time on the infotainment screen. They should make it before sunset. She silently prays there won't be any traffic stops or unexpected delays that could extend their trip into the night.

"So what's this new program you've been working on for the past... what, three months?"

"Six months. It's basically a program that will blah blah blah, computer blah blah, blah blah." Jessie knows how to turn on her laptop, open and compose an email, create a simple spreadsheet, and use copy and paste. Max is talking way over her head. The fact that Max is a techie computer nerd doesn't help their bonding dilemma.

"Sounds cool." She's clueless about anything he just said.

"Yeah, it will be. If we can get it to work."

"We?"

"Did you know bats are almost blind?" Sean doesn't take his

eyes off his iPad or wait for a response as he starts the next episode about chameleons. "I wonder if chameleons are blind, too," he says to no one.

"Something's wrong."

The green cursor blinks in the top left corner of the laptop's black screen. "My home screen still hasn't popped up." Max frowns and frantically taps out multiple keystroke combinations. Nothing happens. He glances up. "Is there any cell service out here?"

Jessie checks the bars on her phone. "There is, but it's weak." She steals a look at his laptop screen while Max continues to tap on the keyboard with a mission. "What's that?"

"It's a chat box." Max senses another question coming and answers before it can be asked. "I'm asking my friend if they've experienced this before."

"Who, Cooper?" Max will be impressed that she remembers Cooper. They've known each other since fifth grade.

"No," Max says as if he's already answered a hundred questions. He hits the Enter key and waits.

"Is it Tyson? He's into computers, right? Remember when I had to drag you two out of the Apple Store?" Max gives her a deadpan look, and Jessie instantly regrets prying further into his life without an invitation. He'd have mentioned the project and his friend if he wanted her to know. She's obviously an outsider and has no business knowing such things.

"It's no one you know."

A mother's favorite answer.

The laptop chimes. Jessie sneaks a peek and notices Max perk up in response to a message from BirdOfPrey431.

"Is that your friend? Bird of Prey four three one?"

"Yeah." Max continues to type.

"What's his real name?" No answer. "Or her real name."

Max sighs. "I don't know, Mom. It's just what he calls himself. I think his school mascot is some sort of bird." New messages blink onto the screen.

*So, it is a he.* And Max doesn't know his name. Tina's questions regarding the Theodore Munson case echo in Jessie's mind. How did this dude's best friend not realize he wasn't who he claimed to be? Can you even call someone your friend if you don't know their real name? How can you know a person if you don't know the most basic information that's been a part of their identity since birth?

The day Jessie asked Jonathan to leave The Agency with her, she told him the name her parents had given her, the one she used for the first eighteen years of her life: Samantha. For the eight years she was with The Agency, Jonathan knew her by the name The Agency gave her, Alex. She thought that if she told him her real name, it would prove just how much she trusted him, and he would wrap her in his arms, eager to start a new life with her. She thought she knew him. But maybe Tina's right. How well can you really know someone when you don't know their real name? Jessie pushes her best friend out of her mind.

"Is this Bird of Prey four three one guy in high school? How old is he?" She tries her best to hide her concern and sound casual.

"Geez, Mom. I don't know. I think he's like my age. We don't grill each other on personal details." He avoids eye contact and impatiently waits for a response to pop up on the screen and rescue him from this interrogation.

*Details can get you killed.* Jessie shakes away Dr. Smith's words. "So, Bird of Prey could literally be a 40-year-old pervert posing as a kid, and you would have no idea." Her tone is harsher than she intended.

"Stranger danger," Sean quips from the back seat.

"Sean, stay out of it. He's not forty. At least he doesn't sound old. He sounds like he's my age, okay? Maybe a year older, he just got a car. And stop using his full handle... just say Bop." Max sounds more irritated over her use of his friend's name than her prying into his personal life.

Since when was forty considered old? Has she really been

oblivious to what he's been doing for the past six months? No need to prepare an acceptance speech for her Mother of the Year award. She doesn't even know who his friends are. It's no wonder they aren't close.

Nick probably knows about this Bird of Prey guy. The three of them probably send each other jokes. Wait, not jokes. Max informed her last month that kids don't do jokes these days. Memes. It's all about memes now. It's obvious why Max hasn't let her into his world. She's completely out of touch. She'll have to ask Sean how to find memes, or maybe you're supposed to make them. She isn't even sure about that.

When Max first mentioned working with a friend on this program, Jessie had assumed he was referring to a classmate from his coding class. Someone he could invite over to hang out with after school. Now she realizes she has no idea who this "friend" is. Her mind races through the dark places on the internet and conjures up images of the vile predators that lurk there.

A shirtless alcoholic with his pants unbuttoned flashes in her thoughts.

Those internet dangers are why Sean can only call or text family members with his phone and has to use the family computer in the living room to get online. He is way too trusting. Max is better at discerning a person's character, but even he can't sense danger through a screen. That's why she asks a hundred questions.

A pothole snaps Jessie from her thoughts, releasing her from the bowels of the internet. They pass another orange construction sign warning of merging lanes up ahead.

Max mutters something as he taps away on the keyboard. "And if I do this command and then..." he types a bit more, "it should be good. As. New." He hits the last key with finality. "What the hell?"

"You can't say that," Sean says. "Mom, he can't say."

Jessie is about to tell Max to watch his language when she glances at his laptop screen and sees columns of random words in

green text filling the screen. She takes a longer look at the screen.
"What is that?"
"I don't know."

# ELEVEN

CHARLIE AND Victor follow the Mercedes down the highway in silence. Victor's uncertainty about what will happen when they find the person with the flash drive makes Charlie's stomach turn. Uncertainty is nothing new to him. Throughout his childhood, he often wondered where his next meal would come from or if he should avoid the latest man in the house. However, this situation with Papa is on a level Charlie has never experienced before, and the fact that Papa's own son doesn't know what to expect leaves Charlie feeling uneasy.

He conceals his hands in the pouch of his hoodie and flicks his pinky nail while counting by fives. It's a trick his middle school counselor taught him to calm his anxiety. When she mentioned that his parents might want to look into anxiety medication, he told her his mom didn't have money for those kinds of drugs and that he didn't have a dad.

The tightness in his chest begins to subside. The counselor's trick, coupled with the rhythmic humming of the highway, calms his nerves. Not being around Oscar also works wonders.

As Charlie releases a deep breath, he shifts in the fully reclined seat, untouched since Oscar sat there.

"You can adjust the seat," Victor says.

Charlie fiddles with the seat controls on the side until he finds a comfortable position.

"I hate it when Oscar rides in here. Asshole," Victor grumbles.

Charlie may not be the sharpest tool in the shed, but if there's anything he knows with certainty, it's how to spot an exceptional asshole. It's a skill his older brother taught him when they were kids.

When Charlie was ten, he and his brother returned home from school to find their mother's latest boyfriend in their bedroom. Charlie's pink ceramic piggy bank lay in pieces on the floor, not a penny in sight. His brother pulled him out of the room before Charlie could open his mouth. "Don't. It'll just make it worse. That guy's an exceptional asshole," he told Charlie. Today Oscar's been an exceptional asshole to Victor, and Charlie hopes he'll be too busy being pissed off at Victor to pay Charlie any more notice.

As they drive past the Chevron, Charlie remembers the time he almost left the city. He had run away from home and made it as far as the Chevron when he realized that he didn't know where to go or what to do next. He borrowed the store clerk's phone and called his brother to pick him up. His brother was pissed he had to leave work, but it was two o'clock in the morning, and nothing good happens at two o'clock in the morning. Especially in Vegas. After a hefty dose of yelling, his brother promised they would move out soon, but Charlie had to promise to stay out of trouble. Charlie agreed, and his brother made good on his promise a few months later.

The Chevron shrinks in the side-view mirror, and Charlie reminds himself that he's not leaving. He'll be back.

He maintains his gaze straight ahead, fighting the urge to acknowledge Victor staring at him.

"You look like a Jason," Victor says.

Charlie isn't sure if he's supposed to respond, but the silence is worse than saying the wrong thing. "Um, yeah. I guess."

"I mean, it suits you. Some people don't look like their name. I wouldn't peg you for a Tom or a Peter. But you look like a Jason."

Charlie looks out the window for a distraction. All he finds is a big, boring desert. Then he sees a construction sign. "Looks like, uh, they're finally gonna fix the highway." Learning to divert attention away from him is another byproduct of his childhood.

"What's my father's number one rule if you work for him?"

Charlie's disappointed his tactic didn't work and steals a glance at Victor before answering. "Don't tell anyone your real name."

"Do you know why?"

"He said it's for safety reasons."

"It's for my safety. My father's safety. Your safety. Hell, even for Oscar's safety." Victor sighs. "And now we all know your real name, Jason." Victor raises his brow at Charlie.

Charlie rubs his sweaty palms on his jeans and glances at the door handle, debating if he should jump at the first chance he sees. The fall would probably kill him at the speed they're going. Even if it didn't, they've left the city, and there's literally nowhere to run or hide in the desert, even if he could distance himself from Victor. He flicks his pinky nail inside his hoodie pouch.

"Dude, calm down. I'm not gonna kill you or anything. If my father were that concerned with us knowing your real name, you wouldn't be here right now." Victor turns to Charlie. He hasn't relaxed. "I mean, he would've fired you back at the mall." He squeezes Charlie's shoulder. "You're gonna be fine."

Victor's words sound like something Charlie's older brother would say to him. But maybe they mean nothing to Victor. That's one thing Charlie's learned about words. To one person, they mean everything. To others, they mean nothing.

From his dad, "I'll be right back." From his mother, "I love you more than anything." From his cousin, "If you don't go along with it, I'll tell everyone at school what your mom does to make money." Charlie aspires to be a person whose words mean something.

The only person Charlie could ever count on was his older brother. He ensured Charlie never went to school unprepared. Even if it meant he went without. Charlie always had clean clothes that fit, school supplies, and a lunch. He didn't particularly like school, but he didn't hate it either. It gave him an escape from his mom and her string of boyfriends.

During his sophomore year, he took wood shop as an elective and discovered he enjoyed working with his hands and creating something from just an idea. At the start of his junior year, his brother gave him the ten-dollar fee to sign up for an after-school woodworking club, but he never got to attend. The week before the club started, his cousin stole one of the power drills and hid it in Charlie's locker. Charlie was able to talk his way out of detention, but he was banned from joining the club. After that, Charlie lost interest in school altogether. His biggest accomplishment in high school was getting voted prettiest eyes in his senior year.

Six months ago, Charlie's brother left the city for a better job and told Charlie he should go with him. At the time, Charlie mistook it as an invitation, not advice. He didn't want to be a burden any longer, so he stayed behind. But in truth, he was scared to leave. He has never ventured beyond the city. His brother was always the brave one.

Charlie supported himself with odd jobs for a while—mowing lawns, scooping dog poop, hauling junk—but that wasn't sustainable. The work was inconsistent, and the pay barely covered necessities. When he met Papa at the diner, he was broke and about to be evicted from his mold-infested apartment. His face fell when the waitress laid the check in front of Charlie. He knew he couldn't pay. As Charlie watched the waitress return behind the counter, he glanced at the door and caught Papa staring at him. A moment later, Papa slid into the booth and sat across from Charlie.

"You can't pay, can you?" Papa asked.

Charlie remained silent.

"That waitress is a single mother. If you skip out on the bill, it comes out of her paycheck."

Still, Charlie said nothing.

"You need a job?" Papa asked.

Charlie nodded.

Last month, Charlie couldn't buy a burger, but this month, he bought his first car.

"Did you like being Jason?" Victor asks.

"Uh, I don't—what do you mean?"

"I mean... did you like your life before? When you were Jason? Before Papa turned you into Charlie." Victor says the last part like it's a bad thing.

"It was okay."

Charlie can't tell if Victor is making small talk or setting a trap. They've known each other for a few weeks, but Charlie hasn't figured him out yet. However, it only took him three encounters with Oscar to realize he's an exceptional asshole.

"When this job is over, go back to being Jason," Victor says.

Charlie knows that was brotherly advice.

# TWELVE

JESSIE EASES off the gas as the Explorer approaches a minivan crawling along at the speed limit. A pickup truck zips past in the left lane, and impatient to get to her in-laws' house, she follows. Just as the truck pulls in front of the van, a line of orange barrels appears, quickly narrowing her lane. Jessie punches the accelerator and slips in front of the van seconds before the barrels cut off her lane. Once clear, she returns the Explorer to its seventy-three miles per hour and taps the cruise control.

Sean sneaks a look between the front seats at Max's computer screen. "What does 'daisy plaid Quebec three cul-da-sac' mean? And cul-de-sac is spelled wrong. It's an e, not an a."

Jessie studies the screen. Beneath the row of gibberish Sean just read, it reads:

teal cowboy Quebec nine casiita.

"And casita is spelled wrong, too," Sean says. "Ms. Burton

would give that person a B minus."

"Go away." Max pushes Sean's face aside with the back of his arm and starts typing in the chat box.

"Where am I supposed to go? We're in a moving car."

Jessie answers an incoming call over Bluetooth. "Please tell me you're on your way," she says.

"I'm leaving the office as soon as I sign..." The sound of a pen scratching paper comes through the speakers. Paper rustles.

"And this one," says a hushed voice in the background.

Jessie recognizes the voice of Nick's assistant. "Hi, Paula."

"Hi, Jessie. I'm trying to get him out of here. I promise." Paula tells Nick to sign one more document, and then the scratching of the pen on paper stops.

Jessie starts to resume their conversation, but Nick cuts her off.

"Hold on one second, Jess."

She hears the sound of his chair rolling and then in the background: "Paula, go ahead and send it, and let Mr. Tashki's assistant know the originals will arrive Monday. And make sure Josh gets the wire out by three."

Papers shuffle, a file drawer thuds, then Nick's chair squeaks under his weight.

His voice is once again clear. "I'm leaving the office now—should be on the road by two. Boys, are you behaving for your mother?" he says this last part louder.

"I am," Sean answers, eyes glued to his iPad.

Max mumbles something incoherent.

"Sounds like you've had a busy day so far," Jessie says.

"It was mostly waiting for IT to fix the servers. But once they were up, it was a mad dash to get the package ready and the wire sent before midnight, so all the dates match and there aren't any hang-ups."

"It's only one-thirty. I think you guys are fine," Jessie says.

"Midnight, Prague time."

Jessie fixes her eyes on the Explorer's screen, where the active call is displayed.

"Did you say Prague?" she says.

"Yeah. Right, Paula? We just closed the Prague deal?" Nick calls out. "I hope that's what I just signed. My brain is fried," he jokes.

A muffled confirmation comes from Paula in the background.

"This thing became a nightmare toward the end," Nick continues. "Thought we were gonna lose it for a minute. I'm so glad it is over."

The only thing Jessie knows about mergers and acquisitions is that they involve deadlines and money—lots of money. When Nick took his current position, he tried explaining the details of his job, but she zoned out for most of it. She was left with the business knowledge she picked up as a kid playing Monopoly: pay money, buy property, collect them all, and make more money. However, Nick dealt with companies, not color-coded real estate.

"Hey, how's the traffic?" Nick asks.

"We just hit some road construction, but it hasn't been bad," says Jessie.

"Maybe it's a good thing you got a late start. You missed all the early travelers," Nick says.

"Yeah, maybe."

Nick lowers his voice. "Hey, pick up."

Jessie switches the call to her cell phone and holds it to her ear.

"Is Max driving?" Nick asks.

Jessie moves the phone to her left ear. "No."

"Is he mad?"

"Yes."

"I told him I'd let him drive so he could get the rest of his hours in," Nick says.

Jessie eyes Max. If he's trying to listen in, she can't tell. She lowers her voice just in case. "The tire pressure was low."

"Ah, crap. I meant to take care of that yesterday," Nick says.

Jessie's tone sharpens. "I told you I didn't mind doing it. I know how to take care of a car."

"I was just trying to help," Nick and Jessie say in unison. She's heard this before.

"I'm so—" Nick's voice cuts out, garbled and broken. "—rry." He says something else, but the connection is so bad Jessie can't make it out.

She calls out his name a few times, catching only bits and pieces of his response. Frustrated, not knowing if he even hears her, she says her goodbyes and hangs up.

"Holy crap! I didn't even see this. It's so small." Max holds something tiny between his thumb and index finger. The flash drive is nothing more than a silver USB connector with a black plastic nub on the other end. The entire thing is barely half an inch long.

Sean sets his iPad on the seat next to him. "That's a quantum node flash drive."

Max turns the flash drive over in his palm, inspecting it with curiosity. "It kinda looks like the USB Bluetooth adapter for my mouse."

"It's definitely a quantum node flash drive. Spies use those. I saw it in a Netflix documentary. They also use special glasses to read encoded messages. I want some of those for my next birthday."

"Where did that come from?" Jessie asks.

"It was in my laptop port. I didn't even notice it until Bop told me to check the port. All those weird words were from this thing."

"I bet it's some sort of spy cryptography," Sean says, like he's about to drop classified intel. He launches into a summary of the Netflix documentary, something about Cold War codebreakers, hidden data in everyday objects, and how spies used to pass messages using hollow coins and modified belt buckles. "But now it's all digital," he adds. "They probably hid some top-secret files in there— like, government-level stuff."

"It's not spies, Sean," Max tries to sound authoritative. "It's probably some sort of diagnostic program they run when they do repairs. One of the tech guys probably forgot to take it out."

Sean turns to Jessie. "Mom, what do you think? Spies or diagnostics? You're the tiebreaker."

Max sighs. "Even if it's a flash drive, it doesn't mean spies are involved," Max says, irritated.

"It's not just a flash drive. It's a *quantum node*, with a built-in power source. It can hold the entire Library of Congress and then blow itself up if the wrong person plugs it in. Which obviously isn't going to happen because we aren't splattered all over the highway."

Max brings it to eye level and inspects it. "How much do you think it's worth?" he mutters.

"Enough to get you kidnapped by three different governments," Sean says.

Sean might be right. Jessie recognizes it. She saw similar flash drives during her final years at The Agency. Those cases involved very dangerous people.

"I think..." She catches Max waiting for her to finish her answer. "... Max is right. The repair guy probably forgot it was in there."

He doesn't acknowledge her or thank her for siding with him and returns his attention to the chat box on his laptop.

"I still think it's spies," Sean says. He presses play on his iPad and gets comfortable.

She loves that he still has an imagination.

# THIRTEEN

THE DESERT is deceiving, with its clear blue skies and bright, relentless sun. There aren't any blossoming trees or changing leaves to signal the transition into spring or fall. Those seasons don't exist in this part of the Mojave Desert. Instead, the weather shifts from dangerously hot to freezing cold and back again. The desert loves to live in extremes. There may be two weeks in March, and two again in October, when the weather is beautiful and locals are grateful for something other than blistering heat or biting cold. But the desert doesn't stay generous for long—it's the kind of place where looks can deceive you.

The landscape to the right gives no hint of the actual temperature outside and might fool a visitor into thinking the real danger is heatstroke. After all, that's what the desert is known for: intense heat. Life-threatening heat. But the locals know the truth. When vapor stops rising from the asphalt, it doesn't mean the danger has passed—it's just taken a new form: black ice. To the left, the snow-capped mountains offer a better clue to the true temperature.

The sight of them might surprise visitors, but Jessie knows it's not the lack of cold that keeps the desert brown. It's the lack of moisture in the air. She awakens to a snowflake icon on her phone on more mornings than one might expect. Still, she knows better than to hope for the elusive white winter to reach the valley.

At a steady seventy-three miles per hour, they should make it to Jessie's in-laws' house just before the sun sets and the temperature plummets. The hum of the highway has lulled Max to sleep. He ignored Sean's objections when he reclined in his seat all the way. But, once fully extended, he realized just how close he was to Sean, who refused to move from the middle seat. Max reluctantly adjusted his seat just enough so Sean was no longer in his peripheral vision. He has Nick's coveted ability to sleep anywhere under any circumstance, as evidenced by his agape mouth and contorted limbs.

His headphones were jostled askew after Jessie hit a pothole a few miles back, but Max hasn't budged in the last hour and a half.

As the highway curves, Jessie moves her sun visor into a wonky position to block the glaring sun. On the podcast, Theodore Munson explains to the host that changing your identity isn't as difficult as people think. The hardest part was remembering to respond to his new name. Jessie never had that problem. The first episode of *The Five-Year Fraud* ends, leaving the Explorer in silence.

Just as the dramatic theme song begins for episode two, Sean says something indiscernible, his words lost under the swelling music. Jessie pauses the podcast and glances in the rearview mirror. "What did you say? I didn't hear you."

"I'm older now," he says, rather loudly despite no competition. Sean has a habit of starting conversations midway through his thoughts.

"Okay." If Jessie doesn't break his train of thought with questioning, he'll get to the point soon enough.

"When I was ten, you told me that you would tell me how your parents died when I was older. Now I'm older. Almost a teenager." He grumbles the last part with dread.

And there it is. Sean is a straight shooter and never one to sugarcoat or beat around the bush. While others may find this quality unsettling or borderline rude, Jessie finds it refreshing. She rarely has to wonder what he's thinking. Max, on the other hand, usually limits his responses to "yeah", "fine", or "whatever". However, it normally takes a little more discussion before it becomes clear what's on Sean's mind. He must have been mulling this over for some time.

Sean always asks the most complicated questions when she's trapped in the car with him. His mind seems at ease when he's secluded from the outside world, free from the stimuli of people, noises, and smells.

Sean started the car interrogations in the fifth grade. One afternoon, on the drive home from school, he asked Jessie what fallopian tubes were. One answer led to another question, which led to another, and luckily, they pulled into the driveway before she had to explain how the man's sperm gets inside the woman. She may have been speeding that day.

Jessie can't speed her way out of this one. She's trapped on the endless stretch of US Route 95. Seeing no way out, she engages. "My parents died in a car accident."

"Oh," Sean says, surprised. He scrunches his eyebrows and tilts his head. "How old were you when they died in the car accident?"

"Eighteen."

He ponders the facts for a moment. "So you weren't like a kid. There's a kid named John in my science class. His parents died, so he lives with his grandma and grandpa. But you weren't a kid, so I guess you could live on your own. I always just thought you were a kid when they died," Sean says.

"Technically, I was seventeen when they died. But I didn't find out until right after I turned eighteen." It didn't matter that she was an adult by age. She still felt like a kid who needed her parents. She wasn't ready to face the world on her own.

"Who told you they died?"

"A doctor." A flicker of Dr. Smith's sympathetic eyes flashes through Jessie's mind.

"I thought the police or someone with a badge tells people when their family dies," Sean says.

"I was a patient in the hospital when he told me." The memory comes quickly of the nurses gathered around her bed, singing *Happy Birthday* while she struggled to smile through the emptiness. It felt like a betrayal to celebrate her life when her parents had just lost their own. "I was in the car with them."

"But you didn't die," Sean says. He contemplates the additional information for a moment. "Were you sitting in the middle seat?"

The memory is fragmented, and Jessie only has bits and pieces of it. The car that hit them was green with a unique silver hood ornament that Jessie still can't identify. Their car spun violently. Then something was dripping on her. The rest of the memory is like a word on the tip of her tongue, she can't quite grasp. It's so close that it frustrates her, and it's the reason why she never wants to talk about it.

"You know, Sean, I don't—" The sudden flood of information cuts off her words. Although painful, the conversation has forced her to really think about what happened, and in doing so, a new piece of the incomplete memory comes into focus.

When the green car caught her attention, it had interrupted something. She had leaned in between the front seats to ask her parents a question. She can't remember the question but feels like it was meant to be funny. And she knows now, without a doubt, she was sitting in the middle seat.

"Actually, yeah, I was sitting in the middle seat," she recalls slowly.

"I knew it. I'm so glad I didn't let Max talk me into moving over so he could recline."

Jessie shakes the memory and sees the road sign for the Lee

Canyon gas station: *exit ahead one mile*. Max is sound asleep, and she could keep driving and claim she forgot about their deal, or she could say she didn't want to wake him. The truth is, she knows letting Max drive will only prolong the trip, but there's no sense provoking an already angsty teenager when they'll be in close quarters all weekend. Besides, stopping gives her an excuse to end this conversation.

"We're going to stop at the gas station up ahead. I want you to go to the bathroom while we're there." Sean begins to object, but Jessie cuts him off. "Even if you don't have to go." She nudges Max, but he doesn't move.

"I can wake him for you."

"No, thank you." She nudges him harder. "Max. Wake up."

Max stirs to consciousness and rubs his eyes.

"Mom, go fast!" Sean pleads as he looks out the front windshield at the dip in the road ahead. Max sits up and plays it cool. He's too old for that now. Years ago, Sean dubbed it the Fun Dip. Because, as he explained, it's a dip, and if you go fast, it's fun.

Jessie punches the gas pedal, and they fly into the descent. She tries to contain a yelp and can't. It gets her every time. "Woo hoo!" Sean giggles in the back. "I definitely have to pee now."

Jessie glances over at Max and catches him holding back a smile.

# FOURTEEN

PAPA RESTS his hand on the windowsill and gently taps his fingers in time with the classical music playing on the radio. Outside, the desert stretches wide, showcasing a seemingly chaotic landscape of bushes, trees, and rocks scattered across the sunbaked earth. But if one were to look closely, there's a rhythm to it. A pattern hides beneath the randomness. Joshua trees grow in loose clusters, their spacing uneven but not accidental. As the sonata continues to play, Papa sees its structure reflected in the landscape, with long breaks in the melody represented by stretches of barren dirt, while the flurry of notes is captured in the sudden bursts of clustered vegetation. The music cuts through his anxiety and calms his thoughts.

Oscar drives the Mercedes well past the speed limit, his jaw tight and his focus on the horizon. He turns the volume down. "Are we close, yet?" Oscar's words intrude on Papa's peace.

Papa checks the GPS unit. They've closed the gap and almost caught up to the red dot. "A couple more miles."

Oscar speeds up as a dark-colored spot becomes visible on the horizon.

"You know, I could have made the drop on my own," Oscar says. Oscar has been trying to prove himself to Papa, to show he's capable of more than just taking orders.

But lately, Papa's confidence in Oscar's judgment has begun to waver. His focus has shifted to Victor, who's shown a growing interest in the business. Papa plans to use today's job to gauge Victor's potential as his successor. "Victor knew I had something important to take care of today and wanted to help. And besides, Charlie needs to learn how things are done."

"You mean, Jason? That whole thing could have gone south back there." Oscar doesn't miss the opportunity to take a swipe at Charlie.

"It could have happened to any of us. You know, you were young once, too. I think he handled himself well," Papa says.

Papa meant what he said. It's not Charlie's fault that an old classmate recognized him, just like it's not Victor's fault that the flash drive wasn't in the laptop port. But without a clear person to blame, Papa doesn't know where to aim his frustration, and this current distraction is eating away at time they can't afford to lose.

The consequence of missing their deadline is nothing short of severe.

Rumor has it that Romeo has a one hundred percent success rate because he doesn't tolerate mistakes. Stories of someone making a mistake on one of his jobs are unheard of. They don't exist—not anymore.

Papa had done a few jobs for Romeo recently, but always alone. This was the first time any of his crew had been brought in. Oscar had been the one to connect him with Romeo's people, and Papa knew Oscar had taken it personally when he wasn't invited to those earlier jobs.

Papa turns the radio volume back up. Beethoven's *Moonlight Sonata* plays. He caresses the gold cross around his neck and stares into the barren desert.

When Papa and Marta were first married, he would sit in his father's hand-me-down recliner, listening to his mother's old classical records. Marta would always ask him why he listened to that kind of music. For her, music was supposed to make a person dance, not sit still. He would tell her, "It quiets my soul"—something he learned from his mother. Over the years, she taught him how to salsa dance, and in turn, he exposed her to the masters. She wasn't keen on classical music until she heard Beethoven's *Symphony No. 5*. Papa wasn't surprised that it became her favorite piece. Marta was always one for the dramatic. She was the spice in his life, and he kept her grounded.

Since losing Marta, Papa has felt adrift at sea. Victor has tried to reach him, but in doing so, he's lost a little of himself. Papa blames himself. Parents are supposed to look out for their children, not drag them along on their path of destruction. Marta would be angry at him for not protecting her boy. Tomorrow, he will ask Marta for forgiveness.

Tomorrow, he will talk to Victor about taking over the business. Tomorrow, Papa will search for the shore and seek some semblance of salvation.

The Mercedes slows as they approach a minivan. Papa looks down at the GPS unit. The little red dot veers off the highway up ahead. The minivan isn't who they're looking for. As they pass the sign for the Lee Canyon gas station, Papa tells Oscar to take the next exit.

# FIFTEEN

IN THE past, Lee Canyon's gas station rarely saw more than a few cars at a time. That changed after a remodel coincided with the Grand Opening of an In-N-Out Burger nearby, turning the area into a popular pit stop for travelers. A small, undeveloped plot separates the two businesses, and years of foot traffic have worn a path between them. A sign on the vacant lot advertises a Chick-fil-A 'coming soon'.

The gas station has since doubled its number of pumps, and the convenience store is twice its original size with a sleek, modern design. The old two-carafe coffee maker has been replaced by an in-store Starbucks. What were once two single restrooms are now spacious, updated facilities, each featuring eight regular stalls and two wheelchair-accessible stalls. Two large family restrooms are located in between. Rusted, leaky faucets have been replaced by automated Dyson units that offer both water and hand drying right at the sink. The decor evokes that of a high-end shopping mall restroom, minus the bathroom attendant. The main entrance to the restrooms has been relocated to the back of the building, reducing foot traffic inside the store. Give the people what they want—burgers, coffee, and a nice place to do their business—and they will come.

Jessie pulls up next to an available pump. The gas station is busier than she expected, given how little traffic they had along the way. Travellers must be heading into the city for the long weekend. Who can blame them? It's Vegas.

"Can I have some money?" Sean asks.

"For what?" Jessie asks.

"So I can buy something."

"I know that. What do you want to buy?"

"Snacks. Plus, some gas stations only let you use the bathroom if you're a paying customer."

"They don't do that anymore," Max chimes in, as he types out a message to Bop: *BRB*. He sets his laptop on the floor and tosses the tiny flash drive into the cup holder. "I could use a snack, too."

Jessie nods to the In-N-Out. "When you guys finish going to the bathroom, why don't you go get some lunch and meet me back here?"

Sean and Max look at each other.

"You're going to let us eat in the car?" Sean asks.

"I'm sure I'll live to regret it, but yes."

He pumps his fist like he just scored the game-winning goal.

The three of them exit the Explorer.

"You two can eat in the car. I have to eat mine there," Max says.

"But Mom said we could eat in the car." Sean doesn't want Max to miss the opportunity of a lifetime.

"I can't. I'm driving the rest of the way. Right, Mom?" Max says, giving Jessie a knowing look.

She swipes her debit card at the machine, selects the middle grade gasoline, and sets the nozzle to pump hands-free.

"Yes, you are." She can't get anything past him. "I'll drive over when I'm done here." Jessie hands Max her debit card. "You remember my PIN?"

"I know it," Sean announces, prompting a questioning look from Jessie.

"Yeah, I got it." Max takes the card. "Do you want anything?"

"Just fries. And a chocolate shake."

Max heads to the back of the building, and Sean hustles to catch up.

As the fuel flows, she opens the driver's side door and gathers the bit of trash that has accumulated in the center console. She reaches for the last receipt and pauses when the flash drive catches her eye. What is it really, and why was it in Max's laptop?

She closes the door and makes a mental note to ask Nick about it later.

—— ·· — — ·—· ·· — —·

Oscar pulls the Mercedes into the gas station and parks at one of the two available pumps. Victor pulls into the one on the other side. As he and Charlie walk over to the Mercedes, Papa lowers his window and holds up the GPS unit. "It's here." They scan the lot, eyeing the parked vehicles and every person passing by.

Charlie mutters his need for a drink and the restroom and heads off.

Oscar gets out of the Mercedes, leans against the driver's side door, and lights up.

"Are you trying to kill us all?" Victor barks as he gestures to their surroundings. "We're surrounded by gasoline, you idiot."

"I don't see anyone pumping," Oscar says. He waits a moment, but when Victor doesn't back down, he reluctantly walks to the designated smoking area.

Papa calls Victor over to his window. "Get the plates off all the cars and have Mike start running them. Have him start with local registrations."

—— ·· — — ·—· ·· — —·

With the cashier's help, Jessie pays for three bottles of water using her Apple Watch after realizing Max had her debit card. She didn't even know she could do that. Maybe technology isn't so bad after all.

As she heads for the door, her attention dives into the abyss at the bottom of her purse, searching for her keys. She's been meaning to downsize. Half the stuff in there seems to have wandered in on its own. A broken laser pointer. A hockey puck. Sean's jock insert?

Focused on the search, she walks right into someone and drops her keys just as she pulls them out. "Sorry," she says, looking up into the face of a young man in his early twenties with bright eyes. If his jeans and hoodie weren't two sizes too big and he did something with his hair, he might pass for the founder of a promising startup.

"No worries," he says, handing her the keys before heading to the drink aisle.

--- ••• – •–• ••• –•

Max exits the men's restroom and pushes through the door, letting it swing closed on Sean. Just as he reaches for the handle, the door opens from the other side.

"Thank you," Sean says automatically, not looking up.

"No problem," says the young man.

Sean steps out. "Max, wait!"

Max keeps walking, pretending not to hear.

"Wait for me!" Sean calls, trotting along the worn footpath that cuts between the gas station and the In-N-Out. He stumbles, glancing down to find his shoelace untied.

Sean stops. He looks at Max, then at his shoelace, then back at Max.

Keeping his eyes on his brother, he crouches and quickly double-knots his shoelace. As soon as the last loop is tight, he pops up just in time to see Max disappear around the corner toward the front entrance of the In-N-Out. Sean takes off like an Olympian.

--- ••• – •–• ••• –•

As Jessie walks back to the Explorer, she catches a glimpse of what looks like a man with jet-black hair taking a picture of her license plate. It's so quick—and so strange—she wonders if she saw it right. There must be a reasonable explanation. But when the man notices her heading his way, he circles away and stands behind a Range Rover, only deepening her suspicion.

Jessie hides behind her sunglasses, pretending to scroll through her phone, while keeping the man in her sight. He says something inaudible to someone sitting in the driver's seat of a black SUV, then lingers near the back of his car, ignoring the nozzle sitting in its cradle—like he's waiting for someone. He shifts his attention between Jessie and a gray-haired man on his phone beside a blue Honda at the pump behind her.

Jessie studies the older man. Nothing about him stands out. She fails to see what the two of them might have in common, warranting this man's attention. The man with jet-black hair is doing a horrible job of being inconspicuous. And her gut won't let it go.

The gas nozzle clicks, and Jessie gives the gray-haired man another once-over as she returns it to its cradle. He doesn't seem like the problem, but something continues to tug at the back of her mind, so she decides to engage. She grabs an old take-out menu from the side compartment of the passenger side door and walks toward a trash can between her pump and his. He ends his call, notices her, and gives a friendly smile.

"How's the gas mileage?" Jessie asks him. Men his age love sharing their knowledge of cars with women her age.

"Can't complain. Has the highest safety rating in its class. And it has latches for my grandson's car seat. Boy, we never had that kind of stuff when I was a kid. I'm actually on my way to Vegas to surprise him," he says.

"Surprise visits are the best," Jessie says. She hates surprise visits.

He finishes pumping and looks ready to continue the conversation, but Jessie heads back to her car and pops the trunk before he gets the chance. He's not the issue. He's just somebody's grandpa.

She spots the man near the Range Rover watching her again. He looks away the moment their eyes meet.

"You headed to Vegas, too?" she asks.

He freezes for a moment, caught off guard. He wasn't expecting to be noticed, much less addressed.

"Oh, yeah. Um, niece's birthday," Victor says, and looks down at his phone.

"Aw, how old?"

He hesitates. "Um... eight. Excuse me." He raises the phone to his ear as he climbs into the driver's seat of the Range Rover.

Jessie lingers, pretending to look through a bag in the trunk. As she watches him on the phone, she notices the driver's side sun visor down—tilted in the same wonky position as hers was when she drove in. It's positioned as if the driver were heading north, out of the city. Not into the city.

That liar probably doesn't even have a niece.

# SIXTEEN

It's well past lunchtime and too early for dinner—even by senior citizen standards—but the In-N-Out dining room is near capacity. Couples, families, and the occasional solo traveler fill the booths and tables. Sean and Max sit on a bench near the pickup counter, listening for their number to be called.

A young boy cries at a nearby table because his mom didn't use the paper cup he'd set out for his ketchup. In her defense, her back was turned when he grabbed one. His older sister stands off to the side, arms crossed, asking if she can sit somewhere else.

Max watches with quiet empathy. He's lived his own version of the ketchup catastrophe—Sean melting down over something small to the world, but enormous to him. Sean sits beside him, tapping his toes in rhythm as he counts ceiling tiles. It's weird. But he looks content, and he isn't bugging Max.

A pimple-faced teenager calls out, "Order thirty-one!" Both boys stand up. Max throws out an arm and pushes Sean back onto the bench, a little too hard.

"Just wait here."

Sean ignores him and weaves through the crowd after Max, careful not to touch anyone.

Max grabs the tray and turns around—right into Sean. One of the French fry boats tips over, scattering fries across the floor.

"I told you to stay there. Ugh." Max storms off to an empty table and drops the tray with a loud clatter.

--- ••- - •-•• ••- -•

Sean crouches and picks up two French fries and immediately drops them. He blows on his oily fingers and examines the little white salt crystals. The familiar smell of the French fries makes his stomach rumble, tempting him to pop one in his mouth, but he knows he shouldn't eat food off the floor. He's been reminded many times. He lifts the bottom of his shirt and makes a pouch. Handling the French fries as little as possible, he starts gathering them.

Sean hears Max let out a heavy sigh. He glances over and sees Max roll his eyes before kneeling beside him, muttering something under his breath.

Sean holds tears in his eyes. "I didn't want to sit there."

"It's a bench. It's made for sitting.

"I don't like sitting by myself with strange people," says Sean.

They continue collecting the French fries as customers step around them.

"You were literally by yourself. No one was even around you. Why do you have to be so weird all the time?" Max says.

Sean picks up a lone fry and glances sideways at Max. His face is tight like it's trying to get really small. Sean knows that look.

He notices dark oil stains blossoming on his shirt and hopes his mom won't get mad. Max is already mad at him. He also knows Max is right. He is weird. All the time.

He tries not to be.

Most kids can sit on a bench and not think about the people around them. Or the people who aren't around them now, but might be soon. They don't think about their brother forgetting about them, sitting on the bench, and leaving them behind. Most kids can probably sit on a bench and not think about all of that.

Sean can't do that.

He tries.

But he can't.

Sometimes, counting ceiling tiles helps.

Sometimes.

After the last French fry is collected, Max returns to the table and takes a big bite from his hamburger. Sean dumps the French fries in a nearby trash can and walks briskly to the restroom.

--- ..- - .-. ..- -.

Every pump at the gas station is now occupied. Jessie shuts the trunk and walks to the windshield cleaning station in front of the Explorer. She grabs a handful of paper towels and the squeegee, glancing at the Range Rover as the driver exits. She walks to her driver's side door, letting the squeegee hang at her side, and uses the reflection in the window to watch the man disappear inside the store behind her.

Jessie drops the squeegee in the rinse water basin and shoves the paper towels back in their holder. She opens her car door to the sound of her phone ringing. The older man in the Honda nods at Jessie as he pulls away, and she gives him a polite smile as she answers the call.

"When are you coming?" Sean's voice is hollow, like he's in a cave.

"I'm heading over now." Jessie recognizes the silence on the other end. "Did something happen?" Silence. "If you're shaking your head, I can't hear it."

"I got my shirt dirty," Sean says, his voice catching. "And Max yelled at me."

"I'll be there in a minute." Jessie drives across the parking lot to the In-N-Out.

A parking spot is available right in front of the In-N-Out, but

Jessie rolls past it and chooses one farther away near the exit. Nothing is worse than being held hostage by a steady flow of traffic and pedestrians when you're ready to leave.

Inside, she spots Max at a table near the hallway that leads to the restrooms.

He's finishing the last bite of his burger, washing it down with a sip of soda. Across from him, Sean's food is untouched.

"Where's Sean?" Jessie asks, taking a drink of her chocolate shake.

"In the bathroom," Max says, nodding toward the hallway.

"I'm going to use the bathroom, too. Then we can go," Jessie says, popping a few French fries in her mouth.

Max holds out his hand.

She hesitates, then hands him the car keys. She takes another sip of her shake, grabs a handful of fries, and heads off, eating as she walks.

When she exits the women's bathroom, Max is still alone. She knocks on the family restroom door.

"Sean, are you in there?"

The door opens, and Sean appears with a red-tipped nose and flushed cheeks.

"Hey, you okay?" Jessie asks.

Sean looks down at his shirt. "I messed up my shirt."

Jessie gives him a quick hug. "You know one cool thing about grandmothers? They can get out any stain. It's like magic."

Sean straightens. "Magic isn't real."

Jessie glances at Max, seated at the table. "What happened—"

Her words are cut short when the dark-haired man from the gas station steps into the lobby. She walks down the hallway toward the lobby and stops short. She watches the man snake his way through the lobby. He's scanning the crowd like he's looking for someone.

Sean appears beside her. "What happened to what?"

Jessie places her hand on his shoulder, guiding him a few steps back with her. Another man, younger, in a hoodie and baggy jeans, stands across the lobby with his back to her. He's scanning the crowd, too.

"Go get Max," she says, keeping her eye on the two men.

Sean hesitates, but nods and heads to their table.

Jessie slinks farther back into the hallway, watching the men as they navigate the crowded lobby.

She watches as Sean slides into his seat. A moment later, the dark-haired man approaches their table just as Max stands. He waits for the man to pass by, then makes his way toward the hallway.

Jessie ducks into the family restroom, peering through the cracked door.

Max nears the restroom, and Jessie steps out, startling him.

His surprise shifts to irritation when he sees her. "I didn't do anything. He bumped into me."

Jessie ignores him. Her words are sharp. "Listen to me." Maybe too sharp.

Max furrows his brow. "What's wrong?"

"I don't know yet."

She didn't mean to say that.

"I mean, I don't know that anything's wrong. I need you to listen to me." She steadies her voice.

Jessie never lies to her kids. Lies have a way of surfacing, no matter how deep you try to bury them. She doesn't always tell the whole truth; some things belong to the adult world, and her boys are still children. But an outright lie? Never.

Her boys know needles prick, medicine tastes awful, and there's no such thing as doggie heaven. She wants her boys to always trust her, so she has made it a point to never outright lie to them.

She's been lucky. They've never asked the kind of questions that would back her into a corner. She's also been trained in constructing answers that could fool a polygraph.

Max and Sean have never thought to question their own mother's name. Why would they?

When Sean once asked if she had a boyfriend before Nick, she said yes. True. When Max asked about the grandparents they would never meet, she told him they had died in a car accident when she was a teenager. Also true. When Sean asked if she had loved that previous boyfriend, she told him she had. True again. But when they asked what she did after her parents died, she said she went to school. True-ish. It was a place where young adults were educated and learned new skills. Technically, it could be thought of as a type of school. Just not the kind of school that hands out diplomas or can be found on the internet.

"I'm going to double-check the air in the tire before we head out." Kind of true. She's going to check something.

"It was fine the whole way here. You just don't want me to drive," Max says. He sounds more disappointed than angry.

"No, I just want to make sure we'll be safe." That part's true. "You and Sean stay inside the restaurant and don't leave until I call you. Got it?"

He doesn't respond.

"Max?" Her voice tightens. "Do you understand?"

"Yeah. I guess."

"No. Not, you guess. What did I say?"

Jessie sneaks a peek at Sean sitting alone. He's examining a stain on his shirt.

The dark-haired man is in the far corner, eyeing a college kid's backpack. She can't see the other guy, but he's not near Sean.

"Don't leave until you call me," Max says finally.

She holds out her hand. He slaps the keys in her palm with a grimace.

# SEVENTEEN

JESSIE STOPS at the exit of the parking lot. In the rearview mirror, she watches a man with a ponytail slip into the driver's seat of the Mercedes. The dark-haired man, the one with the fake niece, gestures impatiently toward someone she can't see, then climbs behind the wheel of the Range Rover.

A Jeep behind her signals its intent to turn left toward the city, and she does the same. Maybe her primal instinct is rearing its head to protect her young, or maybe she's being paranoid. There's a fine line between paranoia and intuition, and sometimes that line is blurry. Whatever the case, she's about to find out if these guys are anything she needs to worry about.

Jessie turns left, and the Jeep does the same. She passes the parking lot and catches a glimpse of the Mercedes and Range Rover pulling up to the parking lot exit. In the rearview mirror, she watches both vehicles turn left onto the highway.

She reaches over and flips down the passenger side visor, adjusting it as best she can. The afternoon sun has reached that annoying position in its descent where it's just below the visor, rendering it useless. She sits up, stretching as tall as she can, and continues down the highway toward the city.

The Jeep stays behind her in the right-hand lane. In the fast lane, a car approaches from farther back, closing the distance.

She pushes the speedometer five miles over the speed limit, but the approaching vehicle keeps gaining. Within seconds, it's close enough for her to make out its large size. It's an SUV, or maybe a van. Her grip on the wheel tightens. Before she can decide whether to increase or maintain her speed, the SUV is passing the Jeep.

Then she sees the light bar on the roof. Her stomach drops. She eases off the gas, anticipating the flashing red and blue lights. But no lights come. No siren. The Highway Patrol SUV blows past her in the fast lane. The patrolman doesn't even glance her way. Whatever he's after, it isn't her.

Jessie checks the rearview mirror. It's just her and the Jeep. Ahead of them, a blue car comes into view. If the men from the gas station were following her, they should've shown up by now.

She signals and moves into the left lane, eyeing the turnaround up ahead. One more glance at the mirror, and her heart stops momentarily.

Several car lengths behind the Jeep, the Mercedes and the Range Rover appear out of nowhere.

The driver of the Range Rover told her he was heading to the city to visit his niece. So, really, there's nothing suspicious about him heading in this direction, but something in Jessie's gut says he lied. She sees the Fun Dip up ahead and comes up with a new plan. The construction barrels blocking part of the northbound lanes will make things tricky, but she's out of time.

Jessie floors the accelerator.

She catches up to the blue car fast. It's her older gentleman friend from the gas station, crawling along at exactly the speed limit. The turnaround flashes by on her left just as she passes him.

Normally, she doesn't drive this recklessly and resists the urge to glance at the driver and mouth, "Sorry."

She's two hundred feet from the beginning of the descent into the dip when she floors it. The speedometer skips by fives: 75, 80, 85. Into the dip she goes. She needs to gain as much distance as possible to turn around at the bottom of the dip unseen.

Given the current situation, Jessie feels silly letting out a little yelp, but it's a reflex she can't control. She nears the bottom and checks her rear-view mirror. Clear. Not even her friend in the Honda has reached the dip yet.

Jessie white-knuckles the wheel, but hesitates. What she's about to do borders on insane.

She eases the wheel to the left just as the Honda crests the dip behind her. The Explorer veers off the highway, cutting wide into the desert that separates the southbound and northbound lanes. The front tires hit the dirt, and the Explorer jolts hard.

Jessie presses the brake with her left foot, her right still hovering over the gas. Another jolt as the rear tires leave the pavement.

The Explorer, now perpendicular to the lanes, starts to skid out on the rocky terrain. She punches the gas and steers into the skid, and for a moment, she's facing the way she just came. She lets off the gas and uses the momentum to her advantage, completing the circle, until she is again perpendicular to the northbound lanes. A cactus and loose rocks attack the undercarriage. The washboard terrain jostles her about.

Jessie accelerates, weaving through the desert divider to avoid a Joshua tree and a rabbit that darts out of nowhere. She checks the northbound lane in her mirror and sees a purple big rig barreling down the hill in the only lane available.

She'll have to angle through a narrow space between the construction barrels to get back onto the highway. And she has to do it before that big rig catches up to her. She commits to the plan and slams the accelerator. The Explorer bounces violently alongside the highway. She targets an opening and turns the wheel to the right.

Her phone rings. It's Max.

She aims for the gap between the barrels and realizes too late that the Explorer is too wide.

A second ring.

The front tires hit the asphalt, and she clips the barrel on her right. It hits hard, jolting the Explorer sideways. Suddenly, she's spun perpendicular to the oncoming big rig. Her seatbelt locks.

A third ring.

Everything slows, and all sound disappears. She looks out the passenger window and sees the little silver bird on the hood of the green car coming down the alley.

A fourth ring snaps her back.

She blinks away the image. The grill of the purple MACK truck fills her vision. It's about to T-bone her.

Jessie smashes the gas pedal. The Explorer rocks as she shoots across the asphalt into the open desert. The big rig blasts its horn and obliterates the barrel she knocked in its path. The truck driver misses Jessie's rear bumper by an inch.

Max's call goes to voicemail.

Jessie lets off the gas and steers north, running parallel to the highway. She begins to breathe again.

Rocks pummel the undercarriage in a relentless barrage, assaulting her ears. She looks across the highway to the southbound lanes just in time to spot the Mercedes and Range Rover dropping down into the dip.

The Explorer loses speed as it climbs the hill, and Jessie punches the accelerator, sacrificing control for speed. The jolt lifts her off the seat, and she tightens her grip on the wheel.

If the men don't notice her or the massive dust trail she's leaving behind, it would be a miracle. But all she can do is hope.

Jessie races alongside the highway and catches up to the big rig. The driver lays on his horn and flails an arm at her.

*Sorry about that.*

In her rearview mirror, the Mercedes and Range Rover climb

out of the dip in the southbound lanes. Jessie presses the accelerator, pulls ahead of the big rig, and veers back onto the highway.

Maybe Jessie is just being paranoid, and a niece does exist. Maybe those men aren't following her after all. For all she knows, they're after her friend in the Honda. Maybe the doting grandfather is a cover.

People aren't always what they seem.

She rounds a bend just before the next exit and checks her mirror for the fifth time. The purple big rig still looms in the distance.

She spots the SUVs behind the big rig, and her stomach knots at the realization. The Range Rover and the Mercedes are the same vehicles she saw earlier in the mall parking lot. Twenty years ago, she would have immediately recognized the SUVs. They belong to the men who were arguing. The dark-haired man lied about heading into the city. They came from the city, just like her. And they were also at the mall, just like her. And they also just made an insane move across the highway.

She calls Max. "Be ready."

# EIGHTEEN

PAPA'S NOT sure what to make of the flash drive's sudden change in direction. It's the latest in a string of aggravations that started with Victor calling him away from the diner. His irritation grew to frustration when Victor announced the flash drive's disappearance. Now, he's simmering. This wild goose chase is fraying whatever patience he has left.

Oscar narrows the gap between them and the purple big rig. "I think we should let Romeo know about the delay."

Papa turns to him. "I don't think that's necessary. We still have time." He says it like he believes it. He doesn't.

His phone rings. He taps the answer button on the Mercedes' dashboard screen.

"What was with the crazy u-turn back there?" Victor's voice fills the cabin, sharp with confusion.

"Whoever has the flash drive turned around." Papa checks the red dot on the GPS unit. "It's a mile ahead."

"That doesn't make any sense. Maybe the signal's not

precise," Victor says. "It was bouncing all over the place earlier. First at the gas station, then briefly at In-N-Out, and then in the parking lot. Why would they head back the way they came?"

"Maybe the person forgot something at the gas station," Charlie offers. No one responds.

Papa runs through the possibilities. One thing is certain: whoever has the flash drive shouldn't. And they know it. That makes them one of Romeo's competitors or someone trying to strike out on their own. Either way, they must know that the information on the flash drive is valuable.

A pro wouldn't turn back for something left at a gas station. There's too much of a chance someone will remember them. People don't register a face the first time they see it. But see someone twice, and the brain flags it. You take notice. An amateur might make the mistake of going back, but they wouldn't have the resources to know about the job in the first place.

That leaves two real possibilities. One: The courier never delivered the flash drive in the first place. Two: Papa has a traitor on his team working with someone on the outside.

Charlie's too green to have the contacts or the guts to pull a double-cross. Victor could've accidentally let something slip. He wasn't as suspicious and consumed with this work as Papa is. And Oscar, he's been nothing but loyal and working to gain status and position with Papa, but maybe he's tired of waiting for his shot.

"Are they still on the highway?" Victor asks.

"Yes. But we can't see around this truck. I'll keep you posted." Papa ends the call.

Oscar slows as they close the distance with the big rig. They're now at the mercy of the truck driver's speed.

Papa lets out a heavy sigh. Suddenly, he slams the heel of his hand into the dashboard repeatedly. "Damn it!"

--- ••• — •—• ••• —•

The desert stretches out in all directions, empty and silent, as if the world has abandoned Jessie. Earlier, she cursed the construction barrels narrowing the highway to one lane. Now she's grateful. The bottleneck has bought her precious seconds, maybe even minutes. And each one counts.

In the rearview, the big rig shrinks in the distance. She can no longer see beyond it, but she doesn't have to. The Range Rover and Mercedes are there. She can feel them.

The feeling is familiar, like an old childhood friend visiting, whispering, "Remember me? We used to be close." It nudged her in the mall parking lot when she caught herself cataloging the height and build of the men arguing. Now it's screaming at her.

Her training, buried with her past, rises to the surface. It confirms her suspicions and takes control.

Muscle memory kicks in as she pushes the speedometer past ninety. Her breathing steadies.

The exit sign blurs past.

There are only so many explanations for these men and their actions. She assesses each of them quickly, methodically, and always ends with the same conclusion.

Jessie eyes the flash drive in the cup holder. It's been over a decade since she's seen one like it. There was a time when computers were reserved for those who could afford such an extravagance. Now, everyone has one in their pocket.

Maybe this kind of flash drive isn't limited to spies and heavily financed individuals anymore. It could be available at the local electronics store, as far as she knows. But people don't tail you across the desert in luxury cars for something you can find at Best Buy.

This flash drive is quantum... whatever Sean said earlier. The information on it must be valuable. Maybe worth killing over.

She lowers her window and hurls the drive into the desert.

# NINETEEN

THE DESERT is calm, quiet, and peaceful. Its cracked earth resembles a jigsaw puzzle with pieces that almost fit but don't quite touch. Overhead, the sky is a crisp, icy blue, clinging onto the weak winter sun for one final hour. Long shadows extend from skeletal creosote bushes and wind-battered Joshua trees. The wind carries a sharp, piercing cry of a red-tailed hawk looking for its dinner.

A mother cottontail nudges her babies toward the narrow mouth of their burrow. They pause, ears twitching at the cry circling above. She pushes them inside, all too familiar with what that sound means. Lizards have gone still, tucked away beneath the rocks. Somewhere beneath the soil, a desert tortoise sleeps through the season, hiding from the cold and the eyes of predators. The coyotes haven't come out yet, but soon they will.

The creatures of the desert know the rules: hide, hunt, or die.

The hum of tires fades as the Mercedes rolls to a stop on the shoulder. The Range Rover pulls in behind it, kicking up a light spray of dust. The desert returns to quiet, except for the wind and ticking sound of hot engines cooling.

Papa and his crew step out, squinting into the sun. The sun may be out, but it offers no warmth. Papa grabs his leather jacket from the front seat.

He glances down at the GPS unit, the small red dot taunting him. "It's over there, " he says, nodding to the stretch of desert dividing the lanes.

He turns to Oscar. "Call Mike and—"

Oscar gives a quick thumbs up, cutting him off, his phone already to his ear.

The others gather near the front of the Mercedes. Victor paces in short loops. Charlie fidgets with his hands in his hoodie. He keeps darting glances back at Papa.

Oscar ends the call. "Mike's twenty minutes out. He just sent over a list of all the makes and models from the license plates we gave him. I'm sending it now."

Phones buzz and ding as the others receive the message.

Charlie leans in close to Victor. "Who's Mike?"

"He's our tech guy," Victor says, scrolling.

Victor studies the list as he speaks. "This still doesn't make sense. It was at the gas station. Then it leaves, doubles back, and then it just stops? He glances up at Papa. "Unless whoever had it threw it into the desert."

Charlie eyes the list on his phone. "Uh, the blue Honda was in front of us. I was watching them the whole time, and I never saw them throw anything out the window."

Oscar exhales sharply. "The flash drive is half an inch long. I doubt you could see it flying through the air." He doesn't bother with the list.

Victor shakes his head. "Not the flash drive, but the motion. To throw it that far, you'd have to have your entire arm out the window. That's a big motion. And I didn't see that. And neither did Charlie," Victor argues. "Besides, I remember the driver. He was old, and I doubt he could have thrown it that hard."

Papa ruminates on Victor's words as he scans the desert like it might offer him an answer. He doesn't like how much of this has become guesswork.

"I think Victor's right. It wasn't the Honda."

Victor puffs with pride and gives Oscar a smirk.

Oscar shakes his head and turns away to light a cigarette.

"There was also a Jeep on the highway," Victor says.

Papa checks the list on his phone. "Not on the list. It wasn't at the gas station." It means nothing if the flash drive changed hands at the In-N-Out. They don't have a record of the vehicles in that parking lot. As he tries to make sense of the situation, he fears the worst. They may never get the flash drive back.

"If we know the flash drive is here, why do we care about finding the driver? We got what we need, right?" The group stops what they're doing, all eyes on Charlie. He instantly regrets speaking.

"If they ditched it while on the move," Oscar says, annoyed, "then they know what's on it. Or worse, they downloaded the information."

Papa cuts in. "We need to find them. And to do that, we need to find the right car. So let's focus on that," Papa says.

Charlie studies the list again. "Oh."

Papa notices his hesitation. "What is it?"

"Uh, well. There's a white Ford Explorer on here. I saw a white SUV driving on the side of the other lanes, like in the desert, when we were going down that big dip." Charlie looks to the group, but no one backs him up. "You guys didn't see it? It looked like it was trying to pass that semi truck. I think it might have been an Explorer."

"Might have been?" Oscar says, unimpressed.

Papa's eyes light up. Passing in the desert is a desperate move to avoid being stuck behind a big rig. The outcome is shifting in his favor. He hands the GPS unit to Victor. "You and Charlie find the flash drive."

He turns to Oscar. "Have Mike bring comms."

"Already told him." Oscar nods, satisfied with himself.

"Oscar and I will drive ahead and see if we can catch up to the guy in the Explorer. Once Mike gets here, he can take over the search, and you and Charlie can meet up with us."

Oscar locks eyes with Victor as he drops his cigarette and crushes it right at Victor's feet. Neither of them backs down.

Papa doesn't know why those two are at each other's throats, but he doesn't have time to deal with them right now. As long as their problems stay their problems and don't affect the job, he'll stay out of it. He turns to leave.

"I don't think it's a guy we're looking for," Victor says.

Papa pauses, then turns back to see Victor still in a stalemate with Oscar.

Victor turns his back on Oscar. "I talked to a lady at the gas station who was driving a white Explorer. I know what she looks like."

Papa caresses his cross pendant and apologizes to Marta for assuming the driver of the Explorer was a man. She would tell him often that women are capable of anything. He should've known the source of his frustration would be a woman.

"Okay. Victor, you drive. Oscar, stay here with Charlie."

Victor bumps past Oscar, pressing the GPS unit into his chest. "Have fun babysitting."

# TWENTY

MAX WIPES his face and tosses the napkin on the food tray. He scrolls through social media on his phone, oblivious to the person barging through the entrance doors.

Jessie rushes to the table. "Where's your brother?"

Max jumps at the question and looks up. "Bathroom. Again." Max returns to his phone.

Jessie bursts into the men's restroom, startling a man on his way out. He gives her a quick once-over, then continues on his way. She calls out for Sean as she checks the open stalls. Sean emerges from the wheelchair-accessible stall at the end, scowling.

"Mom, this bathroom is for men. I made sure before I came in."

She grabs his arm. "We have to go. Now."

He starts to pull away. "But I didn't wash my hands—"

She tightens her grip, dragging him toward the door. Maybe a little too hard. His eyes widen with fear. She loosens her grip. "It's fine, Sean. We have to leave right now."

She ushers him out the door and to their table. "Max, we're leaving."

Max grabs the two drinks and hurries out after her, nearly spilling them. "Geez, Mom, where's the fire?"

As they reach the Explorer, Sean frowns at its appearance. "What happened to the car?" It's coated in a fresh layer of dust and grime.

Jessie ignores both questions, opens the lift gate, and rummages through a bag as the boys climb in. She pulls a sweatshirt over her head, gathers her hair into a bun, and secures it with a desert-tan baseball hat.

Max places the drinks in the cup holders. "Hey, Mom, where'd that little flash drive go?"

Jessie ignores that question, too, and tosses a black baseball hat to him.

"Put this on," she says.

He glances at it: *Bad Hair Day*. It was a gift from Sean for last year's Mother's Day. "Why?" Max asks.

Jessie buckles her seatbelt and orders them to do the same. They're still reaching for their seatbelts when she pulls onto the highway. As she accelerates northbound, she hands Max a pair of aviators from the center console.

"And these."

"Mom, what is going on? You're acting weird," Max says.

"I want a costume too," Sean pipes up.

"You just lie back there until we get to..." Jessie hadn't devised a plan beyond getting back to her boys.

"Grandma's house," Sean finishes for her.

That's an option. But not a good one. They're still two hours away.

Sean lifts his hockey helmet. "I have this. And my stick."

For the first time, she's thankful he didn't listen when she told him to leave his hockey stuff at home.

"Perfect. Put it on and lie down."

Sean doesn't question her and slips on his helmet. He tosses his pillow into the far seat and gets comfortable, twisting his seatbelt so he can prop his iPad on his chest. He cues up the next *Nat Geo Wild* episode. The narrator's calm voice contradicts the violent hunting methods of coyotes.

Jessie looks over at Max. The hat and sunglasses are still in his lap. "Put those on."

"Not until you tell me why." Max locks eyes with her. "You always tell us it's okay to question authority if something doesn't feel right."

He's right. He's doing what she has always taught them. She doesn't want to raise kids who are so afraid of offending an adult or getting into trouble with authority that they would blindly obey even when something felt wrong. If Max or Sean had a legitimate concern, they were allowed and encouraged to speak up, as long as they did so with respect.

Max leans on the center console. "Mom, tell me what's going on."

"Did you know coyotes eat bunnies?" Sean says to no one. He sounds both horrified and fascinated.

Jessie steals a glance at Sean, a grimace on his face as he watches his show. She lowers her voice. "Sean was right. The flash drive you found in your laptop—it's the kind that certain people use."

"What kind of people?"

She exhales and checks the rearview mirror. The highway behind them is empty. "The kind who store and transport sensitive information. People who need assurances that it gets to its destination." She looks at Max. "It can be tracked."

Max's voice trembles. "So, you think someone is tracking it? Tracking us?"

Lying will only make him suspicious and question her every move.

Cooperation without hesitation ensures a mission involving civilians runs smoothly.

"I saw two SUVs in the mall parking lot when you were getting your laptop."

"You mean the guys who were arguing?"

Jessie looks at him, surprised.

"You always tell me to be aware of my surroundings," Max grumbles. Having to admit her advice came in handy clearly pains him.

She's impressed. "Yeah. Them. I saw them again at the gas station."

She checks her rearview mirror. Still clear. She keeps the cruise control at eighty-five.

"We're in the middle of the desert. I bet everyone on the highway stops at that gas station."

Jessie needs to ease Max into her suspicions so he doesn't freak out. Sometimes, hearing the truth is hard for people like Jessie and Max.

"When I told you and Sean to stay at In-N-Out, I wasn't just checking the tire." I was also checking to see if those men would follow me." She hesitates for a moment. "And they did."

"Maybe they just happened to be going the same way."

"When I turned around to come back, they turned around too. I talked to one of them at the gas station, and he told me he was heading south into the city. But he came back north. Why would he do that?"

Jessie has always been straightforward with Max. When he was twelve, he cut his leg while on a family hike. Nick rinsed the wound and was about to bandage it when Jessie stopped him and handed him a bottle of antiseptic. Max had asked her what was in the bottle, and Nick gave her a look, shaking his head. She ignored his unspoken advice and told Max it was medicine used to clean wounds and prevent infection. Max asked if it would hurt. Nick and Jessie gave conflicting answers simultaneously. Max pulled his leg into his chest. Jessie told him it would sting, but hurt worse if it got infected. He hesitated before offering his leg, but said he wanted Jessie to do it.

She doesn't sugarcoat things, and she's not overly dramatic. She hopes that Max trusts she has a valid reason for thinking someone is following them.

"Mom." Max's voice is small, like that time on the hike. "Are we in danger?"

She places her hand on his shoulder. "We're going to be fine." She says, trying to convince herself. "Hey, they didn't see you or Sean. You guys were in the bathroom when I talked to the guy at the gas station. They don't know you exist. If, by some miracle, he remembers talking to me, he'll be looking for a single woman. Not a family." She needs to reassure him. "And besides, I threw the flash drive into the desert on the way back here. So, if they are tracking it, they're probably out there searching for it now."

She checks her rearview mirror for reassurance. Still clear.

Jessie glances over and sees Max staring out the window, unusually quiet. She can't imagine what's running through his head. Just hours ago, he was a kid nobody noticed—no trouble, no drama, at least not outside of Sean. Now he's caught in something so outlandish, even she's struggling to make sense of it. People might actually be after them because of a flash drive he didn't even mean to have.

"Maybe the guy just forgot something at the gas station? Remember when Sean left his hockey puck at the rest stop a few years ago, and we had to drive back to get it so he would stop hyperventilating?"

Jessie shakes her head. "The guy lied about where he was going."

"How do you know he lied?"

"He had the wrong sun visor down."

"A sun visor, Mom? Really?"

"If he were really heading south, like he claimed, then the

passenger's visor would have been down. Not the driver's." She hears Dr. Smith's voice in her head: *Details can get you killed or save your life.* "They left the gas station when I did. And they came back when I did." She glances at him. He's not one hundred percent convinced. "There was no place to turn around. I had to drive across the desert to get back onto the northbound side of the highway." She omits the part about nearly getting splattered by the big rig and passing it alongside the highway.

"That explains the dirt," Max says. She sees his wheels turning. "Since they came back, that means they would've had to drive through the desert, too. But why would they do that?"

Jessie gestures to the hat and sunglasses. "Will you please just put those on? It will give me some peace of mind. If they don't know what you look like, they won't know who to look for if—"

Max complies. "If what?" She can feel him watching her as she scowls in the rearview mirror. "If what, Mom?"

She doesn't answer. She frantically moves her fingers around on the Explorer's navigation screen.

Max turns around, watching the road behind them.

She glances in the mirror.

A black dot lingers on the horizon behind them. She tries to convince herself it could be anyone: a family on vacation, a retired couple on a road trip, or college students getting in one last trip before the new semester starts. But the way her fingers navigate the map shows her desperation to avoid finding out.

"Check our phones for a signal," Jessie says.

"Zero bars," Max says.

According to the map, they're at least an hour away from any civilization.

"Why don't we just go back to the gas station and call the police?"

"It's too dangerous to go back there. The open highway makes us too visible. We need to stay ahead of them to keep out of sight."

Jessie glances at Sean in the rearview mirror. "Hey Sean, give your phone to Max, will you?"

"Why? Is his broken?" Sean takes off his helmet, brushes his hair out of his eyes, and pats it into place.

"No, I just need him to do something for me, okay, bud?"

She hears Sean diggin in his backpack.

Jessie hands Max her phone. "Take the SIM cards out of all our phones."

"Why?" Max sounds so little and so grown up at the same time. The look Jessie gives him answers his question. He takes the SIM card out of his phone, then Jessie's.

Jessie checks her rearview mirror.

Max looks out the back window.

"It could just be another regular person traveling," he says, obviously waiting for reassurance.

"I'd rather be overly cautious," says Jessie.

"You know, taking the SIM cards out won't matter. They can still track the phone and find us if they really wanted to." He opens his hand above the cup holder, and the two SIM cards clink as they fall inside.

If Jessie weren't so distraught by this news, she'd be impressed by his knowledge on the subject.

"But it will make it harder for them." Now she looks to Max for reassurance. "Right?"

Max nods.

A sudden gush of wind and road noise fills the car cabin.

Jessie looks behind her just as Sean chucks something out the window. "What was that?" she asks.

"My phone."

# TWENTY-ONE

VICTOR CHECKS the speedometer. He's not worried about speeding; he just needs to do something to keep himself from zoning out. Staring straight ahead for so long makes his eyes cross, and Papa hasn't uttered a word since they left Oscar and Charlie in the desert.

The silence is suffocating. It's the same silence that hung over them on the way to the funeral for his mother and brother. He had barely survived that drive. After the funeral, he told Papa to head home without him, and he'd find a ride later. Victor couldn't make that drive with Papa again.

Victor has been walking on eggshells ever since the day of the accident. He doesn't know how to be around his father anymore. At first, Victor tried to be there for Papa. He would bring over breakfast and cook dinner almost every night. When that didn't seem to help, he decided to give his father space. Weeks passed, and Victor kept his distance. Soon, it became a safe place to stay.

At that time, Victor was a young adult figuring out what it meant to act like one, and he wished his mother were there to give him advice. She knew Papa better than anyone. In the end, Victor's choice to give Papa time and space turned out to be detrimental. It has been twelve years, and it feels like he's driving down the highway with a stranger.

A shimmer appears on the horizon.

"Looks like there's a car up ahead," Victor says.

Papa doesn't respond.

Victor glances over. Papa looks ahead, but Victor recognizes the empty stare. He has drifted off into another land.

A week after his mother's death, Victor walked into the kitchen during one of these episodes and found Papa muttering his wife's name. He asked Papa if he was okay but got no response. Then he asked again, a bit louder. When Papa finally came around, Victor mentioned he had been daydreaming about her again and suggested it might be time to see someone. Without warning, Papa slapped Victor. They both froze, stunned. Papa played it off like he had been startled by Victor. Victor never mentioned his mother again.

"Papa," Victor says, louder now. Papa snaps his head toward him. "There's a car up ahead."

"Right." Papa straightens and dials a number on the dashboard screen. After one ring, Mike's voice comes through the car's speakers.

"Yeah," Mike says.

"I think we might have a visual. Can you confirm?" Papa says.

Another call beeps in, and Papa puts Mike on hold.

The caller's voice sounds wheezy and impatient. "My assistant tells me you've been delayed."

Victor stiffens. He doesn't recognize the voice, but whoever he is, he sounds like he's not used to things going wrong.

His breathing is labored. "My men need that flash drive tonight. The deliveries can't be made without it."

Victor glances at Papa. He seems surprised by the caller's knowledge of the situation, but his voice stays even.

"Just a slight hiccup. We're sorting it out now," Papa says.

More heavy breathing. "Hiccups tend to come back. Make sure this one doesn't."

"I will."

"I know you will." It wasn't a vote of confidence.

The line goes dead.

Victor hesitates. "Was that Romeo?"

Papa doesn't answer. He switches back to Mike and disconnects the call from Bluetooth. "Mike, I'm back." He listens, then nods and ends the call.

He looks at Victor, something fierce and familiar in his eyes. "She's up ahead."

Victor pushes the speedometer to ninety.

# TWENTY-TWO

THE EXPLORER'S navigation screen shows nothing but the highway and desert stretching for miles. Orange construction barrels continue to block the fast lane with no end in sight. The wide-open landscape offers no cover, making them easy to spot. Trapped, Jessie has no choice but to keep going.

"Um, Mom?" Max sits twisted, his eyes glued to the back window. "The car behind us is getting closer."

Jessie checks her side-view mirror. He's right. The speck has doubled in size. "Sean, lie down and stay out of sight." She slams her foot on the gas. The speedometer jumps past a hundred.

"We're all gonna die." Sean moans, flattening himself across the backseat.

"No one is going to die. Just listen to me, and do exactly what I say." Jessie takes a breath. "Max, check the navigation and find the next exit."

Max zooms out on the map with his fingers and swipes down. He swipes down again. And again.

A chime dings. The tire pressure light shines orange.

"The next exit looks far." Max eyes the light on the dashboard. "Is the tire okay?"

A blur shoots across the road.

Jessie jerks the wheel. The Explorer clips a construction barrel. It spins into another one, which rolls into their path. She can't avoid it. The edge catches underneath the Explorer, lifting the driver's side. For a moment, they are riding high. Then the weight shifts, and the Explorer slams back to the asphalt—a loud pop cracks from outside.

The ride turns violent, like they're driving on a cheese grater.

Flap. Flap. Flap.

Sean's seatbelt locks across his chest. His arms and legs flail.

"Mom! I can't move! I can't move!"

"Help your brother!"

Max unbuckles, scrambles between the seats, and reaches for Sean.

Jessie tightens her grip on the wheel, fighting to keep the Explorer on the highway. She smashes the brakes.

Max lurches forward into the back of the passenger seat just as he frees Sean's seatbelt.

Sean quiets but continues to breathe too fast.

Jessie regains control.

Max climbs back into his seat. Sean sits up slowly and buckles again.

Flap. Flap. Flap. Flap. Flap.

Sean yanks off his helmet and presses his hands over his ears. "What is that sound? I don't like it. Make it stop."

"Is it the rabbit?" Max whispers.

"The tire blew," Jessie says grimly. She eases off the accelerator. "Switch the map to satellite view and see if you can find any building within the next mile or two. I don't care what it is."

Max nods and returns to the screen, dragging the map with shaky fingers. "There. That looks like a shed or a barn or something. It's not that far."

Jessie scans the desert but doesn't see a building. The satellite image shows a small structure in the desert, a quarter mile off the highway. She surveys the desert again and still doesn't see it.

The rhythm of the flapping tire changes as the Explorer slows down. Soon it'll be rim on asphalt.

Jessie grows frustrated as she still can't see the building.

"Maybe it's an old satellite photo," Max says, as if trying to make her feel better. "They probably don't update them often because there's nothing out here."

Jessie spots a power line branching off the main tower by the highway. It veers into the desert and vanishes at the horizon, a quarter mile into the desert. As they approach the tower, a beaten path comes into view. She takes a sharp right turn onto the path and follows it into the desert.

Not a building in sight.

The farther she drives, the lower the power line dips. She follows the path down a shallow slope. Up ahead, the wires disappear behind a plateau.

Thousands of years ago, rivers flowed down the mountains, carving out paths and leaving behind these plateaus. Over time, most of them have eroded into nondescript dirt hills. At the base of the surviving plateaus, smooth river rocks are found, serving as evidence of the former landscape. They seem out of place in the dry, barren desert, but at one time, they belonged.

Jessie slows as she rounds a bend. She breathes a sigh of relief when the building comes into view. It's tucked into the side of the plateau. Whoever built it made sure it wasn't visible from the highway.

To the right, a narrow five-foot gap between the structure and the cliff wall holds a few scattered items. On the left, a small generator hums beside a row of solar panels. Ten feet of hard-packed dirt separates the front door from a neighboring plateau. The building was built on an ancient riverbed.

Jessie considers parking the Explorer in front, where it would be hidden, but there isn't enough space to turn around. The end of the slope looks loose, and she doesn't want to risk getting stuck. She throws the Explorer into park where the ground is still firm.

The building is tiny for living quarters, maybe two hundred square feet at best. It was built from leftover scraps of this and that. The camouflaged roof stands about a foot higher than the floor of the surrounding desert. It blends into the dirt and rocks and isn't noticeable unless you know to look for it.

It doesn't appear anyone is home. No car or other mode of transportation is present.

Jessie puts the SIM card back in her phone. No signal. There aren't any telephone lines nearby. No calling for help here. She takes the card out and puts it back in her pocket. "You guys stay in the car and lock the doors."

Max nods, and Sean lies back down without a word.

Jessie jumps out, reaches under her seat, and pulls out a Glock 9mm handgun. It's a light grey custom model undetectable by X-rays. It was a parting gift from Dr. Smith. She chambers a round and hurries toward the building, weapon raised. Keeping her back against the wall, she listens for any sounds coming from inside.

Nothing.

With one swift motion, she kicks the door open and disappears inside.

Sean bolts up. "What was that?"

"Mom just kicked the door in. And she has a gun," Max says, still processing what he just witnessed.

Sean leans between the front seats. "Mom has a *gun*? Like a *real* gun? Does Dad know?"

Before they can continue their conversation, Jessie taps on the window, causing them to jump.

Max unlocks the doors.

Jessie opens the door and freezes. A breeze carries the faint sound of a vehicle in the distance. "Stay down and out of sight."

Max nods and slides off the seat, wedging himself onto the

floorboard. Sean lies back down, wide-eyed.

Jessie scrambles up the embankment and crouches, ready to shoot anything that comes down the makeshift road.

A few moments pass.

A small hatchback zips along the highway, completely oblivious to her existence. She has some time.

She scrambles back down the embankment, nearly slipping on the loose rock. She yanks open the Explorer's tailgate and throws the luggage to the ground.

"Bring me your backpacks. Quick."

The boys scramble, gathering their things, and rush to the back of the SUV. Jessie grabs a hidden loop on the bottom of the cargo area and pulls with force, revealing a hidden storage area.

Sean and Max exchange a wide-eyed glance.

Jessie grabs a camo backpack, pulls out a belt, and threads it through the loops on her jeans as if she's being timed. She dumps out the contents of Sean's backpack: five fidget toys, three rocks, six pens, a dozen paperclips, snacks, a rubber NHL bracelet, a Rubik's cube, and a book of stamps. She grabs the snacks and one of the pens and throws them back in his backpack, along with a pair of jeans and pajama pants from his suitcase. Jessie clips one of the paper clips on her belt loop and hands Sean his backpack.

She takes inventory of Max's backpack. It's basically empty. She hands it to him. "Grab your sweatshirt and a t-shirt and put them in here." She tosses three bottles of water into her backpack and slings it over her shoulder. "Grab the phones. And your laptop."

Max runs to the front seat, grabs his laptop, the phones, and the SIM cards, and brings them back. She puts the phones and SIM cards in her pockets, takes the laptop, and stows it in the secret compartment in the cargo area.

She turns to the boys. "I'm going to leave the car farther up the road."

"Why?" Max eyes the gun in her waistband.

"Those guys are going to be here any minute. If I leave the car here, they'll see it from the highway. But if they find it up the road with a flat, they might think we hitched a ride."

Max nods, as if he understands.

"You guys go inside and wait for me to come back. Don't come out for anything. No matter what. You got that?"

They nod. Sean grimaces, his face pale.

Jessie locks eyes with Max. "Throw the luggage back inside the car. And keep Sean inside."

She leads Sean inside the shack and takes his hands in hers. "Hey, I'll only be gone a few minutes." She taps the button on his watch to start the stopwatch. "You can time me."

Max opens the secret cargo hold area, slips out his laptop, and quickly shoves it in his backpack.

Then he crawls over the backseats and grabs Sean's hockey stick from the floorboards. He scurries back out, throws the last pieces of luggage inside the Explorer, and closes the tailgate just as Jessie slams the driver's door.

# TWENTY-THREE

MAX LOOKS around the run-down shack for a place to sit. There's a small futon in the corner, littered with old newspapers, beer cans, and several unidentifiable stains. The plywood floor peeks out from beneath two threadbare throw rugs that look like they'll disintegrate if moved. He grabs the least dusty newspapers, spreads them out on the futon, and sits down slowly.

Max knows Sean won't go near the disgusting futon, much less sit on it, so he doesn't even offer. He pulls his laptop from his backpack, powers it on, and switches it to cellular mode. Nothing. No signal. He's about to close it when a message pings through. It's Bop: Bro that took 4ev.

Sean stands in the center of the room, clutching his hockey stick like it's a life preserver, swaying side to side as he watches the numbers tick by on his watch.

"Max, why does Mom have a gun?" He paces in a tight, three-foot radius, all the cramped room will allow.

"I don't know," Max mutters as he types. One day, he had

caught Jessie staring at him with her mouth open, like she was about to say something important. But she blinked, changed the subject, and pretended she had just zoned out. Now, he wonders if whatever she almost said that day has something to do with the fact that she has a gun. A secret gun. That she keeps in a secret compartment.

"What are we supposed to do?" Sean stops pacing and looks around, scanning the room like he's afraid he missed something obvious, some clue about what they're supposed to be doing.

"Wait."

"For what?"

"Mom."

"For how long?"

"I don't know. Stop bothering me."

Sean looks at his watch again and resumes circling like a record stuck in a groove.

Nothing even quasi-interesting ever happens to Max. Bop isn't going to believe this. Max fantasizes about how it all ends as he taps away on his keyboard. Either a bunch of crazy bad guys really are after them, and his mom ends up getting a pat on the back from the cops as they drag the sketchy guys away in handcuffs. Or she's off-the-charts paranoid, and the highlight of their trip will be a blown-out tire.

Max hopes for the former. He can already picture all the comments, likes, and reposts. He might even go viral.

He's so eager to tell Bop what's happening that he doesn't question how they're messaging each other without a cellular connection. He keeps hammering away at the keys while Sean paces in another slow circle. "Bro, you're gonna make yourself dizzy."

Sean stops.

The battery icon on Max's laptop changes from green to red. He digs through his backpack for the charger, rummaging deeper and faster, but comes up empty. It dawns on him: he never grabbed it from the kitchen counter.

"Crap!"

"What happened?" Sean says.

"I forgot my charger."

"Oh. I put that away this morning. I thought you left it out again, and Mom always gets mad when we don't put our chargers away and take hers," Sean says.

"Thanks a lot, Sean," Max grumbles, pounding at the keyboard like it personally wronged him.

"You're welcome."

The shack goes quiet, the only sound the rapid tapping of Max's fingers as he types out the message:

dude! my mom has a GUN!

Message sent.

*— — —  • • —  —  • — •  • • —  — •*

Jessie pulls over a quarter mile up the highway, just past a bend in the road. She throws the Explorer in park, yanks the keys, and grabs her backpack and Glock. In thirty seconds, anyone driving on the highway will have a clear view of her sprinting through the desert.

She takes off at full speed, Nikes slamming the packed earth. She scans the landscape for coyotes, rattlesnakes, and any other predators that might attack. The sound of her feet is muffled by the blood pulsing in her head. Her lungs are screaming. She hasn't run like this in twenty years. Combat-readiness isn't exactly a requirement to join the school PTA.

A breeze carries a faint hum across her ear.

She glances over her shoulder. A black speck crests the bend in the road. It's growing exponentially. She's out of time. Jessie makes a sharp left toward a cluster of Joshua trees about twenty yards away. Seconds later, she throws herself to the ground, skidding on one hip.

Her hand tears against a cactus. Her knee slams into a sharp rock. Her mouth fills with dust. She crawls behind the thickest trunk and lies prone, rolling in the dirt, to dull any shine from her clothing that could give her away. She wedges the 9mm between two twisted trunks, steadies her aim on the Explorer, slows her breathing, and waits.

# TWENTY-FOUR

BEFORE VICTOR can put the Mercedes in park, Papa jumps out and makes a beeline for the Explorer parked alongside the highway. The front passenger tire is shredded, the inner threads exposed. He scans both ends of the highway, shielding his eyes from the glaring sun.

"She can't be too far."

"Someone could have picked her up," Victor says, stepping out and mirroring his father, eyes sweeping the highway in both directions.

"Yeah," Papa replies, distracted. He calls Oscar, relays the situation, then nods toward the open desert. "Let's take a quick look."

Victor sighs as he reluctantly follows. From where he stands, the desert rolls out in every direction, flat, brown, and empty. Nothing but dirt, weathered bushes, and spiny Joshua trees twisting toward the sun. There's no one out here. This will be a waste of time.

They split the landscape. Papa heads left, Victor goes right. A

Joshua tree proudly stands sixty feet ahead, taller and thicker than the rest. Its branches are thicker than the trunks of most other trees. If this desert had a monarch, that tree would wear the crown. Two smaller trees have rooted tightly beside it. Odd for the species.

Shadows from the setting sun warp the terrain. Something flutters in a bush. Possibly fabric. Victor squints as he gets closer. Now fifty feet away. It's just a piece of torn cardboard. He's about to turn when movement near a tree catches his eye. He draws his gun from his waistband and quickens his pace. A sharp rustling comes from that direction. He stops. The rustling stops. He raises his gun, finger hovering beside the trigger, and creeps forward. Another rustle, closer this time. He steadies his breath and moves his finger on the trigger. A squirrel darts out from behind the tree, kicking up a puff of dirt as it bolts into the open desert.

Victor exhales sharply and lowers his gun.

A prickling sensation creeps up the back of his neck. The desert is quiet again, but not peacefully so. Something lurks in the silence. He turns in a slow circle, scanning the brush, but sees nothing out of place. Still, he can't shake the feeling that he's being watched.

Papa chuckles from a distance. "Watch out for those killer squirrels."

Victor is not amused.

He resumes his search. Forty feet away. He'll indulge Papa a minute or two more before he calls it quits. Thirty feet. If she were here, she would have spooked the squirrel before their arrival. Twenty.

Victor's phone rings. It's Oscar.

"What's your status?" Oscar asks.

"No sign of her here. Just her car," Victor says. Papa catches his eye and gestures toward the highway. "We're heading out," Victor says, ending the call. "Mike found the flash drive. Oscar and Charlie are en route."

Papa opens the passenger door and pauses, realizing he's

alone. He looks around.

"Victor, what are you doing? Let's go."

"I need to take a leak," Victor shouts over his shoulder. He continues toward the massive Joshua tree.

"There's no one out here!" Papa spreads his arms wide, gesturing to the desert. "No need for privacy, just go. And hurry up." He shakes his head and climbs into the SUV.

Victor stops where he is.

Ten feet in front of Jessie.

# TWENTY-FIVE

JESSIE LIES motionless behind the Joshua tree, barely daring to breathe. Just ten feet away, the man she saw at the gas station pump stands exposed in every sense of the word, relieving himself. Though she only has a partial profile view, it's enough for her to be sure it's him.

For a moment, she allows herself to be humored by this awkward situation. She thinks about all the toilet humor Max and Sean constantly share. This story will definitely amuse them. Then again, they would probably be mortified that their mother saw a strange man's penis. She once mentioned the word *penis* in front of them, and both boys bolted from the room. She'll keep this one to herself.

An afternoon breeze stirs the air, kicking up a swirl of dust. Jessie turns her head to shield her face, but dirt still finds its way into her nose. The tickling sensation flares. She holds her breath and tightens her core, willing it to pass. For a moment, it does. Then it returns with a vengeance. She clamps her tongue against the roof of her mouth, a trick Sean shared with her after watching a documentary on neural pathways.

It's not working. The pressure builds until she's on the brink. She puts the man in her sights, sliding her finger to the trigger, prepared to drop him once she gives herself away. The sneeze explodes in her throat. She clenches her jaw to keep it silent. Her eyes well with tears as she swallows the reflex to cough. Through the blur, Jessie watches the man zip up and trot back to the Mercedes.

Jessie rolls onto her back, gasping and coughing as though she's just been revived from drowning. She twists her head toward the highway and watches the Mercedes shrink in the distance. She lies still for a few seconds longer, listening to the wind and the receding roar of the engine. Only when the vehicle is a blur on the horizon does she get to her feet.

She takes advantage of the adrenaline coursing through her veins and runs back to the shack at full speed. Coyotes and rattlesnakes be damned. The setting sun casts long, erratic shadows across the uneven desert floor, each one ready to trip her up. She slows to a jog as the shack comes into view, unable to catch her breath. At the top of the embankment, she pauses to scan the rocky descent, moving carefully now. The last thing she needs is an injury slowing her down.

She reaches the bottom and halts when she sees a motorcycle parked on the side.

Jessie draws her gun and creeps toward the front door. With her back pressed against the wall, she listens.

Silence.

She walks backward toward the motorcycle with her eyes fixed on the front door. She starts the bike and cuts the engine a second later.

The door bursts open. A massive, bearded man charges toward the sound. He's at least a foot taller than Jessie and outweighs her by seventy-five pounds, maybe more. It's a wonder he can fit through the door. His black hair is wild underneath a sun-bleached field hat. His beard hangs in thick, matted ropes, cascading down his chest. Jessie points her gun at Black Beard, stopping him mid-stride. She studies him closely. He looks wild and dangerous, yet there is a quiet control about him.

"Anyone else with you?" she demands.

He shakes his head.

She spots a large burn scar on his right forearm and a tattoo on his left. She's seen that tattoo before, when her squad had a joint mission in Europe with an elite special forces team based out of Egypt. This guy is a long way from home, having replaced one desert for another. And he clearly wants to stay hidden.

"Slowly raise your arms above your head."

He obeys, but not to her satisfaction.

"Higher."

He lifts them higher, exposing his tattooed torso and more scars.

"Turn around. Slowly."

He does.

▄▄▄ ••▄ ▄ •▄• ••▄ ▄•

Inside the shack, Max lunges off the futon and tries to stop Sean from going outside. Sean isn't great at recognizing danger. Right before Black Beard showed up, Sean told Max that someday he wants to live all by himself like the person living here. Far away from people.

Max had started to explain that whoever lived in the shack was probably hiding because they were probably a criminal. But Black Beard's arrival cut him off. Max swipes at Sean's arm to grab him, but he's not quick enough.

▄▄▄ ••▄ ▄ •▄• ••▄ ▄•

Just as Jessie spots the gun in Black Beard's back waistband, something catches her eye behind him. Sean is standing just outside the open door with his hockey stick.

Black Beard takes advantage of the split-second distraction

and pulls his gun on Sean.

Sean drops his stick, and it clatters on the ground.

▄▄▄ ••▄ ▄ •▄• ••▄ ▄•

Max is almost to the door when Sean freezes, his stick bouncing end to end as it settles on the ground. Sean would never drop his stick. It has its own birthday, which Sean makes them celebrate.

Max stops short of the doorway and frantically looks around the small shack. He needs something, anything, that he can use as a weapon. His eyes scan every surface. A narrow shaft of sunlight breaks through a crack in the roof, casting a glint on something nearby. Then he sees it— a big-ass hunting knife.

# TWENTY-SIX

Jessie raises her arms, her eyes fixed on Black Beard as he sidesteps to keep her in view, his gun never wavering from Sean. "We don't want any trouble," she says, trying to keep her voice neutral. "We got a flat tire and just—"

"The last person with a gun like yours caused me a lot of trouble." Black Beard nods toward her custom 9mm, invisible on X-ray and engineered to be untraceable. He might look like he's off his rocker, but he isn't stupid. He knows that weapons like hers aren't supposed to exist.

Jessie curses herself for not trying to talk her way out of this situation first. She should've just knocked, feigned helplessness, and politely asked for her kids. Now it's too late to make her acting debut as a stranded motorist. One advantage of being a woman, especially a petite one, is that she's always underestimated. But now she's shown her cards.

"Put it on the ground. Slowly," Black Beard orders.

Jessie eyes Sean as she complies. He hasn't moved, not even an inch. She's never seen him this scared. Fear is a trigger for meltdowns, and she doubts Black Beard would hesitate to pull the trigger just to shut him up. She lowers her gun, praying Sean stays still.

Black Beard swings the barrel toward Jessie, and she relaxes a little.

If they were alone, the situation would've already been handled. But Sean's presence complicates everything. He's in no state to respond to commands, even without the stress of a gun in his face, pragmatic language has always been an issue for him.

She has to treat him as an uncooperative hostage. Usually, hostages were engineers, suppliers, or CEOs of obscure corporations that may or may not have officially existed. She's only dealt with a child once on a mission. It was unexpected and didn't end well. The mission intel didn't include the possibility of a child being on the premises, and it was dumb luck that Jessie even found her. Jessie told the debriefing panel—and herself—that she didn't have time to think, which caused a lot of trouble for her and her partner. She tries not to think about that night and the lies she lives with.

Jessie recalls to mind the things in her vicinity that she can use to regain control of the situation. A stick, stone, glass—anything. There's nothing. The barren desert offers her nothing.

Sean remains a statue, and Max... Jessie realizes he didn't come out with Sean. At first, his absence feels like relief. One less life at risk. Then she imagines him inside, unconscious, possibly injured. Or worse.

"I get it. You don't want anyone knowing you're here. And I won't tell anyone. I have no reason to. I don't care who you are or what you've done. The only thing I care about is getting my boys safely to their grandma's house."

Black Beard listens, but not because her words are persuasive. Jessie recognizes the look in his eyes. She's seen it before, during a mission gone sideways. A man wasn't complying until Jessie showed up. Later, he told her she reminded him of his daughter. The same faraway softness is in Black Beard's eyes now. He may be looking at Jessie, but he's seeing someone else.

"Please. Just let us go." Jessie watches something shift behind his eyes. She desperately hopes that whoever he's picturing is someone he cared about. Or at least didn't kill. "The sooner we can be on the road, the better for you. There are some very bad people after me and my boys. The kind of people who don't leave loose ends."

His face shifts. He seems to understand.

"They've been tracking us. It's only a matter of time before they show up here."

Jessie sees the hesitation in his stance, as if calculating the risk. He looks tired, not just physically, but like someone who has been running for a long time. But that tiredness doesn't mean trust. His expression hardens again as he glances at her gun on the ground. He doesn't know her. And with a weapon like hers, she knows exactly what he must be thinking. She's a government agent, a mercenary, or some kind of trap. She's used this kind of doubt before, to her advantage. Now she watches it turn against her.

Black Beard steps toward her gun. "I can't let you go," he says, almost apologetic.

Max peeks through the doorway and freezes. Black Beard is reaching for the gun at Jessie's feet. Max bolts out the door, grabs Sean's hand, and yanks. Sean's legs don't cooperate, nearly sending them both toppling to the ground. Max throws Sean over his shoulder and runs around the side of the building.

The second Jessie sees Max, she slams her knee into Black Beard's nose. It crunches. His head snaps back, just before she drives her foot into his throat.

His gun flies, clattering against the wall, and slides near the doorway. Black Beard hits the dirt hard, gasping. Jessie dives for her gun, but he sweeps her legs out with a brutal kick, and she crashes to the ground.

She scrambles for Sean's hockey stick, lying just behind Black

Beard, and whips it across his throat as he tries to stand, sending him back down.

Jessie moves fast, scrambling behind him. She plants her feet on his shoulders and holds the hockey stick against his neck. His thick, dreadlocked beard cushions the pressure. She shifts her weight, driving her heels harder into his shoulders, pulling the stick tighter.

Black Beard bucks and thrashes, swinging wildly, trying to throw her off.

Jessie grits her teeth and pulls harder. His veins begin to bulge, his face flushing purple.

He flails one arm, sweeping the ground, desperately searching for his gun.

She digs in harder, tightening the choke. Her legs burn, but she doesn't ease up.

His fist pounds into her calves, over and over, ditching his search for the gun in favor of breathing again.

Jessie feels the cartilage give way beneath the stick. If the kick didn't crush his windpipe, the hockey stick is finishing the job.

A sharp jab to her left knee jolts her loose. Her grip slips, and the stick jerks upward. She grabs for it, catches it, and slaps it back down across his throat, feet digging into his shoulders once again. Fatigue creeps into her shoulders. The veins in her forearms mirror those in his face. Her thighs shake.

Black Beard's assault slows.

Jessie has brought two human beings into this world. Compared to that, then holding this hockey stick for thirty more seconds is nothing.

Black Beard's attack on her legs stops.

Twenty more seconds.

Hot, sharp pain explodes through Jessie's left hand. She loses her grip, the stick flies through the air, slams into the doorway, and clatters next to the gun.

She falls flat on her back.

The odor of iron and wet pennies fills her nostrils. Warm

blood pours from the top of her hand down her forearm.

Black Beard twists in her direction and drags himself to his knees.

Jessie sees the tactical knife gleaming in his hand. He lunges at her.

She blindly stretches for his gun, lying by the doorway, while dodging swipes of the knife. In one smooth, continuous motion, her fingers find the familiar textured handle of a handgun, and she shoots him point-blank. Two shots center mass, one to the forehead. Bits of matter and blood mist her face and torso.

The echo of the gunshot travels across the empty desert. Anyone within a mile would have heard it.

Black Beard freezes. Blood permeates his shirt, creating two circles that soon morph into one.

Jessie scrambles to the side as he falls face forward in the spot she just occupied. She grabs her gun, shoves it in her waistband, along with Black Beard's, and rushes inside. There's no phone. No radio. Nothing to communicate with the outside world.

She grabs Max's backpack and turns to leave, but something on the bed catches her eye. *Max's laptop?* She tucks it under her arm and turns around, bumping into Max.

"What are you doing here?" Jessie gasps. "I saw you guys run away? Where's Sean?"

"I heard gunshots," Max says, eyes widening as they lock on the blood splattered on Jessie's sweatshirt. "Mom! Are you okay? Did you get shot?" His face drains of color. He sways a little, jaw clenched tight against the rising nausea.

"No, I'm fine." Jessie grabs her hat, knocks the dirt off against her leg, and slaps it on her head. "Where's Sean?"

"He's okay. He's around the other side." Max eyes Jessie head to toe. Blood drips steadily from her hand, dotting the dirt below. "Mom, your hand."

The adrenaline has done its job well. Jessie forgot all about the knife attack. As she examines the wound, her brain remembers the trauma, and her hand begins to burn and throb. She needs stitches, and her risk of infection is high given their current environment.

"Maybe there's a first aid kit inside," Max offers, but his voice falters.

Jessie catches the way he looks at her—eyes wide, jaw clenched, as if he doesn't recognize the person in front of him.

She yanks a t-shirt out of Max's backpack. "Go get Sean," she says.

"We need to move. Now."

She turns without waiting for a reply and trudges up the embankment. Jessie grips the shirt in her teeth and shreds it into strips.

Fix the hand. Fix the car. Kill anyone who threatens her boys.

# TWENTY-SEVEN

JESSIE SITS on the rear bumper, pushing a sewing needle through the torn skin on the back of her hand. The wound pulses with each stitch, and she bites down on the tire pressure gauge to keep from swearing. Max crouches by the passenger tire, replacing the lug nuts.

She had insisted he learn how to change a tire before getting his permit. He hadn't wanted her to teach him, but Nick kept putting it off, for one reason or another, and Max didn't want to have to reschedule his test again, so he didn't have a choice. Not surprisingly, he has no trouble with the mechanics. He's always been good at figuring things out. What he couldn't figure out was why he needed to learn how to do it in the first place, since *there's literally an app for that*. Jessie had told him not to rely so much on tech and that changing a tire is something every responsible driver should know how to do. He had rolled his eyes back then. Now, he doesn't complain. If anything, he almost looks like he's enjoying it.

Jessie finishes wrapping her hand in t-shirt strips and crouches next to Max. She checks the lug nuts. "Nice work," she says. A flash of pride crosses his face. She winces as she rolls what's left of the flat tire to Max.

"This thing was a failure." Max gives it a hefty shove into the desert. "Mom, I'm going to…"

His voice trails off as the word *failure* echoes in Jessie's head. She sees Black Beard again, frozen in place. Two bloody holes in his chest. One in his forehead. She has the memory of what happened, but she doesn't remember doing it. Her training has resurfaced and become second nature.

Dr. Smith's voice rises in her mind. *Failure drill. Close proximity. Immediate threat.* Jessie and the other recruits had lined up, backs to their targets. On the whistle, they were to turn, draw, then shoot. Three shots. Two shots center mass. One to the head. She remembers being startled at how close the target was when she turned. It had cost her precious seconds, and she failed her first attempt. Today, she didn't hesitate.

Jessie tosses the lug wrench into the back of the Explorer and stashes Black Beard's gun into one of the suitcases. She climbs into the driver's seat, taking care not to bump her throbbing hand. "Max, why was your laptop—" She cuts herself off. The passenger seat is empty. She whips around. Sean is curled up in the back with a thousand-yard stare. No Max.

She jumps out and scans the desert, panic suffocating her.

Her pulse spikes, and her chest tightens. She turns, searching in all directions. Nothing. A crunching sound travels on a breeze, and she spins in its direction. Relief surges through her when she sees Max jogging toward her, carrying something.

He huffs between breaths, "I figured he probably needs this." He hands her Sean's hockey stick.

Jessie opens the back door and places it gently on the floorboards. "Hey buddy. Max got your stick for you." No response. She brushes the hair from Sean's face and closes the door softly.

As Jessie pulls onto the highway, she catches Max looking at her. "What?"

Max hesitates. "Oh, um, I wanted to ask you…" He trails off. "I was going to ask if I could drive." He tries to convince her with a smile. She knows that's not what he wanted to ask.

Jessie raises an eyebrow.

"I'm kidding." Max jests, before getting serious again as he eyes Jessie's bandaged hand. "Unless, you know, if that hurts. I mean, I could drive for a little while." His concern is genuine, a rare and welcome break from his usual sarcasm.

Jessie follows his eyes to her wounded hand and reassures him she's okay. Her stomach makes an audible growl, reminding her she never finished her French fries and shake. She grabs three granola bars from the center console and hands two to Max. "You guys need to eat something. Adrenaline can make you nauseated."

Sean hasn't moved, and Jessie hopes the granola bar will entice him to come back to planet Earth.

Typically, Max would toss the granola bar at Sean, ready or not. But he doesn't. He gently taps Sean's arm with the granola bar. No response. He tries again. Nothing. He looks at Jessie, waiting for some kind of cue.

She leans toward Max. "Sean needs to snap out of the shock before he has a meltdown. What was the documentary you watched with Sean last week?"

Max shrugs. "Something about toucans, I think. I wasn't really paying attention."

"Okay, play along," Jessie says. Max nods stiffly.

She raises her voice just enough to be heard over the hum of the road. "Hey Max, look at that tree. It looks like there's something in it."

"Yeah," he says, flatly. Jessie gestures for more. He sighs and taps his window. "That tree right there does have something in it."

Jessie resists a groan. Max is awful at improv, but that's oddly reassuring.

"It looks like a toucan," she says, watching Sean for a reaction. If he lets that go, he's worse off than she thought.

"Yep, it's definitely a toucan," adds Max.

Sean pops up and cranes his neck toward the window.

"There is no way you are looking at a toucan bird. They live in the rainforest in Central and/or South America. Not in North America. And not in a desert."

Jessie exhales a quiet breath of relief.

Max rolls with it. "You're right. It must be a bag that blew into the tree. It probably fell off a produce truck, heading from an organic farm in Fresno to a farm in Reno," says Max.

Jessie shoots him a look. He went from deadpan to backstory in under ten seconds.

Max shrugs, as if to say *you wanted improv.* He makes a second attempt with the granola bar. This time, Sean takes it.

Jessie is running on instinct and adrenaline now, but she needs a plan. Her thoughts spiral through her options, none of which are very good. She's about to speak when a flash of green by the highway breaks her concentration. She's unsure why she should care about the green blur, but her subconscious won't let it go. She glances at the navigation screen and makes the connection. It was the sign for Zyzyx Road. The name sits there on the map, just ahead of their location marker.

Her pulse quickens. She hastily digs her SIM card and phone from her pocket and hands them to Max. "Put this back in," she says. "Now."

Max snaps into action, sliding the SIM card into place. The moment Jessie's phone powers on, it starts chiming. Message after message pops up on the screen. Max reads the texts aloud: "Dad says he's running behind because he couldn't find his charger...turned back for his wallet...he's finally on the road..."

Jessie cuts him off. "Call him."

Max taps Nick's contact button. The navigation map disappears, replaced with the Bluetooth interface: Nick's name with the word "calling" underneath. Jessie's shoulders tighten. One ring. Two. Three. The ringing stops. Her eyes snap to the screen. The call timer begins: 0:01, 0:02, 0:03.

"Nick? Hello?" Jessie says, too quickly. For a moment, there's nothing, then a crackle of static, followed by a warped, barely intelligible "hello". Her shoulders loosen as Nick's voice comes through clearly.

"Jessie, did you get my messages?"

"I need you to call the highway patrol," Jessie says. "Give them a description of my car. Tell them we need assistance."

"Jes—you broke—yes, I'm on the highway—be abo—then," Nick says.

"Nick? Call highway—" The call drops. Three short beeps fill the Explorer cabin.

"Call him back," Jessie says.

Max redials. Nothing happens.

"Try again."

Still nothing.

"Try texting. And then call again."

Max hides the call screen, sends a text, then redials.

Jessie stares at the car's call screen, willing a connection to be made. On her phone's screen, the sending bar crawls forward, then stalls at a quarter of the way. Both screens taunt her in Nowhere.

After a minute, Max confirms what she already knows and doesn't want to hear. "We lost it." He takes the SIM card out and gently places her phone and the card in the cup holder between them.

Jessie swears under her breath.

A chime sounds in the Explorer. Jessie wrinkles her brow. "Not again," she mutters, eyeing the dashboard. No warning lights. The tire pressure is fine. She checks her phone, hoping for a miracle. No signal.

Another chime.

"What is that?" she asks.

"Sounds like my laptop when I get a message," Max says, sounding confused. He hesitates until he notices Jessie staring at him like she's waiting for him to move. Then it hits him—his laptop has a signal.

Max frantically unbuckles and scrambles over the center console. Sean flinches but says nothing when Max's feet come within inches of his granola bar. Max teeters on the back seat, legs draping over Sean, as he fishes his laptop from the cargo area. He scrambles back into his seat.

It chimes again.

He flips it open.

Jessie checks the navigation. Wishful thinking hasn't changed their situation. They're in the middle of Nowhere. Well, just past the middle. "How are you getting a signal out here?"

Max shakes his head, baffled. "I don't know. Zyzyx?"

"We're too far past it," Jessie says. Another chime. Her fingers tighten around the steering wheel.

Max grumbles, still confused as the laptop screen comes to life. A box pops up with an unread message.

Sender: BirdOfPrey431

# TWENTY-EIGHT

OSCAR DRIVES with the front windows cracked just enough to let the wind drown out any attempt at conversation. So far, it's worked. Charlie hasn't said a word. Oscar has no interest in small talk or getting to know Charlie. He's a young kid who won't cut it in this line of work. Papa's recent decisions, hiring Charlie and handing Victor the most important job they've ever had, have been questionable. Maybe he's preparing to hand over the reins. If so, Oscar intends to be there when it happens and make sure the reins fall into his hands.

Just last week, Oscar overheard Victor pressing Papa to retire. Papa had pushed back, insisting he wasn't ready to sit around and do nothing like other men his age. Before Victor weaseled his way onto this job, Oscar had seen it as his chance to prove himself as Papa's right-hand man, and maybe get Romeo's attention in the process.

Over the past ten years, Oscar had worked hard to be more than just another name on Papa's payroll. His history with the family ran deep. He'd met Victor's older brother in middle school, and by high school, they were inseparable. During those teenage years, Oscar spent more time at Papa's house than his own. His father walked out when he was thirteen, planting a seed of jealousy that has festered over time. Marta put up with him, and Papa mostly ignored him. Oscar could've been a better influence on their son, but he also could've been worse. They never ended up in jail, but they also never got caught in the real sticky situations they found themselves in.

About a year after the funeral, Oscar ran into Papa again and saw a changed man. He had an edge and a roughness Oscar had never seen before. A week later, Oscar began working for him, and they started building a new relationship. Less father and son. More distant uncle and tolerated nephew.

Even after all this time and Oscar's best efforts, Papa still keeps him at arm's length. But Oscar no longer minds, now that he has his sights on Romeo.

Charlie breaks the silence. "Uh, this should be the spot coming up."

Oscar sighs heavily, silently cursing Victor for sticking him with Charlie.

Charlie holds up his phone. The screen shows a map with a dropped pin from Papa. Oscar ignores him and keeps his eyes on the deserted highway ahead. As they get closer, Charlie points into the desert. "Look. Over there. There's a tire."

Oscar eases the Range Rover to the shoulder and reaches into the back seat for his jacket. The sun has begun its final descent, taking the temperature with it. He steps out and scans the open desert for any sign of life. Nothing. All is silent. Even the winter wind slips by in silence. It feels like the desert is hiding something. Like it knew he was coming.

Charlie furrows his brow and kneels beside the tire, poking at it like it might tell him something. Oscar has no idea what the kid thinks he's doing. Charlie doesn't strike him as someone who knows anything about anything. They haven't spent much time together, but Oscar already finds Charlie's naivety and eagerness nauseating.

Victor, however, seems to have taken Charlie under his wing, playing the role of mentor. Typical. He was always a kiss ass, eager to impress Papa, even when he was a punk kid hanging around the garage trying to act useful. Maybe he's trying to replace his dead brother. If so, he's replacing the star quarterback with the water boy.

But lately, something shifted. Last week, Victor started brushing Charlie off. The kid kept asking to tag along on jobs, and Victor kept dodging with new excuses. Eventually, Charlie came to Oscar and asked if he had done something wrong. Oscar just smirked and said that maybe Victor just didn't like him, now that he had gotten to know him.

Charlie shouldn't even be here. If timing is everything, Charlie had the gods on his side. He happened to be sitting with Papa at the diner when Romeo called, and just like that, he got looped into the job. Just the right place, wrong kid.

Back in the Range Rover, the GPS unit in the center console emits three short beeps. Oscar calls Papa and informs him that Mike has switched the tracking on the GPS unit, and now it's locked on the Explorer. Then he relays Papa's plan to Charlie, not bothering to look at him. "We're tracking her through GPS. She's ahead of us. Papa wants us to continue on the highway. They'll turn around and come at her from the north."

"And then what?" Charlie says.

Oscar keeps his eyes focused ahead. "And then we end this."

# TWENTY-NINE

As Jessie passes the last set of orange construction barrels, the fast lane opens up. The added room to maneuver brings a brief wave of relief. She checks the rearview mirror for what feels like the twentieth time in ten minutes and exhales at the sight of an empty highway. The cruise control holds steady at eighty, the maximum she trusts the spare to handle.

Behind her, Sean snores softly while Max types away at his laptop. The steady speed and hum of the highway paired with familiar sounds of routine threaten to lull Jessie into complacency, but the dull throbbing of her knife wound reminds her to stay vigilant.

"Are you online? How do you have a signal out here?" Jessie asks.

"I don't know. Maybe Nowhere finally got a cell tower." Max shrugs, eyes still locked on his screen.

Jessie scans the barren landscape, nothing but dust and brush to the horizon. If there's a tower, it's nowhere in sight. She holds out hope there's one a few miles up the highway.

"What are you doing?" Her voice tightens with suspicion.

"I'm getting us help."

Without thinking, Jessie slams the laptop shut.

"Ouch! What'd you do that for?"

"We can't involve anyone else in this," she says, voice low and firm.

"Mom, Sean and I almost became dinner for some psycho desert dweller and you..." Max trails off, lowering his head.

"I, what?"

Max hesitates, his mouth opening slightly before closing again. Jessie watches him wrestle with something, his brows pinched tight. It's the same face he makes when he's about to ask for something she'll probably say no to. When he finally speaks, his voice is careful, "Did you kill that guy?"

She stiffens.

"When I went back for Sean's stick...he wasn't moving." He glances at her. "I mean, you didn't have a choice." Another beat. "Right?"

"Right." Jessie keeps her eyes on the road. "I didn't have a choice." The words echo from a previous life, only now, they sound more convincing.

From the back seat, Sean bolts upright, blinking hard. "Where are we?" He rubs his eyes with both fists.

"In the middle of nowhere," Jessie grumbles.

"Good. Can I call Dad real quick?" Sean says.

Max shoots Jessie a quick glance, a silent reminder to be clear with Sean, who always takes things literally. She's the one who usually has to remind him of that. Now here he is, tossing her logic back with the calm assurance of someone starting to stand on his own two feet.

"We already passed the spot. There's no signal out here," Jessie says, trying to keep her voice even.

"But you said—"

"I didn't mean we're literally in the middle of Nowhere," she snaps, then exhales, already regretting the edge in her tone.

"Well, we kind of are," Max says with a shrug.

Jessie shoots him a sharp look. "You're not helping."

The laptop chimes. Max flips it open, but when Jessie reaches to shut it again, he gently blocks her hand. "Mom, if those guys are really after us, we need help."

She pauses, then follows his gaze toward Sean.

Max is usually a typical self-centered teenager, but occasionally, in moments like this, he shows glimpses of adult maturity. Jessie doesn't want to admit it, but she may be in over her head. If she were alone, it would be a different story. But with her boys here, every situation is more complicated, not just logistically. Their presence influences her judgement. Choices made from the heart never follow the same path as those made from the head. She pulls her hand back from the laptop.

"Okay. Is that your online friend?"

Max nods.

"I'm not sure how a 16-year-old kid can help, but maybe he can contact Dad for us," she says.

Max tilts his head and raises a brow. "You underestimate the power of the younger generation. He already knows we got a flat tire."

Jessie eyes him. "And?"

"And that some hostiles might be following us." He watches her reaction carefully, trying to gauge if he's in trouble for saying too much.

*Hostiles?* Kids and their video games these days. "Fine," she says. It's not fine. The last thing she needs is this kid blasting social media with what's happening to Max. Jessie steers with her knee and slides the SIM card back into her phone, wincing as the motion aggravates her injured hand. She powers it up. No signal.

"Is he online now?"

Max nods.

"Why can't I get a signal?"

A message pops up in the chat box with a chime.

"Bop says we aren't using cellular," Max says.

Jessie frowns and tosses her phone in the cup holder. That shouldn't be possible. The only way a signal is possible in Nowhere is via satellite. And Nick bought Max's laptop from the local Best Buy. And how in the heck does this "Bop" kid know they were even talking about cellular service? She's still trying to make sense of it all when she checks the rearview mirror. Her stomach drops.

She moves the navigation map around, searching for an exit. There's a small town ten miles ahead.

"See if your friend can call Dad."

"Dad? What about the police?"

"I just need to get a message to Dad."

"I already gave Bop his number. He said he'll call him. What do you want him to say?"

Jessie is impressed with Max's instincts. She checks the rearview mirror again, her pulse ticking faster. "We need to get off the highway," she mutters.

Max twists in his seat. Jessie catches the subtle flinch that flickers across his face as he squints at the horizon. "That car behind us...is that them?"

Jessie presses harder on the gas. The engine groans, and she silently begs the spare tire to hold together a little longer.

"I need to go to the bathroom," Sean announces from the back, seemingly unaware of the panic rising in the front seat.

Max turns to Sean. "Seriously, how many times do you pee in one day?"

"I have to go number two," he says, as if Max should have known.

A chime sounds. Max reads the screen aloud, puzzled. "Bop said to tell you, 'cheddar apple pie is disgusting'. Whatever that means."

Jessie's grip on the wheel slackens, and her foot slips off the gas. The Explorer drifts lazily into the other lane.

"Mom. Hey, Mom!" Max's voice snaps her back.

Jessie jerks upright, grabs the wheel tight, and punches the gas.

"I really have to go," Sean says, his voice edging toward panic.

"As soon as we can stop, you can go," Jessie says.

Jessie glances at the laptop screen and catches the phrase *cheddar apple pie*. She hasn't thought about that in years. Her grandmother used to make it, cheddar right on top. The last time she mentioned it, her squadmates looked at her like she'd suggested putting ketchup on ice cream. Agents weren't supposed to share personal details, but from their reactions, she figured they were West Coast boys. None of them had heard of the combination.

Derrick and Fletcher, not their real names, had the call signs Eagle and Hawk, respectively. She hasn't thought about them in over a decade, but today, all her ghosts seem to want their turn behind the wheel. They all started as recruits, and after completing The Agency's brutal training program, she and Jonathan completed their four-man squad.

Hawk changed assignments a few times, and Jessie eventually lost track of him. Eagle got benched thanks to an injury, and after nine months of boredom, he bribed the doctor to release him early for the Prague mission. No one realized it would be their last mission together. She and Jonathan worked together most of her time at The Agency, with a steady rotation of agents providing support and backup as needed. She wonders now if any of her old squadmates are still with The Agency.

Jessie nods at Max's laptop. "Type this: You finally got a cheat day?"

Max gives her a confused look, but types the message anyway. A moment later, the laptop chimes. "He said: on April 31st," Max reads aloud.

A hot wave rushes through Jessie from head to toe. BirdOfPrey431. Only Jonathan would use that handle. A nod to his old call sign and April 31st, her and Jonathan's inside joke. The day that didn't exist. They'd say The Agency scheduled everything they looked forward to on April 31ˢᵗ: cheat days, vacation, even graduation.

After eight years in the field, she asked Jonathan to leave The Agency and start a new life together. He held her close, tears in his eyes, and said he would—on April 31ˢᵗ.

"Tell Bob there are only thirty days in April. Not thirty-one. April 31ˢᵗ doesn't exist. And I just farted so I don't think I have to go to the bathroom anymore. I feel better now. Don't tell Bob the part about me farting. Unless he'll think it's funny. Then tell him." Sean says.

"It's Bop. Not Bob," Max says, exaggerating the last consonants.

"Bop sounds weird, and it's easier to say Bob," Sean replies, completely unfazed.

Max huffs. "Whatever. I'm not telling him any of that." He glances at Jessie. "Mom, what do you want Bop to tell Dad?"

Jessie doesn't answer right away. Her eyes are back on the mirror.

The vehicle behind them, now clearly a dark SUV, is gaining fast. At this pace, it will catch up in eight minutes. About the same time it'll take her to reach the edge of the nearest town.

"Tell Falcon we need to get off the highway. Now." Jessie throws Max a look that tells him she knows more than she's letting on.

"Falcon?" Max waits for a response, but doesn't get one.

He hesitates half a second longer, then types the message. Jessie watches his brow furrow as he reads the reply, clearly surprised. Whatever his friend said, it confirmed something for him. He doesn't question her the next time she calls him Falcon.

The SUV is closing in. Jessie scans the map again, but it's useless—no exits, no service roads, nothing but desert. She can't risk taking the spare tire on that terrain. Her only shot is to make it to the upcoming town and lose them there.

A chime sounds.

"Bop—er Falcon—says he contacted highway patrol a little while ago. They're sending someone to escort us into town," Max says. He sounds half relieved, half doubtful.

Before Jessie can ask if Falcon has an ETA, red and blue lights flash in the mirror, coming from the SUV behind them.

Her foot lifts off the gas instinctively. The navigation shows five miles to town, less than five minutes.

"Let him know they're here," she says. Her eyes stay locked on the mirror.

Max taps quickly at the keyboard.

Sean bolts upright in the back seat. "Where?" He squints toward the lights. "Uh, Mom? I think you're in trouble."

*No kidding.* Jessie keeps her voice steady. "Don't worry. Highway patrol is here to make sure we get into town safely. The spare tire's not reliable." It's not a complete lie.

"I thought they were here to arrest you for killing that guy at the shack. Or because those other guys are following us."

Jessie and Max share a surprised glance.

"I have autism, not deafism. I can hear you guys talking, you know."

A loud pop cracks through the air. The Explorer doesn't flinch. Jessie checks the dashboard. No tire pressure warning. Then another pop. And another. Sreeching tires behind them.

In the rearview mirror, she sees the highway patrol vehicle swerve into the left lane, overcorrect, and fishtail wildly. Another shot rings out.

"Get down!" Jessie says.

Max slinks low in the front seat, arms shielding his head. Behind him, Sean drops instantly, curling into a ball on the middle seat.

The patrol car flips, rolling over and over until it crashes onto its side in the middle of the highway. Jessie slams the accelerator.

Beside her, Max reaches for the laptop on the floorboard. As the Explorer hits a pothole, his head knocks against the glove box with a dull *thunk*. "Ow!" He mutters, sliding lower in his seat, laptop tilted in his lap. "Falcon says you need to ditch the car."

"What?" They're still miles from town. The sun is disappearing behind the mountains, and once it's gone, the temperature will nosedive. They can't afford exposure to the elements, not this time of year. She glances at the mirror. The Range Rover is already weaving around the wreckage, back in pursuit.

A chime sounds. "Falcon says they're tracking us through the car's navigation system."

Of course. That's why they took photos of her license plate. License plates are assigned to VINs. VINs are assigned to GPS systems. They're not following her. They're following the Explorer. They need to ditch the car.

"Tell him we can't," Jessie says. "We're too far out."

Max types. Another chime.

"He says he knows," Max says. "Ditch it anyway."

Another chime.

"Now," he pleads.

Jessie checks the rearview mirror. The Range Rover will be on them in less than a minute. The vein in her neck throbs. She checks the tire pressure light. The spare is holding for now.

Up ahead, a car appears in the fast lane. The first they've seen since getting back on the highway. It seems to have come out of nowhere. Within seconds, it's alarmingly close. Too close. Jessie checks the speedometer. Even at ninety, there's no reason she should be gaining on it this fast.

"Falcon says there's a barn one mile into town," Max says. "He can guide us once we get to the main road. We're not that far." He hesitates, then adds, "And he's not happy we're still in the car." His voice trembles, just barely.

Pain shoots through Jessie's left hand like a live wire. She stiffens, her eyes looking at something up ahead. "Tell him we're not going to make it to the main road," Jessie says. "We're getting off the highway. Now."

Max inches up to the screen, tapping through the navigation map. "I don't see a road," he says. "Mom, there's no road coming up."

She wipes her sweaty palm on her pants. What she's about to do will take everything she has. She grits her teeth and grabs the wheel tightly, causing more pain. There's no margin for error.

Max lifts his head from the screen and peers over the dashboard. "Uh... Mom?"

The black Mercedes G Wagon is driving in the middle of both lanes.

Heading straight for them.

# THIRTY

THE LAST bit of sun dips behind the desert mountains, streaking the sky in pink and purple brush strokes. In another minute, the purples will bleed into indigo, and then black. The air cools quickly, and with no city lights to drown them out, the stars will blanket the sky. Papa watches the glorious sunset and thinks about the night he proposed to the love of his life.

The clouds were lit up in wild reds and molten purples, like the sky was on fire. Marta had called it cotton candy on steroids—loud, ridiculous, and beautiful. She's always seen things that way. Bigger. Brighter. Bolder. He envied that about her. She helped him experience things he would've missed. He closes his eyes and makes the sign of the cross across his chest.

The ache of the memory threatens to take hold. Victor says something. Memories are lovely, but he can't be burdened right now. He opens his eyes. The sky is still on fire, but he doesn't feel its warmth anymore.

"What did you say?" Papa asks.

"That's her, up ahead," Victor says.

"Get in the middle," he says, eyes locked on the Explorer in the distance. "Force her off."

Victor hesitates. Then, jaw clenched, he nudges the Mercedes across the dashed line, centering it between both lanes. The last sliver of sun vanishes, and the headlights flick on automatically. Victor's chest tightens. Driving in the middle requires more willpower than entering the highway in the wrong direction. He has established a game of chicken, but has no intention of meeting the same fate as his mother and brother.

Oscar keeps the Range Rover on its course even when the Mercedes drifts into the center lane.

Charlie grabs the bar on the side of his door. "Uh, what is Victor doing?"

Oscar doesn't answer right away. "Trying to get us all killed." No way Victor has the balls for a dangerous move like that. This is all Papa.

The Explorer is only five car lengths ahead. Its tail lights flick off. Smart. He tightens his grip on the wheel. The Mercedes is closing in fast.

The Explorer vanishes into the dark as Jessie kills the headlights. Somewhere behind them, the Range Rover is closing in. Ahead, the Mercedes holds the middle of the road like it owns it. They're trying to pin her in. One in front. One in back. Nowhere to go but off-road.

Jessie's phone chimes. And again. Again. Service is restored. Messages flood in. She ignores them.

"Sean, put your helmet on," she says. "Max, give *your friend* my number. Tell him to call me."

He gives her a quizzical look. "My friend?"

"We need the location of that barn." She doesn't wait for a response. "Grab hold of something." Jessie eases off the gas and jerks the wheel to the right. The front passenger side lifts off the asphalt, then slams back down with a jarring thud that rattles the cabin.

Max shouts and grabs the door handle, one hand against the dash.

Sean yelps as the jolt throws him sideways.

Gravel spits as they begin to fishtail in the desert.

The Mercedes is suddenly on a collision course with the Range Rover as the Explorer breaks off into the desert.

Victor slams on the brakes.

Pulls hard to the right.

Into the fast lane.

Papa braces himself.

Oscar hits the brakes.

Charlie ducks, arms over his head.

The Mercedes tears past—close. Too close.

Oscar fights the drag pulling on the Range Rover.

He yanks right, hitting the desert.

Charlie bounces into the window.

Oscar doesn't flinch.

Jessie steadies the Explorer.

Max's hand bounces along the keyboard, hitting the wrong key. He fixes it with a sharp keystroke and hits Enter.

Sean plants his palms against the front seats, bracing as the SUV bucks beneath him.

Jessie swerves to miss a boulder. The tires lose their grip. The Explorer skids. She punches the gas and turns into it—gravel flying, until the wheels bite and she's back in control.

Victor slows and turns left to join the chase. He switches the Mercedes to four-wheel drive and surges forward.

Papa jolts with the impact, holding onto the dashboard.

"She's not getting away," he says.

Victor doesn't respond. He keeps the wheel steady and the throttle down.

Jessie's phone rings. She reaches for the answer button, but misses as the Explorer tosses her around. She tries again. Success. "Get us out of here!"

Jonathan's voice fills the cabin.

"Alex, an access road on the edge of town will take you to a gas station."

The sound of his voice hits her hard, and she's somewhere else. The rumble of the tires, the way the car shakes beneath her, the headlights chasing her—gone.

She's back at The Agency, new and nervous, running late for orientation. She had opened the wrong door, expecting a classroom. He was standing alone in a janitor's closet, wiping his face with his sleeve. His eyes were red, his nose was running, and he didn't even try to hide it. Jessie froze. Not because of the awkwardness, but because he was beautiful in a way that felt real. Raw. Unpolished. For a second, neither of them spoke.

Then she blurted out, "I'm Alex. Both my parents died."

Jonathan nodded slowly, returning his gaze to the floor. "You're not supposed to share personal information," his voice soft and uneven.

"I know," she said.

He looked up again, met her eyes, and gave a half-smile. "Thanks."

She still isn't sure if she said it for him or for her. But in that moment, she needed someone to know she was sad too.

The Explorer hits a dip hard.

Jessie lurches forward. She flicks the headlights back on.

A boulder leaps out of the dark.

She yanks the wheel.

"I don't see a road!"

The Explorer rips through the brush.

She kills the lights.

Sean yelps, thudding against her seat.

"Alex, has the sun set?"

"Who's Alex?" Max asks.

"Yep. Lights are off. Can't see a thing!"

The Explorer hits the side of a cactus. Spines scrape at the door.

Max's laptop flies to the floor. He bends for it, hits his head.

Jessie checks the mirror. Two sets of headlights are behind them. Closing in.

"What are you driving?" Jonathan asks.

"Explorer."

"How old?"

"Brand new."

"I see you on our satellite. There's a group of Joshua trees up ahead. Pass by them as closely as you can. And when I tell you to, make a sharp left."

Straining her eyes, she scans for anything vertical.

"Mom, who is that? It doesn't sound like Dad," Sean squeezes out between bumps.

Jessie tightens her grip on the wheel. Pain shoots up her left arm.

"Hold on, boys."

Sean hugs his pillow tighter, burying his face.

Max slides his laptop under his legs, grabs the door handle, and braces himself against the dashboard.

Off to the left—a cluster of dark, vertical silhouettes. Joshua trees.

She veers toward them.

Her teeth clench as their dry branches scrape across the paint, trying to get in.

"Now!" Jonathan says.

Jessie hits the brakes and cranks the wheel to the left.

Seconds later, the ground falls out from beneath them.

172

# THIRTY-ONE

TIME SLOWS to a crawl.

Max feels the joyful sensation of his stomach being taken away, the kind that usually comes with a rollercoaster drop or the descent into the Fun Dip. It's a strange contradiction to the tight knots of fear and panic twisting in his chest.

All sound has been bottled up and stored somewhere, like the air itself has gone still.

It's too dark to see, but he knows the tires have left the ground, and for a moment, the Explorer levitates, suspended in the air, like a magic trick.

His body fights against the seatbelt and gravity, wanting to hang in place for a second longer. His chest gets squeezed as the seatbelt draws down, pressing deeper with each inch the Explorer falls. His body pushes against it, resisting the pull. His arms drift upward, unrestrained and weightless. The belt drags his torso down while the rest of him lags behind, suspended in the delay. The pressure builds until the belt pulls him fully into the drop.

He opens his mouth to scream, but his lungs betray him. His chest is tight, every muscle seized, holding the air hostage.

The front end of the Explorer begins to tilt toward the ground, the shift so gradual he only notices it by the way the seatbelt presses a little tighter across his chest. His body leans with the angle, drawn forward by the slow pull of gravity. The silence is broken by the sound of his own breathing—shallow, unsteady, and far away. The vehicle tilts a little more. He can feel it now in his stomach, his spine, and in the muscles of his shoulders, bracing for impact.

The Explorer makes contact at a steep angle.

The front bumper hits first, sending a heavy jolt through the floor and into Max's feet.

Metal twists and screams under the pressure.

Glass bursts somewhere nearby.

Sean's voice tears through the cabin, long and stretched, like he's been yelling the whole time, and Max is only just now hearing it. Momentum snaps Sean forward—just a blur in Max's peripheral vision—then his seatbelt whips him back.

Airbags pop from all directions. The sharp, chemical smell of deployment gas burns Max's nostrils. He begins to cough, finally finding air in his lungs.

The windshield angles toward the ground as the rear end crashes into the wall of the plateau. The impact throws the back end up. For a moment, they're upright on the nose. Then gravity takes over, and the Explorer lands on its roof.

Silence.

Dust begins to settle in the stillness, swirling around the upside-down Explorer.

# THIRTY-TWO

VICTOR SLOWS as they crest a rise. Dust hangs in the air, drifting across the desert in slow, lazy swirls. Visibility is poor, and there's no sign of the Explorer. No lights. No movement. Just the Range Rover, sitting still up ahead like it's waiting for orders.

They pass the cluster of Joshua trees.

Papa watches the dust curling above the landscape, slower now, beginning to settle. The trail doesn't lead anywhere.

Victor pulls alongside the Range Rover.

Papa lowers his window. "Where is she?"

Charlie leans across the center console to speak out Oscar's window. He points toward the Joshua trees. "It looks like there's dust—"

Oscar cuts him off. "Check the GPS."

Charlie fumbles with the screen on the unit. After a few seconds, he shakes his head. "Nothing."

Oscar snatches the GPS unit. "She disappeared," he says. "GPS doesn't show anything. She just disappeared!" He throws the unit at Charlie's feet and slams his palm against the steering wheel, muttering something Papa can't decipher.

Papa doesn't react. The chase is over. For now.

"We're heading to town, he says. He raises his window, not waiting for a response.

Victor turns the wheel. The Mercedes moves forward, cutting through what's left of the dust.

Papa watches the dust fold back into the night and says nothing else. But he is already thinking about where she'll go next—and what he'll do when he gets there first.

# THIRTY-THREE

Anguished grunting stirs Jessie to consciousness. She gasps, choking on dust that hangs in the cabin air. The coughing brings pain, clamping around her chest. The grunting continues, almost primal, but it isn't hers. Jessie tries to turn toward Sean, but her seatbelt and surrounding airbags pin her against the seat. It takes several breaths to realize she's hanging upside down.

Jessie pushes an airbag off her left arm. She tries to press it into the roof for support, but it's uncooperative, dangling broken and useless. Her bandages have ripped off, and fresh blood steadily drains from her reopened knife wound, pooling on the headliner below. A searing pulse shoots through her arm. Jessie quickly removes her watch, feeling her wrist already beginning to swell.

Next to her, Max's blond locks hang toward the roof. The hat and sunglasses are gone. Airbags bury him as he fumbles urgently with his seatbelt. He finally frees himself and drops to the roof with a muffled grunt.

Jessie braces with her right arm, steadying herself as best she can. "Max, undo my seatbelt." As he does, she drops awkwardly and crumples onto the roof beside him. She untangles her limbs and quickly twists toward Sean. He thrashes his head against the headrest, clutching his seatbelt with a death grip. His earlier grunts have morphed into dull whining. "Hold on, buddy," she says.

She turns to Max, "You okay?"

He nods, coughing. She presses gently, needing certainty. "You sure?"

"I'm fine, really," Max says.

Jessie winces as she wedges herself between the front seats, maneuvering awkwardly until she's face-to-face with Sean. She presses the cabin light switch, pleasantly surprised when the dim glow actually comes on. She gives Sean a quick once-over, relieved to find nothing immediately alarming. "Hey, it's a good thing you have that helmet on, huh?" Sean doesn't respond.

Sean's rhythmic whining fills the cabin. Jessie recognizes that he can't process what's happening.

"Sean. Sean. Look at me. Sean." He's not there. Jessie gently grasps the cage of his helmet and turns his head, speaking directly into his ear. She speaks slowly, her voice steady despite the desire to yell and get the hell out of there. "I'm going to release your belt. But you're going to fall when I do, so you need to put your hands up to catch yourself." She releases his helmet, but he doesn't move. "Sean. Did you hear me?" Nothing but heavy, rapid breathing. "Sean, we need to get out of here." Frustration tightens her voice. "If we don't leave now, those men will find us and kill us. We need to go now. Get ready to catch yourself." Even the threat of death doesn't trigger a response.

Max is kneeling outside the back passenger window. He pulls away the sheet of fractured glass, still held together by a thin film, wincing as a shard cuts his finger. Reaching through, he pushes the airbags aside to get closer to Sean. "If you don't listen to Mom, you're going to fall on your head and break your neck."

Jessie looks at Max, startled by his bluntness. She waits, heart hammering, hoping the sharpness of Max's words will break through Sean's panic. She tries not to think about the precious time they're wasting or the deep, steady burn radiating through her injured arm.

"Dude, if you break your neck, no more hockey."

Sean's breathing slows. He looks at Max.

Jessie meets Max's eyes, both surprised that the threat worked.

It takes a moment, but Sean finally releases his grip on the seatbelt and raises his arms, bracing himself.

Max grabs Sean's waistband, ready to break the fall.

Jessie places a finger on the belt release. "One, two, three." The latch clicks, and Sean falls, his arms absorbing the impact with Max's help.

Max slides out of the SUV, pushing the airbags aside to clear a path for Sean.

Jessie sets Max's laptop, backpack, and hat outside the window, then reenters the wreckage, searching for her phone. She pushes a deflated airbag aside, and her phone drops near her knees. She grabs it and her hat, then crawls back out.

With her uninjured arm, Jessie wraps the boys in a careful embrace. Max returns the gesture, slipping his arm around her shoulders. Sean doesn't hug back, but he doesn't pull away like he usually would.

Jessie holds them tighter. She needs just one more moment.

A chill wind sweeps through the desert, raising goosebumps on Jessie's skin. The temperature has dropped sharply since sunset, at least fifteen degrees. Within the hour, it will dip into the low thirties.

Questions flood her mind: How will she keep them safe? Who are these guys? Do they know who she is, or who she used to be? She pushes the thoughts aside, focusing on what needs her immediate attention: injuries, supplies, shelter.

Jessie pulls away and inspects Max quickly, but the darkness makes it difficult. "You sure you're okay?"

"I hit my head on the window and cut my hand, but yeah, I'm fine."

She kneels beside Sean, running her hands carefully over his legs. "What about you?" She moves to his torso and arms. "Does anything hurt?" No answer. She feels the goosebumps on his legs, but finds no protruding bones or noticeable bumps.

Satisfied the boys aren't seriously injured, Jessie rebandages her hand and makes a splint using her belt and the UNLV t-shirt Max got when he toured the campus last week.

She turns her attention to the mess behind them and rummages through their luggage while Max holds up the flashlight on his phone, the steady beam illuminating dusty backpacks and scattered belongings. She grabs her backpack, as well as Sean's.

Nearby, Sean lies in a fetal position, his head resting on his pillow. He has taken off his helmet and changed into a pair of jeans. Under his breath, he commentates the 1980 Olympic hockey game between the USA and Russia. He clutches his hockey stick as if it's protecting him. The sight reminds Jessie of Prague.

She pulls her gaze away, steps farther out, and calls the last number she received on her phone. Although nothing happens on her end, she knows something will, and she waits. A second later, her phone rings.

"Are you guys okay?" Jonathan says.

"Yeah, we're fine." She turns her back on the boys and takes a few more steps away. Her voice trembles with a mix of anger and disbelief as she somehow manages to yell and whisper simultaneously. "What the hell? How long have you been talking to Max? I can't even believe you right now. Pretending to be a teenager. You want to spy on your ex? See what she's up to? That's what social media is for asshole. You used my kid! I don't know who I want to hurt more right now, you or these maniacs trying to kill us!" She stops, but only because she needs oxygen.

Jonathan's voice is calm, but urgent—a trained professional. "Let's focus on the maniacs right now. And yes, they are trying to kill you. So, let's table this conversation and get you guys out of there. Earlier, you said 'boys,' plural, and I heard another voice besides Max. How many in your party?"

"My *party*? This isn't a mission. I don't have a *party*. I have my two boys with me, who were almost just killed, thanks to your crappy directions. And I'm starting to wonder if this whole mess has anything to do with you!" She knows the last part isn't true, but she needs someone to blame.

"Alex, I get you're mad at me right now. But you know I would never put you or anyone you care about in danger. As far as the driving directions..." His voice falters and trails off.

Jessie remains silent, an unspoken demand for him to explain.

Jonathan exhales slowly and finally continues. "It was the only choice I had. I needed to get you guys out of sight."

Jessie would have made the same call, but won't admit it.

"Please believe me when I say it was strictly a coincidence that Max and I ever became friends."

"You are not friends! He thinks you're a sixteen-year-old boy from Arizona."

"Please, let me help you, Alex."

"My name's Jessie."

"Let me help you, Jessie."

A long silence hangs between them as she turns back to her boys. She hates that he's the only option she has right now.

"Tell me where to go."

# THIRTY-FOUR

VICTOR HAS driven the US 95 more times than he can count, but he's never had a reason to stop in Canyon Springs. The name is misleading. There's no canyon and no springs, just an empty promise from early settlers who believed a pretty name might draw people west. But it didn't work here, and the town never flourished. Now, his father's business, reputation, and possibly their lives depend on them finding the owner of the Explorer in this backwater town. With a population of 991, it shouldn't be hard.

Main Street, named with no imagination and even less charm, cuts away from the highway and dead-ends into the Gas & Guzzle. The uninspired naming fits the town perfectly: unoriginal, simple, and boring. Four streetlamps line the road, two on each side, but only one of them works. On either side, four low buildings hold two businesses each, separated by alleys just wide enough for a delivery truck. The last building, nearest the gas station, stirred up the town's only real gossip twenty years ago when word spread that from then on it would house a single tenant.

Not long after, the hopeful owner of The Diner took over the abandoned space next door and knocked down the shared wall, expanding The Diner to nearly the size of a typical restaurant. Before that, it had been cramped, barely more than a lunch counter with a few booths. For the first six months, the novelty drew larger crowds. A few months later, the expanded dining area was used to host a group of stranded travelers waiting out a flash flood. Since then, the added space has been used to store extra restaurant supplies and some of the cook's personal belongings until he can move out of his mom's place.

It's five in the evening, and most businesses are already closed for the day. In one window, a flickering pink neon sign from the 1980s reads "Video Vibes." The Diner and Gas & Guzzle are the only other places still lit. Only one of the lights above the gas pumps is working, and even that one flickers on and off without rhythm.

Victor pulls the Mercedes into the gas station lot, and Oscar and Charlie follow behind in the Range Rover. The men gather in front of their vehicles. Oscar reaches into a canvas bag and pulls out four communication earpieces, holding them out in his open palm. Papa and Victor each grab one, activate them, and position them into their ears. Charlie hesitates, then grabs one too, unsure of what to do.

Victor grabs him by the elbow and steps out of the path of Oscar's cigarette smoke. He shows Charlie how to use the earpiece. Charlie inserts the comm and adjusts it until he finds a semi-comfortable angle.

Papa checks their comms, making sure they're all connected, then asks Oscar for the GPS unit. Oscar takes a slow drag from his cigarette and raises his eyebrows at Charlie. It takes Charlie a second to realize that's his cue. He opens the passenger door, grabs the unit, and returns to the group. He hands it to Papa and stands there a beat too long before realizing it. Then he takes a quick step back, eyes down, as if he's trying to shrink himself out of the moment.

The red dot is absent from the screen.

"I don't always understand how the technology works," Papa says, "but Mike assured me we would have a traceable signal even out here."

Charlie shifts from side to side, eyes darting to the ground and back again. He's clearly holding something in, and he's terrible at hiding it. Victor notes the way Charlie hovers near the group, unsure whether to stay or fade into the background. He wouldn't last ten minutes at a poker table. Victor wouldn't invite him anyway. He likes the kid too much. Oscar, on the other hand, would invite him just to clean him out.

The light above the pumps flickers off, making Charlie flinch. The glow from the gas station storefront is just enough for them to see each other.

"Charlie?" Papa says, sharper now.

Charlie's eyes bounce to Oscar, then drop to the ground.

"Well, what if uh, what if she crashed? That might knock out the navigation or something, right?"

Oscar takes a long drag from his cigarette, then flicks the butt to the pavement and crushes it underfoot. "I think we would've seen her crash in the middle of the open desert."

Charlie glances at Victor, looking for a sign to keep going. Victor gives a slight nod. "Well, uh, it's just that I thought I saw, like, a dust cloud or something. Right before she disappeared." Charlie fidgets. "There's cliffs out in the desert sometimes. One time I was out riding ATVs and my dumbass cousin didn't notice the drop and went right off it. We only found him because there was a big cloud of dust rising up from where he landed. They aren't like huge cliffs or anything, maybe, like, eight to ten feet, but... she was driving pretty fast."

Papa turns to face him fully. His expression tightens. "Why didn't you say something earlier while we were out there?"

Charlie looks to Oscar first, then shifts his eyes to Victor. He opens his mouth, then closes it again, uncertain.

Victor turns to Oscar. "Did Charlie try to tell you he saw

something?"

"It was dark, and things were happening fast," Oscar says. "If he did, he obviously didn't try hard enough." Oscar steps into Charlie's space. "This isn't your cousin's wannabe street gang. If you see something, you make sure we all know."

Charlie stiffens, nodding quickly.

The way Oscar looms over Charlie reminds Victor of an incident with his older brother. They were always close growing up, joined at the hip when they were kids. But in their teenage years, they started to drift. Victor stayed on the straight and narrow. His brother jumped the hedge and made his own path.

One night, during Victor's sophomore year, his brother caught him trying to sneak out to a party. He got in Victor's face, the same way Oscar is doing now with Charlie. Victor had argued it was just a party and that his brother had gone to parties all the time when he was Victor's age. His brother shot back, saying that he would not let his baby brother make the same mistakes he did. He reminded Victor about his college plans and that he couldn't afford to screw it up.

It was the first time Victor saw his brother as more than just a sibling. The way he stepped in felt more like parental protection than brotherly love. It was also the first time Victor saw regret in him for the choices he had made.

Papa breaks the silence. "Alright, let's assume she did crash and is on foot. Victor, what does she look like?"

"Five-five, athletic build. Brown ponytail. Jeans and a grey sweatshirt."

Papa nods. "Oscar, have Mike pull the surveillance from Lee Canyon gas station. See if he can send over a photo of her," Papa says.

Oscar smirks. "Five-five, brown ponytail? Sounds like Danielle. "The other one that got away."

Oscar knows exactly what he's doing. He taunts Victor with a grin, fully aware that he played a part in why Danielle left. After

Victor's mother died, Papa started this new business with unsavory characters. Oscar was part of that shift.

The comment pulls Victor back to the time everything started to change.

Danielle noticed the change in Papa right away, before Victor could admit it. She said that Papa wasn't the same, that something about him turned cold. Victor tried to defend him, saying that losing two people at once would wreck anyone, and that Papa just needed time to come back from it. But Papa didn't come back. He kept going deeper into whatever this life was, and the man Victor knew began to fade away.

It had been almost a year since Danielle and Victor graduated from college, and just as long since he lost his mom and brother. He should have started the brokerage job nine months earlier, but he kept extending his start date, worried about leaving Papa. Eventually, the firm stopped calling. Danielle had tried to be patient, but she watched him stall, each delay tying him tighter to his father's world.

The last time she visited, she came to talk about their future. When she ran into Oscar at Papa's house, she couldn't believe he was the same guy from their childhood. Once an all-state athlete with an easy smile, now a chain-smoking enforcer with a grin that felt more like a threat than a welcome. That's when she told him she couldn't wait forever and warned him that working with Papa and Oscar would change him, too. Victor said he couldn't bear the thought of leaving his father, and Danielle wished them both well. He tried to hold on to everything at once—Danielle, his father, the future they all used to talk about. But one by one, it all slipped away.

The sound of Danielle's name coming from Oscar's mouth makes Victor want to punch him in the throat. He hears his mother's voice in his head, calm and firm. *Don't let him get to you.* He takes a breath and exhales slowly. *I won't, Mama.*

"I'll go check The Diner and see if anyone's seen her." Victor bumps past Oscar and crosses the street.

# THIRTY-FIVE

ON THE other side of the country, a woman in her fifties opens the door to a lavish corner office. Floor-to-ceiling windows overlook the bustling city below, a city that never sleeps. Only a few lights remain in the high-rises across the skyline.

Her long, dark hair is parted clean down the middle and cascades down her back. Designer labels wrap her from head to toe, selected to impress, intimidate, or both.

A photo of two smiling men in their thirties sits on a custom walnut desk the size of a dining table. Behind it sits one of them, now in his sixties. His mother named him Giovanni Amato II. She was the only one who used that name, and he hasn't heard it in over forty years. God rest her soul.

When he moved his operation headquarters to the city twenty-five years ago, this office space wasn't available. Real estate in the concrete jungle was scarce even back then. He spent months trying to persuade, bribe, and intimidate the owner into leasing it. When that failed, he bought the entire building. It wasn't on the market. But in his world, everything and everyone is for sale. He made sure it would take a forensic accountant a miracle and months of overtime to trace the transaction back to him.

He looks up from his screen as the woman pauses inside the doorway.

"He's on line one for you," she says.

"Thanks, Juliet."

She closes the door behind her. He watches the latch click into place before leaning back with a grunt, the extra fifty pounds straining his lungs. He lifts the phone to his ear.

"What's the status?"

His face reddens as he listens. His breathing quickens.

"Send it to me. And call me when you find her. As always, this stays between us."

# THIRTY-SIX

A PASSING cloud blocks the moon and the faint light it was giving. The darkness shrinks the vast desert into a three-foot radius surrounding Jessie and the boys. Her hand aches from Sean's grip. He doesn't like the dark. He hates it. Every few minutes, Sean declares it's too dark to keep going and slows his pace. Jessie gently tugs him forward with whispered words of encouragement that she doesn't even believe. He trips on a rock, knocking her off balance, and his hand slips from hers. She welcomes the brief reprieve, but he quickly regains his footing and grabs hold again.

Max walks alongside them, keeping pace. Usually, when they're out in public, he either leads or lags behind, putting distance between himself and the family so people don't see them together. Teenagers. They'll eat everything in your fridge but won't be caught dead standing next to you. Now, he stays within arm's reach of his mom.

"Are we there yet?" Sean whines. "I can't feel my toes." He pokes at various parts of his body. "Or my face." He sticks a finger in his mouth and mumbles, "Or my tongue."

Jessie touches Sean's cheeks without thinking, a reflex more than anything else. Only then does she realize how numb her own hands are, too cold to tell if he's freezing or not. She's thankful they packed sweatshirts, but wishes they had brought something heavier. The cold in the desert hits differently. It's not crisp and dewy. It's sharp and biting. "A little farther, bud." She keeps her voice low, knowing that with no buildings or trees to absorb the sound, every word carries.

Max keeps exact pace with Jessie. Slow and deliberate makes less noise. Matching their steps helps mask how many people are out here. Jessie didn't even consider asking Sean to do the same. It might have distracted him from the dark, but if he fell out of sync, he'd insist on starting over. That would mean stopping and resetting his steps, wasting time they don't have.

Jessie compromised and let Sean bring his hockey stick, but the helmet had to stay behind. She told him Max's online friend knew where to find it and agreed to get it for him. Another lie. She never wanted to be the kind of mother who lied to her kids. How many lies did that make today? Three? Four? Does it count if they come from good intentions?

It doesn't matter. Today's lies pale compared to the truth she's been hiding their entire lives.

Sean uses his hockey stick as a walking stick. It helps him maintain a steady pace. Every so often, his steps align with Jessie and Max's. Their footsteps drag, heavy with exhaustion, but stopping isn't an option.

In the distance, the faint gas station light glows, giving Jessie a glimmer of hope. Maybe the worst is behind them. Jonathan has already sent help their way. They just have to reach the barn, about a mile into town, and wait. He told her he wasn't close. Otherwise, he would come himself. She believes him. One foot in front of the other. Almost there. They'll be okay.

A coyote howls in the distance, and Sean stops, yanking

Jessie's arm mid-step, nearly pulling her to the ground.

After a few steps, Max realizes Jessie and Sean have stopped behind him and turns around.

Another howl cuts through the air, closer this time.

"It's okay. They're just talking to each other," Jessie whispers.

"They're warning the intruders to stay out of their territory. We're the intruders. It's not ok. They want to eat us," Sean says.

"Sean, those coyotes are miles away." Jessie has no idea how close they actually are, but they sound disturbingly close. "See that light up ahead? That's where we're going. We'll be there long before any coyotes get close enough to eat us." Another lie. At their current pace, they're at least twenty minutes from the gas station. Even if the coyotes are five miles out, they could reach Jessie and the boys in half that time.

Jessie's phone vibrates in her pocket. She pulls it out and sees Nick's name, giving her a brief moment of comfort before the pain in her arm pulls her back to reality. She hands Sean off to Max and tells them to walk together. She falls a few steps behind and answers the call.

"Are you and the boys alright?" Nick talks a mile a minute, and Jessie misses pieces of what he's saying. "I just got a call from some guy. I don't remember his name."

"Jonathan."

"Yeah, Jonathan. He said he knows you and that you and the boys were in some kind of car accident. Are you okay? Are you hurt? What about—"

"We're fine. Everyone's okay," Jessie says. "I had a tire blowout, no one got hurt." That's true.

"Who is this guy, Jess? Was he with you?"

"No. He's an old friend... who called at the right time, I guess."

"Why have you never mentioned him before?" Nick has never been good at hiding his emotions. Some might hear jealousy or anger in his voice, but Jessie knows better. He's worried. Nick has always trusted her judgement. He even makes her do the social screening when they meet new people, claiming she has a gift for weeding out the weeds.

Another thing Jessie loves about Nick is that he feels things openly. The Agency trained her to shut out emotion, to treat it as something that clouded judgment. For so long, she was careful not to feel too much of anything. Nick's the one who's helped her believe it's safe to feel again. She lets a few tears fall.

Jonathan hasn't told Nick everything. He wouldn't do that to Nick or Jessie. If Nick knew the whole truth, he might call the authorities, and she wants to avoid endangering more innocent people. The less he knows, the safer they all are.

"We can trust him. He's going to help us get to your parents' house." She's met with silence. Maybe it was a mistake to have Jonathan call him. "Nick?"

"Hold on a second." He sighs. "Sorry, I was reading a sign. Traffic is being diverted through Lee Canyon because of an accident. Did you guys have to deal with that?"

"No, we must have just missed it." It's not a lie, not exactly. Just another carefully constructed truth.

"How's Sean holding up?"

She clears her throat as she wipes away the tears. "He's doing surprisingly well."

"Max?"

"He's fine too."

"Can I talk to them?"

She hears a beep on the line. Her phone screen shows an unknown caller. It's Jonathan.

"I think our ride is calling. I'll try to call you when we..." *don't have a murderous gang trying to kill us.* Another beep. "... when we get back on the road."

"Love you. And tell the boys I love them and give them a hug."

She closes her eyes for a second, just long enough to let his words embrace her.

"I will. Love you, too." She stifles the tears that want to return, pressing her lips together until the moment passes.

The beeping from the other line stops. Two rings, then a hang-up. That's their old signal.

Her phone rings again, and she sends it straight to voicemail. Protocol. A minute later, the new voicemail comes through. She hits play: "Hey, babe." The voice carries the tone of a loving partner. Once upon a time, she would've taken it at face value. But now, she knows Jonathan says it for whoever might be listening.

"I'll be quick. My battery is going to run out. I found a different floor plan. Maybe five hundred more square feet, similar to what we have now. It's five bedrooms, four baths, in a quiet neighborhood near a golf course. Others were also looking, and of course, everyone loved it. No speed bumps in the neighborhood, either. And it has a casita. I sent you a letter, which should be there within the week. I'll use my laptop to write a review of this place, since my battery is going to die right now."

None of that is good news.

# THIRTY-SEVEN

JESSIE CLOSES the gap, bringing the two silhouettes ahead of her within arm's reach. The adrenaline from the car crash is starting to wear off, and her body feels the aftermath. Pain radiates from her broken arm into her shoulder. Fatigue creeps in. Nausea swirls in her gut. The biting cold makes everything worse. As she tries to focus on Jonathan's voicemail, her mind wanders.

As a kid, she loved puzzles—jigsaw, crossword, logic. At the academy, she discovered a new kind of puzzle: coded language. It quickly became one of her favorite areas of training.

Unlike Morse Code or encryption that relies on a cipher, this system was personal. Agents and their counterparts developed it together, and proficiency required regular practice. She likened it to sharing an inside joke and how a single word or glance could carry layers of meaning.

By the time she and Jonathan graduated from the academy, they had mastered it and could send layered messages no one could interpret.

Jessie stumbles over a cactus but catches herself, forcing her body to ignore the spike of pain and the steady ache of cold and exhaustion. She plays the voicemail again, telling herself it's only to decode the message.

"I'll be quick. My battery is going to run out." That part's easy. Jessie needs to ditch her phone as soon as possible. Someone is listening, tracking, or both. Keeping it could put them in danger, but it still feels like a lifeline she isn't ready to cut. If she were alone, she would have tossed it already, right along with the flash drive.

She reaches the end of the message. "...my battery is going to die right now." Silence. She's listened to it three times and knows it's over, yet she lingers anyway, wanting something more. Be careful. Stay safe. Bye. None of that comes. And why would it? 'BYE' had once meant something. 'Be Yours Every day'. It was how they said 'I love you' back when that still meant something. But that was another life. He isn't that man anymore. He's on a mission, and she's his asset, not his partner. He's not thinking about her like that. He's thinking about the objective. And why does she even care? She loves Nick.

She turns off her phone and rips out the SIM card. She bites it in two and spits the pieces into the dirt.

Jessie once read about people writing their fears and troubles on paper and then burning it. She stares at the phone. Men are chasing her over a piece of technology, threatening her life and the lives of her children. Her husband is helpless and miles away. And now Jonathan is back in her life after seventeen years of radio silence. She channels all her fear, rage, and exhaustion and hurls the phone into the dark. It lands with an anticlimactic thud.

The boys stop walking. Up ahead, their silhouettes freeze. "What was that?" Sean asks.

"Nothing." And that's how she feels. No peace. No calm. No relief. Just nothing. *Catharsis my ass.*

She takes Sean's hand, relieving Max. They continue walking toward the glow of the gas station. Jessie forces herself to focus on

Jonathan's message.

It was something about him finding a different floor plan. Her stomach growls as pain shoots through her arm. *Focus.* That part means the barn is compromised, and he's come up with a new plan. "Maybe five hundred more square feet, similar to what we have now. It has five bedrooms and four baths in a quiet neighborhood near a golf course". Five hundred more can't mean five hundred miles, so it must be five miles. "...similar to what we have now..." means on the opposite side of the highway. "It's five bedrooms, four baths." Five times four is twenty.

Twenty miles. He's got to be kidding. They need a vehicle if he expects them to travel that far. "...quiet neighborhood near a golf course..." quiet neighborhood means no immediate neighbors and golf, gulf... probably water. Something near a stream or a creek?

A wave of nausea washes over Jessie, a mix of hunger and adrenaline on an empty stomach. Her pace has slowed, but Sean keeps moving, causing her to stumble. She regains her footing and matches his stride.

Jessie arches her back and breathes into the stretch, trying to focus. "Others were also looking..." Of course. They had a trace on her phone. That's why Jonathan told her to ditch it.

Jessie estimates they're about a quarter mile from town. She runs through the message again: ditch the phone—done. The barn is compromised. They need a vehicle and have to travel twenty miles out, probably near a creek or stream on the west side of the highway. Part of her still wants to head straight to the gas station and call the authorities. But a flash of the highway patrol car rolling across the highway reminds her of what making that call would bring. She pushes the thought aside. It's not an option.

Sean stumbles, and Max reaches for him. Jessie takes Sean's hand and passes him to Max so she can focus. "And it has a casita..." That means a cabin or some kind of small building. "I sent you a letter..." Thank God. He's sent an agent to meet them there. "... should be there in a week." Which really means an hour, though even that feels like forever. "I'll use my laptop to write a review of this place..." Jonathan has uploaded something to Max's laptop. Presumably, a name. Hopefully a face.

As they near the gas station, the lights tempt her, offering safety she knows isn't real. If they follow Jonathan's plan, it means pushing the boys even harder: more exposure, more risk, more chance they don't make it. Maybe she could hide them, draw the men away, and turn herself in. They're still looking for a woman travelling alone. She pictures it: stepping forward, getting shot before she can even speak. And then what?

Her heart says the boys are safest with her. For once, her head agrees.

She takes a deep breath and regroups. Help will arrive at the rendezvous point in an hour. Max's laptop should have the name and picture of the person Jonathan sent.

She runs through the new plan: drive five miles past town, locate a creek on the west side of the highway, follow it for twenty miles until they reach a cabin with no nearby neighbors. Help will be waiting.

Sounds like a well-laid plan.

# THIRTY-EIGHT

JANICE SITS alone in a booth, a cigarette balanced between two fingers of her sun-spotted hand. Red nail polish clings to the center of each nail, chipped away until only small islands of color remain. She looks every bit her sixty-something years, worn by four decades of smoking and circumstance. If not for the red-stitched 'The Diner' on her faded polo, Victor might have mistaken her for a customer. "Nope, sorry, Hon," she says.

Victor pushes his phone across the table. "Would you mind checking again?"

She glances again at the surveillance photo, humoring him. "Ain't a soul been in here for the last hour." Janice has worked at The Diner since high school, bound by an ill parent, an unplanned pregnancy, and a bad marriage. It's the kind of life that roots deep before you realize you never moved on.

She stubs out her cigarette next to a mountain of ash on a dessert plate and hollers toward the kitchen. "Fred, let's call it a night." She slides out of the booth, taking her plate with her. "You wanna order something before Fred shuts the kitchen down?"

Fred pokes his head out, waiting.

Victor isn't hungry, but even if he were, he'd rather starve than eat anything from Fred's kitchen. "No, thanks."

━━━ ••━ ━ •━• ••━ ━•

Main Street sits quiet, the only sound the low, electric buzz of the one working streetlamp. Charlie rubs his hands together and blows warm breath into his palms. He and Papa walk down the sidewalk, scanning for any businesses that still have lights on. So far, no luck. The silent vacancy reminds Charlie of a trip to a ghost town with his aunt and uncle. At the time, he couldn't understand wasting vacation days on a place no one lived in anymore, but at least he wasn't at home.

As they approach Video Vibes, Charlie states the obvious. "This place looks open."

The pink neon sign in the front window hums faintly, its washed-out glow bleeding into the glass as if it's been shining too long. He leans in to peer through the windows. Floor-to-ceiling shelves are crammed with DVDs, some with cracked cases, others stacked sideways where space has run out. A cardboard cutout of Bruce Willis slouches in the corner, duct-taped at the knees. Charlie lets out a chuckle. "Dude. It's a video store. I've heard of these."

Papa doesn't respond. He barely slows as he veers off toward the alley, heading around to the back entrance like he's done this a hundred times before.

Inside, a group of teens loiters in a corner near the "New Releases" shelf. A few gray-haired couples peruse the VHS wall, mostly movies from the 1980s and 1990s. In the neglected "Family" section, two siblings, maybe five and six years old, argue over a DVD. The girl's hair is a ratty nest, and the boy's pajamas are stained in a rainbow of spills.

It's January, and neither is wearing shoes. Their parents ignore them, focused on reading the back covers of two slasher flicks with screaming women on the covers.

Papa takes a slow look around. "You take the teenagers and the clerk. I'll talk to the family and the mature folks." He and Charlie split up.

A few minutes later, they reconvene at the entrance.

Papa shakes his head, "No one's seen her."

"Same."

Victor's voice crackles in Charlie's earpiece, making him jump. The Diner was a bust. Charlie jumps again when Oscar comes through next, reporting no luck at the gas station either. He adds that Mike intercepted a phone call and part of a voicemail and he has a plan.

# THIRTY-NINE

JESSIE CAN'T feel her nose, and her cheeks burn from the cold. Even the slightest breeze hits like a frozen blast, making her gasp. Her right hand hides at the bottom of her sleeve, trying to stay warm. But her left hand isn't so lucky. She had to cut the sleeve to accommodate the swelling in her broken arm, leaving her skin exposed to the elements. The makeshift sling offers some protection, but not much.

Sean has slowed to a zombie-like pace. His arm hangs limp at his side, dragging his hockey stick through the dirt. The scraping sound breaks the desert's silence, sharp and rhythmic, announcing their presence to anyone nearby who might be listening.

Jessie doesn't know how close their pursuers are, but if they tracked her phone signal, they had to be nearby. She reaches over and takes the stick from Sean. He doesn't resist. He doesn't even seem to notice.

To a stranger, Sean would look spaced out. Jessie knows better. He is hyper-focused, no doubt counting in his head. One of his doctors suggested this strategy when he experienced long lines or waiting rooms. So far, it seems to be working.

If it comes to it, Jessie and Max could carry Sean the rest of the way. But even Max's steps have deteriorated into a shuffle. He outweighs Jessie by at least twenty pounds, maybe more, and stands four inches taller than her. Possibly five. He has no choice but to keep going. And he has, without a single complaint about being cold, tired, or hungry.

"Is that where we're going?" Max sounds like he just rolled out of bed.

It's too dark for Jessie to see where he's pointing, but the gas station is the only thing visible, even with its dimmed, flickering lights. It seems like the most logical choice to get help, which is precisely why they shouldn't go there. But unfortunately, she has no choice.

"Only to get a car," Jessie says. "We need to get to the other side of town and across the highway."

There's no way they're trekking two miles to the highway, much less twenty more, up the mountain. Jonathan's message mentioned a body of water, which means they'll be at a high enough elevation for cooler temperatures and probably snow. They need a car, and the gas station is their best shot. It'd be nice if someone left their keys inside while they ran in to pay. This town looks like the kind of place where people leave their belongings in an unlocked car.

Sean's teeth chatter, and his shuffle is getting slower. "967, 968, 980... no, that's not right," his voice barely audible. "968, 969, 907. Ugh. When are we going to be at Grandma's?" he whines. He sniffs and wipes his nose on his sleeve. "Mom, I can't."

The 'Mom, I can't' is how he communicates that he wants to escape the situation. Sean struggles to change a plan once it's set in motion, even if he knows it's going badly. And today's plan hasn't just changed multiple times; it keeps going from bad to worse.

Jessie tells the boys to stop and take a break. They plop to the ground without hesitation and grab their drinks from their backpacks.

Sean gives up on the numbers and switches to reciting the words from Max's laptop under his breath. "Daisy, plaid, three, cul-de-sac. Daisy, plaid, three, cut-de-sac." As his anxiety fades and his thinking sharpens, he goes quiet, after muttering something about coyotes.

They're close enough now that Jessie can see two silhouetted vehicles parked at the gas station. Finally, it seems something is going her way. She scans the desert in all directions. No headlights, flashlights, or shadowy figures. It looks like they're all alone.

Her plan was for all of them to walk to the gas station together. But the boys are spent. They should be fine waiting for her where they are. The gas station is directly ahead, so theoretically, if she drives back in a straight line, she should run right into them. Easy enough.

She turns her back to Max and tells him to dig the flashlight out of her backpack. She can't remember the last time she checked the batteries. Back when she still kept track of things like that, she used to replace them on the first of the month. Checking the go bag she kept in her car was just part of her monthly routine. She hates to admit that, as she became more comfortable in her new life, she grew less diligent about those kinds of things.

As Alex disappeared, checking her go bag for fresh batteries was replaced with checking her diaper bag for diapers and wipes. The boys needed more of her attention, and her priorities shifted. She would postpone checking on supplies, get distracted, and then forget altogether until lying in bed. Then, she would dismiss the idea of leaving her nice warm bed to check for fresh batteries in a go bag she would probably never use again. Every year, around Max's birthday, she contemplated getting rid of the bag. For some reason, she could never bring herself to do it. Right now, she's thankful for that.

Jessie turns her back on the gas station, covers the flashlight with her thigh, and flicks it on and off. Good news: the batteries work. Not-so-good news: the light won't be visible from the gas station. She'll have to enter the desert before it can be seen. Still, if she drives straight out from the gas station without veering, she should run right into Max and Sean.

There's no sign of anyone around either of the parked cars. Both drivers must be inside, paying, grabbing snacks, or using the restroom. If she's lucky, they're friends, caught up in a conversation about last night's game.

She blinks hard, pushing back the exhaustion, and waits another minute. Still no movement.

Having a plan brings her a brief sense of calm. Hopefully, the warmth of a car will give them newfound energy. She hands the flashlight to Max and walks him through the plan. The boys understand what they need to do and reassure her that they'll be fine. But she still has to force herself to walk away.

She treads lightly, but with purpose, wanting to return to her boys as soon as possible. *The boys will be fine. It won't take long.* Besides, she's pretty confident the men aren't in the desert lurking in the shadows like boogeymen. If they were, she'd know. Alex would've noticed something.

But is Jessie still that sharp? She's injured, exhausted, and hungry. And now her mind is working against her. *Stop overthinking. Just walk.*

The light above the gas pumps flickers back on. Jessie freezes. Her assumptions are confirmed. The men aren't in the desert.

The Range Rover and Mercedes are parked at the gas station.

# FORTY

ROMEO OPENS an email attachment. A still image appears on his computer screen: Jessie, frozen in mid-gesture, tapping her watch to the card reader at the Lee Canyon gas station. He leans closer to the screen, enlarges the photo, then applies a filter to sharpen the resolution. His jaw drops.

"Juliet!"

He doesn't bother with the intercom.

Juliet bursts through the door, scanning for the emergency. "Are you okay?"

"Get me all the files from 2007. Now."

Before Juliet finishes placing the stack on his desk, Romeo starts tearing through them. He forms a messy discard pile, folders sliding to the floor with each impatient addition. As the pile grows and the untouched pile shrinks, his heart rate kicks up. His toss becomes a throw.

With only a few files left, he finds what he's looking for and pushes the rest aside without a glance.

Romeo opens the file and flips through the reports like he's racing against something only he can see. Pages blur past. A few tear free from the metal prongs, as he lifts too hard, too fast. He finally stops on a heavily redacted document.

Muttering a string of numbers under his breath, he stands abruptly. One of the chair's wheels snags on a fallen file, nearly toppling him. He curses, kicks it aside, and crosses to a wall. Behind a plaque for Distinguished Philanthropy, he opens a concealed safe and removes a small metal box. He plops into the leather high-back chair and rips open the lid, his breathing heavy. Plastic clinks against metal as he rummages through its contents. He pulls out a flash drive labeled 4-07420 and inserts it into his computer.

After a few clicks, the screen fills with folder icons. He opens the one labeled Off Sur Vid, revealing a chronological list of dates. After a few more clicks, a low-resolution video starts playing in a small window. He enlarges it to fill half the screen and fast-forwards until someone enters the frame. He pauses when the person faces the hidden camera.

Heat rushes to his face. His breaths come sharp and fast. He drags the surveillance photo from the gas station across the screen and places it next to the paused video from 2007.

Wild rage boils inside as he stares at his brother's killer.

# FORTY-ONE

SEAN GRABS for the flashlight. "It's my turn."

"Dude, just stop. Mom told me to hold it." The beam swings between them as they engage in a tug of war.

They both jump when Jessie snatches the flashlight and clicks it off. "You two knock it off."

"Where's the car?" Max asks.

Jessie doesn't answer. She hands the hockey stick to Sean. "Here, you can hold this." She scans Main Street, keeping an eye on the gas station. Everything is still. A few seconds pass. Then, movement. A shadow shifts at the end of an alley.

She waits. Two figures pass through the next gap between the buildings. She tracks their path, anticipating their next appearance. They emerge again, headed for the Gas & Guzzle. Another figure steps out of The Diner. A fourth exits the gas station. They gather by the Range Rover and the Mercedes.

A scratching sound fills the air. Sean is drawing in the dirt with his hockey stick.

"Stop making noise," Max hisses.

"Why? No one is here except us," Sean keeps dragging his stick.

"You want the coyotes to think that noise is a bunny?"

Sean frowns and plops to the ground, fiddling with his fingers.

Content that the bickering is over, Jessie turns west, angling toward the highway, and scans for any other buildings with light. The gas station is no longer an option. Finally, she spots a pink glow bleeding through the gap between two buildings. She can't make out the whole sign, just a fragment: "Vid." Hopefully, it means the business is open and has customers who drove there.

She walks back to the boys and explains the change of plans. Instead of waiting for her, they need to walk to the highway, where she'll pick them up. The three of them begin the trek. Sean's exhaustion works in her favor. Normally, he'd fire off a million questions: Where is she getting a car? Why can't they come with her? How long will it take? How much will the car cost? Does she have that much money with her? But he's too tired to care and continues shuffling forward.

Max moves to Jessie's other side, putting her between them. He leans in. "Those are the guys at the gas station, aren't they?"

"Yes. And I don't think they know you and Sean exist, and I'd like to keep it that way as long as possible. Understand?"

"That's why we can't go with you."

"Yes." Jessie glances toward the highway. No headlights. No engine noise. "Since I'll be coming from the road instead of through the desert, I'll have the headlights on. When I turn onto the highway, I'll flash them once. Use the flashlight to flash back and get to the edge of the highway as fast as you can. Stay low until I stop. Got it?"

Max doesn't answer right away. Jessie can feel his tension and knows the full weight of their situation is finally setting in. Everything's gone from weird to dangerous to something else entirely.

"Max?" she asks. She can barely make out his nod.

"Yeah. You want me to flash the light once and wait at the edge of the highway."

"Yes. And make sure Sean understands you guys need to move fast when I get there."

"Okay, yeah."

As the boys continue toward the highway, Jessie turns and heads toward Main Street. When she looks back, she can't see them anymore. It unsettles her for a second until she reminds herself that if she can't see them, no one else can see them either. She quickens her pace.

Jessie emerges from the desert and crosses an empty lot behind what appears to be an auto parts store. A discarded bumper leans against the building, and the cracked pavement is littered with fast food wrappers and broken glass. She moves quickly, head down, hugging the building until she reaches the alley between it and the bakery.

Jessie tucks her hair under her hat and rolls her shoulders forward. Then she heads down the alley, pretending to scroll through a phone that doesn't exist. From a distance and in the darkness, she could pass for one of Max's classmates.

Keeping her head down, she scans the area as she walks. She passes the end of the alley and glances at the gas station. Four men are gathered around the Range Rover and Mercedes, deep in conversation. She doesn't stop. The pink glow ahead sharpens, and through the front window of Video Vibes, she sees a handful of customers browsing the shelves.

Her heart races as she crosses the street. She makes it to the storefront without hearing a shout or the sound of footsteps running toward her. She takes a deep breath.

She circles to the back of the building and exhales slowly.

Jackpot. Five cars are parked behind the video store. Without making a sound, she slips over to a Ford Focus and checks the handles. Locked. Voices carry through the alley between the video store and the laundromat. She ducks behind a dumpster and crouches low.

Three teenagers emerge from the alley, laughing as they pile into a faded red Trans Am. The engine sputters before they tear out of the parking lot and down Main Street. Jessie waits a moment longer, then resumes her search. Chrysler 300. Locked. Buick Regal. Locked. Dodge Caravan. Unlocked.

A minivan wouldn't be her first choice, but beggars can't be choosers. On the upside, these older vans are easy to hotwire. She quietly opens the driver's side door and is hit with an odor that can only be described as sewer sludge. By the looks of the debris littering the dashboard, there's likely old food rotting under the seat. Jessie kills the interior lights and has the engine rumbling in under twenty seconds.

A minute later, she's driving on the wrong side of the highway. She flashes the headlights once. No response. Her hand chokes the steering wheel. Maybe they haven't made it close enough to the highway yet. She leans forward, squinting through the darkness. Maybe the flashlight died. She should have checked the batteries last month. She speeds up. The van's engine groans, and the chassis begins to shake. What if one of them got injured? Sharp rocks, cacti, rattlesnakes, coyotes, mountain lions, they're all possibilities.

She flashes again. This time, a beam cuts across the dark in response. Two shadowy figures rise from the bushes as Jessie makes a U-turn and pulls alongside them.

She curses at the van as she searches for the button to open the sliding door.

Max opens the door from the outside and ushers Sean and his stick inside.

Sean flinches at the foul odor. "Ew! Did you fart?"

"Get in and shut the door. Hurry up."

Sean does as he's told.

Max climbs into the passenger seat and recoils at the stench.

"Geez, Sean." He twists to face Sean.

"It wasn't me," says Sean.

Max turns back to Jessie. "Mom. We have a little problem." He nods toward the back.

Irritated, she turns to look at Sean. "What?"

He's pointing to the seat behind her. She shifts in her seat, twists around more, and freezes.

"Shit."

# FORTY-TWO

MIKE LETS the spool of copper wire spin in his gloved hand as he walks backward around the living room perimeter, leaving a trail in front of him. The wooden floor creaks underneath his black tactical boots as he maneuvers around the handmade furniture, returning to his starting point. He steps over a dog-chewed slipper and passes a recliner patched with duct tape. The air is thick with the smell of stale tobacco, canned soup, and old newspapers. He snips the wire and places the new end into a clay brick, pressing down until it holds.

The steps are burned into muscle memory after years of doing this kind of job. Each setup goes faster than the one before. Papa told him his plan was overkill, and Mike said it was insurance.

The walkie-talkie on his hip chirps. Mike is old-school and doesn't appreciate fancy communication earpieces, finding them irritating. He enjoys the freedom of ignoring anyone on the other end if necessary. He presses the button harder than necessary. "Yeah."

Oscar's voice comes over the walkie-talkie. "ETA?"

"Twenty minutes."

"Can you make it fifteen?"

"If I could make it fifteen, I would have said fifteen."

"Did you send the photo?"

"I said I would do it, didn't I? Now, if you would stop bothering me with extra work and pointless conversation, I could finish up here." Mike tosses his walkie-talkie on a blue TALAtools bag.

"Copy," Oscar says, his voice muffled by the walkie-talkie lying face down. Mike finishes the job, gathers his gear, and shuts the door behind him.

# FORTY-THREE

JESSIE STARES into the big green eyes of a toddler, the undeniable source of the foul odor. "Shit."

"Scit," the toddler mimics.

Max bursts out laughing.

"Don't say that," Sean snaps. He covers the toddler's mouth with his hand, trying to muffle the word. The kid peels his hand away, undeterred.

"Scit," it repeats.

Max giggles again.

The toddler joins in, loving the reaction.

Jessie pulls back onto the highway and speeds up. "Oh, now you're gonna speak up," she mutters. She can't believe parents these days. So lazy. They're supposed to protect their children, not put them in danger. No sooner does she finish the thought than she realizes the hypocrisy of it. She's put her own boys in danger: crossing paths with Black Beard, crashing the car, then roaming the desert in coyote country. "Who the hell leaves their kid in the car?"

"Hell," says the tiny voice. More giggles from Max and the baby.

"Mom! You kidnapped someone's kid! And you're teaching it swear words."

Sean rattles off the potential jail time she'll receive and what will happen to him, and Max, and Dad while she rots away in jail because her lawyer was inexperienced with kidnapping cases. He adds the possibility of additional charges for teaching a baby how to swear, which he isn't sure is a crime, but should be, and probably is, because adults always tell kids not to swear. "Just don't drive across the state line. Then the Feds will be after us, too."

By the time Sean stops to take a breath, they're pulling into the video store parking lot.

She parks the van back in its original spot next to the Buick. The door to the video store chimes as it opens.

"Get out! Get out!" She kills the engine and jumps out.

Max gets out and slides open the other door for Sean.

"Hide behind the dumpster."

Max closes the door, and the boys run off. The dumpster smells just like the inside of the van.

Jessie stays low as she moves around the front of the van.

An elderly couple exits the store and stops just outside.

Jessie ducks behind the van.

After ensuring that one of them grabbed the DVD from the counter, the couple continues walking and discussing their favorite actress, who stars in the movie they just rented. They pause next to the neighboring Buick. For a moment, neither of them speaks, as if they forgot they were having a conversation. Jessie bites her lip, sure she's been made, and runs through possible cover stories in her head.

Then the woman breaks the silence, gushing about how she loved the actress in her last rom-com. The man agrees and says he can't wait to see this one, even though it's a decade old and they already know how it ends. *Geez, just get in the car already.*

Jessie creeps up and peeks at the dumpster through the van's finger-smudged side window. The area is dark, and she can't see the boys, which means the Chatty Cathys won't be able to either.

The husband pats down all twelve thousand pockets for the car keys while his wife launches into a story about a scandalous article she read about their favorite actress. Or perhaps it was the actress in the movie they rented last week.

The wife's cell phone rings. She digs through a purse big enough to double as a beach bag and finally finds her flip phone. "Cathy here." *Seriously?* Cathy tells Edna all about the movie they just rented with their favorite actress, Julie Robertson. *Close.* She plunges half of her arm back into her purse and pulls out a set of keys, which she jingles at her husband. He painstakingly walks around to retrieve them. His journey back to the driver's side takes even longer. He gestures for her to get in like she's the one holding things up. Her door is locked. He presses the key fob, opens his door, and slowly lowers himself into the seat. Her door still doesn't open. He grumbles and presses the door unlock button on his door. Cathy settles in. At last, the Buick rolls out of the lot.

Jessie starts toward the dumpster, but faint movement in the corner of her eye makes her pause. She turns around. The van's sliding door is cracked open. When she reaches to close it, the toddler's wide, emerald eyes lock onto hers. She huffs under her breath, slides the door open, and comes face to face with Mr. or Mrs. Poopy Pants.

She quickly scans the interior and grabs a lone diaper peeking out from the mesh pocket on the back of the driver's seat. The car seat buckle sticks when she presses the button, and she has to wiggle the strap free. Cradling its head, she lays the baby on the floor, trying not to be wooed by its charming smile. Jessie used to take pride in her fifteen-second diaper changes back when her boys were babies, always racing the clock before the fire hose went off. She undoes the sagging diaper, its tabs barely clinging to the sides. Okay, the baby's a Mr. That explains the giggling at the swear words. *Boys.*

It's not her best work, and the diaper's velcro tabs are

stretched to capacity, but it's the best she can do with no time, no wipes, and a diaper two sizes too small. She checks the car seat and is surprised to find it installed correctly. Jessie puts Mr. Poopy Pants back where she found him and buckles him in with the bar across his chest, not across his stomach, which is how she found it. A part of her wants to take him back out.

"I'm rooting for you, kid." She goes to teach him how to do knuckles, but he already knows how. *Boys.*

She grabs the deadly diaper, closes the van, and tosses the diaper in the dumpster just as the family from the video store opens the back door.

Jessie crouches next to her own boys as she watches Mr. Poopy Pants drive away.

# FORTY-FOUR

MAX FEELS an emptiness in his stomach as he watches his mom disappear down the alley between the video store and the laundromat. She told them to wait while she searched for another vehicle. Both cars still in the parking lot were locked, and breaking a window wasn't worth the risk.

He and Sean should be at their grandparents' house right now, finishing slices of apple pie and scoops of ice cream. Grandma always insisted on serving a light dinner course, followed by a heavy dessert course, whenever the grandkids visited. Then they'd play a couple of board games before crawling into beds with new memory foam mattresses that Grandpa bought just for them. Their mom and dad would sleep on the lumpy old mattress in the guest room and complain about sore body parts in the morning.

Instead, Max and Sean squat behind a dumpster, pinching their noses and sharing a long-forgotten package of fruit snacks that Sean found squished in a pocket of his backpack along with a crumpled five-dollar bill.

A strong odor of urine clings in the air, but it's too dark to see the source, so sitting on the pavement isn't an option, even though their legs are going numb. Max chews his last two fruit bits, yet the emptiness remains. It won't go away until his mom is back beside them, hidden behind this disgusting dumpster.

Max breaks a granola bar and hands Sean the smaller piece. Sean asks if Grandma and Grandpa know where they are. Max shrugs and says Dad probably filled them in on what he knows. They were in a car accident, and now a man Mom knows, named Jonathan, is helping them. Max had to explain to Sean what the phrase "fill them in" meant. No, Dad wasn't going to pour something down their throats.

Sometimes Max wonders how Sean will survive when he leaves for college in two years. Other times, he tries not to think about it.

So far, Max has pieced together that his mom and BirdOfPrey431—his sixteen-year-old online friend who turned out to be a forty-something-year-old man named Jonathan—have known each other for a long time. He hates that she was right about Jonathan not being who Max thought he was. Through his eavesdropping, Max is almost certain their dad didn't know about Jonathan until today, which means his mom must have known him before she met Dad.

Maybe Jonathan is an ex-boyfriend. It's hard for Max to picture his mom with anyone other than his dad. He wonders if Jonathan ever met Max's other grandparents before they died. Mom never talks about them, and Max never asks. He doesn't like to see her sad.

Max's thoughts drift to the toddler swearing in the backseat of the stolen van, repeating every curse word like it was a game. He chuckles under his breath. Sean never did that as a toddler. He didn't start talking until he was much older. Now, Max can't get him to shut up. However, Sean is doing an impressive job of staying quiet while they wait for their mom.

Max turns to offer him the rest of his granola bar, only to find an empty space.

"Sean?" Max whispers. He looks behind him. Nothing. To his left. He's not there. Max steps out and scans the parking lot. No sign of Sean.

Jessie scurries from the alley and crouches beside Max, catching her breath. "I'm going to get us another car. The men left the gas station, and there's a truck that just pulled—"

"He's gone." Max's voice cracks.

The words don't register. "Who?" Jessie leans past him and sees Sean's backpack on the ground, but no Sean. "Where's Sean?"

"I don't know, one second he was here and the next he was gone," Max says in one breath.

Sean has always been a wanderer. When he was seven, he walked into Jessie and Nick's bedroom and declared that morning to be the day he would start making his own breakfast. Half-asleep, Jessie stumbled into the kitchen, hoping to intercept the inevitable mess of milk and cereal. But there wasn't a mess or a seven-year-old in sight. Instead, a bowl, spoon, and cereal box formed a neat line on the counter. Jessie searched the living room, bathroom, and laundry room. No Sean. Upstairs, outside, in the garage—he was nowhere to be found. Nick was on the phone with the police, and Jessie was calling neighbors when Max walked in the front door with his little brother. Sean was holding a carton of milk and a cup of sugar.

Apparently, Sean had gone next door to borrow milk from Mrs. Wilson. Nick had forgotten to pick some up on his way home the night before, and Sean took matters into his own hands. He also asked for a cup of sugar because, as he explained later, that's what people do on TV when they borrow from neighbors. Those five minutes had been the scariest of Jessie's life. Until now.

Jessie steps out into the open, her eyes scanning in all directions. "Sean." It takes everything she has not to scream his name. Her heart tries to break free from her chest. Her broken arm pulses with pain. "Sean." Her head spins. She steps further into the parking lot, exposed.

A car door slams in the distance, the sound echoing down the alley from Main Street. Then a man's voice follows. "I left it on the counter. It'll only be a minute." Seconds later, a shadowed figure begins walking in her direction.

Jessie scrambles back behind the dumpster, crouching beside Max.

"Mom," he whispers, nodding toward the video store.

Sean is inside, standing in line behind a young couple who can't keep their hands off each other.

The shadowed figure walks at a steady pace, his stature and gait oddly familiar. As he reaches the light cast by the parking lot lamp, Jessie freezes. It's the young man with poor posture, baggy jeans, and a hoodie—her gut twists.

Jessie clamps a hand on Max's arm, either to keep him from giving up their position or prevent herself from pouncing. She's not sure which. "He's one of them," she breathes, barely a whisper. Blood drains from her head. Adrenaline pumps double time. Chills run from her scalp to her fingertips.

The young man heads for the door.

Jessie bolts up.

Max yanks her down.

She can't breathe.

"They're only looking for you," Max whispers.

Jessie doesn't move. She takes a breath as his words echo in her ears. There is no reason to think the men are aware of Sean. They've only ever seen her. Just her. Not the boys. Not Max. Not Sean.

She crouches next to the dumpster, Glock in hand, and watches the young man enter the store. Her heart and her head battle for control over her decisions. The couple steps up to the counter just as Sean bends to inspect the candy selection on the bottom row of a display. The young man walks past Sean and stands in line behind the couple.

"Don't stand up," Jessie whispers as she inches away from the dumpster. "Don't stand up." She crouches low, weight forward, ready to pounce if necessary. "Just stay where you are." She wills her words to magically reach Sean's ears.

The young man rises onto his tiptoes and looks over the couple at the counter. He says something to grab the cashier's attention and gestures to the counter. The cashier nods, completes the transaction with the young couple, and rummages through the drawers behind the register.

Jessie watches the young man scan the store. His gaze catches on something.

He makes a beeline straight toward Sean.

# FORTY-FIVE

JESSIE AND Max watch the young man head toward Sean as he continues to crouch at the candy display. He steps past Sean and bends to grab a bag of peanut M&M's. At the exact moment, Sean stands up and raises a candy bar toward the cashier. The cashier finally turns toward Sean.

"For once, just stop talking," Max mutters.

Jessie doesn't respond. She places her Glock on the ground and wipes her palm on her jeans. Her gaze stays locked on the young man.

The cashier says something to Sean, who crouches again just as the young man stands and steps forward to the counter, like two ships passing in the night. Jessie doesn't blink.

The cashier passes a phone to the young man. He slips it into his hoodie pouch, pays for the M&M's, nods a thank-you, and heads for the door.

Jessie ducks back behind the dumpster and pulls Max with her. They remain still as footsteps cross the parking lot into the alley.

Moments later, a car door slams, echoing down the alleyway. The engine rumbles, then fades into the distance.

Jessie secures her gun in her waistband as Sean walks up to the dumpster. She grabs him by the shoulder before he can speak.

"What were you thinking?"

"I—"

"You can't just take off like that! Do you know what kind of danger we are in right now?"

Sean stiffens in Jessie's grasp, his chin lifted but unmoving.

Her words come fast, too fast. "Those men are looking for us, and they will not hesitate to kill you. You put us all at risk when you do reckless things like that. What were you think—"

A hand grasps her arm. Jessie turns to Max, his eyes pleading. She looks at Sean and suddenly notices the tears rolling down his cheeks.

She immediately releases her grip and pulls him into a mama bear hug. He remains a marble statue. Jessie swallows hard and whispers in his ear, "I'm sorry."

She kisses his head and looks him in the eye, wiping away his tears and hers. "Hey, I didn't mean to yell. I panicked when I couldn't find you. And then I saw one of those guys inside with you... and thought—"

"I didn't go inside with a guy," Sean says. "I know not to talk to strangers or go anywhere with them. I'm not a little kid."

Jessie nods and brushes his hair from his eyes. "I know, bud. I know you're not a little kid. That's not what I meant." She remains calm. "While you were looking at the candy, one of the guys who's looking for us went inside the store and stood right next to you. It made me really scared."

Sean thinks for a moment. "Like when I borrowed the sugar and milk?"

Jessie exhales a half-chuckle. "Yeah. Just like the sugar and milk."

"Oh," He goes quiet, thinking some more. "But you said they

don't know that Max and I are here. So, we are basically like ghosts to them."

Jessie can't separate her existence from that of her sons. If she exists, they exist, and vice versa. Part of her purpose is to love and protect them. Helplessly watching Sean so close to danger felt like relinquishing control to the universe. She has seen too many terrible things happen in the universe to put her trust in it. She can't balance their existence in the universe without her protection.

But the boys are right. There's no reason for the men to suspect she's traveling with anyone, let alone children. The guy at the gas station only saw her at the pumps. And Sean was lying in the backseat during the desert fiasco. Besides, it was too dark for anyone to see inside the Explorer. There's no logical reason for them to think she's not alone.

"We need to be extra careful, though, okay? No more leaving on your own. We stay together," Jessie says.

Sean nods. Looking down, he hands Max a candy bar. "It was buy one, get one free."

"Thanks, bud." Max offers Jessie a piece, but she declines. Her nerves have wrecked her stomach.

"I'm going to get us a car." Jessie straightens and starts for the alley.

Sean grabs her sleeve. "You just said we stay together. Plus, the last two times you left, some crazy beard guy was going to eat us, and then you stole somebody's baby. And you taught it how to swear."

Max shrugs, talking with a full mouth. "He's not wrong."

Trying to separate them from danger hasn't worked. It still finds its way to them. "Okay, but you have to do exactly what I tell you. No questions. No hesitation." She looks at Max. He nods. She looks at Sean. Nothing. "Sean, do you understand?"

"Yes. I understand." He snaps a sharp salute.

She gives a slight nod. "Walk on the sidewalk toward the gas station. If anyone shows up, keep going and wait inside until I get you."

"Okay," Max says, voice muffled by the wrapper.

Jessie looks up and down Main Street. Empty. No cars at The Diner either. The rusty Datsun truck still sits at the pumps unattended.

"Let's go," she whispers.

--- ••- - •-• ••- -•

The three of them remain silent as Jessie drives the Datsun down Main Street onto the highway. She pulls off her baseball cap and lets her hair fall free. The boys lay contorted beside her on the bench seat. After five minutes on the highway, she tells them they can sit up. Max shifts into an upright position, and Sean's head flops into his lap.

"He's out," Max says.

"Good. He needs some rest. So do you."

Jessie could use some rest herself. She's so tired that she almost forgot she's supposed to watch for a road off the southbound lanes that leads up into the mountains. After several hard blinks, she forces her eyes wide, determined to stave off sleepiness.

Another mile up the highway, and the road she wants is announced by the reflective letters on the street sign. Kyle Canyon, next exit. Rest is near.

"Mom?" says Max.

"Yeah?" Jessie exits the highway, crosses underneath, and merges onto the southbound lanes.

"Why do you know how to hot wire a car?"

Jessie glances at him. The tightrope walk between lies and truths begins. She knows she can't keep this up forever, but now isn't the time to come clean.

"I used to work for a place," she chooses her words carefully, "that taught me how to do that."

"And how to drive like that? Like when we were in the desert?"

She hesitates. "Yes."

As a recruit, Jessie learned to answer yes-or-no questions with a simple "yes" or "no." Only offer what's necessary.

Max swallows and won't look her in the eye. He picks at his cuticles. "Are you—are you a criminal? Like a thief or something? Is that why those men are after you?"

The last few hours have been crazy. Jessie would have questions, too, if she didn't know the whole truth.

Jessie chuckles. She's very much the opposite of a criminal. She's the person governments and powerful people call to deal with the criminals. She *was* that person. Max deserves more than a one-word answer. "I'm not a criminal. I have no idea who those guys are, or why there was a flash drive in your laptop, or what was on it. But I will do everything I have to to protect you and Sean. Even if it means borrowing a car or two."

The Datsun slows to a crawl and leaves the highway, turning west onto the mountain road. Less than a mile up, a creek appears on her right. "There it is." On the other side, a gravel road runs alongside and follows the creek's bend. As Jessie crosses the creek, the jostling wakes Sean.

"Are we there yet?" he asks.

"Almost." She hopes.

▬▬▬ ••▬ ▬ •▬• ••▬ ▬•

The desert transforms as the altitude climbs. Joshua trees give way to rising pines, and the hard, cracked soil turns into a patchy blanket of melting snow. Recent snowfall has left the road slick with slush.

Jonathan's instructions were to follow the creek twenty miles to a small building Jessie assumes is a cabin. The speedometer needle dances around, as if it wants to break through the glass. She estimates they've been averaging forty miles an hour. At that rate, it should take thirty minutes to reach the cabin.

She ditched her phone and watch hours ago. And of course, the clock in the Datsun doesn't work. Hardly anything works. She thinks they should reach the cabin in about ten more minutes.

For the third time, Jessie turns the thermostat knob, hoping by some miracle the heater will kick on. No luck. She's closed all the vents except for the broken one on her side to keep the cold winter from entering the truck. A dusty blanket drapes over the boys' legs. It had covered the holes that revealed the innards of the seat back cushion, so they use their backpacks to prevent the springs from poking them.

"I need to pee. Bad," Sean announces.

She doesn't need to ask, but does anyway, feeling optimistic. "Can you wait ten more minutes?"

"No."

Jessie knows he's not exaggerating. Sean doesn't exaggerate. He has to go now. They could be ten minutes out or thirty. She has no way of knowing. Her sense of time has been distorted by fatigue, hunger, stress, and the pain from her broken arm and sliced hand. It should be fine to stop for a couple of minutes. Besides, she has to go too. She eases the Datsun onto the narrow shoulder as far as she can.

The three of them climb out of the truck. Max grabs the flashlight from his backpack and clicks it on.

"Turn that off," Jessie snaps, voice low. "Put it back in your bag."

Max grumbles and shoves the flashlight in his back pocket.

They move into the forest, the chilly winter air biting at them from all sides. Each footstep crunches on the frozen earth, echoing through the silence that surrounds them.

# FORTY-SIX

MIKE TAKES off his wool beanie and rubs his bald head. He listens to the local law enforcement radio channel as he drives down the mountain in his lifted Silverado. He glances down at the nick on his finger. His knuckles are stiff, and the wound keeps reopening each time he grips the wheel. The cut is shallow, but it's reopened again. He wipes the blood on his jeans without flinching. It's been quiet regarding actual calls. He can't imagine a place like this sees much action.

On his way up the mountain, the radio traffic consisted of the dispatcher and Officer Plunket awkwardly flirting amidst the gossip about the incident that occurred just outside of town.

Either a highway patrolman got a flat tire, was involved in an accident, or shot a stranded motorist. No one really knows what happened.

Since then, the dispatchers have had a shift change. What a relief. The new dispatcher comes to life. She reports that a Datsun pickup truck has been stolen from the Gas and Guzzle, last seen approximately fifteen minutes ago.

The owner, Jimmy Wilson, is positive that his brother didn't take it this time. The dispatcher confirms that his brother is currently locked up, so she's pretty sure it wasn't him.

Mike relays the information to the rest of the crew via text. Papa messages him to return to his location and check if she shows up. Officer Plunket comes over the radio, putting the moves on dispatcher number two. Mike shakes his head, amused but unamused, and makes a U-turn.

# FORTY-SEVEN

PAPA STANDS on the rickety porch of a double-wide mobile home and thanks Gertie for her time, wishing her luck with her cold case podcast. Oscar had left and returned to the Mercedes as soon as Gertie had told them she hadn't seen the missing woman.

Papa lets her ramble a minute longer, still playing the part of a concerned uncle. She assures him that if someone suspicious were lurking nearby, she would spot them the second they set foot in town, thanks to her crime-detecting skills. As Papa walks down the porch steps into freedom, he reassures her, again, that it isn't necessary to leave his number in case she "uncovers new information." Gertie offers tips and advice even as Papa walks away.

An incoming phone call from Victor saves him from the incessant woman. Papa answers on the second ring.

Victor tells Papa that Charlie retrieved his phone from the video store, and they're heading into town to help canvass the neighborhoods. Papa advises Victor to meet Mike at his last location instead and to keep an eye out for a recently stolen Datsun pickup truck.

Papa and Oscar ride in silence to the next street over. None of the neighbors have seen anyone or anything suspicious tonight, or at least, nothing that fits the description of the woman they are searching for.

Several have asked whether the missing woman was connected to the highway patrol car crash earlier, and more than a few have speculated that she was a criminal who caused the accident in order to escape. Papa dismisses the theories with calm indifference, though each time he is met with narrowed eyes watching him too closely.

The next house they visit is a narrow stick-built structure wedged between two aging mobile homes, as if it were added as an afterthought. There are no outdoor lights, and the weedy grass grows right up to the front door. As they approach, a sharp click of a lighter snaps through the air. Oscar flinches and reaches for his gun, but Papa catches his arm, a silent cue that there is no threat.

In the dark sits Dan, a town resident for forty years. A sharp metallic *clink* sounds as he lights a cigarette. His robe falls open as he stands, revealing pale legs and boxers. Papa slows his approach, and Oscar's hand hovers near his hip.

Dan takes another drag from his cigarette and exhales through his nose. He coughs into his fist before waving the smoke away. "What do you want?" he asks, not bothering to tighten the robe.

Oscar steps forward and raises his phone, the screen already lit with the gas station surveillance photo. "We're looking for this woman. Have you seen her?"

Dan squints at the screen through the rising smoke of his cigarette, takes a long drag, holds it, then exhales in a slow stream. "Maybe," he says.

Oscar shifts his stance. "Have you or not?"

Dan doesn't blink. He takes another pull on the cigarette, completely unfazed. Judging by his crooked nose and missing teeth, Dan has been in his fair share of fights.

Papa doesn't waste time. He pulls a twenty from his wallet and holds it out. He knows how to speak Dan's language. Dan snatches the bill and shoves it in his sock.

"Yeah, I seen her," Dan says, flicking ashes in the weeds. Oscar takes a step back.

"When?" Papa doesn't raise his voice, but there's weight behind it.

Dan shrugs like it's a chore to recall. "Can't remember."

Oscar takes a step toward him.

Papa reaches into his wallet and pulls out another twenty. He doesn't wave it or offer it up. He just holds it, like bait.

Dan snatches it. "Two hours ago."

Papa does the math. Less than two hours ago, he and his crew were chasing her through the desert. If she made it to town, she's been here for less than an hour. Papa fantasizes about knocking out the rest of Dan's teeth, but they can't afford to draw any attention. They already stick out like a sore thumb in this town.

"He doesn't know anything," Papa says, returning to the Mercedes.

The neighbors on the following two streets proved just as useless. Papa had walked up to each door with a polite knock and a neutral expression. His patience was tested with every repeated "no." He only needs one yes.

Oscar drives to the next neighborhood while Papa calls Mike.

"We haven't had any luck," Papa says.

Mike's voice fills the Mercedes. "What do you want me—" His words cut off as a voice crackles over his end.

"Dispatch to Plunket. Be advised, Frank just called and said he saw Jimmy's truck while walking Betsy. It's pulled over to the side of Canyon Road. Over."

Mike comes back on. "Did you catch that?"

"I heard."

"There's a back road just north of Canyon Road, behind the treeline. I can check out the area from that side without being noticed," Mike says.

"Victor and Charlie should be closer. Have them do it," Papa says. "We're almost done here. I'll let you know when we're heading that way." He ends the call without waiting for a response.

Oscar turns left into the newest neighborhood, a ten-year-old planned tract with fewer than twenty houses and a neglected park. Most of the porch lights are off or burned out. It shouldn't take long to get twenty more no's from the residents, especially if they split up, as Oscar suggests.

Papa shakes his head. He wants the people to feel comfortable enough to talk. Oscar doesn't know how to fake friendly, let alone be it.

"Maybe it's time we loop Romeo in on this," Oscar says. He toggles the climate switch up a notch, activating the heater with a soft hum.

"I don't see the need," Papa replies. "Mike has the flash drive, and if she doesn't show up, then we forget about her, and still make the drop before midnight. There's a good chance she's long gone."

"Romeo won't like that."

"Romeo only cares about getting the information to his people," Papa says. "We have the flash drive, and we'll get it to them." He shifts in his seat and gazes at the quiet road ahead. "It's looking more and more like Victor was right. She probably came into possession of it by accident."

Oscar tilts his head, unconvinced. "Then why did she drive back to the city, turn around, and drive through the desert to pass a truck?"

Papa exhales slowly and looks at Oscar. "She's a woman travelling alone in the middle of the desert. She realized she was being followed and panicked. Let me worry about Romeo. And let me do all the talking this time."

Oscar throws the Mercedes into park in front of a single-story house where a couple waits outside for them. News travels fast in a small town.

Porch lights from nearby homes flicker on, one after another, like a domino effect of curiosity. Papa adjusts his coat and steps out. The couple offers weary smiles and waves. Papa returns the wave, maintaining a relaxed posture. He doesn't like the way the neighborhood is paying attention.

Oscar joins him at the walkway. "Twenty more no's?"

Papa watches a curtain twitch next door. "Maybe not," he says. "But let's make it quick." This is dragging on too long, and he's losing interest. They don't need the woman to finish the job.

Papa steals a glance at Oscar and wonders why he's still hell bent on finding her.

# FORTY-EIGHT

Twigs and snow crunch beneath Jessie's Nikes as she climbs the incline. The ground levels into a small, sloped clearing, spotted with a couple of rogue trees. She pauses to scan the dark treeline opposite her. They're alone.

On her way back down to the spot where she told the boys to wait, a faint buzz draws her attention skyward. "Hey, look," she says, pointing up. "Power lines. We're probably close to the cabin." Her words hang in the cold air, meant to spur them on, but neither boy acknowledges her comment.

"Max, let's check your laptop for the info Jonathan sent."

"Yeah," he mumbles.

"Mom, I'm going to pee my pants," Sean says, shifting side to side.

"Okay, we'll check it when we're done. You guys head up there. There's a small clearing. Stay together and be quiet. I'll stay down here and keep an eye on the truck."

Max and Sean trudge up the incline without a word, their

breath visible. Jessie watches until they're nearly out of sight, then hears Max's voice cut through the quiet. "Stop following me. Go over there." She glances just in time to see him point to the right and drop his backpack. Sean disappears in the direction Max pointed.

Jessie keeps the truck in her sight and conducts her business behind a bush. The silence is eerie yet calming, as if the world has paused just so she can catch her breath. Then a branch creaks somewhere beyond. She jolts upright and cocks her head, listening. Jessie recognizes the sound of deliberately placed footsteps that are attempting, but failing, to remain quiet. Those footsteps are too measured to belong to the Baltimore boys. Jessie scrambles to collect herself, draws her gun, and treads lightly up the incline as she hunts for the source.

The moonlight filters through the branches as Jessie steps into the clearing, each movement slow and deliberate. Thirty feet ahead on her left, Max's profile emerges from behind a tree. She looks to her right but can't see Sean. She walks back down the incline and stops when he comes into view. He stands twenty feet ahead on her right, angled so she sees his three-quarter profile. From there, she can no longer see Max. With light steps, Jessie inches up the incline until she sees Max's head, just shy of the tree, while still keeping sight of Sean. She alternates her gaze between them, breath catching in her chest. Another twig creaks. It wasn't Jessie, and neither boy has moved. She freezes.

Two figures emerge from the shadows at the clearing's edge near the treeline. They separate, one moving toward Max from behind, the other closing in on Sean, guns drawn.

The silhouettes advance on the boys. There's no way Jessie can shoot both men before one of them takes a shot. She has mere seconds to calculate distances, visibility, and accuracy before she must make a decision.

Sean struggles with his pants zipper.

Max is looking down as if putting himself back together.

Neither boy glances up. They're completely oblivious to the

danger silently approaching from behind.
Jessie says a silent prayer and takes the shot.

# FORTY-NINE

MAX'S HANDS jerk mid-button as the gunshot echoes through the clearing. He turns around to see a young man pointing a gun at him. He looks just as shocked as Max.

"You're a kid," the young man chokes out.

Max's eyes go wide, and his legs tremble. He doesn't feel any heat or pain, but he's never been shot, so he doesn't know what it should feel like.

He's heard that sometimes shooting victims don't realize they've been shot until later because of shock or adrenaline, or maybe both. His throat seizes as adrenaline floods his veins, preventing him from yelling.

The young man runs his hands through his hair, gun still in hand. "You're just a kid," he repeats. "I could have..." He glances behind him.

Max tries to see what he's looking at, but there's nothing there. Not even Sean.

Jessie rushes toward the body, keeping her gun trained on it. The man's right eye socket gapes open, spilling blood into the foliage and staining leftover bits of snow crimson. She pivots to Sean and puts her finger to her lips. He wipes a tear from his cheek and nods, shoulders trembling. His eyes are wide, and his breathing is uneven. She takes his hand and clamps it on the back of her waistband, signaling him to hold on. He nods again.

Her head tells her to hide Sean and go after the other man. Her heart isn't allowing Sean out of her sight again. With Sean trailing, Jessie takes calculated steps up the incline until Max comes into view.

The young man whirls back to Max. "Run," he snaps. He looks over his shoulder, back to where the body lies. "Run. Now."

Max doesn't move.

Jessie moves her finger to the trigger.

The young man lunges forward.

She loses sight of him behind the tree. Heart pounding, she circles like a big game cat and ascends the incline with Sean in tow. She glimpses a hand shove Max in the shoulder. As she continues up the incline, she catches a blur of Max stumbling over his uncooperative feet, then loses sight of him as he runs through the forest. She now has a clear shot at the young man. Twigs and snow crunch underfoot as Jessie closes in on him, but he doesn't notice her presence.

He falls to his knees and sobs.

# FIFTY

JESSIE IGNORES the man sobbing on the ground and runs back to the Datsun, dragging Sean by the hand. Nothing in the world could make her let go. She yanks open the passenger door and orders, "Get in."

Sean hesitates. His face scrunches, and breaks into fresh tears, snot and saliva joining the stream. He utters something, but Jessie can't understand him.

She pats him down, checking for injuries. "Are you hurt?" He shakes his head, gasping between sobs. Then the smell hits her. "You wet your pants?" He nods, shoulders shaking. "It's okay. You can change when we get to the cabin, okay? Right now, we need to get out of here and find your brother." She ushers him into the truck.

After a few minutes on the road, Sean's hysterical crying eases into quiet whimpers. Jessie glances at him and suddenly recalls Mr. Poopy Pants. She pulls over.

She rummages in Sean's backpack and pulls out a pair of pajama pants. "Here, put these on. But make it fast."

Sean clutches the pajama pants but stays still. "I don't have any clean underwear," he whispers.

Jessie leans close. "I'm going to tell you a secret, but don't tell Dad. He doesn't wear any underwear under his pajama pants." She raises her eyebrows. *What do you think about that?*

Sean grimaces at the new information. "But these are for bedtime. It's not bedtime yet."

"But it is nighttime, so I think we're good."

Sean counts aloud as he changes into the dry pajama pants, twenty-seven seconds. He beams at his timing and the fact that he didn't fall over when his foot got caught in the turned-out leg. He throws his soaked clothes into the truck bed and slides back inside wearing the pajama pants.

"Better?"

He nods and gives a half-smile.

Jessie wasn't too far off in her calculations. A cabin comes into view a short time later. There are no visible vehicles or signs of anyone being home. Max knew they were heading to a cabin, and she hopes that he will continue with the plan. There's no way he could have beaten them here on foot, even if he ran the entire way. Jessie stops sixty feet from the cabin and kills the headlights.

Sean lies motionless in his seat, not making a sound. He isn't picking at his fingers, or humming, or counting. He's just lying there. Jessie strokes his hair as her gaze sweeps the cabin's perimeter, searching for Max.

Time moves infinitely slower when you don't know where your child is. When Jessie became a mother, she realized her worst fear was that her child would go missing.

Not that they might die. Death brings closure. But missing means there's always hope of the worst kind. Hope without answers. Hope that tortures.

After what feels like an eternity—but Jessie calculates to be fifteen minutes—she decides to check the cabin. It's possible Max slipped in through the back. She leaves Sean sleeping in the truck and silently walks the perimeter, her gun at her side. No sign of Max outside.

The porch creaks underneath her steps just as the front door swings open.

# FIFTY-ONE

CHARLIE CAN'T tear his gaze from Victor's body. Blood trickles from a gaping hole where his right eye should be. It can't be real. This can't be real. Everything blurs until the desert air feels thick and unreal. He must be hallucinating a scene from a horror movie franchise.

This can't be happening. His phone's sharp ring shatters the moment. He stares at it and lets it ring twice more, then answers.

"You were supposed to check in five minutes ago. What's going on? Victor isn't answering his phone," Papa says.

Charlie closes his eyes and shakes his head. Maybe if he blinks hard enough, the hallucination will vanish, and Victor will sit up.

Papa's voice crackles again, louder this time, "Charlie?"

Charlie turns away from Victor. He drags a shallow breath and utters a hesitant "Yeah."

"What's your status? Any sign of the woman?" Papa demands.

"Uh." Charlie rubs his temple, searching for words. Any

words. He's never seen a dead body before. He's never had to tell someone they lost a loved one, especially to murder. Only one word breaks free. "Dead."

There's subtle glee in Papa's voice. "She's dead? You guys found her?" Charlie hears Papa tell Oscar, "They found her. She's dead."

Charlie forces out the truth. "Victor."

"What?"

Charlie inhales in short, uneven gasps. "Victor. He's dead." He wants to explain how they heard a car stop and spotted movement in the forest clearing. They saw a man taking a leak and a smaller figure nearby. They believed the smaller person was the woman. Victor said it made sense why she had evaded them for so long. She wasn't alone. Charlie wants to explain to Papa that the man was actually just a scared kid. But he can't find any of those words. Instead, he simply says, "She killed him." He instantly regrets the words and answering the call.

Silence fills the air. Charlie isn't sure if the call dropped until a low growl vibrates through his ear, followed by a long inhale. His pulse races.

Papa roars, "I can't believe she killed my boy!" Charlie pulls the phone from his ear as rage spills through the line. When the tirade stops, Charlie presses the phone back to his cheek. "Do you have her? Tell me you have her," Papa demands.

Charlie's throat tightens, and he forces the words out. "Uh, no. She took off."

"Was she alone?" Papa asks, each word measured.

Charlie's eyes dart to Victor's body. The kid's ghostly, wide-eyed face flashes in his mind. He swallows. "Uh...yeah, she was alone." As soon as Charlie says it, he knows the lie will come back to bite him in the ass. Lies tend to do that.

"I'll have Mike meet you there and help get Victor into the car. I don't want him dragged through the dirt like an animal. Oscar and I are on our way," Papa says, back to business.

Charlie is uneasy with how quickly Papa regains his composure, as if he hadn't just received the worst news of his life. The terseness in Papa's words sends a chill through Charlie. He may not know the proper response to receiving news like that, but he knows it's not what just transpired.

Charlie hopes the lady and her kid find a safe hiding place before Papa and Oscar arrive. Maybe they'll get help and return to wherever they belong, and Papa will never know Charlie lied to him.

And maybe they'll all live to see another day. Maybe.

# FIFTY-TWO

JESSIE STARTLES when a man suddenly appears in the doorway. She slides her hand behind her leg, hiding her gun. She's been watching the cabin for the last fifteen minutes without seeing any movement or hearing any sounds inside. The cabin doesn't have a garage, and no vehicle is parked in front or at the back.

Then again, an agent wouldn't leave a car where anyone could see it. Jonathan's message said help would arrive in an hour... has it already been an hour? The agent must have been waiting for her to approach him, not wanting to spook her after the ordeal she's been through. He's much older than she expected.

He pulls his hand from his pocket, revealing a tattoo. That's not right. The Agency didn't allow tattoos, especially on the hands. They are too identifiable and too hard to cover up.

Jessie's thoughts ping-pong inside her head. Maybe he's ex-agency. That would make sense. Jonathan probably couldn't get official approval to send an active agent, so he called in a favor from someone he knew. A person she knows nothing about. They once shared the same circle of friends. Reality hits: they both have different lives now, not just her.

Before Jessie can get a word out, the stranger says, "Oh, hi there." That's not what she was expecting.

"Hi," she says, unsure of where this is going.

He nods to her left arm in the bloody sling. "You, okay?"

She nods. "Looks worse than it is." She struggles to recall whether she told Jonathan about her arm. Everything that's happened in the last few hours blurs together. She didn't get a chance to check Jonathan's email and has no idea what the agent looks like or if there's a code phrase to confirm identity. She doesn't even know if the person he sent is a man. She could be at the wrong cabin, talking to a random mountain resident. It wouldn't surprise her if the Datsun's odometer was broken and she didn't travel far enough. Her mind races, figuring out the best way to play this.

He nods to the truck. "You got car trouble?"

Wouldn't Jonathan have mentioned the crash? He should know about her terrible vehicle situation. But maybe he's simply verifying if she's the person he's waiting for or just a random traveler having car trouble. The truck is clearly a piece of junk. Jessie has just entered a very dangerous game of flinch, as they begin to suss out one another. Dr. Smith's rule echoes in her head: Only answer a yes-or-no question with a "yes" or a "no."

"Yeah." She waits for his response. He who talks the most gives away the most.

"You want to come inside and get out of the cold while I grab my tools? I can take a look for ya?" He opens the door wider, and she catches an Irish lilt beneath a bad American accent.

There's no way she's going inside with him until she knows who he really is. "I'm fine out here, but thank you."

He wasn't expecting that answer. "Okay, then. I'll be right back." He turns and heads back inside.

Suspicions flare when Jessie realizes he never gave his name, which would've been in Jonathan's email even if there wasn't a code phrase. At the very least, he would've let her know who he is. Maybe she really is at the wrong cabin. Anything is possible.

The man returns with a regular-looking blue tool bag, except for the brand name, which Jessie doesn't recognize. She shifts to the side, keeping her gun hidden behind her thigh as he steps onto the creaky porch. She secures her gun in her waistband and follows him down the steps.

Another detail sinks in: he hasn't asked about the boys. She's certain Jonathan would have mentioned them. As the man approaches the front of the truck, her heart rate quickens. The truck. Sean.

Jessie quickly walks up behind him and blurts out, "On second thought, can I get something hot to drink?"

The man stops and turns around.

"It is pretty cold out here," she adds, offering a weak grin.

His face softens in a way that feels forced. "Certainly." He glances sideways at the truck as they walk back to the cabin.

The thought occurs to Jessie that Max might very well be in the cabin. Perhaps he arrived before them and is tied up inside—or worse.

The porch creaks beneath their steps as they enter. She notices a limp as he walks to the kitchen and sets his tool bag on the counter. She takes a quick look around. The cabin is sparse but livable, and there's no sign of Max.

"Make yourself comfortable," he says over his shoulder. He grabs two mugs from the upper cabinet and fills the coffeepot with water.

Jessie examines a picture on a nearby wall. It looks about twenty years old—two men in a fishing boat. She's trying to imagine them bald. Maybe one of them could be this man. Too hard to tell.

"Coffee, okay?"

"Yes."

"So, how do ya know Jimmy?" He fills the coffeemaker with water and begins the brew cycle. He turns back to lean on the counter, folding his arms.

She remains fixed on the photo, heart pounding, afraid her poker face isn't what it used to be. *Who the hell is Jimmy? Why would she know him?* She can't recall any code word "Jimmy" from her time at The Agency, and she can't ignore him forever. She turns to face him. "I'm sorry?"

"Jimmy, how do ya know him?" He pushes off the counter.

He clearly knows this Jimmy guy and believes she does, too. She racks her brain for a moment longer. Any further procrastination will raise suspicion. Then, she figures it out.

"Cousin. Second or third, I can't remember. I'm about to disown him after he loaned me that piece of crap truck of his. Reliable, my ass."

The man chuckles. The coffee stops brewing, and he reaches for the cabinet above the machine. Jessie begins to reach for her Glock.

"Cream or sugar?" He turns toward her.

She quickly scratches at her waist. "Both. Do you mind if I use your bathroom?" Jessie can't shake the thought that Max might still be inside somewhere.

"Sure, follow me." As they walk down the hall, he closes a door on the left, leading her past it. "That toilet's broken." They continue into the main bedroom, and he points to a small bathroom before returning to the kitchen.

When Jessie is certain she's alone, she kneels and checks under the bed. Nothing. She moves quickly to the closet and peers behind hanging coats. Empty. Nothing behind the shower curtain. No sign of Max. Her pulse pounds as she creeps down the hallway back toward the living area.

She stops short when a walkie-talkie chirps to life: "Mike, any sign of that bitch?"

Mike rounds the corner, gun aimed at Jessie.

*He has green eyes. Not many people do.*

The gunshot echoes through the forest.

# FIFTY-THREE

A LOUD noise startles Sean awake. He bolts upright, heart hammering, and blinks at the unfamiliar cab around him. Wires dangle from the steering column like tangled earbuds, and for a moment, he doesn't recognize where he is. Outside the window, tall pine trees block the moonlight, and a cabin sits back in the shadows. Now he remembers. Mom killed a guy at the shack, crashed the car, then stole another car with a baby, taught it to swear, stole this truck, killed another guy, and lost Max. And he peed his pants.

The driver's side door swings open, and Sean jolts. Jessie slides behind the wheel and tucks a gun in the glove box. Sean watched *Guns: The Evolution of Firearms* last week and knows the gun in the glove box has a safety. The one his mom secretly kept in the Explorer doesn't. Now she has two guns.

"There was a loud noise," Sean says.

Jessie doesn't reply and hands the walkie-talkie to him. "Do you know what that is?"

"Of course, Mom. I'm not six. When I was six, I didn't know

what a walkie-talkie was, but then when I was seven and we went to Grandma and Grandpa's house, Grandpa let me play with an old set he had." Sean turns it over in his hand, inspecting it.

"So, you know how it works?"

"Yeah, you just press this button to talk—"

Jessie snatches the walkie-talkie before his thumb can press it. "Yes, but I just want you to listen to it. Here." She hands it back to him along with a black marker she took from the tool bag. She uses her teeth to pull her sleeve up to her elbow and offers her right forearm. "I want you to write down the names we hear, okay?"

Sean scrunches his face. "On your arm?"

"I saw a guy do it in a movie once. Write down the name Mike."

He looks at the walkie-talkie, afraid he has already missed something. "But I didn't hear anyone say that."

"Someone said it while I was still inside the cabin."

"Was Max inside?" He asks, even though he knows Max would be sitting next to him if he were. But he needs to make sure.

She scans the surrounding area around the cabin. "No. But we're going to go find him. Now, write down the name Mike."

Sean uncaps the marker and hesitates before writing M-I-K-E, his hand trembling.

Just as Sean finishes writing the name, the walkie-talkie squawks to life, and Sean flinches, thankful he wasn't still writing. He holds it in his open palm to avoid accidentally pressing the button.

The operator on the other end doesn't keep the button fully pressed, and the message comes across choppy. "Uh, Mike, I hope you can hear this. This is Charlie, by the way." Sean's heart lurches when he hears the name, and he snaps his head toward Jessie. She nods to her arm.

Sean hesitates again. Mrs. Wilkes always reminded students not to write on their skin because cheap pens have toxic ink. But, according to *How It's Made*, ink pens aren't allowed to use toxic ink anymore. Sean feels guilty writing on his mom's arm, but he also feels a weird excitement because she told him to do it, so it's okay. He lowers the marker and pauses, worried that he might hurt her, even though he knows from experience that writing on your arm doesn't hurt at all. Unless you use a sharp pencil like Philip from his fourth-grade class. But Sean isn't that dumb. He writes the name "Charlie" underneath "Mike" and glances at his mom. She seems fine.

Charlie's voice returns, not as choppy, but still not smooth. "Maybe you're driving and can't reach your walkie right now, but I hope you can hear this, so I'll just, uh, tell you and not expect a response. Anyway, I'm with... uh, I'm with Victor. Well, I guess his body. Papa said you were coming to help me with that."

Sean adds "Victor" and "Papa" to the list on Jessie's arm.

Charlie continues. "I hope you're on your way. He also said that, uh, no one should be in contact with Juliet or Romeo except him. I think that has something to do with Oscar...not you or me. I don't even know who those people are." After a pause, he mutters, "Okay, I hope you're close. See you soon. I hope."

Sean inspects his work: Mike, Charlie, Victor, Papa, Juliet, Romeo, Oscar. Mrs. Wilkes would be proud of his penmanship. If he had to graffiti his mom's arm, it would be his best work.

Jessie starts the truck, then extends her arm back to Sean. "Put a line through Mike and Victor."

Sean drags the marker across both names and looks at Jessie.

She answers the look. "We don't need to worry about those two anymore."

He thinks he understands, but isn't going to ask for clarification.

"Did you know that nobody really knows for certain when William Shakespeare wrote Romeo and Juliet?" Sean says. Jessie raises her eyebrows. He points to the names at the bottom of the list near her elbow: Juliet and Romeo.

She nods. "Good observation. Now, let's go find your

brother. Maybe he couldn't find the cabin in the dark."

"He has a flashlight," Sean says, as he gently lays the walkie-talkie in his lap.

Her jaw tightens. "Yeah, but he might have been too afr—" she doesn't finish, eyes narrowing on the forest.

Sean's eyes dart around. He's gotten better at making inferences and knows what his mom is thinking. She thinks Max would be too afraid to use his flashlight because someone might see it and follow him. "You're right, he's too smart for that," Sean reassures her. It's better to think Max is being smart rather than think he's afraid. In the movies, the people who are afraid usually make stupid decisions and get hurt or die. People who are smart usually make it to the credits.

Jessie mutters options on where they should start looking. After she dismisses a few of her initial suggestions, Sean asserts himself. "I think I know where he is."

She turns to him. "Where?"

"Back by where you killed that guy," he says.

"The shack in the desert? That's too far away."

"No, the other one."

She looks back at the cabin. "I checked the cabin. He's not inside."

"Mom! How many guys have you killed?"

"You mean where we stopped to go to the bathroom?"

"Yes," Sean says.

"Why do you think he's back there?"

"Every time we play hide and seek, Max *never* wins. He checks a place, and when I'm not there, he moves on. Then I leave the place I'm hiding in and go hide in the place he just checked because he never checks the same place twice. My gift to him last Christmas was telling him about my strategy.

If you were a bad guy looking for someone, would you look for them in the place they just ran from? Also, Max never looks up."

Jessie presses her hand against Sean's head and draws him

closer. He tenses, then relaxes when she kisses his hair.
The Datsun rumbles down the mountain.

265

# FIFTY-FOUR

A YOUNG woman stands outside the door and closes her eyes. Thirty seconds usually does the trick. Any longer and she drifts into the fantasies of a boyfriend picking her up for dinner and a movie, or becoming a singer or dancer on Broadway, anything but this room. Twenty more seconds. Her choir teacher once told her she had talent. Her English teacher told her she'd probably end up a barista. She's never been good at school, but she loves singing. Loved singing. Ten more seconds. Another girl told her about the trick of closing her eyes before entering. *It helps prepare your eyes for the darkness, one less shock to the system.* It worked the first time she tried it. It even calms her nerves. She vaguely remembers a science teacher mentioning that sudden physical shocks can induce anxiety, but she was never good at science. That teacher told her she'd make a good fashion blogger. Nobody blogs anymore. Except old people.

She quietly enters the room and opens her eyes. The room is painted a soft seafoam green, the kind of color you'd find in a spa or a coastal cottage. A glass wall cabinet displays various body lotions and oils, his favorites obvious by how empty some bottles are. Nothing hides behind that glass. Beside it, crisp white towels are folded into neat stacks on glass shelves. Compared to the rest of the mansion, the ceilings here are low, yet they would be standard height in a suburban home. The lighting is soft in the windowless room, and because of her little trick, her eyes need almost no time to adjust.

When she was little, she refused to go down the dark hallway in her house because of the monsters hiding there. Her mother assured her that monsters didn't hide in the dark. She was right. They hide in plain sight.

The room's construction and interior design serve a purpose. Its small size makes him seem bigger and more powerful. The lack of windows and lighting makes the room feel intimate and personal. White towels, white sheets, white robes, white everything. If she ever gets married, her dress will be anything but white. To anyone else, this room is just an ordinary spa treatment room. But she knows the truth. It's less spa and more prison.

This is her third visit in as many days. She tries to hide her loathing. Any hint of reluctance only makes matters worse. The one thing she appreciates about the room is the darkness. At first, it was unnerving, but now it's a welcome veil of protection for at least one of her senses. It's dim enough that sometimes he doesn't notice when she closes her eyes.

She never breathes through her nose if she can help it. The mingled smell of sweat, whiskey, and cigarettes seeps through his pores, making her stomach turn. Once, his odor was so bad that she vomited as soon as he left the room. And she knows he showers; she's been in there with him, yet the stench clings, as if it's a core part of his being.

She hangs her robe on a hook by the door. There isn't a tangible lock on the door, but she's a prisoner nonetheless. Her skin instantly turns to gooseflesh. Her bra and panties do little to protect her from the sixty-five-degree room. The other girls say he keeps it that cold because he's fat. She agrees. It also gives him an excuse to rub his greasy hands all over her to "warm her up."

As her shaky hands adjust a tiny pink bow on the side of her panties, she notices her hip bone sticks out a little more than it did six months ago. She doesn't hate it. It reminds her of the models she's seen on social media. Maybe this is sexy. Her mother has asked more than once if everything is fine. She has noticed the weight loss and the slipping grades. "Yeah, everything's... fine." *I'm making money, and I look like a model. Living the teenage dream, right?*

She walks to the massage table where he lies face up, phone pressed to his ear. This happens often, and she prefers it this way. The more distracted he is, the better. However, if he's on a stressful call, it takes him longer to "get ready," and that's always worse.

One of the older girls said stress can affect old men that way. She has no idea how old he is, but he's definitely older than her mom. She's not sure about her dad; she's never met him.

Whenever he's on the phone, she distracts herself by singing in her head. But today, something grabs her attention. *Did he mention a son?* She can't imagine him having children. And God help them if they exist.

"I agree. He should have put you in charge instead of his son. But then you'd be the one who's dead right now," Romeo says into the phone.

Apparently, it isn't his son they're discussing. The world will be a better place if he never reproduces. She walks around to the head of the table and massages his shoulders. She hears a muffled voice on the other end, but can't make out the words.

"It wasn't a lucky shot. She's a pro." Romeo snaps his fingers out to his side.

She stands where he snapped, waiting as his eyes travel up and down her body. She hopes the call distracts him enough that he doesn't realize she's kept her bra on.

He continues on the phone, "I want her brought in alive." He snaps his fingers again. She slips off her bra. "Get him under control and bring her to me." He ends the call and hands her the phone.

Usually, the towel draped over his hips has risen by now.

"What's your name, again?" He tosses the towel on the floor.

This isn't going to be quick.

"Susie." She isn't Susie. She likes to mess with him whenever she thinks she can get away with it. Playing this game is her only form of power in this room. She knows he won't remember who she is when he asks again next week. She could be Stacey, or Amy, or Veronica. It doesn't matter. She could be anyone.

# FIFTY-FIVE

A PASSING cloud hides the moon, and a winter breeze whistles through the Datsun's vents. Sean shivers, bouncing his legs on the worn bench seat. Jessie regrets not grabbing a blanket from the cabin and tries not to think about Max, who's out there somewhere, freezing.

The Datsun sputters. Jessie's surprised that the piece-of-crap truck is still running and will do anything to keep it alive a little longer. Another gust of wind parts the clouds, and the moonlight washes over the power lines. Jessie recognizes the clearing from their earlier pit stop. She throws the gearshift into park, kills the engine, and grabs the walkie-talkie from the seat.

She turns to Sean, but before she can get a word out, he's already on a Ramble Report—that's Max's nickname for when Sean unloads a torrent of facts without pausing to breathe. It always happens after he watches a documentary.

"I am not staying here. Nah-uh, no way. Do not even say it. Do not even think about it. Do you remember way back when I was ten?" Of course she does. It was only two years ago. "I got my black belt. And Dad said when I got my black belt, I could walk to the park by myself. And you told him that was not happening unless it was over your dead body. And I asked you why. And you said there were bad people who like to take kids when they are by themselves. And Dad got mad at you for telling me that, even though you said it was the truth—just turn on the news. And I said I had my black belt now, so I could fight someone trying to take me. And you said that there was no way I could fight off a grown man trying to take me."

Sean finally takes a breath. Jessie knows there's more and lets him finish. It's best not to interrupt.

"Well, back then, I Googled what the average adult man weighs, and I did the math, and there is no way, even though I'm bigger now, there is still no way I could fight an adult man and win. So, that means you were right. I will not win, so you have to take me with you." He's not sure if he's won her over yet. "Because some people like to take kids when they are by themselves."

"I was going to tell you to grab your backpack," Jessie says.

"Oh."

Jessie allows her eyes to adjust to the darkness. She uses the power lines to orient herself and finds the clearing where she last saw Max before he ran off. Slivers of moonlight slice through the pines, illuminating their path as the breeze weaves through the forest. She takes the gun out of her sling and aims it just below eye level.

Jessie keeps her voice hushed, loud enough only for Sean to hear. "Stay behind me, okay?" He nods. "And don't forget to look behind you and to the sides—alternate."

Sean snaps his head around: first left, then right, then behind, then right again, and finally left. He's going to make himself dizzy. Jessie taps his shoulder and demonstrates a slow, methodical scan. He mimics her and gives a thumbs-up. She nods in approval.

Jessie quickly surveys the clearing. No sign of Max. Or anyone else. She scans left, scans right—nothing. They move fifteen feet across frozen dirt that crunches under each step. In the distance, she spots Victor's body, exactly where she left him. No sign of the other guy.

If Jessie were Max, where would she go? She senses Sean is right, and Max would come back here. But where? The clearing stretches far, and the moon hides behind uncooperative clouds. A flashlight would draw attention, and the psychos trying to kill her could be anywhere. It took her twenty minutes to reach the mountain in a crappy truck. If the other guys are on their way up, they could make it in half the time in their hundred-thousand-dollar SUV.

They might already be in the area. She might be leading her lamb to slaughter, but her other lamb is lost out here somewhere. She has no choice but to proceed.

She scans again. Still nothing. Then she remembers the other thing Sean said: Max never looks up when they play hide and seek. Jessie lifts her gaze to the night sky. Nothing but trees and more trees until... a faint reflection catches her eye. It's at the top of the power lines.

She taps Sean's shoulder and points toward the power lines. He nods. They move forward, January's chill biting at their cheeks.

The walkie-talkie crackles to life on Jessie's waistband. "Yo, Mike. Where are you?" says the voice. Jessie shoves her gun in her sling, clenching her jaw at the searing pain. She crouches, pulling Sean with her. She presses a finger to her lips. Sean nods, eyes wide. The voice on the other end sounds like it's coming across in stereo. "I'm freezing my balls off, dude."

She kills the walkie-talkie.

The man freezing his balls off is within earshot.

# FIFTY-SIX

THE CLOUDS clear, and moonlight falls on Charlie as he paces in front of Victor's body. A gust of wind ruffles his hair. He retrieves a flannel from the Range Rover's backseat and pulls it on over his hoodie. He presses the button on the walkie-talkie. "Mike? It's Charlie. Where are you, man?" He resumes pacing and stares at the walkie-talkie, waiting. He talks to himself. "Where the heck is he? This is bullshit." His patience cracks. Mockingly, he says, "It's just a dead drop. It'll be easy. You'll be home in time for dinner."

Charlie kicks at the rocks, sending small stones skittering across frozen ground. He stops at Victor's body and kicks the ground harder, sending more frozen gravel into the air. "Bullshit! Your dad is full of bullshit! This is all bullshit!" He paces faster. "Now people are dying."

He turns and hurls another rock with his foot. "Nope. Nope. Just take the car and go, Charlie."

"You should take your own advice," Jessie says.

Charlie startles and spins around to Jessie, pointing a gun at him. As he puts his hands in the air, his phone rings in his pocket.

"Take it out slowly and put it on speaker," Jessie says.

Charlie slides the phone out, swipes to answer, and taps the speaker button.

"Is Mike there yet?" asks the caller. He glances at Jessie. She nods.

"Uh, yeah. He just got here," Charlie says.

"We're on our way," says the caller. Another man in the background curses in Spanish. "And if you see her again, try not to kill her. Romeo wants her brought in alive." Charlie ends the call and begins to put his phone away.

"Stop!" Jessie commands. Charlie jerks and almost drops the phone. "Slowly put the phone on the ground." His fingers tremble as he lowers it. "And any weapons."

"I put the gun in the car."

She notices he says "the" gun, not "my" gun. Amateur. Jessie steps forward and pats him down. He wasn't lying; he's clean. "Sit on your hands with your feet out in front and cross your ankles." He listens better than her kids.

Jessie can't place where she's seen him before, besides the mall parking lot. His bright eyes are familiar. Before she can ask, a twig snaps behind her. She whips around to glimpse Sean darting back behind the tree where she told him to wait. She turns back to Charlie. He hasn't even tried to move. She keeps her eye on Charlie and calls out, "Come here." She doesn't need to say his name. She's using the Mom Voice.

Sean stands by her side, clutching his hockey stick. Jessie steals a glance at Sean and sees fear in his eyes. She knows Sean and the dark don't get along. She tells him he can hold the flashlight from her backpack and reassures him that everything is okay.

She's not as gentle with Charlie. "I'm going to ask you questions. If you don't answer them, or I think you're lying, I'll shoot you." Charlie nods so hard his shoulders shake. "I'll know if you're lying."

"She will," Sean says.

"Who called?"

"That was Oscar," Charlie says.

"Who was yelling in the background?"

"Uh, that's Papa. Our boss."

A bright beam of white light hits Charlie in the face. He flinches and almost tips over.

Jessie turns to see Sean, arm outstretched, pointing the flashlight straight at Charlie's face.

"Sean," Jessie says.

"That's what cops do when they question criminals."

"Not now."

Sean clicks it off.

Jessie refocuses on Charlie. "Why was Mike coming?"

"To help me with him." He nods to Victor's body.

Jessie notices the substantial size difference between the two men.

"Why didn't you pull the trigger earlier?" Jessie says.

Charlie's shoulders slump, and he tilts his head. "You mean shoot the kid?" He swallows. "Because he's a fucking kid!"

Sean's eyes widen.

"Sorry, bro," Charlie says to Sean. Then to Jessie, "He's a freaking kid. I'm not—"

"What about your dead partner over there?" Her impatience cuts him off. She shifts her gaze from Charlie to Victor's body. "He was about to kill this kid," she nods at Sean.

Charlie's face tightens. "I don't think he would have hurt him. I don't think he was like that." He pauses, "He thought it was you."

Sean is only an inch shorter than Jessie. She understands how, from a distance in the dark, he might look like a small woman. She'll give him that.

Charlie's voice cracks. "I don't do this. I'm not a murderer. I don't even know why I pointed the gun at him." He looks at Victor's body and shakes his head. "I didn't know him for long, but...he wouldn't have—he really did think it was you."

Jessie believes him. People see what they're looking for.

Charlie continues, "Victor's not.... he wasn't like that." He moves to wipe a tear.

"Hands!" Jessie snaps.

Charlie freezes and slides his hands back under his butt. "I'm not a murderer," he insists, hanging his head.

"Why are you after me? I don't have your flash drive anymore."

Charlie lifts his head and looks Jessie in the eyes. "Honestly? I don't have a fu—", he catches himself, "freaking clue, lady. We were supposed to do a dead drop. That's where one person—" Jessie cuts him off with a raised hand. He nods.

"It was the flash drive. Victor was supposed to pick it up from the computer shop. I guess that's how it usually works. I don't know what happened to the guy who usually picks it up, but this was our first time. But by the time Victor went to get it, you had already taken it. We followed the trace and figured out what car you were driving. Once you tossed it, I don't know why we didn't forget about you and finish the job."

This kid is too naïve to fabricate a believable lie. He's telling her the truth.

"Where's the flash drive now?" she says.

"Mike has it. He's gonna be here any minute."

"Mike isn't coming."

"Mike isn't coming."

Charlie's face crumples with confusion.

Sean speaks up. "We crossed him off the list. That means he's dead."

# FIFTY-SEVEN

PAPA AND Oscar walk down the porch of the last house in the neighborhood. Charlie's message about Victor's death hangs heavy in Papa's mind. Luckily, no one answered the door and witnessed his outburst. After the initial rage, Papa settled into an eerie calm. He understands the importance of this job and knows when to be professional. The calm always comes first.

As they head back to the car, Papa spots a wooden baseball bat lying in the yard. He nonchalantly picks it up as if moving a tripping hazard.

Oscar reaches the Mercedes when a sharp crack echoes through the quiet street. Oscar turns to see Papa bludgeoning an innocent tree until it bleeds, and the bat snaps in two. The smaller half sails into the air and lands in the grass.

Papa's breath is unsteady, his knuckles white around the handle. He wipes his brow, drops the handle, and climbs into the passenger seat.

Now they sit in silence as Oscar drives down Main Street and toward the highway. The silence feels empty and echoes the new state of Papa's life. He rubs his thumb over the gold crucifix hanging from his necklace, a habit he didn't realize began during the funeral of his wife and oldest son. To distract himself, he tunes the satellite radio to the classical station.

Beethoven's Piano Concerto No. 5 finishes, and his Fifth Symphony begins. The first four notes pound through the speakers, and Papa's soul resonates with the beat. As they repeat, he invites the heaviness settling within him, but before the despair consumes him, Beethoven pulls him out with airy violins and soft wind instruments. Papa knows he only has to wait seconds before the timpani drum and French horns usher in the four notes of despair clinging to his heart. As the music builds, Papa is reminded of each of his losses: Victor is dead. His oldest son, dead. Marta. They're all dead. What is life without them?

The movement's orchestral chaos prevents Papa from settling on any single emotion. The lower strings whisper hope, and the winds beckon him forward, but the timpani beats underneath, keeping the pulse of his heartache alive. The music turns and builds to a joyful place. Papa and Victor were working together; business was good. He stopped drinking and started making plans for the future. Life was turning a corner, and Papa wasn't opposed to going along for the ride. But life can be cruel.

The music pauses and the horns reemerge, betraying Papa by inviting the gentle playfulness of the lower strings, followed by the jubilant upper strings. Marta dances along the beach while his two boys chase each other with crab carcasses and seaweed. They laugh at an intense game of Uno, as the flute and piccolo join in the fun. Papa and his boys praise Marta's overdone Thanksgiving dinner. They were a happy family until the timpani builds, the violins lower, and the orchestra fades only to return in full volume with a vengeance.

It's not long before the oboe solo reminds Papa of all that was and what will never be. And then the chaos starts all over again. Violin. Graduation day. Horn. Empty beds. Flute. Birthdays. Viola.

Anniversary dinners. Bass. Drunk driver. Timpani. Murder.

The beautiful commotion swells into the full orchestra, and Beethoven ends the first movement with a forceful fortissimo, leaving Papa with an emotion on which to settle. His jaw clenches, and he turns off the radio.

"What's the plan when we get there?" Oscar asks.

"Find her." Papa hides his crucifix inside his shirt. "And then I kill her."

# FIFTY-EIGHT

SEAN'S TEETH chatter in the cold. He both hates and loves it when his teeth chatter. It fascinates him because he has no control over it, but it also annoys the crap out of him because he can't make it stop. He rocks back and forth to get warmer, but it doesn't really help much.

"Do you want to wait in the truck?" Jessie asks.

Sean shakes his head quickly. "I'm fine. I want to stay with you." He's afraid to leave his mother's side. She might kill this guy if he does.

Sean knows he's not supposed to listen to other people's conversations, but this seems like a special situation where the rules might be different.

So far, he's learned that the person his mom is talking to is named Charlie. The guy named Papa is in charge, but there's someone above him he is working for named Romeo. Classic bad guy hierarchy. Sean learned what a hierarchy is in a WWII documentary. Romeo has a girlfriend or an assistant named Juliet.

Maybe she's both. Ew. Why would anyone want to date a bad guy?

Charlie thinks Romeo and Juliet are in a time zone three hours ahead or three hours behind. He's not sure which. Luckily, they don't have to worry about those two being after them, too. Papa and Oscar are on their way up the mountain to help Charlie and Mike find his mom. But Mike is dead now, so he won't be any help. Charlie said Victor was the only other person who knew she wasn't alone. But he's dead too.

So that means Papa and Oscar still don't know Max and Sean are with her. Well, at least they don't know about Sean. Max is lost, so maybe they found him. Sean hopes all those times they played hide-and-seek taught Max how to pick a really good hiding spot.

"How are you communicating?" Jessie asks.

"We have comms. Mine's in the Rover. I don't like always having someone in my ear. I say sh—tuff and forget they can hear me, and Oscar gets all pissy about it. But Mike and I were using the walkies."

"Does anyone else have one?"

"I don't know. Maybe."

"How long until the others get here?"

"Maybe fifteen minutes," Charlie says.

Jessie wipes her forearm across her forehead.

Charlie shifts his weight around, and she quickly points her gun at him. "Sorry, just trying to readjust," he says.

Jessie lowers her weapon. "Well, don't."

Sean doesn't think this guy is a real threat, and he thinks his mom feels the same way. She's treating him like she does Max after he does something really stupid and she has to punish him. This guy had the chance to shoot Max. And he didn't. He even told him to run. Killers never release their prey.

"You can sit cross-legged if you want," Jessie says.

Charlie looks confused, so Sean helps. "Crisscross applesauce." That's what they used to call it in elementary school.

Charlie nods and rearranges his legs.

"But keep your hands where they are," Jessie demands, but not as harshly as before.

Charlie makes a show of shoving his hands even further underneath his rear.

Jessie furrows her brow and purses her lips.

"Take the Rover," Charlie says suddenly. He sounds excited.

She stops in front of Charlie. "What?"

"Take the Range Rover. You and your kid need to get out of here."

"My other son is somewhere out here, and I'm not going anywhere without him."

Charlie looks disappointed. "Maybe... uh, maybe he went to the cabin."

"We were just there." She glares at him. "With your friend Mike."

"You can use my phone to call someone," Charlie says.

Sean's not sure who she could call. His dad is too far away to help, and the last law enforcement officer who tried to help ended up toppled on the highway. And she probably doesn't know Jonathan's number because he was using Max's laptop to send them messages.

"They monitor your phone. They'd hear every word," Jessie says.

Charlie's eyebrows scrunch up like he's surprised.

"Don't move." She glares at Charlie until he nods. She trots to the area where Max had been standing before he ran away.

"Psst. Hey, kid," Charlie whispers to Sean.

Sean looks at him from the corner of his eye and fidgets with his fingers.

"Hey, you hungry? I have a bag of M&M's in my coat pocket."

The thought of anything resembling food makes Sean's stomach rumble. He tries not to think about the candy-coated, chocolate-covered peanuts, but now it's all he can think about.

"I'm just gonna reach into my pocket." Charlie pulls his right hand out from under his rear.

Sean looks around for his mom, but can't see her in the dark. He starts to panic and almost yells for her when something lands by his feet with a soft thud. He jumps and stares at the candy for a moment before grabbing it.

His mom always told him not to accept things from strangers, especially candy, but he's really hungry now that Charlie mentioned food. He'll only have one. He opens the bag and pours a few into his hand.

"Wait," Charlie says loud enough to startle Sean, but not so loud for Jessie to hear. "Are you allergic to nuts?"

Before Sean can answer, Jessie comes back. "My son had a backpack. It wasn't on his back when he ran. Where is it?"

Charlie nods toward the Range Rover.

"Stand behind the tailgate," Jessie says to Sean.

He shoves the M&Ms in his pocket before she sees them. Sean peeks around the back of the Range Rover and watches Jessie grab Max's backpack from the front seat, along with the gun Charlie said was in the glove box. She takes out the magazine and the chambered bullet, placing them and the gun into Max's backpack.

Jessie continues watching Charlie as she turns on the laptop. When it makes the start-up sound, she tells Sean to watch Charlie and let her know if he moves.

Sean steps closer to Jessie and glances at the laptop screen.

She opens a chat box and types two words: cabin compromised. The screen goes black before she can hit Enter.

"Damn it! You've got to be kidding me!"

"What's wrong?" Charlie asks.

Jessie gives him the same look she gave a supermarket employee when they commented on her parenting during one of Sean's meltdowns.

"Maybe I can help," he says, his voice low.

"Mom, what's wrong?" Sean takes a step closer.

"The battery's dead."

"I can get you a power bank," Charlie blurts out.

Jessie storms toward him, gun in hand. "Why are you so eager to help? It wasn't that long ago that you had a gun to my son's head! What's your angle?"

He cowers as she gets closer. "I know! I know! But I didn't know he was a kid! I swear. I don't even know why I did it. I wasn't going to shoot him. I don't shoot people! I deal weed and occasionally fence some shit. And I'm not even good at it!"

Even in the darkness, Sean sees that the color has drained from Charlie's face. His mom's gun is pointed at his chest. "Mom," Sean whispers. She lowers her gun.

Charlie's voice gets higher as he talks faster. "My mom was a piece of work. I mean, a real winner. The only reason I survived my childhood is because of my big brother. He got me out of that toxic dump as soon as he turned eighteen. We walked out the front door with all our stuff, and she didn't even ask where we were going."

He chokes back tears, his voice steadying. "She never considered for one moment kicking out her lousy boyfriends." He swallows. "And you freaking killed a guy for your kid. Two guys."

"Three," Sean interjects.

"Geez, lady. Who are you?"

"She's my mom," Sean says. He stands next to Jessie, puffing out his chest.

"You're just a mom?"

Jessie steps into Charlie's personal space. "Don't ever say that to a woman. And threatening her kids—that's a death sentence." Her eyes shift to Victor's body.

Sean thinks his mom should trust Charlie. He can help them contact Jonathan so that they can find Max.

Jessie shoves the laptop into Max's backpack and slings it over her shoulder.

"Where's the power bank?" she finally asks.

# FIFTY-NINE

CHARLIE'S GLAD Badass Mom agreed to let him help. She didn't offer her name, and he wasn't about to ask. Actually, badass doesn't even begin to cover it. These days, everyone's got a bumper sticker or hat claiming the title. She's something else entirely. She's ready to go to war over her kids. Battle Mom feels more accurate.

A power bank doesn't seem like enough, not after pulling a gun on her kid. He offered to call the local police, but she said that would cause more problems. He can tell she doesn't completely trust him, and he doesn't blame her. His brother would be so disappointed in him. As soon as he gets off this mountain, Charlie will call him and see if the offer still stands for Charlie to stay with him. Just long enough for him to get on his feet. He needs a fresh start. Away from here.

Charlie tells her that Mike was their tech guy and that he should have all kinds of power banks, chargers, cell phones, and similar items. They agree to use the walkie-talkies to communicate with each other. She explains that the walkie-talkies aren't encrypted, so they should change frequencies after every message. Remembering which frequency to use was too difficult for Charlie, so they scrapped that plan. She tells him to keep his messages brief and avoid using names or mentioning the kids.

Mike usually kept items like power banks and extra batteries in his work bag. She didn't notice anything like that in the tool bag when she took the marker, but she also wasn't looking for power banks and batteries. People see what they're looking for. Charlie agrees to return to the cabin and find her a power bank.

Battle Mom and her kid will search the area for her other son, Max, and meet Charlie back at the cabin. She reminds him about Mike's body, and he offers to move it before she arrives with the boys. She appreciates that.

"In ten minutes, check in with the other guys and see how far out they are and which way they are coming from," she says. Charlie checks his watch. "When they're three minutes away, you need to leave in the opposite direction. Even if we're not back." He begins to argue with her. She interrupts him. "They will kill you."

The words hit Charlie like a sucker punch. His stomach drops, and cold sweat breaks out across his forehead. He's known it was a possibility—hell, he's seen what they're capable of—but hearing it said so plainly makes his hands shake. The forest around him seems to close in, and he remembers Papa's face when he talked about finding the woman. That cold calculation. Charlie had mistaken it for business focus, but now he understands. Papa doesn't see her as a person anymore. Just an obstacle.

Charlie remembers a month ago, when Papa had smiled and clapped him on the shoulder after Charlie helped him move some equipment. "You're a good kid, Charlie. Loyal. I respect that." He'd felt proud then, chosen.

Now the memory turns his stomach.

"Okay," he murmurs.

He doesn't know how things got so messed up. Charlie realizes how naïve he's been. He thought they would find this lady, explain the mix-up, retrieve the flash drive, and be on their merry way. Now he understands that whatever is on the flash drive matters more to Romeo than anything else. People be damned.

His brother's face flashes in his mind. They'd been sitting in their shared apartment waiting for his brother's rideshare to the airport. His brother had noticed Charlie had gotten another job through someone else's connection, the third time that year.

"You let other people make too many decisions for you," his brother said quietly. "When someone tells you what to do, what to think, ask yourself what you're really giving up." His brother had leaned forward. "You're smart enough to figure things out on your own. You don't need someone else calling the shots for your life."

Charlie had gotten defensive, insisted he was just being practical, that it was easier to let people with more experience guide him. His brother had just shaken his head. "Easier isn't always better. It's never too late to do the right thing." The words echo in his head as he watches Battle Mom and her kid disappear into the forest.

━━━ ••━ ━ •━• ••━ ━•

There's significantly less blood around Mike's body than Charlie expected. He's thankful for that; blood makes him nauseous. Still, the metallic smell hangs in the air, mixing with the cabin's mustiness and the lingering scent of coffee. Charlie tries to breathe through his mouth as he steps around the body.

He searches inside the blue tool bag on the kitchen counter, methodically removing each item. His fingers are steady now that he has a task to focus on, but his mind keeps drifting to the ten-minute deadline he was given. Screwdrivers, wire strippers, electrical tape. It's mostly tools.

The tech items must be in Mike's truck, but Charlie didn't see a vehicle parked out front or in the back. Now that he thinks about it, Mike probably parked the truck where it wouldn't be visible to Battle Mom.

He still can't believe she killed Victor with one shot. In the eye. Charlie went to the shooting range a few times to get familiar with the gun Papa had given him. However, he could never make a headshot from any substantial distance. He figured if the worst came to worst, he would just point and shoot until he ran out of bullets. But after what happened earlier, he's confident he doesn't have it in him to shoot someone unless it's in self-defense. And maybe not even then.

Charlie moves systematically through the cabin, checking drawers, cabinets, and even under the couch cushions. He doesn't find a power bank. He has no choice but to call Oscar.

Oscar answers his call with a 'what'—his usual charm.

"Hey, uh, we're back at the cabin. Do you know where Mike parked his truck?" Charlie says, working to keep his voice casual. "I got here before him, and, uh, I don't see his truck outside."

"Why don't you ask him?"

Charlie's pulse spikes. "Uh, yeah, I would, but he asked me to get something out of his truck for him and…" Charlie should have thought this through before he made the call. His eyes dart around wildly: living room, kitchen, bathroom. He lowers his voice. "He's in the bathroom. I don't want him to be mad when he gets out and I didn't get what he needed."

The silence lasts too long. Charlie can hear his heartbeat in his ears.

"Unbelievable. Just a minute," Oscar grumbles. Charlie hears him ask Papa if he has the location. He wipes his sweaty palms across his jeans and notices the time on his watch. It's been ten minutes since Battle Mom left.

Oscar gets back on the line. "It's on the west side, behind a row of pines."

"How long until you—" the line goes dead before Charlie can finish. He stares at the phone, wondering if Oscar suspected anything. Wondering how much time he has left before he needs to run.

# SIXTY

Sean walks beside Jessie in Charlie's oversized flannel. Charlie also gifted them another flashlight, which Sean slid into the side pocket of his backpack. They walk in silence, except for Jessie whispering Max's name every few feet. The clouds have finally dispersed for the evening, providing enough moonlight to keep their lights off.

Jessie sees the reflection of the power line pole she pointed out earlier, indicating they're close to the clearing where they made the pit stop. Her pulse quickens. If Sean is right about Max using Sean's hiding strategy, they should find him soon.

Sean whispers, "Do you think there's coyotes in the mountain?"

"No." Jessie doesn't tell him she thinks the mountain lions keep the coyotes away. They approach a small patch of snow that the canopy has protected. It's smooth and undisturbed until they reach the edge, where two footprints have left an impression. The prints point in the direction they're walking.

Jessie's heart flutters. Please be Max. Please be alive.

The forest is dense, making it hard to see anything more than five feet ahead. She worries they might miss him by just a few feet. What if he's injured? What if he fell while running and hit his head? She saw him stumble just before he took off running. He could be unconscious somewhere in the darkness.

Jessie takes a risk and briefly scans the area with her light. Nothing. She clicks it off, hands it to Sean, and returns to her gun. Her training kicks in, weapon ready, finger resting near the trigger.

Sean stumbles over a branch and steadies himself.

In her peripheral vision, she catches something, a brief gleam, there and gone.

"Did you see that?" she whispers. "Shine the light over there," she says, nodding to her left. He does. Nothing's there. "Okay." He turns it off.

Her frozen hand makes it difficult to feel the trigger. She slides the gun into her back waistband and rubs her hand against her jeans to warm it up. Then, she sees it again. That was definitely a flash of light, quick but deliberate, high near the treetops.

"Mom," Sean whispers. He saw it too.

Before she can respond, Sean raises the flashlight and signals: short, short, short. Pause. Short.

Jessie snatches the light from him. "What are you doing?" Her voice is sharp with alarm. Every instinct screams that he's just given away their position.

"I think it's..." he doesn't finish, concentrating on the flashing light in the distance. Two long pulses. Pause. Short, long. Pause. Long, short, short, long.

"Sean no." But he's already pulling out the second flashlight Charlie gave them. Jessie reaches for it, but he steps back, continuing his pattern. Short, long. Pause. Long, short.

There's a response. Long, short, long.

"Stop," Jessie hisses. "You're giving us away. Those guys could be—"

"It's Max," he says, excited but keeping his voice low.

"You don't know that. Anyone could know Morse Code."

"He just spelled his name. And I spelled mine. We always end with 'K', so we know it's really us.

Jessie stares at him. Smart. If Sean was right about Max returning to the place he ran from, he could be right about this. Or he could have just alerted the men to their presence. "Sean, if you're wrong—"

"I'm not wrong, Mom. It's Max."

He's already moving in the direction of the light. Jessie has no choice but to follow. Scanning the shadows for threats, every step feels like walking into an ambush. They move in the direction of the light, but it's been several minutes since they've seen anything.

They're ten feet from the power line pole when a pile of leaves and branches suddenly erupts. Max emerges like a woodland creature, dirt and pine needles in his hair, and launches himself at Jessie. The impact nearly knocks her over, and she's grateful she isn't holding her gun.

"Max." The name comes out as a sob. She wraps her good arm around him, feeling his body tremble against her. "Are you okay? Are you hurt?" She pulls back to study his face in the moonlight.

"I'm fine, Mom. Really."

But she can see the exhaustion in his eyes, the way he keeps glancing over his shoulder. She lifts his hair with gentle fingers, checking for injuries, turning him around to examine his back and arms.

"I heard you calling, but I wasn't sure it was really you until Sean used the code. Then I climbed down from the power line pole and hid."

Jessie hugs him again, and this time he clings to her like she might disappear. She lets him hold on as long as he needs.

"I knew it," Sean says, and Max finally releases their mother to accept his brother's awkward but heartfelt embrace.

"Good job, bro." Max tousles Sean's hair as he releases his hug.

"When did you guys learn Morse Code?" Jessie says.

There's just enough moonlight for Jessie to catch the look between Max and Sean. She knows there's a story there, but she doesn't press the issue. Brothers need to keep some secrets. She hands Max his backpack, and they head back to the truck.

Jessie settles into the driver's seat of the Datsun with both her boys beside her. Max is safe. Sean is safe. Her arm is broken, but it will heal. They're less than a mile from the cabin. That's less than a mile from warmth and being able to power up the laptop and contact Jonathan.

Jessie exhales, and her shoulders relax. Sleepiness tugs at her eyelids, and she blinks hard to stay focused.

"Mom," Max says. "What happens next?"

"We get to the cabin. Contact Jonathan. And get off this mountain."

The Datsun sputters.

Jessie frowns and presses the accelerator. The engine responds reluctantly, then sputters again. She can feel the boys tensing beside her.

"Mom?" Sean's voice is careful.

The truck lurches once more, then dies completely. Jessie tries the ignition. Nothing. She tries again. The starter turns over weakly, but the engine won't catch.

"We're out of gas."

# SIXTY-ONE

MAX'S HANDS and toes are numb, but he hardly notices. He's deep in thought about what happened in the forest. The man. The gun. The crack of the gunshot breaking the silence and chasing him while he ran.

Sean's words break through his thoughts. "I swear I'm never walking again. Ever. In my entire life." With every step, Sean stabs the ground hard with his hockey stick.

"Stop whining. We're almost there," Max snaps.

"How do you know?"

"I can see the top of the next power line pole." Max's tone is full of superiority.

"Good observation, Max," Jessie says.

"Whatever."

"Hey, we're all tired. No need to be snippy."

Max mumbles something under his breath and rolls his eyes freely—it's too dark for Jessie to catch him. They've been butting heads a lot lately, especially during driving practice because she always acts like they're going to die. She also asks him to do chores at the worst possible time, usually when he's in the middle of a breakthrough on a new coding project. He can't wait to leave for college.

"Besides the obvious, what's wrong?" Jessie asks.

"Nothing," Max says, accentuating each syllable.

"Then why the attitude?"

"Because. You did nothing. Absolutely nothing." Max's voice cracks as he gets worked up. "Well, you did something for Sean. As always." He's holding back tears now. "You always do everything for him. You chose to save him over me." The dam breaks. "It's always about him!"

Jessie tells Sean to stop and pulls Max a few feet back. "What are you talking about?"

Max pushes the words out through sobs. "You shot the guy who was going to kill Sean. You didn't even try to save me."

Jessie puts her hand on Max's arm. "Oh, Max. If I could have shot both of them at once, I would have. It had nothing to do with you or Sean. If you two had been in each other's places, I would have made the same choice. It's the only choice I had."

Max hangs his head and digs a rock out of the snow with the tip of his shoe.

She wipes a tear from his cheek. "I could only see part of Charlie's arm from where I was. He was the guy behind you. I had a clear shot of the guy behind Sean. I was one hundred percent positive I could make that shot. If I had tried to shoot Charlie, the best I would have done is wound him and alert them to my presence. I went for the sure thing."

Max kicks at the ground. What she said makes sense, but he still takes it personally. "But he didn't shoot. He didn't even try."

"I know. I was about to..." Jessie pauses. "I saw that he was letting you go. That's the only reason he's not dead, too."

The words hit Max. She was ready to kill Charlie to protect him. The thought makes him feel better for a moment, and then instantly worse. His emotions are playing a vicious game of ping-pong.

Max isn't the kind of person who takes pleasure in other people's pain. Maybe it's because he's watched Sean struggle with things he's never had to think twice about, like trying on new clothes. It's made him appreciate how simple life is for him.

However, he's not giving these teenage years a five-star review.

He thinks about how his dad opens doors for people, lets drivers merge, and even gave away the last roast at the supermarket to a woman cooking her college son's favorite meal. Nick always thinks of others first. Max aspires to be a man just like his dad. The more he reflects on Jessie's words, the more he realizes she was thinking about him and Sean, while he's been focused only on himself.

He tries to put himself in her shoes. If he had to choose between saving his mom or his dad, who would he choose? It's an impossible choice. So impossible that there must be an outside force influencing the decision. In Jessie's case, that influence was tactical—who she had the clearest shot at.

"So, what happened to the other guy? Charlie?" Max asks.

"He said he didn't realize you and Sean were kids. He seems to have gotten mixed up in all this. He's at the cabin now, looking for a power bank for your laptop so we can contact Jonathan."

"Guess it's a good thing you didn't shoot him. Why don't we just charge it at the cabin?" Max wipes his face with his sleeve.

"I'm not sure Charlie's a threat, but I also don't trust him, yet. We need to stay on the move," Jessie says.

Max nods. All the excitement has left him devoid of energy. He really wishes they could stay at the cabin at least until his toes defrost.

They continue walking. Jessie grabs Max's hand and kisses the top of it. Normally, he would object, but he appreciates the gesture. Before she releases his hand, he sees her forearm covered in writing and grabs it. He brings it to his face, trying to read it in the dark.

"What's this?"

"It's a list of the names we heard over the radio," Jessie says.

"We crossed out the ones Mom has killed," Sean says matter-of-factly.

Sometimes, Max envies Sean. He takes things at face value. Sean is like, *Mom kills guys, and we cross them off a list on her arm.* While Max is like, *How is this my life right now?*

He notices Mike's name is the second one crossed out. That makes three people his mom has killed. He doesn't know what to think, and before he can go down that rabbit hole, he welcomes another interruption by Sean.

"And they're all military," Sean adds.

"It's possible they're ex-military. Except for Charlie," Jessie responds.

"Even Charlie," Sean says.

"I guarantee you, Charlie was not in the military."

"No, they are all military Morse Code alphabet names," Sean says.

Jessie brings her arm close to her face, and Max scoots closer —Sean's right: Charlie, Mike, Victor, Papa, Juliet, Romeo, Oscar.

She unclips the walkie-talkie, presses the button for half a second, releases it, waits a full second, and then presses it again. If it's safe to talk, Charlie should respond.

A moment passes. No response. Max isn't sure if that's good news or bad news.

Jessie slows her pace. Max does the same. She tries to signal Charlie again. Radio silence. She tells the boys to stop.

Max decides the silence is bad news.

The walkie-talkie squawks to life. "Hey, I found a toolbox of stuff in Mike's truck. I'm not sure what kind of cord you need, so I grabbed the whole thing. There's lots of stuff in it. You could see if anything else would be helpful."

This guy is definitely not ex-anything. He talks way too much.

Jessie quickens her pace, and Max follows by her side. They catch up to Sean, and she presses the button. "Where are the others?"

"Papa and Oscar are on their way up here. You close? They're gonna be here soon. I don't know exactly when, but the Mercedes has four-wheel drive, so they shouldn't have a problem getting up here. And Oscar drives like a maniac."

Max can practically feel Jessie's frustration as Charlie rambles on. Finally, he signals he's done, and she responds. "Ran out of gas. Walking. I'm ten out."

No response. Even Max knows you should always respond so the person on the other end knows you heard them. This can't be good. Another moment passes. Max can feel the tension radiating from Jessie.

Finally, the walkie-talkie crackles back to life with Charlie's voice, "Okay."

Max and Jessie exhale.

# SIXTY-TWO

THE TEMPERATURE has dropped into the twenties. Jessie's face is frozen. She readjusts Mike's gun deeper into the back of her waistband. Her fingers are numb, and she doubts her ability to pull the trigger if needed. They've been walking for fifteen minutes, despite what her body tells her. Her legs ache, and every step tempts her to stop and huddle with the boys for warmth and rest. No matter how inviting the notion is, she knows they can't stop.

They round a bend, and the cabin's outline appears against the treeline. Next to it, the Range Rover sits, half-hidden in the shadows. Relief washes over Jessie. She turns to Max. "When you ran away from Charlie in the woods, why didn't you head to the cabin?"

Max's breath catches as a cold gust hits them. "I did, but I got a little turned around and ended up behind the tree line on the backside of the cabin. I saw a guy sitting in a truck parked behind the trees, and I went to ask him for help." Max pauses and swallows.

"And?" Jessie prompts.

"The guy had been shot in the head."

Jessie recalls the first time she saw a dead body. "I'm sorry you had to see that." She can't help but wonder if they would have reached the cabin before Mike if they hadn't stopped to pee. Then maybe they would have met up with Jonathan's guy. Or maybe they would be dead along with him.

Max straightens. "Then I thought about where else you might look for me."

"So, you came back to where you had already been," Jessie says.

"My hide and seek strategy," Sean says.

"It worked," Max tells Sean.

"It always does." Sean beams.

Jessie grabs Sean by the arm and tells them to stop. She closes her eyes and listens, trying to determine the direction from which the noise came, but the sound doesn't occur again.

"What's wrong?" Max asks.

She presses her ear against the chill air for a moment longer before letting go of Sean and resuming their walk. "I thought I heard a car."

Max glances into the forest. "I didn't hear anything."

"Me neither," says Sean.

Jessie shakes it off. Exhaustion is probably the culprit, but she still takes precautions. She clicks off the walkie-talkie. "Stay silent until we're inside." She scans the treeline. Twenty yards separate them from the cabin.

Gravel crunches under their steps as Jessie and the boys walk down the path leading to the front porch. She guides the boys up the stairs onto the creaky porch. Using the tip of her Glock, she knocks on the front door.

Nothing.

She knocks again. "It's Jessie," she says in a low voice.

Still nothing.

Jessie realizes she never gave Charlie her name. But it's not like he's expecting another woman to show up. "Charlie?" she says louder.

The door flies open, and Charlie herds them inside without a word. Jessie motions for the boys to remain quiet and stand next to Charlie by the front door. Sean sets his hockey stick on the ground as if it's a bomb about to explode.

Jessie clears the living area, then the bedroom, and the bathroom. They're alone. The smell of bleach mingled with stale vomit lingers in the air. Charlie did a good job cleaning up in such a short time. The only evidence of Mike's death is a faint smear of blood along the baseboard.

Now that she sees Charlie in better lighting, she notices how young he is. How did this kid get mixed up with these guys? She looks at her own kids, their chapped red cheeks and dark circles under their eyes, and makes them drink some water. She tells Max and Sean to sit on the couch.

Charlie shifts his weight from side to side. He's acting more nervous than when Jessie was holding him at gunpoint. "I tried calling them like you said to, but no one answered. I even tried the walkie-talkie and the comm. They could be close. They probably are." Charlie runs his hands through his hair and paces. "You need to hurry. If you're here when they get here, I don't know. Papa seemed really pissed when I told him you killed Victor. I mean, why wouldn't he be? But then he was like, really calm, you know." Charlie stops in front of Jessie, breathing too fast. "None of this was supposed to happen."

"Breathe. In and out." He's going to pass out if he doesn't gain control of himself. Jessie takes a deep breath, and Charlie does the same. "Where's the power bank?"

Charlie leads her to the dining room table, where a blue metal toolbox sits. It matches the tool bag on the kitchen counter, exactly where she left it. She opens the toolbox and peeks inside. It's filled with various outlet adapters, cords, plugs, batteries, wires, and small electronics. She rummages through it and finds a power bank.

Charlie bites his thumbnail and rocks back and forth on his

heels.

"Max, come see if this will work," Jessie says, holding up a power bank.

Charlie passes Max and looks out the front door peephole.

Max takes the power bank from Jessie and peeks into the toolbox. "Whoa. Is this what I think it is?" He pulls a detonator from the bottom.

Jessie grabs it from Max and turns toward Charlie. "Why do you have this?" she asks, holding up the detonator.

"I don't know. What is it?" he whispers quickly. He returns his attention to the peephole and taps his toes, clearly not interested in what she's showing him.

Max picks up a Bluetooth speaker, admires it, and then puts it back. "This should work," he says, taking the power bank with him to the couch.

Jessie places the detonator back in the toolbox and closes it. Finding explosive equipment sends a chill through her that has nothing to do with the cold.

Sean pulls Max's laptop from his backpack and passes it to him.

"I've told you before not to go through my stuff," Max adds.

Sean puts his hands in his lap.

"But you were just helping. Thanks," Max says.

Sean looks Max in the eyes, offering his equivalent of a forgiving smile.

Max plugs the power bank into his laptop and sets it on the end table next to the couch. It will need a few minutes before it has enough battery to power on. As he waits, he notices that the rug by the far wall looks like it has an extension cord running underneath it, and he eyes the lump on the other side. Upon further examination, he realizes it's not a cord; it's thick wire.

He gets up and follows the wire running along the baseboard into the bathroom.

Jessie hears a creak and looks back at the couch. Max is gone.

She glances around and sees him emerging from the bathroom. Another creak fills the silent cabin, and this time she knows it's not from any of them.

"I think—" Max's words are cut short by Jessie's hand, still holding her gun.

# SIXTY-THREE

Jessie releases her hand from Max's mouth and shoves her Glock in her sling. He stares wide-eyed, surveying the room as she snaps her fingers at Sean and presses a finger to her lips. He nods in understanding.

Sean remains still while his eyes dart around, searching for the threat. The old wooden floors groan with the slightest movement.

Jessie draws her gun as she walks over to Sean and nods for Max to follow. He tugs at her sleeve and points to the bathroom. She disregards him and nods toward Sean again. Max needs to move over to the couch.

She signals for the boys to lie on the ground, and they comply. Jessie positions herself in the middle of the room, uncertain about where the threat will arise. Currently, she is outnumbered two to one and not operating at full capacity. She needs to even the odds.

Jessie puts her gun in her sling and hastily unzips the front pocket of Max's backpack, pausing when she hears another creak. The sound comes from above, footsteps on the roof, or the aging structure settling under snow. She can't be sure, but her instincts sense a threat. She hands Charlie his gun and magazine and waits for him to chamber a round. He doesn't. He's probably never fired that thing.

She places her Glock in her waistband, next to Mike's gun, and grabs Charlie's magazine, wedging it between her knees. Charlie hands her his gun, and she marries the magazine to the grip. She slides the gun halfway down before releasing the magazine from her knees and tilting the gun so the magazine doesn't fall. With lightning speed, she jams the magazine base into her thigh to seat it, then chambers a round by pushing the slide against her waistband in one swift motion. She hands the gun to Charlie.

His hands shake as he takes it, sweat beading on his forehead despite the cabin's chill. His grip is weak and unsure.

Max and Sean look at each other in disbelief. They didn't see her kill Black Beard, but they heard a single gunshot and made that assumption. Max doesn't know how Mike died, but he guesses she shot him, too. Victor died from a bullet wound to his eye.

Until now, Max had leaned towards the idea that Jessie might have stolen a couple of cars in her youth. That would explain the evasive driving and hot wiring. Max believed that everything she had done that day was a result of hanging around with the wrong crowd. Now, he isn't so sure.

He thinks back to their earlier conversation about her decision to shoot Victor instead of Charlie. She said it was calculated. And she killed him in one shot. Black Beard in one shot. Probably Mike, too.

Three shots, three kills.

Max realizes his mother hasn't been getting lucky—she's been trained for this. Most people would panic and empty their gun. His mom calculates, plans, and executes. She hasn't panicked once, not even when she stole a baby.

Sean glances at his waistband, grateful Jessie's wearing jeans instead of her usual yoga pants. She wouldn't have been able to do that cool gun trick if she were in yoga pants. He's never seen that done before. Maybe Grandpa taught her how to do that, like he taught Max and him Morse Code. He also showed them how to shoot a rifle and a handgun that day. Max also got to try the shotgun, but Grandpa said Sean wasn't quite big enough yet. Maybe next year, which was supposed to be last year. Grandpa told them not to tell Jessie about their shooting adventures because she might disapprove.

Sean thinks he's definitely ready for the shotgun this year, and maybe Jessie can teach him that cool gun trick. If Grandpa hadn't shown her, maybe it's just something moms know, because his mom knows how to do everything. Once, Sean asked how she knew how to take care of Max when he was a baby, even though she had never had a baby before, and she told him it was because of her mother's instinct.

That's probably why she knew how to do that with the gun. Charlie didn't know what to do. He's not a mother.

Jessie scans the back door, then the front. The wind picks up, rattling the windows and masking any sounds that might give away the presence of anyone outside. She strains to listen beyond the natural noise, her training forcing her to identify every potential threat before making a move.

She trains her gun on the front door, listening for sounds from outside. Nothing. She gets the boys' attention with a "psst". Keeping the gun muzzle down, she gestures to them, then to herself, then to the front door. They're leaving through the front. She gestures for Charlie to exit out the back.

They all nod.

The boys stand up and fall in line behind Jessie. Charlie heads toward the back door. She rests her gun in the sling and reaches for the door handle when wood explodes behind them. She spins around, almost knocking Sean to the ground. The back door flies off

its hinges, missing Charlie by inches, as splinters shower the room.
Oscar fills the doorway, gun trained on them.

# SIXTY-FOUR

JESSIE WATCHES as Oscar steps through the doorway.

She turns back to the front door and opens it to find Papa pointing a gun at her. Her instinct is to grab her gun and shoot him, but she knows Oscar has a clear shot at both boys standing behind her. Jessie's jaw tightens as she calculates distances and angles, factoring in her broken arm, searching for any opening that won't cost the boys their lives. Her eyes never leave Papa's face as she raises her uninjured arm in defeat.

--- ••- - •-• ••- --•

Charlie sits at the dining room table with Oscar's gun pointed at him. He glances over at Jessie and the boys sitting on the couch under Papa's threat and feels the familiar weight of responsibility crushing down on him.

This is his fault. Papa wouldn't have known about the white Explorer if Charlie hadn't mentioned it. He also told Papa she might have crashed in the desert and might be on foot. If he had kept his mouth shut, none of them would be here right now. And Victor and

Mike would be alive.

He should have told her to run the moment he opened the door.

Why didn't he? The answer sits heavy in his chest. Because he's a coward, he always has been.

Charlie's mind drifts despite the gun aimed at him. He thinks of his older brother, who tried to intervene on Charlie's behalf even when it made his life worse. By the time his brother took him away from their home, Charlie had convinced himself their mother deserved everything that happened to her.

But watching Jessie now—seeing the desperation in her eyes—he finally understands.

His mother hadn't chosen those men. She'd been trapped by them, weighed down by daily struggles that felt impossible to escape. Starting over with two kids required courage and a safety net that didn't exist.

Charlie remembers the shouting, the slamming doors, the look in his mother's eyes when she thought he wasn't looking. As a kid, he didn't understand the look. Now he sees something similar in Jessie, but different. His mother's despair came from defeat. Jessie's desperation burns with rage.

Looking back, Charlie recognizes the toll those moments took on his mother and how they aged her spirit. He finally comprehends that she would never abandon him and his brother to save herself from her abusers. She was a woman always on the verge of crumbling under the crushing weight of fear and hopelessness. Charlie feels a deep sense of empathy for her choices, understanding that her love for her children was her anchor in the face of unbearable circumstances.

A memory surfaces. One that has been buried under years of self-protection.

He was four or five. For years, he remembered it as a game of hide and seek, running to find a hiding spot while his brother was already hiding somewhere. But now the pieces rearrange themselves into the truth.

His brother hadn't been hiding. He had run to the neighbor's for help.

His mother didn't trip on the rug. She threw herself in front of Charlie to take the blow meant for him. And Charlie wasn't playing. He was running because his mother screamed at him to run and hide. They never saw that boyfriend again.

And they didn't see their mother until she was released from the hospital two weeks later. The realization rewrites everything he thought he knew. She had saved him.

By middle school, Charlie spent more time on the streets than at home. His brother worked while in high school and saved every penny he earned. Charlie never saw him with anything new. When their mom's boyfriend, at that time, tried to take that money, Charlie's brother fought back and broke the man's nose. The boyfriend backed down, but he never left.

When his brother finally saved enough money for their own place, Charlie protested. They couldn't abandon their mother.

"We can't save her," his brother had said. "But I can save you." They left that night. Charlie hasn't seen his mother since. The guilt of that night gnaws at him. He can still picture his mother's face in the window as they drove away—not angry or hurt, but relieved. She had mouthed 'I love you' through the glass, and Charlie had turned away. He'd spent years telling himself that she was weak, that she chose those men over her children. But the truth was simpler and more painful: she had chosen to endure hell so her sons could escape it.

Oscar shifts his weight, bringing Charlie back to the present. His own gun is tucked into Oscar's waistband—another reminder of the power imbalance that has defined his entire life.

But now, Charlie understands something he'd missed before. His hands tremble slightly as he realizes the pattern he's been living —the same cycle of fear and submission that trapped his mother. But unlike her, he doesn't have children depending on him for their survival. He has a choice she never had. The recognition fills him with something he hasn't felt in years: clarity. The mental hold those men had on his mother was stronger than any physical restraint. Just like Papa's hold on him.

Until this moment.

He looks at Jessie and the boys sitting on the couch. He couldn't save his mother, but maybe he can save the one sitting there now.

Time to tip the scales.

# SIXTY-FIVE

JULIET GENTLY knocks as she opens the door to Romeo's office. Her voice has a blend of concern and irritation. "It keeps going to voicemail. Do you want me to keep trying?"

Romeo looks up from the family photo in his hands, the silver frame catching the light from his desk lamp. Behind him, city lights flicker through the floor-to-ceiling windows. "No. I'll call from my line."

His tone is sharp enough that Juliet simply nods and quietly closes the door as she backs out.

Once alone, Romeo sets the photo face down on the mahogany surface and retrieves a cell phone from his desk drawer. He dials with urgency, his free hand drumming against the leather chair arm.

"I haven't heard from you."

"I've been a little busy," comes the voice on the other end. "She killed Mike."

Romeo's drumming stops. He stands and moves to the

window, staring down at the traffic below. "Do you have her?"

"Yes. And her two kids."

The words hit Romeo unexpectedly. He turns from the window, his reflection ghosting across the glass. His jaw tightens as he processes the complication and its benefits.

"Don't kill her," he says, his voice controlled and deadly quiet. "I want to question her myself." A pause. Romeo's eyes drift back to the overturned photo on his desk.

"If she won't come willingly, use the kids."

# SIXTY-SIX

JESSIE HEARS only the tail end of Oscar's conversation: "Not a problem." Oscar glares at her as he pockets his phone and returns to Charlie, gun trained on him. Jessie glances down at the names on her forearm. Besides Mike and Victor, everyone else on the list is in this cabin except for Romeo and Juliet, who, Charlie said, are in another state. One of them must have been the caller. *But why call Oscar instead of Papa?*

Something catches her eye, and she steals a glance down. The butt of her gun protrudes from her sling by half an inch. Moving at a snail's pace, she slides her left arm across her torso, tucking her fingers under her right arm to cover the opening.

She should make her move now, but Papa appears in front of her before she can act. He leans close until she can feel his rapid, adrenaline-fueled breathing on her face. During her time at the academy, Jessie learned to control her breathing and heart rate. Papa's intimidation tactics don't faze her. His hot breath hits her forehead as he reaches around her and grabs Mike's gun from her back waistband. *He's right-handed.* She uses the opportunity to shove her gun further into her sling, wincing at the pain.

Papa releases the magazine from Mike's gun, catching it in his left hand. With deliberate theatricality, he slides each bullet out with his thumb, letting them fall to the floor one by one.

Jessie refuses to react, maintaining her gaze straight ahead as she listens to their chances of survival diminish with each metallic clink.

When the magazine is empty, Papa tosses both it and the gun aside while pulling his gun from his waistband. He looks Sean up and down, then Max. "You know, I used to have two sons. Yours, they don't really look alike." His voice takes on a conversational tone that's somehow more unsettling than his rage. "My boys, they looked alike. People thought they were twins as teenagers. That's how much they resembled each other."

Papa turns his attention to Jessie. "Stand up."

She complies.

He gestures at Sean and Max with his gun. "You too."

Max looks at Jessie. She gives him the slightest nod. He grabs Sean's elbow, helping lift his rigid body as they both stand.

Papa traces the gun's barrel around Jessie's face. The cold metal burns against her flushed skin. When he locks eyes with her, she refuses to look away. "They had their mother's eyes. Charlie tells me you shot my boy in his eye. In his mother's eye."

Jessie closes her right eye as he presses his gun against it. The pressure makes both eyes water and sends throbbing pain through her skull.

If her children weren't here, she would have never let the situation reach this point. She would have never surrendered, never let him intimidate her like this. With Max and Sean present, she won't take the same risks she did as an agent. When she worked for The Agency, a ninety-five percent success rate was not just acceptable—it was commendable. Now, anything less than absolute certainty is unacceptable. She won't make a move based on a ninety-five percent chance of success.

She's not that desperate. Not yet.

Tears cascade down Sean's cheeks. Papa moves his gun away from Jessie and turns toward Sean. Every maternal instinct screams at her to attack, but any sudden movement might cause an accidental discharge. Or an intentional one. She forces herself to think past the roar of protective fury in her heart.

Papa swipes his thumb across Sean's cheek, wiping away his tears.

Jessie clenches her jaw. *I'm going to rip you apart.*

"Don't worry. This will all be over soon," Papa tells Sean.

Sean begins to shake. Max squeezes his hand and looks past his brother at their mother. Her knuckles are white from gripping her pant leg, her teeth clenched, nostrils flared, cheeks flushed. Max has never seen her look so intense. It scares him, but she has to have a plan. She always has a plan. And backup plans.

Unlike his mother, Max figures things out as he goes—one reason for their recent arguments. Jessie expects him to plan for everything, and he never saw the point until now. Her preparedness has gotten them this far. She had a gun in the car that he didn't even know about, plus a backpack with a flashlight, food, water, a first aid kit, and who knows what else. He doesn't know what her plan is, but he'll be ready to act when the moment comes.

He hopes he recognizes it.

Papa steps in front of Jessie. "You killed my son. Shot him in the eye."

Jessie doesn't respond.

Papa's voice drops to a whisper, his fingers finding the gold crucifix around his neck. "An eye for an eye."

She glances at the gold cross. "You might want to read the New Testament sometime."

The words stop Papa cold. Something snaps behind his eyes, and laughter erupts from deep in his chest—wild, unhinged laughter that makes even Oscar shift uncomfortably. "Oh, you're

"That's not what Romeo wants," Oscar says.

Papa freezes. As he turns toward Oscar, he loses his focus and lowers his gun to Jessie's torso.

It's the perfect opportunity to go for his gun, but the boys are too close.

"And how exactly would you know what Romeo wants?" Papa asks, taking steps toward Oscar.

Oscar clenches his jaw and raises his head slightly without responding.

Understanding dawns on Papa's face. "You're the reason he knows things went south."

"You didn't think he would let you do a job without eyes on the inside, did you?" Oscar says, as if talking to a child.

Papa takes another step toward Oscar. "Romeo's not here, is he?"

Oscar raises his gun, pointing it directly at Papa. "No, he's not."

The cabin falls silent except for Sean's quiet breathing and the distant sound of wind through the trees. Jessie feels the shift in power and sees her moment approaching.

# SIXTY-SEVEN

PAPA AND Oscar face each other across the small cabin, guns raised, the air crackling with tension. They size each other up, neither willing to back down. Oscar has youth and size, Papa has nothing to lose, and an untamable need for revenge. It's only a matter of seconds before one of them loses control.

Oscar breaks the silence. "We can't kill her. Romeo wants to question her. We have to bring her in alive."

"I don't have to do anything!" Papa jabs his gun into the air at Oscar. "She killed my boy!"

Jessie makes eye contact with Charlie. Sweat beads on his forehead, and his leg bounces nervously. She gives a slight nod toward the table. He glances at the blue toolbox in front of him and looks back at Jessie. She gives an almost undetectable affirmative nod.

"Then take it out on her son instead," Oscar says, calculated and cold. "An eye for an eye. Isn't that what you want? But Romeo still needs her alive and talking."

Jessie's heart stops. "No!" She steps back to close the gap between her and the boys.

"You even have two to pick from. Hell, threaten them both if you want. Just don't shoot them in here," Oscar says, as his eyes dart around the room. He's desperate to keep her alive, but not as desperate as she is to keep Sean and Max alive. His willingness to sacrifice her children as leverage chills her to the bone. Especially since she doesn't know anything about a download and has no information to give them.

Jessie stares intensely at Charlie, hoping he can feel the weight of her gaze. He does and turns toward her. She eyes the metal toolbox again. Charlie follows with his eyes. She shifts her gaze to the ground, then to the toolbox, then back to the ground. *Knock it over.*

Papa swings his gun toward Jessie. "Pick."

The words don't register. "What?"

"Pick one." He jerks his head toward Max and Sean. "Choose which one dies."

Jessie stares blankly, unable to process what he's demanding. Her mind rejects the concept entirely, as if refusing to understand might make it untrue.

"You have three seconds to decide, or I kill them both."

For Jessie, the next few seconds stretch and collapse like taffy. Sound becomes muffled, as if she's underwater. The words take forever to reach her ears, yet they also slam into her all at once. The last time she experienced this warping of reality was when her family's station wagon was crushed by a green car with that distinctive silver hood ornament. Both of her parents died in that twisted metal. And now she might lose both of her sons.

Her vision tunnels. Her hands begin to tremble. Each heartbeat thunders in her ears.

Jessie hears Papa's voice as if from a great distance, traveling through her fractured world. "Two..."

*Two? What happened to one? Or three?* She's unsure if he was counting up or down. It's irrelevant. Either way, she has one second left with both her boys. Time distorts around her, each moment stretching into eternity while simultaneously rushing past.

The sharp crack of splintering wood cuts through her mental fog like a blade.

Papa and Oscar spin toward the source of the crash.

327

# SIXTY-EIGHT

THE FORCE of the impact pops open the toolbox lid, scattering its contents across the floor. Charlie sees a sea of cords strewn between the dining room table and the kitchen. He's pretty sure Jessie wanted him to do that, but he's uncertain about what he's supposed to do next. He's never been good at making plans. Whenever he's hung out with friends, he usually waits until one of them makes the plans and then goes along with it. His brother is a leader. He makes plans. He devised the plan to get a job, save money, and get Charlie away from their mother's toxic environment.

Charlie sees a blur of movement behind Jessie; it's Max.

Max jumps when the toolbox crashes to the ground. The Bluetooth speaker, two batteries, and a small rectangular object slide across the floor toward the back door. The rest of the cords and plugs lie in a tangled pile between the dining room table and the kitchen area. He sees everyone except Jessie looking at what made the sound. He scoops up his laptop and power bank from the end table and grabs

Sean's arm.

Sean lets out a small yelp when the tools crash to the floor. He hopes nobody heard him. His voice remains high-pitched and squeaky, even though many of his friends' voices are changing. He's still trying to figure out what the guy said about killing Jessie's son. Was he talking about killing him or Max? Apparently, the guy she shot in the eye was this guy's son, and he is really pissed off about it. But his son was going to kill Sean, so his mom had no choice. Sean thinks he's got it figured out when he feels a vice grip on his arm. He turns to see Max grabbing hold.

Jessie leaps onto Papa. They both hit the ground. His gun slides underneath the couch.

Charlie sees what she's doing and follows her lead, pouncing on Oscar and bringing him down in front of the dining room table.

As soon as Max spots Charlie and Oscar on the ground, he yanks Sean off the couch, but Papa and Jessie are blocking their only path.

Papa heaves his body toward the ceiling, throwing Jessie off of him. She rolls across the cramped living space and smacks her head on the leg of the cast-iron fireplace. Her gun falls from her sling upon impact and slides under the fireplace. Papa advances in pursuit.

Max pulls Sean by the arm and runs for the back door.

Jessie feels dazed and slow to move. She sees a blurry Charlie on top of a blurry Oscar. A pair of legs runs past her toward the back of the cabin, followed by another pair. She blinks hard, and her vision begins to clear.

Charlie and Oscar wrestle on the floor for Oscar's gun. Charlie bites

Oscar's arm and grabs the gun, but Oscar punches him in the chest, sending him flat on his back. Oscar stands, gun in hand, and turns to the boys running behind him.

As Max and Sean run toward the door, Max sees the rectangular object that fell out of the toolbox lying near the door. He recognizes it and snatches it up as they exit.

Charlie yells with all his might and tackles Oscar from behind. They crash into the kitchen just as the gun fires.

For a moment, Charlie thinks a second shot was fired, but then realizes it was the sound of Oscar's head hitting the tile countertop.

Jessie hears a gunshot, then the sound of a body hitting the floor. Or maybe it was the other way around.

Papa charges at Jessie. She rolls to her left, narrowly avoiding an incoming kick from Papa. She jumps to her feet, scrambles to the front door, and swings it open. A sharp kick to her back sends her tumbling down the front porch steps. Papa follows.

Charlie scrambles away from Oscar. Blood oozes from Oscar's head, but he's still moving. Charlie scans the room. He doesn't see Papa. Or Jessie. Or the boys. Through the open front door, he spots Papa pursuing Jessie at the bottom of the porch. He looks out the back door and sees only darkness. He checks the front again and fights his instinct to help Jessie as Papa closes in on her. Charlie darts out the back door in search of Max and Sean—that's what their mother would want.

Oscar winces at the sharp, searing pain in the back of his head. The warm blood trails down the back of his neck and into his shirt collar. He's been hit in the head enough times to know he'll be fine. A moderate concussion and deep laceration won't slow him down. He'll have a massive headache for a while and will probably throw up in the next twenty to thirty minutes. Stitches wouldn't be a bad idea. Surveying the room, he stands, dazed, realizing he's alone in the cabin.

For a split second, Oscar feels proud of Charlie. He really didn't think he had it in him to do something so bold. Maybe he would've made it in this business after all. It's too bad he has to kill him now. Oscar picks up his gun and steps through the back door into the cold, dark night.

# SIXTY-NINE

JESSIE TUMBLES down the porch steps head over heels onto the walkway. Gravel cuts into the flesh on her cheek as she skids to a stop. The sharp stones bite into her skin, and she tastes blood mixed with dirt.

Her feet flail beneath her as she tries to regain her footing on the loose gravel. It sounds like someone attempting to start a stalled engine as small rocks fly into the air.

The cold night air burns her lungs as she gasps for breath. She thinks the boys ran out the back door. Regardless, she's going to draw Papa as far from the cabin as possible. Max and Sean need time—time to get away, time to hide, time to survive. She scrambles to her feet and manages only one step before her head snaps back.

Papa yanks hard on her hair. The pain shoots across her scalp like fire. Jessie twists around to break his grasp, ripping hair from her scalp in the process. A clump comes away in his fist. She tightens her abs, preparing for the punch from his right. She's fought enough men to know their patterns, and she's learned Papa's a right-handed brawler, heavy on his feet.

Papa does exactly as she expected, and she immediately delivers a kick to his left side. Her Nike connects with his ribs, and she feels the satisfying give of flesh and bone. He doesn't anticipate this and stumbles backwards, his breath coming out in a sharp grunt.

Jessie turns to run. Her legs are swept out from under her, and she lands hard on her knees, catching herself before her face hits the gravel. Pain sears up and down her broken arm, white-hot agony that makes her vision blur. The makeshift sling has come loose, and her arm lies useless at her side. She spins as if being unrolled like a rug.

The distance she has created gives her enough time to stand. In the background, the cabin's porch light casts long shadows across the gravel walkway, but beyond the cabin lies only darkness. The woods are maybe thirty yards away, too far to reach before he catches her again. She has resigned herself to the fact that she cannot outrun him. Running would waste energy—energy she does not have.

Papa circles her slowly, like a predator sizing up wounded prey. His breathing is controlled, methodical. This isn't rage anymore, this is business. He's done this before, probably many times. A cold dread settles in her chest.

It's time to fight.

# SEVENTY

A HUNDRED yards into the woods, Max calls to Sean. "You know where to go?"

"Yeah." Sean has the intense stare he gets when he becomes hyper-focused.

Max slows to a brisk walk, shoving his laptop and power bank into his backpack while grabbing his flashlight. He runs to catch up with Sean and tells him to take out his flashlight. Looking over his shoulder, Max sees that Charlie is not far behind. For a moment, he questions whether Charlie is running after them or coming toward them. A moment later, his doubt is erased.

"Don't stop!" Charlie yells as he closes the gap.

Max increases his speed, and Sean matches him.

"Get ready!" Max tells Sean. He knows it's a dangerous plan, but at this point, he feels like they've been surviving on miracles as it is, and this is the only shot they have. He glances behind them; Charlie's ten feet away. And Oscar is closing in. Max looks over at Sean and has second thoughts. If anything happens to Sean, he'll never forgive himself. He can't think about what it would do to their mom. No other plan is coming to mind. He prays this will work.

"Go!" Max says.

On Max's command, Sean accelerates and veers to the right. Max diverges to the left. Charlie hesitates briefly, then follows Sean. Oscar does the same. So far, so good. Max knew that he and Sean shouldn't stay together. He had already seen Papa pit their lives against each other with Jessie. He didn't want either him or Sean to end up in the same situation. Especially Sean.

One thing Max admires about Sean is his sheer determination. That boy does not know the meaning of quit. He is driven by an obsessive compulsion to finish things. When they were little, Nick used to take them to a parking lot near the airport to watch the incoming planes land. On their initial trip, Sean had a meltdown when they tried to leave before every single plane in the sky had touched down on the tarmac. Given how busy the Las Vegas airport is, Nick was stuck there for twenty minutes longer than he had planned, and they were late for dinner.

From that day on, they could only stay for twenty plane landings. As soon as the twentieth plane hit the tarmac, without a word, Sean would jump off the tailgate and get in the truck to go home. Usually, Sean's need to finish things is annoying, but right now, Max thanks God wholeheartedly for giving him a special brother.

People underestimate Sean's physical abilities based on his stature, but Max learned years ago that Sean is much stronger and faster than he appears. His mind instructs his body to accomplish things it shouldn't be able to. That darn stubborn mind of his, right now, Max loves it.

Their plan is to force Oscar to pick one kid to run after. Max bet Oscar would assume Sean was the easier of the two boys to catch, given his age and size. He was right. Oscar picked the wrong kid because what Oscar doesn't know is that Sean is at the ice rink five to seven times a week. His endurance is insane. And he's wicked fast.

What he lacks in size, he compensates for in speed. He has to; otherwise, he wouldn't survive playing hockey. And he doesn't just survive. He excels at it. Max is four years older than Sean and knows he can't outrun Sean. He's tried.

Max looks to his right, and in the distance, he sees Sean's light grow smaller and dimmer. Good. He shines the light, searching for Charlie, and sees him trip over a fallen branch and stumble to the ground. He slows his pace and continues watching as Charlie struggles to get up and hobbles in the direction Sean was heading. Max can no longer see Sean's light and hesitates before making a wide berth and U-turning.

He turns off his light and moves carefully through the darkness, running past where he thinks he saw Charlie. The darkness plays tricks on his eyes, causing him to mistake a few trees for a person. After his eyes adjust, he takes cover behind a tree, drops his backpack, and scans the area for Charlie. He's a few yards ahead, limping. Charlie turns his head in every direction, clearly lost. Max is about to run over and help Charlie when he hears Oscar's voice cutting through the dark.

"You always were lost."

Charlie turns around. Oscar is pointing a gun at him. Max moves closer behind his tree as Oscar approaches Charlie.

"And you were always looking out for no one but yourself," Charlie replies. "When did you flip on Papa? From the very start? Traitor."

Oscar laughs. "Traitor? You're lecturing me on loyalty?" He walks toward Charlie. "You actively helped our hostages escape."

"Hostages? They're kids!"

"Not my problem," says Oscar.

"You're a monster."

"So, I've been told. I saw an opportunity with Romeo, and I took it." Oscar stands a foot away from Charlie, gun aimed at his head.

Charlie sees a glint rising above Oscar's back. "Don't think about it. Just do it."

Max drives the hunting knife toward Oscar's back as he leaps onto him. Oscar lurches forward, but remains upright, the blade catching more shoulder than spine.

The gun goes off.

Charlie falls back, his thigh erupting in fire.

Oscar knocks the knife from Max's hand and loses his gun during the scuffle. Charlie sits up, clutching his thigh, watching his blood pulse between his fingers with each heartbeat. The warmth spreads down his leg, soaking through his jeans.

Oscar twists wildly.

Max lands hard, knocking the wind out of him.

Oscar grabs the knife and lunges at Max.

Another gunshot echoes through the trees.

Oscar's shoulders round as his torso thrusts forward. Blood permeates the front of his shirt, forming a circle around his heart that expands with each passing second. His eyes grow dark and vacant as he drops to the ground.

Behind Oscar, Charlie lies with the smoking gun, the recoil having knocked him backward from his seated position. His face is pale, his breathing shallow.

Max rushes over, grabs Charlie's arm, and tries to lift him to his feet. "Come on, let's go."

Charlie doesn't resist, but he also can't help. Max scoots under Charlie's arm and attempts to stand. "We have to go."

The excruciating pain Charlie felt moments ago is masked by adrenaline and shock. He releases his arm from Max's neck and sits, propping himself up with one hand while gripping his thigh with the other. "Max, go. You need to find your brother."

"No, I'm not leaving you here," Max says, his voice breaking. "I know where Sean is. He's safe. We have a plan."

Charlie's pulse races, fighting against the rapid loss of blood gushing over his fingers. He's lightheaded, tired, and doesn't have enough time left to argue with a defiant teenager. In one swift motion, he grabs Max's shirt and pulls him close. "Good. You need to go finish your plan. Then you can come back for me." It takes all of Charlie's energy to stay upright.

"I'm not leaving you. Now get up," Max says, wiping away tears. He tries to stand with Charlie, but Charlie pulls him back down.

Charlie looks Max in the eye. "Go. Sean needs you. You're his big brother; he'll always need you."

Max nods, understanding finally settling in his eyes. Charlie releases him.

Max retrieves his backpack, promises Charlie he will return for him, and then runs back toward the cabin.

Charlie watches Max disappear through the trees before falling back onto the cold, damp ground. The white specks above wink at him in a pattern, as if trying to tell him something. He has never appreciated their beauty until now, and he finds the contrast between the bright stars and their black background striking. As he ponders the Morse code sent by the twinkling lights, he is reminded of his fifth-grade science teacher. Mr. Campbell had stunned the class when he told them that light and darkness weren't opposing entities.

He explained that light can be created, but darkness cannot; it only exists in the absence of light. If only Charlie's light hadn't been dimmed so early in life, perhaps things would have turned out differently.

He looks to the stars and wonders if his light shone bright enough in the end to make a difference. They wink back and remind him that it's because of him that Max has a chance to do something Charlie never could: save his mother. A tear escapes and runs down his cheek as the twinkling stars blur and fade to black.

# SEVENTY-ONE

PAPA AND Jessie stand locked in a deadly stare, each knowing only one of them will walk away. Their motivations fuel the same fire; both fight for their children. He wants to avenge. She wants to protect. Papa has forgotten all about the flash drive and Romeo. Romeo can kill him later. What does he care? He has nothing left in this life. Death is welcome after he gets his revenge. Death will reunite him with his family.

Papa stares at Jessie, seeing not a mother protecting her children, but a woman who murdered his last remaining son. Nothing matters anymore. Only revenge. Only making her feel the same devastating loss that has already hollowed him out twice.

His recent jobs had lived in the moral gray areas, but this, this was black and white justice. Most of his business has had questionable legality, but he decided to let the lawyers handle those types of questions. Sometimes people get injured, but that hasn't always been the case. Over the years, Papa has become more tolerant of the violence, learning to justify it. He's balanced it out with good works. He tried to channel his grief into preventing others' tragedies through speaking engagements, but reliving that night only made the pain sharper. As his jobs became more dangerous and paid more money, he donated substantial amounts to organizations where he once volunteered. He believes that when weighed on the scales of justice, the life he led with his family and his charitable efforts will outweigh his recent endeavors.

But standing here, face to face with Victor's killer, those justifications crumble. She took his last child. His baby boy.

Papa's eyes bore into Jessie. He's desperate to share his misery with her. Her stare unnerves him, and he reminds himself of what she is: a murderer. He advances toward Jessie and breaks the silence. "Oscar will catch your boys. And when he does, you will watch them beg for their lives. That will be the last thing you see in this life."

He lunges at her.

▬▬▬ •• ▬ •▬• •• ▬•

The world slows as Jessie sees him coming. Her training takes over, and she turns and ducks. As he sails over her, she pushes off with her legs, launching him into the air.

He regains his footing and charges at her, wrapping his arms around her hips and bringing her to the ground. The gravel feels like a million tiny jabs into her back.

Jessie kicks her legs.

Papa loses his grip.

She shimmies farther from his grasp and thrusts her knee into his chin.

His head snaps back, and he rolls to Jessie's side.

She sits up.

Still lying on his side, Papa swings his leg into her ribs.

They both scramble to their feet and take a breath. The moment is over.

Papa swings with his right hand—predictable.

Jessie twists and blocks the punch, but her broken arm

screams in protest, as it dangles at her side.

He pivots, targeting her weakness, his boot connecting with her broken arm. She feels the broken bones shift against each other.

Pain explodes through her arm as she screams, bending forward. Through the agony, one thought cuts clear. *Max and Sean need me to survive this.*

He drives his knee into her face.

Jessie hears the cartilage in her nose give way. The warm, sticky blood flows into her mouth.

Papa follows up with an uppercut to her jaw.

The crack of her teeth echoes in her head, followed by a ringing in her ears.

A hook to her right eye.

It feels as though her eye has been ejected from its socket. Swelling and tears blur Jessie's vision. She swings violently but misses her target, throwing herself off balance. She has lost focus on strategy and fights out of desperation and survival.

Papa lands a punch to her ribs.

Then another.

Jessie feels the searing pain with every snap of her ribcage. Her ribs and nose make it impossible to breathe, forcing her to take short, shallow breaths. Her right eye has swollen to a useless sliver, and her left eye isn't much better. Blood drips down her puffed-up face and into her mouth, where she can taste the wet pennies. Jessie fights to remain standing, swaying as if she's had too much to drink.

For a moment, the assault ceases. Papa turns away from her and gazes at the front of the cabin.

Beyond the ringing in her ears, Jessie hears something. She tries to focus on the sound. Something about it is familiar. The ringing subsides enough for her to recognize the voice coming from inside the cabin.

"Mom!"

# SEVENTY-TWO

Jessie must be hallucinating. She thought she saw the boys escape through the back door, but maybe Oscar stopped them.

"Mom! Help!" It's definitely Max's voice. "It's Sean. He needs you!"

"Max." Jessie tries to scream but can't find enough breath to fill her lungs.

A kick to the gut sends Jessie onto her back. "Stay here."

Jessie rolls onto her side and watches a blurry version of Papa walk across the gravel. Every breath feels like drowning, filling her chest with more pain than oxygen. Papa's footsteps fade toward the cabin, and silence settles over her like a shroud. Jessie lies motionless in the gravel, tasting blood and dirt. Her blinks become longer, until they stop altogether.

She gave up her entire life for this one, and this is how it ends —broken and alone. She gave up everything she was to become a mother. The decision that changed everything...

Ms. Johnson was in her office reading a book. The décor was

exactly as one would expect: elegant and sophisticated, perfectly representing Ms. Johnson. A light knock on the doorframe caught her attention. Jessie stood in the doorway. Ms. Johnson removed her glasses and invited Jessie to take a seat, as if she had been expecting her.

"Sorry to bother you." Jessie's voice trembled as she sat down on the couch.

"Not at all." She held up the book. "I've already read it. Twice." Ms. Johnson eyed Jessie's knee as it bounced up and down. Last week during the Prague debriefing, Jessie admitted to shooting the unarmed man and never wavered in her account of the events; however, Ms. Johnson had been in the business long enough to know that Jessie was keeping something back. Jessie's disciplinary hearing was in two days, and she undoubtedly sought Ms. Johnson's advice on the matter.

"I'm pregnant," Jessie blurted out. She still had the habit of mouth vomit in front of Ms. Johnson.

"Oh." Ms. Johnson took a seat next to Jessie. Clearly, this was not the conversation she was expecting. "And are congratulations in order?"

Jessie shrugged and was silent for a moment. "I don't know. Maybe."

"And the father…"

"Isn't here."

"Ah. I see." Ms. Johnson sighed. "What can I do for you, Alex?"

Jessie began to tear up. "I don't know what to do."

"It is a big decision."

"Do you have kids?" Jessie asked. She had never considered the possibility of Ms. Johnson having children until that moment. For some reason, she had simply assumed that she didn't. It's like when kids see their teacher at the movie theater or grocery shopping with their family. It's a shock to realize that their teacher is more than just their teacher. Jessie never envisioned Ms. Johnson as anything other than... Ms. Johnson, Dr. Smith's partner in their training.

"No, I don't." There was no hint of regret or disappointment in Ms. Johnson's voice. There was also no sign of any other emotion connected to the statement. It was merely a response to a question.

"Did you want them?" It came out before Jessie could stop herself.

"Yes. At one point, I did."

Jessie hesitated to ask her next question. "Why didn't you? Are you even married? I mean, not that you have to be married. Or even in a relationship. We're in the new millennium, women should be able to—"

Ms. Johnson touched Jessie's knee to stop the train wreck. "I loved the thought of having kids." She took a moment. "But I loved the job more." She gestured around the room. "I wasn't always in an office. I, too, was once trotting the globe, rappelling out of helicopters in the middle of the night. It's kind of hard to find a nanny who keeps those hours."

The agents were relatively safe, but sometimes their identities became known, and they had to relocate. Keeping one person safe is much easier than protecting an entire family.

Ms. Johnson leaned in toward Jessie. "You are only the third person alive to know what I'm about to tell you." Jessie wasn't sure if she was joking or serious. "Ms. Johnson is my maiden name. I'm actually Mrs. Smith." She leaned back and gave Jessie a wink.

Jessie's mouth fell open. There were some assumptions about Dr. Smith and Ms. Johnson because neither of them ever mentioned a spouse or significant other. Still, there was absolutely no suspicion of them being together. Why were they wasting their talents working at The Agency? Those two should be in the CIA.

"We both loved the idea of kids. We talked about it many times. Ultimately, the decision was mine. It would be me letting the little tike take up residence, and Dr. Smith didn't want me to feel pressured into giving him something he may have wanted more than me." She paused. "Trust me. It wasn't an easy decision. There are a lot of 'what-ifs' either way you decide. Don't go down that rabbit hole. Our situation was a little unique in that we both work for The Agency, and I never became pregnant. Had it just been me working here, I could have quit and led a normal life with a family. But since we both work here, he wouldn't have been able to stay either."

"It would have been too dangerous for all of you," Jessie concluded.

"Yes. No point in bringing a child into the world if you're just going to worry about them constantly. Although I hear that's what mothers end up doing anyhow." Ms. Johnson had let out a little laugh.

"I can attest to that. My mother was a bit of a worrywart. Luckily, my dad balanced her out. The stuff we did behind my mother's back..." She looked at the ceiling. "Sorry, Mom."

"Had I chosen to have kids, it would have also meant that I was choosing for him to leave a job he absolutely loves."

Jessie leaned forward, resting her head in her palms.

"Have you talked to the father?"

Jessie shook her head in her hands.

"I'm sorry I can't be of much help. I will say that becoming a mother will change your life entirely. Of that I am certain. I made the decision that was right for me. You must make the decision that is right for you."

The words linger in Jessie's mind as the memory dissolves. She chose to give up her life for her child once before; she can do it again. But first, she needs to get inside the cabin.

It doesn't end like this.

Jessie opens her eyes and coughs up blood. She attempts to spit it out, but can't. Her jaw is broken or maybe dislocated. The blood and saliva run down her chin onto the ground.

"Mom, where are you? We need you." She hears Max's voice from the cabin.

His voice ignites a primal energy she can't describe.

*I'm coming.*

Jessie staggers to her feet and stumbles. She summons all her strength, ignoring the pain radiating from every inch of her body, and takes a step forward. Then another. She can hear the guttural sound of her breathing. Another step forward. More shooting pain.

Every limb feels like cement, yet she continues her pursuit, an invisible force pulling her in. She takes another step, and another, inching closer to her children.

Her heart drops as she watches Papa's silhouette cross the threshold and disappear into the cabin. With sheer willpower, she forces her feet forward. *Almost there.* A thunderous boom erupts, throwing her back to the ground.

# SEVENTY-THREE

JESSIE BURIES her head in her arm as the world explodes around her. The initial blast, a deep, bone-rattling boom, sends the cabin's front door spinning through the air in splintered wooden fragments.

She presses herself against the gravel as debris rains down like deadly hail, each piece striking the ground with a violent symphony of destruction.

The heat hits her next, a wave of searing air that penetrates her sweatshirt and makes her skin feel like it's shrinking. The choking smell of burning wood and melted plastic fills her nostrils, mixing with something else—the sharp, bitter scent of her own singed hair. She frantically pats her head, her palm connecting with a piece of red-hot metal that brands her skin instantly. The pain doesn't register.

Through her swollen right eye, she watches the secondary explosion tear through what remains of the structure. The propane tank erupts with a thunderous roar, sending chunks of the Range Rover cartwheeling through the air. One piece, she thinks it might be a door, slams into the ground mere feet from where she lies curled in a ball. When the final echoes fade and the last fragments settle, Jessie forces herself to look.

"No." The word comes out as barely a whisper. Her body shakes with rage and grief that threaten to tear her apart from the inside. Snot and tears run down her face as she silently curses Papa. Her body convulses with every tear. The cabin is gone. Not damaged —gone. Obliterated.

Where walls once stood, there are only pieces of splintered wood and twisted metal. The cast iron fireplace, knocked from its foundation, lies on its side like a fallen monument. Orange flames lick at the debris, casting dancing shadows that make the destruction seem alive and hungry.

This was always their plan: to get her inside and destroy everything. A propane explosion at an old cabin could be easily written off as an accident due to poor maintenance and a gas leak. Tragic, but not suspicious. No one would question it.

Jessie rolls onto her back and stares into the smoke-hazed night sky. The fire's glow has swallowed the stars, leaving only an empty orange dome above her. *It's beautiful.* She feels her own light dimming, not from her injuries, though they're extensive, but from choice. From the crushing weight of her failure.

She had one job: protect her children, love them, keep them safe, give them a chance at the life she never had. Instead, she'd led them straight into a trap. She'd gotten them killed.

The thought of facing Nick, of explaining how she'd failed their boys, is unbearable. But living without Max and Sean? That's impossible. The grief cuts through her worse than any physical wound.

Her hand finds the plastic baggie in her back pocket, one of the few remnants of her old life she'd kept. She tears it open with her teeth. Two yellow capsules spill onto her chest and roll to the ground. She puts the baggie in her mouth and uses her teeth to slide one of the remaining capsules into her mouth.

The fire crackles and pops, consuming what little remains of the cabin. A crash echoes as the remaining wall and roof sections shift under the blaze's destruction and collapse. The sky above glows beautifully. The sound of the hungry flames is soothing, like the sound of ocean waves. Funny how one destroys the other, yet they both produce a calming rhythm.

Jessie positions the capsule between her back teeth and begins to apply pressure.

Crunching gravel. Something moving.

The final fragments of the cabin collapse with a thud.

Jessie shuts her eyes.

Faster crunching.

She bites down harder.

"Mom! Mom!"

Jessie turns her head, expecting to see nothing. A figment emerges from behind the now destroyed cabin. As the image approaches, she recognizes the hazy silhouette. Max.

He rushes toward her, his face streaked with tears and dirt. When he drops to his knees beside her, his touch is undeniably real —warm, trembling, and alive. Not a figment, coming to welcome her to join him and Sean in death.

"Mom!" Max chokes on his tears as he takes in her battered body. He gently pushes the bloody, matted hair from her face.

Jessie's mouth is too dry to spit out the capsule. She digs it out with her finger and flicks it away.

"Max." Her breathing is slow and labored. "Sean?"

"He's safe." Max wipes his tears and then hers. "He's at the top of the power line tower. Charlie—Charlie helped us get away from Oscar."

Jessie's body tenses. She tries to form the question with her eyes since her mouth won't cooperate.

"Charlie killed him," Max says, understanding. "They're dead. They're all dead." He chokes back more tears. "Charlie, too," he adds quietly.

Blood wells up in Jessie's throat, and she coughs, splattering crimson across her lips.

"Don't die." Max's voice is small, younger than his years. "Please don't die."

She's never seen him this scared, not even during the terror of the last few hours. His fear is raw, honest, and it breaks something inside her that she thought was already broken.

She squeezes his hand, the gesture taking enormous effort.

"Don't leave me with Sean," he says, attempting a joke through the tears. "You know how he is."

Despite everything—the pain, the blood, the labored breathing—Jessie laughs. It turns into another coughing fit, but she doesn't care.

"Sorry," he says, quickly. "I probably shouldn't make you laugh."

*Yes. Make me laugh. It's been a long time since you tried to make me laugh. Too long.*

Max takes out his flashlight and aims it toward the power line tower, flashing it in a pattern. Within minutes, Sean appears, running toward them with the stride of an athlete that's uniquely his.

Jessie decides it's not her time to die.

# SEVENTY-FOUR

MAX WATCHES Sean circle their mother, keeping his distance, kicking debris, and occasionally picking up pieces to examine them. He knows Sean is struggling with how different she looks and the way trauma has changed her face. Sean has always been unsettled by anything that makes people look different from what is normal. Even when she wears makeup, for rare nights out with Nick, Sean will tell her, "You don't look like you." It's never about looking good or bad with Sean; it's about different, because different is hard for him.

Something behind their mother grabs Sean's attention, and he runs toward it. When he returns, he's clutching a piece of black composite. The CCM logo is the only indication of what it once was. "My stick!" The excitement in Sean's voice surprises Max. Most of the hockey stick has been shattered into bits, leaving only this small fragment, but Sean holds it like he's found treasure. He doesn't seem to care that it's unusable, having even a piece of his beloved stick is enough.

Max walks toward the treeline behind what used to be the

cabin. The Ford F-250 sits where Jonathan said it would be, and Max tries not to think about the body he has to move from the driver's seat. Jonathan had suggested he use his feet to avoid direct contact, advice Max is grateful for.

After settling into the driver's seat, Max opens his laptop, navigates to the maps app, and drops a pin on his current location. He takes a breath, opens the chat box, and exhales, awaiting further instructions.

The gravel road jolts the truck with every bump, and Max can hear their mother wince in the back seat. He's driving slowly to minimize the jostling, but she keeps urging him to speed up and get them the hell out of there. Her instructions are simple: drive until they reach the highway and run over anything or anyone that gets in their way.

The freedom in that command unnerves him. Usually, she micromanages every aspect of his driving—speed, lane position, and following distance. Now she's given him carte blanche to drive recklessly, and all he wants is the comfort of his mother's control. He wishes she would tell him how to handle the gravel road, how to navigate the curves, how to manage a four-wheel drive vehicle he's never driven before. Instead, there's just silence from the backseat and one simple instruction on how to get there that makes him feel completely untethered.

Sean launches into a detailed report of their plan, his voice animated despite everything they've been through. Max finds himself impressed by how well Sean remembers the sequence of events. Usually, their retellings dissolve into arguments about who's getting the details wrong. But this time, there is no bickering, no snide remarks, or accusations. Just a hint of excitement that their desperate gamble worked.

"When we split up, I ran to the power line tower and climbed to the top," Sean explains to their mother. "And I wasn't even afraid of the dark." Max can hear the pride in his brother's voice.

Sean continues the story while Max fills in the parts about

rigging the Bluetooth speaker he found in the toolbox and luring Papa into the cabin. "That's what I was trying to tell you right before those other guys barged in," Max interjects, remembering how frantic he'd felt trying to warn her about the explosives he'd spotted.

When Charlie knocked over the toolbox, Max saw the detonator by the back door and grabbed it as he and Sean ran out. The whole plan had been a gamble based on his assumption that whoever rigged the cabin had finished the job.

"It was Max's plan," Sean concludes.

"Yeah, but it wouldn't have worked without you," Max replies, meaning it. Sean's role as lookout from the power line tower had been crucial. Without Sean's view and walkie-talkie signal, Max wouldn't have known when to detonate the explosives.

"You guys did great," their mother wheezes from the back seat, her voice barely audible.

Max lifts himself out of the seat to check the rearview mirror, catching a glimpse of her battered face. She looks bad, really bad. When he settles back into his seat, he swerves slightly before correcting course. He waits for the usual sharp comment about paying attention to the road, but there's only silence. She's not moving, just lying there. Why isn't she moving? Maybe it hurts too much to move. Maybe she's worse off than he realized. Maybe she's dying.

The maybes attack him from the inside. His gut aches, his heart pounds, his mind races. The unknown is consuming him, and that's when it hits him. She isn't afraid of the independence that driving will give him. She's afraid of the unknown and the anxiety it will give her.

Right now, he has anxiety about the unknowns, even though he can see her in the mirror and knows she's breathing and alive. But when he's finally able to get in a car and leave on his own, she won't have that comfort. She won't be able to see him, and know if he's safe. Or alive.

The realization sends Max down a rabbit hole of what-ifs as he tries to concentrate on the dark road ahead. All these times she criticized his lane changes, questioned his speed, gripped the dashboard when he took corners, maybe it wasn't about controlling him.

Maybe it was about trying to control all the things that would make it impossible for her to protect him once he was on his own.

Driving represents his first taste of real freedom as he approaches adulthood. When the day comes that he drives away by himself, he'll leave her protection and enter a world of unknowns she can't control or predict.

For the first time, Max thinks he understands. And understanding makes his own chest tight with emotion he can't quite name—something between gratitude and guilt, love and the terrible weight of growing up.

# SEVENTY-FIVE

THE LIVING room of the hotel suite buzzes with activity around Romeo. Two six-foot banquet tables hold an elaborate breakfast spread meant to feed the thirty or so people milling about. He catches Juliet's eye from across the room as she nods for him to follow her into one of the bedrooms. A muted TV broadcast shows a news story about the teachers' union threatening to strike. She shuts the door behind them, the sounds of conversation from the other room becoming a muffled hum.

"Is this going to be a problem?" Romeo asks, nodding to the TV.

"It's just a threat. On another note... I'm still unable to contact Oscar," she says, her voice carrying an edge of concern she rarely lets show.

"Same with Papa." Romeo begins pacing, his movements sharp and agitated. Rage builds in his chest like a fire catching kindling. "I had twenty deliveries that didn't get made last night. Twenty!" The words tear from his throat, and he feels that blaze igniting behind his eyes, the one that makes people step back when they see it.

He knows Juliet won't try to calm him down. She's known him long enough to recognize when he's past the point of reasoning, when he's more like a caged animal than the controlled businessman he usually presents to the world. It's better this way—let the fury burn itself out so they can move forward. The crowd in the other room is the only reason furniture isn't flying right now.

"If those two aren't already dead, I'll kill them myself," he hisses through gritted teeth.

He sees Juliet glance toward the door, and knows she's worried someone might have heard. She knows, as well as he does, that he has never killed anyone and never would.

He's too smart to put that kind of spotlight on himself. There are people for that sort of thing. His business holds too many secrets for him to risk an investigation anywhere near him. Romeo has spent the last three decades building his operation, perfecting his business model, and creating his philanthropic persona through various foundations. He takes every precaution to avoid so much as a parking ticket. There are many arms to his operation, and he makes sure none of them ever touch each other. Anonymity keeps him from getting caught. The promise of anonymity keeps him rich.

"I've already told the courier to send next week's list immediately. You'll be back on track tomorrow. It was just a minor snag," Juliet says.

Romeo stops pacing and faces her with a stare. The heat in his chest spreads outward, making his hands shake slightly. "You know how powerful some of these people are. If their confidence in me is shaken... who knows what they might do in a panic?"

He walks over to a bar cart and pours himself a drink. The crystal decanter clinks against the glass, penetrating the thick silence in the room. The whiskey burns, but it's nothing compared to the fire already consuming him from inside.

"We've attributed it to a clerical error in the dates. As far as anyone is concerned, the delivery date was always supposed to be for tomorrow," she says, though Romeo can hear the lack of conviction in her tone.

He gives her a knowing look over his glass. Even she isn't buying what she's selling. And Juliet is the best saleswoman of them all. If she can't sell it to herself, what chance do they have with their clients?

"Find out where Oscar and Papa are and bring them here. I need answers now."

Romeo notices Juliet staring past him, her attention suddenly caught by something on the TV screen. She grabs the remote and turns up the volume. "I think I just found them."

The newscast shows yellow caution tape fluttering in the breeze around the charred remains of the cabin. Romeo's blood turns to ice as he reads the headline in bold red letters: BREAKING NEWS: MULTIPLE BODIES FOUND. In the foreground, a news correspondent speaks directly into the camera, her expression grave.

"So far, remains have been found both inside the cabin and near the perimeter. Investigators believe at least one victim was inside when the explosion occurred. A neglected propane tank is the suspected cause of the lethal blast. Several neighbors in the area reported hearing two loud explosions late last night. One such neighbor, Frank Willis, lives a mile up the road and went out to investigate."

Romeo's chest tightens as the broadcast cuts to footage of a gray-haired man in his fifties standing on a wooden porch. The man looks exactly like someone who belongs in these mountains. Next to him sits a yellow Labrador retriever, her tail occasionally thumping against the porch boards.

"I had just settled in bed when I heard the explosions. It shook my walls so bad I thought we was having an earthquake," Frank says. "There's a tree out front that got a broken branch from the last windstorm, and I wanted to make sure it didn't fall on my tank. It's important to take care of those sorts of things. Betsy here followed me outside." He gently pats the dog's head. "She seemed a little shook up still, like she didn't want to leave my side just yet."

Romeo's hands clench into fists as Frank continues, his weathered face serious in the camera. "When we got outside, I saw the flames in the distance, so naturally I went to check it out. Sometimes Bill burns his trash at night 'cause he knows he ain't supposed to be doing that. Betsy and I walked on to Bill's, and when we got closer, I could see that the place down the road from his was up in flames. I ran over, of course, but that's when Betsy started barking." Frank points to the area behind the cabin. "She's the one who found the poor guy over there."

"I was headed back to my place to call 9-1-1, but Betsy wouldn't come. She was looking at something in the dark. I could see a SUV, one of those fancy kinds, parked kind of out of the way so you couldn't see it if you were coming up the road. Then I thought I saw someone running away from the area, but my eyes were tired, and when I blinked, it was just a tree branch," Frank says, shaking his head.

Romeo's heart pounds.

The broadcast returns to the news correspondent, who presses her ear and squints, as if straining to hear. "It appears the second victim, found near the cabin, had been shot in the head at close range. Shortly after authorities arrived, a third body was found in one of the nearby SUVs. That victim had a fatal eye injury. Not too long after that, two more bodies were found in the woods within a mile of the cabin. Both gunshot victims."

The rage in Romeo's chest transforms into something colder, more dangerous. He watches the news correspondent press her ear again and squint harder. "I just received word that yet another body has just been found beyond that tree line." The cameraman follows her gesture to the trees behind the burning cabin. "Also, with a gunshot wound. That brings the total body count to six," she says, as the camera refocuses on her face. "Official causes of death, of course, will be pending autopsy reports."

Romeo sees Juliet standing with her mouth hanging open, the remote still in her hand. She mutes the rest of the news report. "What the hell happened up there?"

"Confirm it's Papa's crew as soon as you can," Romeo says, forcing his voice to remain steady.

"What about the flash drive? There's no way to find it in that mess."

"It doesn't matter anymore. Someone downloaded a copy of it. The information is out there." He pours himself another drink, then turns back to Juliet. "We need to find out who has it."

He catches Juliet eying the glass in his hand. "You go on in twenty minutes," she says.

The reminder of his public appearance and the careful facade he must maintain sends a fresh wave of fury through him. He slams the glass down hard enough to make both the brown liquid and Juliet jump. Droplets splatter across the bar cart's clean, polished surface. Thirty years of careful construction, and it could all come crashing down because of one missing flash drive.

There's a soft knock on the door before it opens. A man in his early thirties steps in with a leather portfolio cradled in his arm. "Sir, your revised speech is ready."

Romeo straightens his shoulders and smoothes his expression into the mask he wears for the world. The philanthropist. The pillar of the community. The man who donates to schools.

"Five minutes," he says, his voice perfectly controlled.

But inside, the monster hungers for revenge.

# SEVENTY-SIX

THE RHYTHMIC beeping pulls Jessie from the depths of consciousness. Her eyelashes are crusted shut, and when she finally wipes them free, she discovers an IV taped to the back of her hand. Everything hurts. Her nose throbs, and her ribs protest with every breath. Blinking hard, she focuses on the hallway beyond her doorway. A doctor walks past, and for a moment, she thinks his face looks familiar. When he passes by again, her brain has fully woken, and his name surfaces from her clouded memory along with a terrible certainty. Dr. Smith is coming to tell her that her parents are dead and she's all alone. But this time, he turns at the nurses' station and disappears, leaving her unsure if she even saw him at all.

Scattered fragments of the night before flood back. Someone walked beside her gurney as it rolled from the helicopter to the ER, stroking her hair and speaking in a low, reassuring voice. His touch had made her feel safe and protected. She knew he would make everything alright. He wouldn't let there be any more explosions.

The cabin had exploded.

Max and Sean were in the cabin.

Panic jolts through her, and she tries to sit upright. Pain radiates outward in every direction. Her heart monitor spikes. Then she sees Sean curled up asleep in an oversized chair across the room and Max sitting beside her bed.

As her heart rate settles, a sharp sensation shoots down her left arm, where a purple cast stretches from her hand to her bicep. She examines the signatures and can't help but smile. Sean claimed the entire top portion with his name in quarter-inch-thick letters, complete with a crude hockey stick drawing. Max's name appears in neat script with a tiny smiley face.

She turns the cast over, searching for one more signature, but it's not there. Her smile fades. Of course, Nick wouldn't sign it. He's not into childish things like that.

Sean's signature makes her smile. It's bold, just like him. She watches his chest rise and fall with each snore. His oversized hospital scrubs make him look like the tiny baby she brought home from the hospital twelve years ago. The smell of smoke from Sean's clothes probably made him nauseous; he's sensitive to smells. Knowing Sean, she wouldn't be surprised if he threw them in the garbage before anyone could stop him. The thought triggers a faint smell of campfire, and she notices Charlie's flannel hanging on the bathroom door. Sean kept it.

Max sits watching YouTube on his phone with earbuds, looking older somehow. On the brink of adulthood. Maybe it's the confidence he showed while driving down the mountain, or the way he wears his dad's hoodie over blue scrubs, or the near-death experience they survived. But somehow, he's changed.

Jessie attempts to sit up and immediately regrets it.

Max tosses his phone and earbuds onto the bedside tray and grabs the bed controller. "Lay back, I got it." The motor whirs as the head of the bed rises. Sean stirs but doesn't wake. Max helps her lean forward and readjusts the pillows behind her. She winces as she lies back.

"Thanks." She lifts her cast. "Purple?"

"Sean insisted they give you a purple cast. I'm pretty sure he told every single person in scrubs. 'Make sure my mom gets a purple cast. Not pink. Not blue. Not red. Purple.'" Max grins. "Team colors, so it matches your jersey at his hockey games."

She nods. Of course, Sean would think of that. "Would you believe this is my very first cast?"

"Seriously? You never broke a bone as a kid?" Max takes his seat.

"Nope. Never. But you and Sean have definitely made up for all my missed ER visits." She studies the two names on her cast. "Is Dad here?" The memory of someone meeting them at the helicopter feels dreamlike. She could have confused it with a scene from an old hospital TV drama. Just like her thinking she saw Dr. Smith in the hallway.

"Yeah, you don't remember? He met us when we landed. The hospital guys yelled at him for running out onto the landing pad." Max settles back in his chair. "He's eating in the cafeteria. The nurse said he looked like crap and guilt-tripped him into eating something."

"What about you two? Have you eaten?" She takes a sip from the water cup and can't stop. Her throat feels like sandpaper, and despite the IV, her mouth feels like cotton. She downs the whole cup in seconds.

"Are you kidding? The first thing Sean asked for was the bathroom, and then food. I had a sandwich. It was disgusting." He waves his phone in the air. "But I'm good. If I really need something edible, I've got Uber Eats."

"Hey, bud, think you can get me some ice chips?"

"No problem. Be right back." Max heads for the door.

Jessie takes a deep breath, immediately regretting it as pain flares through her ribs. She needs more pain medication, but first, she wants to convince Nick to take the boys to his parents' house.

In that moment, she realizes she doesn't have a clue where

they are. They were about halfway to her in-laws' house when all hell broke loose. Did they fly back to the city? Or maybe to her in-laws' town? Looking around the room, she doesn't see any hospital-branded items to clue her in, and the room looks like it could belong in General Hospital, Anytown, USA.

A nurse enters with a cart. He has to be at least six-three, with a tattoo peeking out from underneath his sleeve. His skin is dark and smooth. Jessie thinks he belongs in a firefighter calendar. On the cover.

He introduces himself as Damien and asks Jessie how she's feeling. "Fine," she lies.

This isn't his first rodeo, and he offers her some pain meds, which she gladly accepts. She thought she could wait until the boys left before getting dosed up and loopy. She was wrong. After checking her vitals and administering the drugs, Damien leaves.

Within moments, Jessie struggles to keep her eyes open. She's drifting toward sleep when she sees him in the doorway. The sight gives her a boost of adrenaline, prolonging her consciousness for a few minutes longer. All she can do is smile. Her heart feels warm. She knows it's probably the medication, but all her pain seems to evaporate the moment she sees him.

He's here. With her.

He peeks his head in and notices Sean. She gives an affirmative nod to his questioning look, and he takes Max's chair. His voice is tight and low.

"Hi, Alex."

# SEVENTY-SEVEN

JONATHAN'S VOICE cracks like it did on their orientation day at the academy, when Jessie found him in the janitor's closet. Tears pool in her eyes as she looks at him for the first time in years, hoping it's not a dream.

"Hi. It's Jessie now."

"Right. Jessie." His questioning look is so recognizable, it feels like no time has passed.

She still knows what he's thinking before he even asks. Why did she pick the name Jessie?

"Owens."

"Jesse Owens." He nods, slowly. "Did you find the good?"

His eyes follow hers to Sean, sleeping peacefully.

"I did."

"Is that Sean?"

"Yeah." She wipes away a tear that escapes.

"Max?"

"Getting ice." Another tear escapes, and this time Jonathan

reaches out, his thumb brushing it away. The familiar touch sends warmth flooding her cheeks, and she has to look away.

"He's okay, though?"

"He will be." The words come out stronger than she feels. Every instinct tempts her to reach for him, to close the distance between them until there's no space left for all the years and choices that separated them. "We're all okay. Thanks to you."

"I'm not taking the heat for the six bodies you left scattered across that mountain," he says. She can hear him forcing lightness into this tone, trying to ease the weight of everything unsaid between them.

"I'm only responsible for three bodies. Max caused the explosion that killed Papa."

Jonathan's eyes widen. "Damn. That kid really is his mother's son."

The laugh bubbles out of her before she can stop it, followed by a grunt of pain that makes her press her hand to her ribs.

"Sorry. I probably shouldn't make you laugh." He makes an exaggerated guilty face at her. "What about the others?"

"The one they called Mike is responsible for your guy." She offers him a look that carries all the sympathy she can't put into words. "The two in the woods took each other out. The younger one, Charlie, helped us get away. He wasn't like the others. He got caught up in something he didn't understand and paid for it." Jessie wipes her eye.

"That's a total of seven. They only found six bodies on the mountain."

"You'll find a guy a quarter mile south of town in the desert, on the east side of the highway." Jessie tries to readjust her pillow, but Jonathan's hands are there before she can struggle with it. She nestles her head and turns toward him, already feeling the medication softening the careful walls she's built around her thoughts.

Jonathan takes her hand, cradling it carefully between both of his. His thumbs gently trace patterns across her knuckles, avoiding the IV line. "I'm glad...I'm glad you're here," he says, choking back tears.

"Same."

He releases her hand to wipe away his own tears, and she almost protests the loss of contact before catching herself.

"They said we downloaded information from the flash drive," she says quickly, needing to steer them back to safer ground. "But we didn't. Max swears he didn't, and I—"

"Can barely turn on a computer without help?" he gently teases.

She chuckles and winces at the same time.

"Sorry, old habit." His hands go up in playful surrender. His voice lowers, and she almost doesn't hear him, "I love making you laugh." For a heartbeat, they just look at each other, and she sees the man she used to love looking back at her. Jessie feels her resolve weakening and is grateful when Jonathan clears his throat and breaks eye contact with her. "The download was me. As soon as I saw what was on Max's screen, I pulled the file to our server. Sorry if that caused you more grief. If they were able to detect the download, then those guys are some heavy players."

"Were. They were heavy players."

He moves to the window, staring out at the parking lot below. When he turns back, his expression is serious. "We copied the file onto a laptop and planted it in the Mercedes before first responders arrived. It's hidden well enough that local police won't find it, but if there are others involved and they get the laptop from police evidence..."

"They'll think Papa took it for himself," Jessie finishes.

"The information was worth killing over. Someone's going to come looking."

"Yeah, I guess." Jessie's eyes drift shut as the medication pulls at her consciousness. "What was on it? It just looked like a bunch of random words to us." She opens her eyes, now mere slits as the medicine works its way through her veins.

"Same. Our guys are working on it. But you don't need to worry about that. You just focus on healing."

Jessie's eyelids lose the fight, and Jonathan watches the last of her defenses fade away.

He studies her face. She looks tired. And broken. He has never seen her look this vulnerable, and it cuts him to the core. He knows he's partly responsible. She had once asked him to leave The Agency with her and choose something different. But he'd let duty and fear make that choice for him.

He thinks about Derrick, also known as Eagle, who'd left five years ago. Six months later, Jonathan received a postcard from Alaska, with no words, just a bald eagle against snow-capped mountains. Most of the women who left The Agency did so in their late twenties or early thirties. When he mentioned this to a female agent, she explained that they likely wanted to have children and saw their window of opportunity closing.

Looking at Sean now, Jonathan feels something shift in his understanding. Jessie didn't miss her window. She'd seized it, built something beautiful and real.

He wants to tell her that the chances of this being over are slim. He wants to explain that the guys she killed in the mountains were likely the bottom rung of a long and dangerous ladder, and that he wants to protect her, but doesn't know if she'll let him.

He wants to tell her how often he thinks about the life they might have had, and how empty his world feels without her laugh echoing through it.

But it wouldn't be fair to share these thoughts. She needs her rest and her family. She doesn't need him. Not anymore.

He approaches her bedside quietly and presses a gentle kiss to her forehead. Her skin is warm beneath his lips, and for a moment, he lets himself remember what it felt like when she was his to protect, his to love.

She's already drifting away, surrendering to the peace the

medication offers, leaving him alone with all the words he'll never say.

373

# SEVENTY-EIGHT

THE AGENCY vetted all the nurses as thoroughly as possible on such short notice, and Damien was the most qualified for the job. He's a Marine with an exemplary record who was discharged due to a combat injury. He stands at the nurse's station, filling out paperwork, when Jonathan approaches from behind.

"Damien?"

Damien turns, "Yeah? Can I help you?"

Jonathan notices the bewilderment on Damien's face at being addressed by name. He steps closer and lowers his voice, sliding a business card across the counter. It only has his first name and a phone number. "If anyone comes around asking for information on the patient in room 431, call me immediately."

"And who are you exactly..." Damien examines the card with the thoroughness Jonathan expected. "... Jonathan?"

"I'm someone who wants to make sure nothing happens to her or her family."

Jonathan knows that Damien will need more than that. It's

time to leverage the connection he researched. "Francis Mercer is a mutual friend, and he vouched for you."

He sees the recognition wash over Damien. Very few people knew Frank as Francis, and that information couldn't be found online. Frank changed his legal name over fifty years ago, a fact Jonathan would only know if he were the real deal.

"Yeah, okay," Damien says, but Jonathan can see the questions forming.

Jonathan leans closer. "Anyone looking for information on your patient will go to any lengths to get it. If you have a family and these people contact you, believe me, they already have a plan to extract information. Your only shot at protecting them and yourself is to call me immediately."

Jonathan doesn't need to mention Damien's daughter specifically. He watches the man's face tighten as the implication sinks in. Besides, mentioning his daughter could give Damien the wrong impression about Jonathan. He needs Damien to trust him, not fear him.

"What about her doctor and the night nurse?" Damien glances over at the far end of the nurse's station, where Dr. Smith and Ms. Johnson are discussing a chart. "I've never seen them before." Now he understands why. Whoever his patient is, she must be important.

"They've already been informed."

Damien nods. "Will do. Do you need my number or anything?"

"That's not necessary."

"You already have it, don't you?"

Jonathan offers a faint smile that confirms Damien's suspicion. He shakes Damien's hand before turning to leave.

As he rounds the corner, Jonathan sends a text message to Dr. Smith, informing him that the nurse has been briefed. The response comes quickly—perimeter secured, all assets in place. Jonathan reads the confirmation when he bumps into someone and looks up, catching a glimpse of himself.

The world stops.

Jonathan's thumbs hover over the letters on his phone, his tactical operational mindset dissolving as he watches the boy pick up ice from the floor. He has Jonathan's face. Not similar, but identical, just a sixteen-year-old version. Same bone structure that will sharpen with age, same wavy blond hair that complements his angular jawline, same ocean-blue eyes.

"Max, let me help you," another voice says. A man, presumably Nick, joins Max on the floor, scooping ice into the cup. His attention stays on the mess. "Sorry about that. Our minds are... somewhere else." He tosses a few pieces of ice into the cup Max is holding.

Jonathan can't find his words or his voice, for that matter. His training is the only reason he can keep his composure. "Oh, uh, no. Totally my fault."

Max stands, coming face-to-face with Jonathan. It's as if he's looking into a mirror reflecting his future self. When Max tilts his head, studying Jonathan with apparent confusion, it's a gesture Jonathan recognizes. It's the same questioning angle he makes when trying to figure something out.

"I wasn't paying attention," Jonathan manages.

Was he paying attention seventeen years ago when Jessie asked him to leave The Agency with her? At that time, he believed her impulsiveness stemmed from the aftermath of the Prague mission. She hadn't mentioned a baby, never giving him the chance to choose differently.

But would he have chosen differently? The Agency was his identity, his entire existence. If he wouldn't leave for Jessie, what would make her think he would leave for a person he hadn't met yet? Looking at Max now, seeing his own features reflected back at him, Jonathan realizes he'll never know what he might have chosen because Jessie never gave him the opportunity to choose.

And that stings.

Just as Nick stands back up, Max releases his grip on the cup, and it falls back to the floor, ice sprawling between them. Max mimics the frozen pose Jonathan just had. He stares at Jonathan, his eyes wide and questioning.

Jonathan breaks free from his gaze and helps Nick collect the ice. The melting ice slides around with every attempt to grasp it.

"Thanks. He's not quite himself. He's had a rough night," Nick says.

"Same."

Jonathan dumps the ice he's collected into the cup. They both stand.

"Thanks ag—" Nick finally looks at Jonathan. Then at Max. And back to Jonathan. The realization dawns across his features like a slow, devastating sunrise. "Oh my... you're..."

"Jonathan," Jonathan finishes for him.

Max finally snaps back to reality upon hearing the name. "Falcon? What are—? Why do you look..." He looks at his dad, and Nick doesn't have to say a word. His stricken face says everything. Tears fill Max's eyes. He runs into Jessie's room. Nick and Jonathan both watch, but neither of them follows.

"I didn't know." Jonathan holds back his tears, his professional composure fracturing completely. "I didn't know about him."

"Me neither. I mean, I knew she was pregnant when we met, but she told me the father had died." Nick hangs his head and picks at his finger, his voice tightening with every word. He looks back at Jonathan. "I feel like there's a lot she hasn't told me."

Jonathan wants to help Nick understand why she wouldn't tell him about her time with The Agency, and why she's kept so many secrets. But even he doesn't know the answer. The Agency trains agents on what they can and cannot share, as well as how to best answer or evade questions about their work. Leaving The Agency is almost as lengthy a process as joining it. But why she would keep the pregnancy, keep Max's existence a secret from him—

that goes beyond any protocol he knows.

His mind is reeling with the discovery of his child, the son who just ran away from him in tears. He's useless to Nick right now.

--- ... - .-. ... -.

Nick has a tornado of emotions raging inside him and doesn't know where he should land at this moment. Betrayal, concern, anger, sadness, love, they cycle through him like a destructive storm. Standing in this sterile hospital corridor, he can feel seventeen years of certainty crumbling beneath his feet.

The revelation that Jessie told him Max's father was dead when the man is standing right here, very much alive, causes him pain he can't describe. How many other conversations have been carefully constructed lies? How many times had she deflected questions about her past? Nick's mind reeled back to the beginning, to when he'd believed their life together was built on truth.

The day Max was born, Nick had been in awe of him. He was so tiny, and Jessie had endured an arduous labor. Max was stubborn even back then. His oxygen and bilirubin levels weren't where they needed to be, and he stayed in the NICU for a week. Jessie was discharged four days after giving birth, but refused to leave without him. She camped out in the NICU as much as the hospital allowed. Nick admired her fierce protectiveness, something he had attributed to new mother instincts.

The hospital had been on the verge of kicking them out when a doctor Nick had never met before told him he had worked it out so Jessie could stay as long as Max was in the NICU. Nick doesn't remember the doctor's name, but has been eternally grateful to him. Now he wonders if that had been a coincidence, or if the same hands providing her private room and security had been pulling strings even then.

Sean's birth was quite the opposite. Jessie almost didn't make it to the hospital in time. Once Sean was delivered, he seemed content to be a part of the outside world. To Nick, newborns all seemed the same. A cute pink head attached to a blanket, too tired from the journey to bother opening their eyes. But Sean was different. Nick still swears Sean gave him a look that said, 'I was in there and now I'm here. Let's go home.'

Two boys. Two completely different births. Two sons he'd loved without question.

His boys. The possessive pronoun feels uncertain now.

When Nick realized he was falling in love with Jessie, he had no qualms about raising Max as his own. The night they met, he found her attractive and easy to talk to, but he wasn't looking for a relationship. His career was taking off, and he was focused on that. They met through Jessie's friend Kacey, who took her out to lift her spirits, accusing her of having pregnancy mope. After Kacey introduced them, Jessie cut her off and said, "Hi, I'm Jessie. I'm pregnant."

Nick had laughed, thinking it an odd way of introducing herself and unsure if she was totally serious. She explained that she had no filter when she was nervous, but was glad to have all her cards on the table.

Except, apparently, she hadn't. Not even close.

When Nick asked Jessie why she was nervous, she didn't have an answer. Kacey ratted her out, telling him Jessie thought he was cute. Nick blushed and told her the feeling was mutual. The following week, they ran into each other again. And then again, a couple of days later. Nick joked that the universe was trying to tell them something. Jessie laughed and told him it was probably telling her she had a stalker.

Looking back now, Nick wonders how much of their entire relationship was built on carefully constructed fiction. What other truths is Jessie hiding? What other secrets might surface when she wakes up?

"I better go check on him," Nick says, finally.

"Of course."

Jonathan watches Nick enter Jessie's hospital room. The same room his son ran into, where the woman he once loved heals from her wounds, and where a family he never knew existed tries to make sense of a truth that changes everything.

381

# SEVENTY-NINE

JESSIE DRIFTS into her memories as the morphine takes hold. The last time she experienced this level of pain in a hospital bed, she was just two years older than Max. Within ten minutes of waking up, she wished she were dead.

Every plan she had made for her future became irrelevant. Dorm shopping, choosing classes, the careful timeline she had mapped out—none of it mattered anymore. Nothing mattered at all. She felt nothing but despair and anguish. Life wasn't fair. She had done everything right: she had listened to her parents, earned good grades, and helped others. By all standards, she was a good person. She didn't deserve what had happened.

Both her parents were gone. She had no siblings, and no aunts or uncles that she was aware of, and no grandparents were still living. She felt utterly alone. The anxiety about attending college and taking on real adult responsibilities was intensified by the knowledge that she would face these challenges without support. Although people her age managed it without family or encouragement, it felt like an overwhelming challenge in that moment.

Her life had been derailed, but she got it back on track, choosing a different destination—one filled with adventure, intrigue, and danger. While some people retreat and build walls after experiencing tragedy, fearing that the worst might happen again, she took the opposite approach and embraced danger. She would taunt death, sometimes getting reprimanded by The Agency for it.

She made risky decisions far too many times to remember, all while falling in love. Even her love for Jonathan couldn't stop her from dancing with death. In her mind, he would also be taken from her someday, just like her parents. She always held him loosely, or so she believed, to avoid the pain when he was ripped from her grasp.

Her fellow agents would call her fearless. What they didn't realize was that she was so full of fear that she couldn't let herself pause long enough to confront it. She feared that death would come for the newest person in her life. She would flirt with it and seduce it, daring it to go after her instead of him. But it never did.

Instead, life was created, and everything changed. For the first time since her parents' death, Jessie felt hopeful. Alive. Excited. The last time she remembered feeling that way was the day she received her college acceptance letter. While she feared venturing out on her own, far from home, there was also excitement in that fear, along with a hint of hope. Jessie never had the opportunity to discover where that excitement and hope would lead her.

When she told Ms. Johnson about the pregnancy, she didn't receive the advice she was looking for, but Ms. Johnson offered her something better: wisdom. Later that evening, Jessie had a dream. She couldn't recall the details, but it was one of those dreams that leaves behind heavy emotions. She woke up feeling excited and hopeful. This time, she would find out where excitement and hope would lead her.

For a second time, her life was derailed. And for a second time, she put herself on a new track. She has never looked back.

The last time Jessie experienced this level of pain in a hospital bed, she wanted to die. This time, she is thankful to be alive. She is grateful for her family and Jonathan's brief return to her life.

She anticipates a lot of therapy for them in the future, especially for Max, but she remains optimistic. Max is just like his mother—stubborn and resourceful. And forgiving, just like his father. He will get through this.

Sean could go either way. The last eighteen hours might negate all the progress he's made over the past several years or become just something that happened once, something he tells his friends like a campfire ghost story. Sean is the wildcard. You never know how he'll react. He definitely keeps things interesting.

Something falls to the floor in the hallway, jolting her from her peaceful state. She blinks her eyes open, and her gaze lands on the names of her children written in Sharpie, making her chest tight with joy. There's a bit of black marker peeking from the cast's underside that wasn't there earlier.

She turns her arm, and her breath catches.

The handwriting is unmistakable. Her throat closes around the word, around the finality of it. She traces the letters with trembling fingers, knowing this might be all she has left of him.

The morphine pulls her under again, but she holds tight to the strange peace that comes with knowing some endings are also beginnings. She clings to those letters because they mean everything.

BYE.

# EIGHTY

June 21, 2026
Las Vegas, NV

*THUNK. THUNK. Thunk.* Jessie's cherished personal quiet time is shattered by the sound of a heavy object being dragged down the stairs. It grows louder as it approaches. *Thunk.* It's not a body. *Thunk.* If it were a body, its owner would be screaming her name. *Thunk.* Surprisingly, that scenario has never occurred in the Baltimore household. *Thunk. Thunk.*

"I'm ready," Sean says. He rolls his suitcase to the kitchen island and sits on a bar stool next to Jessie. "Where's Dad and Max?"

Jessie studies his face—alert, purposeful, not the reluctant camper she'd expected to drag kicking and screaming from bed. She chugs the last of her coffee, mourning the loss of serenity. "Sleeping in, like you should be." She walks to the sink and rinses the lopsided coffee mug. As the tan water swirls around inside, Jessie does a quick calculation and confirms what she didn't think was possible. It's been a decade since Max proudly presented her with the coffee mug and a toothless smile on her twenty-eighth birthday. No, it was her thirty-third birthday. Years of hand washing have left a faded spot, and a chipped rim forces her to use it left-handed, which always feels awkward. As she dries it, the dish towel gets caught on the chip, pulling out a fiber and causing a pucker. Every dish towel in the kitchen bears the mark of the mug.

"I got up at 6:10," Sean says.

"That's not sleeping in." At the start of the school year, Nick and Jessie had agreed to send Sean to summer camp this year. However, since their ordeal in January, Jessie has been hesitant to let Sean go. Sean's therapist, however, "highly encouraged" the idea when Nick brought it up. Jessie eventually caved, knowing that when the time came, Sean would push back. And Nick wouldn't want to rock the unsteady boat they were all living in, nor would he force the issue. She was wrong. Sean is dressed, and his suitcase is packed, which tells her that some part of him wants to go. Perhaps he's curious, or maybe he's ready for some independence. She can't quite read him yet.

Jessie begins the did-you-pack-everything interrogation. "Did you pack extra underwear?" she asks.

"Yes."

"Toothbrush?"

"Yes."

"Pajamas?"

"Of course. What else would I sleep in? My clothes?"

She smacks her palms on the counter. "Alright, my expert packer, you are indeed ready." Before they leave, she will double-check the contents of his suitcase.

"Yes, I am." He slaps the Camper's Packing List on the counter and slides it to Jessie. Every box is checked. Twice. "And you do not need to double-check. I already did."

Jessie looks at the list and nods. He's nothing if not thorough. She's still going to double-check when he isn't looking.

Max trudges into the kitchen, wiping sleep from his eyes, and rummages inside the walk-in pantry. He exits the pantry, gulping a

Gatorade between bites of a protein bar. His new Mario Wasted t-shirt is creased with the manufacturer's fold lines, complementing the wrinkles in his basketball shorts.

Jessie's happy he's eating something other than his usual breakfast of nothing. "You're up early."

Max glares at Sean with the universal look of an older brother whose sleep has been disturbed. "Not by choice." He finishes the protein bar and tosses the wrapper into the trash. "I'm going back to bed."

"You all packed up?" she asks.

"Yep."

"Toothbrush?"

"Me and Jon— my dad—we're going to pick one up to keep at his place."

Jessie notices the slight hesitation before "my dad" and wonders how comfortable Max is with that title.

"Extra underwear?"

"I stopped pooping my pants a long time ago." Max starts up the stairs.

"Pajamas?" Jessie calls after him.

"Wearing them," Max says, his voice trailing as he disappears upstairs.

Jessie faces the bathroom mirror and stares at a single short hair standing at attention in the middle of her head. She smooths the hair, sprays it with hairspray, and holds it in place as she dries it with a hairdryer. After a moment, she turns off the dryer and gently releases her hand. She waits and watches as the hair holds for a second, two seconds, three seconds, and then bends and rises to full attention. Again, she attempts to tame the rogue hair. She leans into the mirror and examines the lone hair sticking straight up, mocking her efforts. Her first gray hair. Jessie lets out a frustrated sigh and yanks the hair.

She walks to the bedside and gazes at Nick, who is sleeping

entangled in the duvet. While showering, she dropped her razor twice, let out a rather loud yelp when she nicked her knee, and slammed the shower door shut when she lost her grip getting out. Through all that noise and the hair dryer, Nick hasn't stirred. She will always be envious. It's not fair that he can sleep through anything, while the sound of flapping butterfly wings will end her slumber since day one of motherhood. The clock reads 9:17 a.m. Nick told her he would only need fifteen minutes to get ready. Jessie shakes his shoulder like an irritated corrections officer waking a prisoner, trying not to enjoy it too much. "Time to get up," she says.

Forty-three minutes later, Jessie and her family are pulling out of the driveway. Right on time.

The Baltimore family rides in silence down the freeway. Jessie glances in the rearview mirror. Max's thumbs fly across his phone—texting Katie Bridgewater, no doubt. She's the first girl he's really paid attention to, and Jessie knows what that means. Her little boy will be dating soon, and she's not ready for that. Sean stares out at the passing landscape and is probably wondering if his cabin mates will smell weird, a concern he shared with her earlier. Beside her, Nick drives with that focused calm he gets when he's trying not to think about something difficult. Jessie knows he's dreading their first therapy session this afternoon as much as she is, but they've agreed it's necessary. A new beginning starts today for everyone, whether they're ready or not.

First, they'll drop Sean off at camp. Jessie is nervous about Sean being gone for six days. Nick seems optimistic and thinks it will be good for him, though she catches him glancing at Sean more than usual. In the backseat, Max shifts in his seat, and Jessie suspects he's looking forward to having a Sean-free house for the next week. They'll drop Max off next. He's staying at Jonathan's overnight for the first time. For the past three months, Jonathan has been slowly reintroduced into Max's life as a father, rather than his faceless online friend. Jonathan usually picks Max up once or twice a week and takes him to dinner or a movie. One day, they spent the afternoon at the

Pinball Hall of Fame, and when Max came home, he actually shared details, using more than five words—a minor miracle. Nick had joked that Max would end up liking Jonathan more than him. But Jessie recognized the genuine worry in his statement. Nick isn't the only one with newfound concerns. She wonders what Max and Jonathan talk about during their visits and if they ever discuss her.

Camp drop-off goes better than expected. Jessie watches Sean walk toward his counselor with steady steps and no backward glances, and feels guilty for wishing Sean had been more reluctant. She wants him to need her, but is proud that he doesn't. Five miles down the road, and she already misses him, but she's happy for the memories he'll make. The other kids had better be nice to him.

Thirty minutes later, they pull into Jonathan's luxury apartment complex, which could be mistaken for a small resort. The manicured landscaping and fountains make Jessie feel underdressed in her jeans and t-shirt.

Nick waits in the car while Jessie walks Max inside. She watches him check out the big-screen TV and the pool table in the fancy clubhouse, his eyes taking in details as he records a video.

Jonathan and Jessie sit at a table in the back corner while Max explores. He offers her a bottle of Evian from the clubhouse kitchen, and she accepts. The tension is reminiscent of a first date and a job interview rolled into one. She takes a drink, giving Jonathan the chance to break the ice. He doesn't. After a year-long ten seconds of silence, they talk over each other.

"How were you able to message Max on his laptop?" Jessie says.

"What time do you want me to drop him off tomorrow?" Jonathan says.

They both let out a nervous half-chuckle. Jonathan gestures for Jessie to speak first. "Whatever time is good for you. I'll be home all day," she says. She takes a drink. "I know you probably told me in the hospital, but I have some blank spots. Max's laptop must have had satellite capabilities for you to message him, right?" Jonathan confirms with a nod. "And you somehow made that happen?" she asks. He nods again. She waits for more details, studying his laugh lines, wondering who's responsible for them.

Jonathan gives her a quick rundown, his tone professional but not unkind. "The Agency was on the trail of a hacker, and Max was in one of the coding chat rooms the hacker had been known to frequent. Max was asking some very complicated questions. He's really smart, you know."

"I do," Jessie says.

"Anyway, I engaged with him for a few months and remotely uploaded a virus to his laptop so he would take it to get fixed. That's when we switched his laptop with one equipped with satellite so we could keep tabs on him. Our investigation received an internal hit on your new name, and we determined Max wasn't our guy. I had every intention of breaking communication, but then he told me his mom had a gun and he was hiding in the desert."

Jessie nods, the memory surfacing in fragments. Some of what he has said sounds familiar, like déjà vu with sharper edges. "I'm glad it's over." But Jonathan's expression shifts, his mouth tightening, and she feels her stomach drop. "What is it?"

"The laptop we planted in the SUV at the crime scene went missing from police custody two days ago," Jonathan says.

She sighs, feeling the weight settle back on her shoulders. "And it had the information from the flash drive on it." Jonathan nods. "So, someone tied to this is picking up where they left off."

Jonathan places his hand on hers, and she's surprised how warm and steady it is. "You don't have to worry. We have scrubbed all the footage from the mall, street cameras, gas stations, rest stops, and anywhere you went that day; we've cleaned it. The Agency will find them. We'll handle it." He notices Jessie eyeing his hand and gently removes it, the gesture somehow more intimate than if he'd left it there.

"Thank you," she says, meaning it. The cracking of billiard balls captures her attention. Max is lining up another shot, his phone propped on the edge of the table, recording. He looks comfortable here in a way that both pleases and worries her.

Jonathan slides a nylon bag to Jessie. "I thought you'd want this back. Don't ask how I got it."

Jessie unzips the bag and looks at the 9mm Glock from Dr. Smith. She was certain it had been destroyed in the explosion or the massive fire that followed. It's a little nicked up, but she's glad it's back where it belongs. She stands and resists the urge to hug Jonathan, not sure what the gesture would mean or how he'd receive it, or how long would be too long. Instead, they exchange a look that conveys all they need to say.

Max approaches with an extra pool stick for Jonathan, and Jessie wonders if this is what father-son bonding looks like when you're starting from scratch. She ignores the guilt creeping in and hugs a reluctant son goodbye for the second time today.

On the way home, Nick and Jessie talk about nothing—the weather, what they should have for dinner, whether they need to stop for gas. He doesn't question her about the bag or what's inside it, and she appreciates his patience and trust.

Nick waits for Jessie downstairs. He suggested they go to lunch before their therapy session. Despite her efforts, Jessie isn't hiding her anxiety about the boys leaving, and he said the distraction will be good for her. And maybe he just wants to spend time with his wife without the background noise of family logistics and teenage attitudes. She tells him she's going to change real quick before they leave and disappears up the stairs.

Jessie stands inside her bedroom closet, loading the Glock's magazine, as precisely and efficiently as when she was an agent. She takes a deep breath and holds it until the lump in her throat disappears. This will be the first time both of her children are in the overnight care of someone other than Grandma and Grandpa, and it doesn't sit well with her.

But she doesn't have a choice. She has to let them grow up and have their own lives, even when every maternal instinct begs her to keep them close.

The Baltimores haven't figured out how Jonathan fits into their family, but they're working together to figure it out. Jessie is grateful for the men in her life, both young and grown. They have been patient, understanding, and loving. Toward her and each other. Jessie slams the loaded magazine into her Glock and places it in a newly installed biometric safe mounted on the closet wall. More than anything, she is grateful because her family is safe.

For now.

# EPILOGUE

June 22, 2026
New York, NY

THE CAMPAIGN headquarters buzzes with the electric tension that comes before an election. Tomorrow, New Yorkers will decide whether Giovanni Amato II—a name that emerged from relative obscurity just six months ago—will unseat the incumbent in what many are calling the upset of the congressional primary election.

Romeo loosens his tie and surveys the organized chaos around him. The merit-based interns are still there at eleven PM, fine-tuning voter outreach lists and double-checking polling locations. The nepotism hires left hours ago to celebrate a victory they haven't yet earned. He makes a mental note to remember who stayed. Loyalty has always been currency in his world, and he rewards those who prioritize his interests over their own.

"Sir?" One of the remaining interns approaches with a tablet. "The final polling numbers just came in. You're up by twelve points."

Romeo nods, maintaining the measured confidence he's

perfected over thirty years. "Thank you, Marcus. You should head home and get some rest. Tomorrow will be a long day."

As the office empties, Juliet appears in his peripheral vision, moving with the efficient grace of someone who's orchestrated a thousand operations more complex than a congressional campaign. She pours two drinks from the bar cart.

"You know I still think this is insane," she says, settling into the chair across from his desk.

Romeo accepts his glass and leans back. "You've made your position clear."

"Have I? Because running for public office when you've spent three decades avoiding any spotlight seems like the opposite of your usual methodology."

He takes a measured sip. Juliet is one of the few people who can challenge him directly, a privilege earned through years of flawless execution and an understanding of his business. "Sometimes hiding in plain sight is the most effective camouflage."

"And sometimes it's just hiding with better lighting."

Romeo laughs—a genuine sound that surprises them both. "You worry too much. Besides, we both know I understand people. What they want, what they need, how to give them just enough of both to keep them satisfied."

Juliet raises an eyebrow. "Your clients weren't exactly thrilled about your political ambitions."

"My clients learned to adjust their expectations. Especially after Senator Gates received those rather unfortunate photographs." Romeo's smile doesn't reach his eyes. "Funny how quickly threats evaporate when people remember how much they have to lose."

The mention of Gates's about-face brings them both back to the reality of their situation. Romeo may be campaigning on education reform and infrastructure improvement, but the real business never stops.

"Speaking of losing things," Juliet says, her tone shifting to the crisp efficiency he's come to associate with good news, "we got the laptop out of evidence." Romeo sets down his glass with care. "It took months, but our contact managed to extract it during a routine inventory check. He found the downloaded file, and the courier is confirming the list. He can have everything back in circulation in the next week or two, assuming the product is still on the shelf."

For the first time in months, Romeo feels a sincere smile tugging at the corners of his mouth. "That is fantastic news."

"I thought you'd be pleased." Juliet finishes her drink and reaches for the bottle. "The courier arrangement continues to exceed expectations, by the way. Your initial skepticism was noted but ultimately unfounded."

"Your idea," Romeo acknowledges. "Though I still marvel at how you conceived it."

"Sometimes you have to think like a woman.

They drink in comfortable silence, happy to ignore the weight of tomorrow's election for the time being.

Romeo stands and walks to a shelf of photographs—years of charity galas, foundation events, and carefully orchestrated public appearances. He finds a frame in the front and examines it. He and his brother donned tuxedos and smiles for the camera at some long-forgotten fundraiser.

Juliet takes the whiskey bottle to him and pours him another drink. "That was the last time you saw him, wasn't it?" Her voice carries an uncharacteristic gentleness.

"Yes." Romeo doesn't elaborate.

He sets that frame down and reaches for a smaller silver one tucked between two larger photos in the back row. It's unremarkable among the collection of family photos and professional shots with CEOs and dignitaries.

Juliet studies the innocuous image of a woman at a convenience store, captured by security cameras in what appears to be a routine transaction.

Romeo places the photo in the front row, rearranging the others to ensure it sits perfectly among them.

"You know that's reckless," Juliet says.

"You never noticed it before tonight," Romeo counters. "And you notice everything."

"That's different."

"Hiding in plain sight, remember? Besides, I want to see her face every day. I don't want her hiding anymore."

To everyone glancing at the shelf, she's a cousin, a niece, or an old friend. She could be anyone. But Romeo knows exactly who stares back at him from the grainy surveillance footage. A murderer.

Revenge is just another business transaction waiting for the right time to close.

About the Author

Ivy Bronson has always loved writing. She has held two jobs that couldn't be more different, but require some of the same attributes from those who do them. Her favorite movie is based on a book she has never read. Ivy graduated from a university with a couple of degrees. If she weren't a writer, she would still be a creator, in a very different medium. Ivy lives in the United States.

For more information and bonus content, sign up for Ivy's newsletter at www.ivybronson.com.

# OUTWIT

A JESSIE BALTIMORE NOVEL

COMING

2026

# IVY
# BRONSON

SHE TOOK THE JOB TO FIND A GIRL,
THEN ANOTHER ONE DISAPPEARED.